Praise for the Men of Mercy Series

"Lindsay Cross delivers high-powered action, alpha heroes and an exciting conclusion!"

- **ELLE JAMES**
New York Times and USA Today bestselling author

"This is one of those books that the phrase sit down, shut up and hang on would be used because it's a wild ride from page one to the end."

- **5 Star Goodreads Review**, Redemption River

"This book was wall to wall action. Once the danger hit, it never slowed down. I was late leaving my house because there was no way I could stop reading."

- **5 Star NetGalley Review**, Redemption River

BOOKS BY LINDSAY CROSS

MEN OF MERCY NOVELS
REDEMPTION RIVER
RESURRECTION RIVER
RECKLESS RIVER
RAVAGED RIVER
ETHAN'S PROMISE – MAY 2016
AARON'S HONOR – JULY 2016
MERC'S STORY – FALL 2016
SHERIFF LAWSON'S STORY – FALL 2016
ANTICIPATION - 2015

Resurrection River

Men of Mercy, Book 2

Lindsay Cross

Copyright Warning

Published by Cypress Bend Publishing LLC

Cover Design by Kari March

Resurrection River
All Rights Are Reserved. Copyright 2015 by Lindsay Cross.

First electronic publication: October 2015
First print publication: October 2015

Digital ISBN: **978-0-9968360-0-5**

Print ISBN: **978-0-9968360-4-3**

To my family and friends whose unwavering support saw me through the tough spots.

DOSSIER

TASK FORCE SCORPION (TF-S)

A branch of Joint Special Operations Command (JSOC)
Ft. Grenada, MS

MACK GREY: Detachment Commander, Captain
 ➢ Recruited from the 75th Ranger Regiment, Ft. Benning, GA
 ➢ Specialized Skills: direct action, unconventional warfare, special reconnaissance, interrogations specialist, psychological warfare
 ➢ First in Command. Responsible for ensuring and maintaining operational readiness.
 ➢ Height: 6'
 ➢ Weight: 195lbs
 ➢ Combat Experience: Operation Gothic Serpent, Somalia. Operation Desert Storm, Operation Iraqi Freedom, Operation Crescent Wind, Operation Rhino, Operation Anaconda, Operation Jacan, Operation Mountain Viper, Operation Eagle Fury, Operation Condor, Operation Summit, Operation Volcano, Operation Achilles

HUNTER JAMES: Warrant Officer, Detachment Commander

> Recruited from the 75th Ranger Regiment, Ft. Benning, GA
> Specialized Skills: direct action, unconventional warfare, special reconnaissance, psychological warfare
> Responsible for overseeing all Team ops. Commands in absence of detachment commander.
> Height: 6'3"
> Weight: 230lbs
> Combat Experience: Operation Enduring Freedom, Operation Crescent Wind, Operation Anaconda, Operation Jacana, Operation Mountain Viper, Operation Eagle Fury

RANGER JAMES: Team Daddy/Team Sergeant, Master Sgt.

> Recruited from the 75th Ranger Regiment, Ft. Benning, GA
> Specialized Skills: direct action, unconventional warfare, special reconnaissance
> Plans, coordinates & directs Team intelligence, analysis and dissemination.
> Height: 6'2"
> Weight: 225lbs
> Combat Experience: Operation Enduring Freedom, Operation Crescent Wind, Operation Anaconda, Operation Jacana, Operation Mountain Viper, Operation Eagle Fur

JARED CROWE: Weapons Sergeant, Sgt. 1st Class
- Recruited from Delta Force, Ft. Bragg, NC
- Specialized Skills: direct action, unconventional warfare, special reconnaissance, Sniper
- Weapons expert. Capable of firing and employing all small arm and crew served weapons
- Height: 6'0"
- Weight: 220lbs
- Combat Experience: Operation Enduring Freedom, Operation Crescent Wind, Operation Anaconda, Operation Jacana, Operation Condor, Operation Summit, Operation Volcano, Operation Achilles

HOYT CROWE: Asst. Weapons Sergeant, Staff Sgt.
- Recruited from Delta Force, Ft. Bragg, NC
- Specialized Skills: direct action, unconventional warfare, special reconnaissance, Sniper
- Weapons expert. Capable of firing and employing all small arm and crew served weapons
- Height: 6'0"
- Weight: 210lbs
- Combat Experience: Operation Enduring Freedom, Operation Crescent Wind, Operation Anaconda, Operation Jacana, Operation Condor, Operation Summit, Operation Volcano, Operation Achilles

AARON SPEIRS: Medical Sergeant, Sgt. 1st Class
- ➤ Recruited from Delta Force, Ft. Bragg, NC
- ➤ Specialized Skills: direct action, unconventional warfare, special reconnaissance, medic
- ➤ The life-saver. Employs the latest field medical technology and limited surgical procedures
- ➤ Height: 6'1"
- ➤ Weight: 195lbs
- ➤ Combat Experience: Operation Anaconda, Operation Jacana, Operation Condor, Operation Summit, Operation Volcano,

RISER MALLON: Asst. Medical Sergeant, Staff Sgt.
- ➤ Recruited from Delta Force, Ft. Bragg, NC
- ➤ Specialized Skills: direct action, unconventional warfare, special reconnaissance, medic
- ➤ The life-saver. Employs the latest field medical technology and limited surgical procedures
- ➤ Height: 6'2"
- ➤ Weight: 215lbs
- ➤ Combat Experience: Operation Anaconda, Operation Jacana, Operation Condor, Operation Summit, Operation Volcano, Operation Achilles

MERC: Engineer Sergeant, Sgt. 1st Class
- ➤ Recruited from Special Operations Group (SOG) of the Central Intelligence Agency (CIA)
- ➤ Specialized Skills: direct action, unconventional warfare, special reconnaissance, Demolitions, psychological operations
- ➤ Demolition expert. Trained in psychological warfare, conducts field interrogations.
- ➤ Height: 6'5"
- ➤ Weight: 250lbs
- ➤ Combat Experience: Classified

ETHAN SLADE: Communications Sergeant/Commo Guy, Sgt. 1st Class

- Recruited from the 75th Ranger Regiment, Ft. Benning, GA
- Specialized Skills: direct action, unconventional warfare, special reconnaissance, communications
- Communications expert. Employ latest FM, multi-channel, and satellite communication devices.
- Height: 6'0"
- Weight: 200lbs
- Combat Experience: Operation Condor, Operation Summit, Operation Volcano, Operation Achilles

SHANE CARTER: Weapons Sergeant, Staff Sgt.

- Recruited from the Marine Corps Forces Special Operations Command (MARSOC), Camp Lejeune, NC
- Specialized Skills: direct action, unconventional warfare, special reconnaissance, weapons expert/sniper
- Weapons expert. Capable of firing and employing all small arm and crew served weapons
- Height: 5'11"
- Weight: 180lbs
- Combat Experience: Operation Iraqi Freedom, Operation Condor, Operation Summit, Operation Volcano, Operation Achilles

CORD CARTER: Weapons Sergeant, Staff Sgt.
- ➤ Recruited from the Marine Corps Forces Special Operations Command (MARSOC), Camp Lejeune, NC
- ➤ Specialized Skills: direct action, unconventional warfare, special reconnaissance, weapons expert/sniper
- ➤ Weapons expert. Capable of firing and employing all small arm and crew served weapons
- ➤ Height: 6'1"
- ➤ Weight: 210lbs
- ➤ Combat Experience: Operation Iraqi Freedom, Operation Condor, Operation Summit, Operation Volcano, Operation Achilles

MR J: CIA Liaison, Embedded with ISA
- ➤ Special Activities Division (SAD) of the Central Intelligence Agency (CIA)
- ➤ Specialized Skills: Classified
- ➤ Training: Classified
- ➤ Height: 5'10"
- ➤ Weight: 170lbs
- ➤ Combat Experience: Classified

.

Chapter One

Amy's day started at sunrise and ended after midnight. Feed the chickens. Feed the cows. Feed herself. Then, after five, feed the alcoholics.

The rest of the time she spent pretending her husband hadn't left for deployment with a good-bye fight instead of a good-bye kiss.

Six months was a little long for a stand-off between husband and wife. And if Shane were home, that time would shrink to hours. But the damn man hadn't called. Hadn't written. She'd gotten nothing but a cold shoulder from a third world country. And Shane should have been home from deployment two-weeks ago.

She paused painting the new nursery pink and put a hand to her aching back. She'd been on her feet for five hours straight trying to finish painting before her shift at the bar. Over three hours ago her feet had swollen past the confines of her tennis shoes and she'd switched to flip-flops. Now she just had to make it through the night without some drunk stepping on her feet and mashing her bare toes. Amy probably should have taken a break, but she was determined to make a place for her daughter.

Someone knocked on her front door. Eight o'clock. Who would be knocking on her door this late? Most of the residents of Mercy, Mississippi considered this bedtime. Her hand immediately went to her belly, covering her unborn child. Amy was seven months along, only finding out about her condition the week after Shane left. If he were regular military, she could tell him. Let him know he was going to be a father. But when Task Force Scorpion, TF-S, an elite branch of Special Forces deployed, they went off grid.

Nothing and no one could contact them.

They knocked again. Amy carefully balanced her wet paintbrush on the open bucket at her feet and headed to the front door, stopping for a quick peek in the mirror. A few smudges of paint dotted her cheek and her ponytail sagged a little. They knocked again. This time more forceful. *Two-weeks late.*

Could be someone needed help or her best friends wanting to drag her out of the house and make her pretend to be happy.

Could be an all-together different reason. One she never wanted to know.

Don't answer it.
Don't answer it.
Don't answer it.

"Amy, it's me."

Ranger James. The man she should have married.

Why was he on her front porch and not her husband? They were both in the same unit. If Ranger was home and not Shane…

Her unborn daughter, Chloe, shoved an elbow into her ribs and Amy rubbed soothing circles over the skin. She took a calming breath. Her doctor told her no undue stress. It's okay. He's just letting me know Shane had to stay in the country longer than expected…

She pasted on her I'm-sure-it's-nothing-important smile and opened the door.

The roar of the battering rain immediately surrounded her. A drenched and dripping Ranger stood on her front porch, his truck headlights shining through the downpour. His blond hair plastered to his head. His t-shirt plastered to his chest.

Do not look at his chest.

"Amy." Ranger's voice still had that edge, the one that always managed to scrape across her nerves. But right now his voice had something else. Something frightening.

She stepped onto the porch. Lighting flashed, highlighting his expression, and she jerked like she'd been struck in the chest. The raw pain in Ranger's gaze made her tremble. "No."

"Shane." His voice slammed through her with the force of an eighteen-wheeler.

Her heart stopped.

"Shane. He's..."

Ranger's words faded under the roaring in her ears. Her hands went numb. He kept talking, but she couldn't hear. Couldn't process anything but the oxygen seeping from her lungs in horror. Just because she hadn't talked to Shane recently didn't mean something had happened to him.

Didn't mean he was dead.

She wanted to run. To close the door, curl up in a ball and sob. Instead, Ranger's eyes filling with tears trapped her. "I'm so sorry. The condolences officer showed up at headquarters. I beat him here. I thought you should hear it from me."

No. No. No.

Not her. Not him. Not her husband.

Shane. Shane hadn't failed to call because of their fight. Not because they were flirting with separation. Not because he didn't love her. He hadn't called because he was dead.

Oh God.

Her stomach twisted, and sharp pain ripped across her back. Amy doubled over and Ranger grabbed her arms, barely keeping her from falling. "Amy, holy shit. You're... you're..."

Pregnant.

A stabbing cramp ripped through her stomach again. She gasped out loud. "Something's wrong."

* * *

That night, Amy delivered a healthy baby girl, with Ranger at her side. When the doctors proclaimed everyone healthy enough to leave, he drove them home. Cheri and

Evie, her best friends, basically moved in to help take care of Chloe while Amy grieved and tried to care for her newborn baby girl.

The next week passed in a daze of flowers and cribs and caskets.

Ranger finished painting the nursery and put her daughter's crib together. He did everything her husband should have done.

The day of the funeral, Cheri and Evie rode in the limo with her. Mrs. Trudy, Amy's godmother, volunteered to stay home with Chloe. Amy couldn't bring herself to take her baby to the funeral. Not now.

Her best friends sat across from her, crying and talking nonsense. Amy sat to the side, staring out the tinted window, watching all the people showing up for the funeral. Shane's unit lined the cemetery drive, all of them in their dress blues and standing at attention.

Cops. Firemen. Soldiers. People she knew and people she didn't recognize. All of them there to honor her husband.

Amy sat straighter in her seat and dried her tears. She wasn't just a grieving widow. She was the wife of Staff Sergeant Shane Carter, killed by terrorists. Purple Heart recipient. Fatally injured saving the lives of everyone in his squad.

They passed a news van. National News America. The same station that had shown Shane's assassination on national TV the week after she'd learned of his death. She'd been standing in the living room after getting Chloe to sleep for the night. The ten o'clock news flashed an alert right before showing the new viral video. Shane, on his knees, a black hood covering his face and an automatic rifle pressed to his head. The retort of gunfire had erupted. His body falling to the floor. *How many women got to watch their husband murdered on live television?*

"Damn leeches. How dare they show up here." Cheri sat forward in the seat and flipped them off. Too bad the windows were tinted black.

"Want me to get them out of here?" Evie took Amy's

hand. She stared down at her friend's grip, seeing but not feeling her touch. Amy blacked out after watching the video and when she'd woken, her body had been blessedly numb, as if anesthetized by a powerful drug. A distant part of her recognized this non-feeling as a sort of shock. A shock she was sure to come crashing out of at some point, but one she held on to with a grip of steel.

"Let them feed. Mavis will soak it up." Mavis, Shane's mother, rode the high of her son's death like a starved pit bull, seizing and chewing every scrap of attention the anchors threw her way.

"Why do you put up with her?" Cheri said.

"Because she's his mother. I know she's grieving, too." Somewhere in that deep dark pit of a soul.

Evie snorted, "You're a better woman than me. If she talked to me the way she talks to you, I'd slap her in her big fat face."

The image brought a smile to Amy's lips, however brief. The limo stopped. A huge crowd surrounded the graveside service, ringed by men in uniform. Amy took a deep breath, closed her eyes and let the ice creep through her veins. If the media wanted a show, she'd give it to them.

Hunter, Shane's team leader and Evie's husband, stepped to the door and opened it, offering his hand. They'd all grown up together, here in Mercy. Hunter, Ranger, Shane, Evie and Amy. Evie exited and then Cheri. Evie leaned up and whispered something in her husband's ear. Hunter nodded and motioned a soldier over to him. After a brief talk, the other man walked off, shoulder's squared as if on a mission. He poked his head inside the car and held out his hand. "Don't worry. We'll take care of them."

She didn't have to ask who he meant. As she emerged from the car, a team of uniformed men surrounded the news anchors and tightened, cutting off their access like a noose. Amy heard their protests and stiffened. The last thing she wanted was a circus show today. Hunter placed her hand on his forearm and gave her a reassuring squeeze. "We've got this."

Amy bit her lip, helpless to do anything but watch. The circle of men started to move away, the media trapped in its confines. The journalists in the middle yelling and snapping pictures and threatening lawsuits. Everyone stared.

A strange sort of hysteria crept up her spine and wrapped around her throat. This wasn't supposed to happen. Not here. Not today.

Today she buried her husband.

Her hands and feet started tingling and the humid air grew thick like mossy pond water, stifling her oxygen. Evie appeared in front of her. "Breathe, hon. Just breathe. They will be gone in a minute."

Amy saw her friend's lips moving, but her words seemed blurry and distorted. What kind of monsters fed on grieving families?

"Crap. She's going comatose again."

"Move." Cheri pushed Evie to the side and grabbed Amy's face between her palms. "Focus on me. Look at me."

But I am looking at you.

"Dammit Amy, if you don't look at me right now I'm going to slap you and give those bastards something real to report on."

I can't move.

"Someone get me some water."

Come on girl, get it together. You promised to be strong. You can't break down now. Not here. Later. Compartmentalize. You just have to get through today. Tomorrow you can fall apart.

Amy reached inside and forced herself to move something. Anything.

She blinked.

"That's a girl. Now drink."

Cheri took her hand and closed her fingers around a water bottle. Amy lifted her hand, the movement feeling strange and disjointed. She took a drink of the lukewarm water.

"Good. Now we're going to walk forward. Focus on getting to your seat, okay?" Cheri stayed right in front of her face.

Amy nodded. Good. Focus. *Move your feet.*

Hunter still stood on her right side, her hand held on his arm. Cheri stepped to her left, took the water bottle, passed it off to Evie and took Amy's other hand. The crowd parted, her vision tunneled on the green canopy tent about twenty feet ahead.

"You ready?" Hunter leaned down, his six foot four inch frame dwarfing her by a good foot.

Would she ever be ready? "Yes."

The trio moved forward as one. They got halfway there and Amy became aware of the silence. No more screaming news anchors. Not one sound. Like God himself had thrown a blanket of tranquility over the proceedings.

A weak wind stirred and the black netting covering her face snagged a stray strand of hair. Dark grey clouds hung low and heavy in the summer heat. Thunder grumbled in the distance. Amy couldn't help but peek back over her shoulder. A wall of men and women blocked the entrance to the cemetery, holding the rabid scavengers at bay.

Tears pricked her eyes. This was why she loved a man in uniform. They weren't afraid to show their respect. She stepped under the tent and stopped.

The bold colors of the American flag stood out over her husband's coffin. Colors of honor. Colors of freedom. Colors of sacrifice.

She'd never thought they'd be the colors of death.

She sat on a padded metal chair. Shane two feet away. Separated by two inches of wood. Patriot. Warrior. Hero. The words carved in bold script across the side of the polished mahogany coffin, gleaming even in the absence of sunlight.

Patriot. That's what they called the men who joined the military.

Warrior. That's what they called the men who fought for their country.

Hero. That's what they called the men who died for their country.

Shane was a hero.

The row of chairs behind her remained empty. No one approached. As if they were afraid to sit too close. As if death was infectious and would contaminate their lives.

She couldn't blame them for not getting close. Death had infected and destroyed her life with the opening of a door. Amy choked, took a breath and reined in her control.

She wanted to reach out. Touch him. Remember how his skin felt. But he wasn't in that coffin. His body lay somewhere in some unknown desert, in an unmarked grave.

"It's your fault he joined the military. It's your fault my son is dead." Mavis Carter, the only person sitting in the second row of chairs, leaned forward and spewed her venom.

Chills spread across Amy's arms and neck.

Cheri hissed in a breath beside her and turned to face the dragon lady. "You're bat-shit crazy."

Amy didn't turn, didn't speak. She didn't need to see how her over-weight mother-in-law's bloodshot eyes glowed with hate.

"You say another word, Mavis, and I'll have you thrown out." Ranger appeared not one foot away. His dress blues making him seem bigger, more threatening.

Amy's gaze collided with Ranger's. Shane's best friend. The man who'd told her of Shane's death. He'd caught her when her knees gave out. He'd fought with her to make sure she ate and drank. He'd fought to make sure she survived.

Now he fought for her.

Ranger turned, his heels clicked together, and marched to the end of Shane's coffin. Hunter took position at the other end.

They grasped the corners of the flag lying on the coffin and lifted, keeping the flag high and tight.

Seven soldiers in dress blues stood off to the side, their line precise. No more than a foot apart, their rifles rose in unison. They moved in perfect synchronization, nothing out of order. Flawless.

The first round of gunshots exploded into the sky. Amy jerked and clutched Evie's hand.

Bang. Another round. Fire seared through her chest, like the bullets had lodged in her heart.

Bang. The last round of the twenty-one-gun salute blasted with finality. Tears she had fought hard to contain slipped free.

Was a gunshot the last sound Shane heard before he died?

A lone soldier raised a horn to his lips, the mournful sound of Taps filled the cemetery.

Hunter walked toward Ranger, folding the flag corner to corner into a tight triangle. They took their time. Made it perfect.

Then Ranger took the flag and Hunter saluted. His white gloves stark against tanned skin. Both of them stood tall. Stiff.

Amy started praying.

Ranger knelt at her feet, head bowed.

No. No. No.

He raised his head, his blue eyes red-rimmed and staring at her like a dark bruise. She couldn't move. Couldn't reach out and take that flag.

She kept her hands clasped in her lap, white knuckle tight. Ranger pried them apart and laid her right palm open. He placed the flag in her hand. Pulled her left hand down on top of the smooth triangle.

Her heart hit hard and fast, like a train speeding out of control. About to go off track and kill anything within striking distance.

"People die all the time, honey. If I die, I'll die for a worthy cause." Shane's words whispered through her mind.

She clutched the flag to her chest, clutched it for everything she was worth. She held on to the one thing her husband had believed in with all his soul.

.

Chapter Two

Amy soared. Just her, the sky and the sixty-acre stretch of soybeans below. She pulled up her Air Tractor crop duster at the end of the field, swooped out right, turned back left and lined up for the next round.

Long straight rows stretched out in front of her in GPS mapped perfection. She pushed the control stick forward, swooped down at a smooth one hundred forty miles per hour and hit the chemical release button. The plane hovered five feet above the crops. She'd already sprayed ten fields today, but her stomach flew up into her throat with each dive. Adrenaline zinged through her limbs from the rush of crops coming at her at high speed.

Hardwood trees running perpendicular to the field grew bigger by the nanosecond. She held straight and steady. The flow of chemicals had to be maintained until the last minute or she'd waste precious herbicide. And money.

When the trees got up close and high-def she eased back, missing the tops by a good four feet. Her stomach plopped back down from her throat, leaving a tingling tickle in its wake. Her hand loosened on the control, the thrill made her feel as weightless as the fluffy white cumulus clouds above her.

She didn't need drugs. Nor alcohol. No, those were too slow. She needed air speeds over two hundred mph, mere feet from the ground. She needed to zip beneath power lines with almost zero clearance. She needed to tempt death to feel alive.

And damn if she wasn't addicted.

Amy banked into a wide turn. The sun would set in two hours. She had at least another good hour of flying. And she wanted every second she could steal.

Because when she was up here, she wasn't thinking about her dead husband. She wasn't thinking about his best friend. She wasn't thinking about anything except the rush.

Amy dropped the plane for her fifth pass at Smith's field. Fat and skinny shadows broke up the earth as she sped past. The sun painted shades of apple green to evergreen.

Next pass, she saw him. His bright red four by four truck pulled over at the other end of the field. She swooped down and her heart jumped. But not from the drop in altitude.

Ranger James.

That truck might as well have a flashing neon sign – warning hot male will make panties drop.

She'd warned him to stay away.

Her response to Ranger was as natural and hot as lava erupting from Mt. Vesuvius

Reckless rage followed the thrill of anticipation coursing through her veins. She flew closer. Ranger leaned against his truck, long jean clad legs crossed ankle over ankle. That gleaming head of blond hair. Her mouth watered. She could see his biceps from here.

Power lines. Oh shit. Amy whipped beneath them at the last second, buzzing within feet of her own version of regret. Get it together. Mistakes. Distractions. Death sentence.

Her entire body hummed with energy. Fury. And unmistakable lust. Amy gritted her teeth. Any southerner with half a cylinder firing knew the people of Mercy would shred her reputation like a John Deere tractor shredded grass.

A widow only eight months after the funeral wasn't allowed to date. It wouldn't matter that her bed was as empty as her bank account.

And had been empty way before he left.

Her bank account was in desperate need of funds. She'd bet all her money on the farm. Literally. Ranger and his too tempting lips could sink her fast.

If she didn't fly, she and her daughter didn't eat.

Two more passes. That's all she had to do. Two more. Keep it level. Precise. Her plane shook, metal rattled but she kept going. Grandpa Silo promised her his fifty-year-old plane could get the job done.

She made the wide turn, slowed a split second and took a breath. Ranger was just a man. Just a man. Just a man.

A man she'd been secretly in love with since high school.

Calm was definitely not on her radar. She pushed down, increased speed, wanting to rip a little hair off his head as she whipped past. The ground rushed up. Her muscles contracted. She gripped the stick. Hard.

She hit the chemical release button too early and gave Ranger a bath in herbicide.

That would teach the man not to show up at Smith's field. On her time clock.

She finished this pass going ten miles an hour faster and barely yanked up in time. The treetops slapped her wheels. Then she was flying toward the clouds. Last round. Forget another hour of work.

She couldn't stop the flash of images in her mind. Her fight with Shane. Her dreams about Ranger. Her husband's coffin. Her heart squeezed tight. She leveled out too close to the field but didn't care. She hit the release.

Ranger wasn't leaning against his truck anymore. He was waving his arms like a mad man and yelling. She didn't have to get close to know he was cursing.

Amy flew so low she risked taking the tops off the soybeans. She lined up. A few feet behind Ranger's truck. Throttled the engine. The crop duster groaned, shimmied, but held together. One hundred twenty mph. She kept a careful eye to make sure her spray speeds didn't saturate the plants. One hundred mph.

Ranger stopped doing the angry dance and backed up to his truck. Amy let go of the chemical button. Skimmed beneath the power lines and lifted her hand to Ranger in a

salute that conveyed every emotion in her body.
And she did it with a smile

Chapter Three

She flipped him the bird.

Shock rooted Ranger's boots in the gravel as good as instant cement. Anger struck up a strong beat in his chest. Amy Carter had lost her ever-loving mind.

His eyes stung, watered. He ran to his truck and grabbed a towel from the back seat. Scrubbing his face with the cloth made the sting worse. His arms and legs prickled.

Ranger stripped to his boxers like fire ants invaded his pants. Then he threw his soaked clothes in the back and grabbed a fresh pair of jeans from his duffle. At least she was spraying herbicide today. That particular chemical wasn't poisonous.

He'd been on his way to a new undercover op. One that required some overnighters. And he'd wanted to see Amy before he left. Make sure she was okay. Even if she'd told him to stop coming around. He just couldn't get the woman off his mind.

The chemical bath made her opinion all too clear. She wasn't just scared of a relationship, she was angry. And he hadn't done a damn thing to deserve it. But he sure as hell wasn't about to tuck tail like a whipped puppy.

He heard a car coming and ran behind his truck. Gravel crunched. Ranger spun around just as a little black sports car stopped right next to him. He clutched his jeans in front of his boxer briefs.

"My, my. If I knew I'd get this kind of show I'd a done my hair." The sweet southern drawl had too much Georgia in it for Mississippi. Like she'd put two cups of sugar in her tea instead of one.

Ranger cringed, unable to stop the instinctive response. Tonya Lee Swopes, Mercy's second hairdresser and first-rate gossip. Ranger had made the mistake of kissing her after high school graduation and she'd been after him non-stop ever since.

"Tonya."

Fate must have it out for him.

Her black hair seemed too black. Almost blue. Her eye make-up more along drag queen lines than southern belle.

Tonya took her time, her mud brown eyes trailed him from top to bottom. "Come on over here and let's have a taste."

"Listen, I'm running late for a date. Sorry, but I don't have time to visit. Maybe later." Almost to his door.

"Oh yeah, and just who is this hot date?"

"Amy. She's waiting right now." Liar. He wanted a date with Amy. Right after he tanned her ass for her little prank.

"That grease monkey? You want her when you can have this?" Tonya flicked her hair and gave him a look that clearly indicated she thought he'd lost his mind.

"Not every woman needs makeup to be attractive." Oh shit. Shoulda kept his mouth shut. His father, Hank James, always said his lack of filter between brain and mouth would get him in trouble.

"And I do?" Tonya's voice rose, part of her accent disappearing into a shriek.

Ranger jumped in his truck. The hot leather burned his ass and bare thighs but he didn't stop to curse the pain. "Sorry," Ranger yelled through the open window. "Gotta go."

He cranked the engine, but the roar wasn't loud enough to mask out her voice. "You can't run forever, Ranger

James."

He slammed the gas pedal to the floor, spinning out in his haste to escape. Ranger spared one last look in the rearview. Tonya stuck her hand through her window and flipped him off.

Two times in one day. Great. Today was turning out to be his record for pissing off females.

Ranger sped down Smith's Road, hung a sharp right onto the highway and squealed tires when his truck spun from gravel to pavement. He was late for a self-imposed date with a redhead whose temper outranked his commander's.

Fields of soybeans, cotton, rice, and corn blew by in a blur. He took Deadman's curve going seventy. A feat in itself. A few minutes later, Amy's drive appeared on the left and he turned between the two rows of pear trees lining her driveway. He didn't stop at the white farmhouse though. He sped past to the airplane hangar a few hundred feet behind.

By the time he parked in front of the tan metal building, sweat dripped down his naked back and soaked his seat.

Ranger jumped out, not bothering to dress. She'd put him in this state. She could deal. He stomped through the open hangar door, bare-foot and half-naked, with every intention of cuttin' loose on the woman who haunted his daydreams.

Ranger entered the airplane hangar and crossed the concrete floor tattooed with oil stains. A small breeze swirled dust and stirred up the summer heat. A heat matched by his boiling temper and simmering blood.

The source of his frustration climbed a ladder to the nose of the airplane, popped the hood and stuck her head down into the engine compartment. Ranger stopped, his visual field shrinking to one perfectly rounded ass in serious need of a spanking.

Amy kicked a booted foot into the air. Metal clanked on metal and a wrench flew over her shoulder at Ranger's feet. "Come on, baby. Come on. I'm sorry I pushed you so hard. I shouldn't expect so much out of you." Amy's voice echoed, her head and torso hidden in the open nose of the small plane.

"Please, I promise I'll never do that again if you just give me another chance," she pleaded with the archaic plane like it could do anything but fall apart.

Ranger's mouth went dry like he'd swallowed every dust particle in the air. Her curves baited him, drew him in. Dazed, he walked forward, his anger merging with lust.

Something banged, she jerked, and then a panel from the belly of the plane clanged to the ground. "Please don't do this." Amy pushed up out of the plane and climbed down the ladder. Her gasp when she saw the missing panel filled up the entire hangar.

Ranger smiled, crossed his arms over his chest, enjoying her distress. She deserved it for her stunt. And for the months of frustration she'd put him through. If he had his prayers answered, her Amelia-Earhart-era-airplane would never fly again.

But then she leaned her head sideways and rested it on the side of the plane. Her eyes drifted shut and the look of utter hopelessness filled her features.

His anger melted. "You know, beating the engine with a wrench isn't a good way to get it to work."

Amy spun around, the yellow airplane a perfect backdrop to her beautiful face. "What are you doing here?"

Ranger let his gaze travel from her scruffy boots, torn jeans and gloriously figure hugging tank, to the top of her dark red head. Her pink cheeks flushed.

"Like what you see?"

Ranger approached, her dark brown gaze turned wary. Good. She should be worried. She'd doused him in chemicals. His skin still itched. He reached forward, plucked an oil stick from her ponytail and sent her hair spilling to her shoulders. He caught the brief scent of flowers and oil.

Amy grabbed her hair, lips parted. Angry. Stubborn. Sexy.

He held up the stick right in front of her face. "Oil stick." Amy snatched it from his fingers and tossed it across the room. "I told you to stay away from me."

Ranger shrugged, his brain still caught on the image of her jean-clad ass hanging out of that airplane. Forget *Sports Illustrated*. He had farm fucking fantastic right here.

"Don't you think dropping that all-natural excuse for chemicals on me is a bit dramatic? If you want to get me naked all you had to do is ask." Ranger gestured to himself, sweeping his hand from his head down to his torso, Amy's eyes followed.

That definitely wasn't desperation or anger in her gaze.

The desire he'd been trying to hold in check for months reared up inside him.

"You think I want to see you naked?" Amy snorted, then lifted her chin. "Besides, I figured anything would be an improvement to your normal smell." So much for her vulnerability.

The wind picked up, blew into the hangar. Ranger shifted, praying the wind wouldn't open the fly on his boxers, and almost covered himself. Almost. Until he remembered she was the reason for his stench. Instead, he stood tall. "You've never had a problem with the way I smelled before."

"My manners were just too good to say anything." She strode past him, punishing him with the sexy sway of her hips.

Dammit, he was so hard for her, even her walk had his mind blanking. He stood there, nearly naked, and drenched in herbicide, and she walked past him like a stranger on a sidewalk.

Running from him. Again.

"Amy Ann." He didn't yell, but she stopped mid-stride. Turned. Lips parted.

"You did that on purpose," Ranger said. She'd been hard headed even in high school, when he tried to break up with her, explaining that he needed a little space to see if life in Mercy was what he really wanted. Jumping on the marriage and kids bandwagon at eighteen years old had scared the shit out of him. But he'd obliterated any chance for reconnecting with Amy when she'd seen him making out with Tonya at the football game senior year.

He hadn't thought that leaving her to sow the wild oats of his youth would be a self-fulfilling prophecy of regret. Or that his best friend would move in on Amy so fast and fill the void that Ranger had left in her heart.

"You bet your ass I did."

"What the hell for?" He couldn't get her smell, her taste, her touch out of his head. But she'd dumped shit on him for the last time.

Her eyes narrowed and her lips flattened. "I warned you."

Yeah, she'd warned him to stay away from her. He'd stayed with her for weeks, helping her after the funeral. She'd healed physically, but remained an emotional tomb.

"I promised Shane, if anything ever happened to him, I'd look out for you." He wanted to take her in his arms and kiss that angry expression right off her face. He'd wanted her since high school, but when she'd married Shane, he'd vowed to put those feelings away. Forever. But the attraction hadn't disappeared. And he knew it never would. "I know the chemistry between us is weird. Scary. But dammit it's real and it's here and now. You're just flying through the clouds because you don't want to see what's on the ground right in front of you."

If he hadn't been studying every minute expression on her face he would have missed the brief flash of vulnerability in her gaze. Then her anger slid back in place. "The only thing I feel is annoyance. Are you so desperate that you have to chase after what you can't have? You dumped me first, remember?"

Him? Desperate? No. He'd never had a problem getting women. Until Amy.

If he hadn't been so young and stupid he would have been the one she'd married. Not Shane.

Now all he could think, all he could see, was the small sprinkle of freckles across her pert nose. He could be on a mission in a third world country or down the road. It didn't matter. She affected him.

He had an all-consuming need for his best friend's

wife. He hadn't counted on lust eating him alive.

But he had honor. He had loyalty. Ranger had vowed over Shane's grave to take care of Amy. "Do you have a death wish?"

"A what?"

"You could have tangled in those electric wires today. You touched the goddamn treetops. Are you trying to commit suicide by plane and join Shane in the ground?"

Fury flashed across her gaze. Fury and something else. Something like pain and fear. "How I do my business is none of your business."

"It is my business if you're endangering yourself." He ground the words through clenched teeth.

"No. It's not. It used to be Shane's business. But he's dead." Her voice rose with each word and cracked on the last.

"Shane may be dead, but you're not. Chloe's not." Ranger moved closer, took her hand and placed it on his chest. "I'm here, Amy. I'm standing right in front of you. Can you not see me? Feel me?"

Her breathing increased, sharp, short and fast. She wasn't immune to him, he knew it in his bones. He just had to convince her.

He held her gaze and stepped closer. Her eyes widened a fraction. Satisfaction rolled through him. She wanted him. He could see it in the parting of her lips, the pulse racing at the hollow of her throat. "You're scared. Admit it."

Unable to help himself, Ranger pulled her to him. The air around them sparked. If they stood any closer to the gas tank, the whole place would go up in flames.

"Afraid? Of you?" Her voice was breathy.

"Yes. You're afraid of me."

She shook her head. "No. I'm not afraid of you. I'm afraid of losing my business. My farm. My respect in this town."

"There's no way I'd ever disrespect you. I'm not looking for a one night stand." Ranger cupped her cheek, his gaze drawn to her plump lips, surprised at the tremble he saw there. "I want all of you."

He spoke slow, careful not to scare her away. But his heart pounded so fast he was afraid it would punch out of his chest. He had gone too long without tasting those lips.

"You can't stop people from gossiping. And even if most don't say anything, my mother-in-law will eviscerate me. I'll be ruined," Amy said.

He wanted to squeeze her, tell her everything would be fine. He'd shut the mother-in-law's mouth, permanently, if he had to. He wanted Amy enough to sacrifice everything. But he couldn't stand the fear in her gaze. "You aren't married anymore. You are free to date whoever you want." *Free to be with me.*

Amy grabbed his hand, turned into his palm and kissed him there. That small touch shooting electric currents straight to his chest. "But I'm not free. Not yet."

He lowered his head, his need for her overtaking every other cell in his brain. Amy. Her smile. Her laugh. Her heart.

"Let me go."

"Never. Someone's got to put a stop to this. To you being so scared of the townspeople that you risk death in that crop duster, instead of facing what you really want."

"Scared? When Rand owns Mercy Chemical? You think Mavis will let her new husband continue to supply my business if she finds out about us?"

Ranger was beginning to hate hearing the name Mavis. The woman was pure evil. And she had an undeniable power position in Mercy. She all but controlled the congregation at the First Baptist Church. She basically owned her group of gossip cronies. Now that she had a hand in Mercy Chemical, she could manipulate her daughter-in-law.

But Ranger could take care of Amy and Chloe. "You have to stop before you get hurt."

"The only person that had the right to tell me what to do was my husband. Not you. I didn't choose you." Amy's voice dropped low, but her words burned into his chest with the accuracy of a sniper's bullet.

"You're right. I might not have ever had the right, but I promised Shane I would look after you." He would make her understand, even if he had to turn her over his knee. He tangled a hand in her hair, tilted her face to his. "I've already lost one Carter. And I'll be damned if I lose another."

Ranger captured her mouth in a kiss meant to dominate. She filled his senses. He slanted his mouth over hers, thrusting his tongue deep, forcing her to respond to his kiss. He couldn't lose her. He couldn't stay away. She was his everything. His hope. And she was going to quit endangering herself, even if he had to chain her to his bed.

She whimpered, the small sound breaking into his insanity. He became aware of her nails digging into his flesh. Her shaking. Guilt gut punched him.

He had to stop, to break free of this...madness.

Ranger eased up, pulled back, but before he could separate from her, she wrapped her hands around his neck. Her tongue met his, and he was lost.

Chapter Four

Amy relinquished control. She couldn't think. Couldn't find her anger or her logic. Not when Ranger held her like this.

The loneliness she refused to admit to anyone, even herself, urged her onward. This was what she needed. This volcanic explosion of lust.

Ranger trailed kisses across her cheek, down her neck. She really shouldn't be kissing him. Touching him. If anyone found out...

Ranger bit down on her neck, drew her skin into his mouth. She gasped, grabbed his shoulders for support. Nothing about the man was soft. His corded muscles felt like satin encased steel.

His hands fell to her bottom, lifted and she wrapped her legs around his waist. He walked them backwards, propped her inside the cockpit of her plane and continued his onslaught.

Amy couldn't be still any more. Her hands roamed across his wide shoulders, down his biceps, exploring his hard muscular chest. Ranger used his teeth to tug the strap of her tank to the side and expose her breast. She held him close. The possibility of a tarnished reputation becoming more of an absent thought than a life or death decision.

When he sucked a nipple into his hot mouth, she arched, cried out. He stripped her defenses. Exposed her. He pulled her other strap down and continued to torture her sensitive skin. She didn't try to stop him. She couldn't.

Heat flooded her thighs, her body a burning mass of need. The entire town could walk in right now and she wouldn't care. By the time his lips returned to hers, Amy was out of breath and ready to climb on top.

Her hand shot south between them, straight into his boxers and wrapped around his hard length. His girth so big her fingers didn't touch. She found the moisture beading his tip and he groaned, bucking forward into her palm. A heady sense of power heightened her arousal and she squeezed him harder, wanting to make him lose control.

He growled, the deep rumble of his chest vibrating through her entire body, and ripped open the button on her blue jeans. "You feel so fucking good." His words were dark and desperate.

"Yes." Amy thumbed his tip again. He sucked her nipple deep, bit down.

"No, Signor. No, I cannot do this." A man's voice broke through their silent struggle to rip each other's clothes off. Amy froze.

Another man's voice, this one more guttural, spoke in a fast stream of Spanish, his anger evident despite the fact she couldn't understand a single word of the foreign language.

"No. Please, I beg you." Pedro. That was Pedro's voice begging the other man. In her hangar. And she was half naked with Ranger between her legs.

Oh no. Amy shoved Ranger away so quickly she nearly fell out of the cockpit. Ranger turned, caged her behind him. She pushed against him, but she might as well have been pushing a hundred year old oak tree.

"Move." She kept her voice low, almost to a whisper, silently praying the other men wouldn't see them.

"Quiet." Ranger held a finger to his lips.

The Spanish stranger spoke again. Amy heard a thump then Pedro answered in Spanish, their speech patterns the only way she could tell them apart. The men were on the other side of the plane.

Rangers ice blue gaze slammed into hers. "We're not finished."

Amy wiped the back of her hand across her mouth, as if she could wipe away the memory of his touch. As if his taste wasn't permanently imprinted on her lips. Her hand trembled and she shoved it in her back pocket before he noticed the betraying movement. "Yes, we are. You took advantage of me."

Had she thought his gaze was hot before? The look of pure menace filling his features caused her to take a step back. He placed a hand on either side of her head, pinning her between him and the plane. His voice was low, but it impacted her just the same. "I didn't make you shove your hands in my pants."

The breath expelled from her lungs. He was right. She couldn't think straight when he got within a half mile. Where was her control? "I didn't ask you to come here. I didn't ask for any of this."

Ranger's smile disappeared and he slammed a palm flat against her plane. Metal rattled, the entire plane shook beneath his attack. Another screw broke free and clanged to the floor.

"You broke my plane."

He slapped her plane again. "You can't break a rust bucket. This piece of shit is barely holding together." As if to emphasize his point, another piece of her precious plane fell to the ground. The crash seemed louder. Final.

She didn't even turn to see what broke. "This pile of garbage puts food on the table."

"Why can't you do something safe? Wait tables full-time instead of just on the weekends? Get a job as a secretary? That puts food on the table. Hell, if you would let me, I would put food on your table."

"What, now were going caveman?" She thumped a fist on her chest. "Me caveman, you woman."

Ranger's face turned red. "Damn you hard headed woman. Just because I want to take care of you doesn't make me a Neanderthal."

She rose up on her toes, nose to nose with him. "No, it just makes you an overbearing chauvinist. In case you missed the past, oh I don't know, fifty years or so, women can make a living any way they want."

"Miss Amy?" Pedro walked around the plane, a short stocky man she didn't recognize right behind him.

Amy shoved past Ranger, needing to put as much physical distance between them as possible and cover her embarrassment at being caught. "Pedro, who's your friend?"

Pedro's gaze dropped, the brim of his faded red baseball hat hiding his eyes. ""No one, signora. He leave."

"No hurry, amigo. Introduce me to your boss lady." The man walked forward, held out his hand. "I am Santos."

Amy moved to extend hers, and hesitated. Pedro's fear snaked across the empty space between them, wrapping around her. Warning her.

Hostility rolled off Ranger with all the subtlety of a tidal wave and Amy's stomach knotted. She trusted Pedro, as much as she would a brother. And although Ranger drove her crazy, she trusted him too. She pulled her hand back at the last minute and let it fall to her side.

Santos dropped his hand, but his dark eyes traveled the length of her body, the lewd look filled her with repulsion. "Be careful, you don't want to piss me off."

Before Amy could react, Ranger pushed her behind him. His wide stance completely blocking Santos. "Care to repeat that?"

She swallowed, sensing the raw power barely contained inside.

"I see the señorita means much to you. You should be careful with the things you love. They are precious and easily broken."

Amy's entire body was a mass of nerves, but she couldn't resist peeking around Ranger's broad shoulders. Any look of congeniality disappeared from the Mexican's face. He lowered a beefy hand to the bottom of his shirt and slowly lifted it up. A small black pistol nestled between his jeans waistband and bulging stomach.

Ranger took a step forward, when a sane man would have backed up. He towered over the Mexican by a good foot. Needing to do something besides stand there like an idiot, Amy sidestepped and crossed her arms, intending to tell Santos to kiss off. But Ranger shoved her back behind him.

"You could say the same thing about necks. So delicate, so easily broken." Ranger took another step. Santos lowered his hand, resting it on the butt of the gun.

Pedro eased closer to Santos, his gaze locked on the weapon. "Santos, you come here for me. Let them alone."

Amy had brought Pedro and his son into her home. Gave him a job. Gave him a chance at a life in the US. And now he put himself between her and Santos.

"Yes, mi amigo, I did. But now I see what you've been hiding." Santos's black eyes slid to her. Amy lifted her chin and narrowed her gaze, while inside she shivered.

She'd never been threatened before. Never.

"Miss Amy," Pedro's son, Arturo, rushed from the back door of the hangar to her. His little voice was the only warning before he launched himself into her arms. She caught him mid-leap, his legs wrapped around her waist, his arms locked around her neck.

"Ah, so this is Arturo. A strong young man." Santos's eyes reflected his black soul.

Amy had no idea what he had planned for Artie, but she instinctively turned, shielding the boy from his view.

"Lobello. I see the tattoos on your face. I know what you do to women and children." Ranger's voice was harsh. Deadly. "You need to leave and never come back, or your gang won't be able to do anything but bury the pieces left when I'm done."

Even Artie kept quiet, his usually prolific talking silent, and buried his face against her neck.

"Please, Santos. I told you, I cannot help. Please, do as he says." Pedro said.

Amy glanced back to see the hard line of Santos mouth break into a grin more menacing than Hannibal Lecter. "You are right. I will go." Santos wrapped a hand around the back of Pedro's neck and yanked him close. "But you and I, we will speak again."

Santos looked at Amy "I will see you soon, bonita."

Maybe, if she were smart, she'd ignore the threat. But not today, not now. He'd threatened Pedro. He'd threatened her. He'd threatened Artie. And she'd be damned if he touched a hair on the boy's head. "Get off my property before I call the cops."

* * *

Ranger used every ounce of control to keep his arms at his sides and not wrap his hands around Santos's neck. The small L shaped tattoos trailing from the corners of the man's eyes clearly labeled him as a Lobello. The gang of Mexican cartel wannabes and un-documented murderers used a small L, instead of a teardrop, to mark all of their rapes and kills. And Santos had enough to prove that he wasn't all talk.

"Nice tattoos." Ranger said,

"Si señor, and if my friend here is not careful, I'm going to add two more."

Pedro visibly fought to stay brave although his fear was palpable. And as much as Ranger wanted to kill Santos, he couldn't sacrifice his mission. The Lobellos were his mission. He had been heading to their territory a mere two hours ago.

But if the asshole didn't stop looking at Amy like she was naked, Ranger would forget the mission. He'd forget the law. He'd forget everything honorable in his body and murder the Mexican. Fuck the mission.

"I'll be in touch, Pedro. Give you a day to think about it." Santos said.

"No thinking, get the hell out." Ranger crowded Santos's space, forced the smaller man back a step. He couldn't give a dick if the fucker was packing. He'd killed under worse circumstances.

Santos raised his dirty hands and backed up. He turned and walked out. But Ranger had the feeling the man wouldn't heed his warning. And he'd have to be dealt with.

But not until Ranger took care of Amy. She clutched Arturo like a mamma bear protecting her cub, not one hint of

fear on her beautiful face. Only fury. Ranger's chest swelled
with pride. His woman was fierce.

"Miss Amy, I sorry. I told him not to come here."
Pedro pulled off his ball cap and knocked it on his leg,
sending a cloud of dust puffing into the air.

"It's not your fault." Amy said.

"Damned if it's not his fault. What the hell are you
doing getting involved with the Lobellos?" Ranger couldn't
suppress his anger. Not after Santos threatened Amy. And no
matter how grateful Pedro was for taking his family in off the
street, he was mixed up with the worst gang within three
states. Which meant danger to anyone Pedro knew.

"Don't talk to him like that." Amy snapped. Ranger
ignored her, keeping his gaze focused on Pedro.

"The Lobellos got us to the US. I gave him everything,
all my money. They said that's all they need. Me and Arturo,
we come here, look for work. I thought we were finally free.
Then Santos showed up. Said I owe him." Pedro fidgeted,
looked down. His stance deflated.

"They can't do that." Amy said. "We will call the
police."

"No. The police no help illegals. They would send us
back. Arturo will be U.S. Citizen." Pedro shook his head,
pushed his shoulders back. "No. We will leave. Tonight. That
way Santos have no reason to come back."

"No, Papa. I don't want to go." Arturo cried out,
squeezing his little arms around Amy's neck in a death grip.

Amy petted the boy's hair, soothed him. "No, you're
not leaving. I won't let you."

"Leaving isn't going to solve the problem. Not now."
Ranger said. Not after seeing the look of lust in Santos gaze
when he looked at Amy. The man would be back, whether
Pedro left or not.

The woman was crazy. And he wanted her so bad he'd
give up breathing for a kiss. He would stay here. He would
protect her. He just had to figure out a way not to totally
screw his mission.

Amy finally set Arturo on the ground, the five-year-old

took off running to his father, but stopped halfway. Staring up at Ranger. "Why you naked, signor?"

Chapter Five

"Arturo. It's bedtime. No more talking tonight." Pedro tipped his hat down, a perfect shield. If the man shrank any further he'd go to migit-mode. "Miss Amy, I sorry. I not intend to bring trouble."

"But papa, the sun is still up."

"Hush," Pedro eased his harsh tone by soothing a hand over Artie's curly black hair. He faced Amy, the look in his eyes way too intense for Ranger. Too intense and too familiar.

Rangers gut twisted with a feeling he'd so far only harbored for his dead best friend. Jealousy.

"We leave before we bring you trouble," Pedro said.

"No. You two aren't going anywhere. I'll call the sheriff and let him know so he can keep an eye out. I can't run this place without you."

"I can help. I know how to deal with people like Santos." Ranger had no intention of letting the pair leave and break Amy's heart. Even if Pedro was giving her goo-goo eyes. He would stake out her place, camp on her front lawn if he had to, whether she wanted it or not.

"Don't need your help. We've got it. Right Pedro?" Amy forged on.

"Please papa, I don't want to go." Artie's baby brown

eyes pleaded worse than a lost puppy. No way anyone could turn that kid down.

"Yes, miss. We stay. You want to run the plane tomorrow? I have it ready."

"I can't tomorrow. I've got something else to do." Amy grabbed Artie and gave him a quick kiss on the forehead. "I can't run this place without you either little man."

"I'm going to make you a special present, Miss Amy." Artie gave her a quick hug. "But no painting."

Pedro and Arturo said their goodbyes. She'd given her old farmhouse to them rent-free earlier this year when Pedro had shown up looking for work. When any other single woman would have hid behind a locked door, she had let them in. Given them a home. A job. A chance at life. His woman had a kind heart. An innocent heart. "You're a good woman."

And one that would get her killed if she didn't get help with the Lobellos.

"Anyone would do it," she said.

The sun sank lower, and the shadows stretched across the hangar. Heavy air pressed him down almost as much as his worry. A threat from the Lobellos wasn't anything to take lightly. His recon on the gang had been so far from small-town-wanna-be-gang, they almost qualified for the Mexican Mafia.

In fact, they operated a lot like ISA, the Islamic State of Afghanistan, which Ranger fought overseas. The same ISA that killed Shane.

The Lobello's initiation required a "triple." One drug deal. One rape. One kill. By the time a member reached the next level, their face was tattooed with an L from cheek to chin. Santos had most definitely reached level five.

Amy and her innocent heart would be trampled in a second. "Not just anybody would take in a complete stranger." Ranger tugged her to him. "Amy, I'm going to run home and take a shower, grab an overnight bag. I'll stay here. Make sure Santos doesn't come back."

"Ranger, I can't do this. We can't do this." She tugged

back, but he held firm.

She had to understand. He wasn't letting her go. His muscles pulled tighter than rigger cord beneath an open parachute canopy on a HALO jump. He wasn't leaving her alone to be trapped and tortured by a psychotic gang. "You might not want me to, but there is no way I'm letting you stay here, alone, with Santos's threat. He will come back."

"I'm not alone. Pedro is here. I have a gun. We'll be fine." She crossed her arms, looked at him like he would just say okay and leave.

Not on her life.

"No, you won't. I've fought men like him. They're dirty and dangerous. And if you think some puny shotgun and an illegal immigrant with a five-year-old can protect you, your nuts. Think of Chloe. Do you want to risk her? Santos is coming back. He might not tonight, but he wants you. I saw it. And if he gets you, I might not be able to save you."

Amy's face drained of any color. Her lip trembled and Ranger wanted to hold her, tell her she would be okay. The look of desperate fear on her face ripped his heart. But she had to understand, and if he had to use her baby to make her realize the danger, he would. He'd seen too much death in his job to just let her go. Let her fend for herself. Ranger gripped her arms hard and fought the images flashing in his mind. Images of women and children from battle zones, bloody and broken. He'd seen too many hurt and killed because of evil men. Only this time, stranger's faces were replaced with Amy's. Fury refueled his determination.

"Ranger, please, let go. You're holding on too tight."

He immediately relaxed his grip, but he couldn't let go of the fear for her. "I've seen what they can do. Is that what you want? You want to get hurt? You want them to take Arturo and make him Lobello? And you and Chloe? I promise, once he is through using you he will sell you both and you will disappear. He knows you live alone, out here, on this farm. He could do anything and by the time I got here, it would be too late."

The last bit of resolve melted from her face. Ranger

fought the regret climbing up his spine. All he wanted today was to talk to her, hope for a date, maybe a kiss. Instead, a goddamn Mexican cartel honed its sights on his woman.

His woman.

No, Shane's woman. He shouldn't think of her like that. Like he had a right to her body. But more and more he found himself wanting more than her body. He wanted her heart. Her soul. Her love.

He wanted to be there to protect her and Chloe. The thought of children, or raising a child, had never before entered his mind. But seeing her with Chloe in her arms did things to him. Made him feel deeper. No, he shouldn't want Amy Carter or her baby. He should honor his promise to look out for her, a promise he'd made to Shane at his graveside. But he did want her. He wanted all of her.

"You can't stay here. Not tonight." Amy placed a hand, gently, on his chest. He felt like she shoved her fist into his chest and gripped his heart. "I'm not stupid. I understand that this guy is a threat. But it can't be you protecting us. I'll call Bo."

"Why are you so damn scared of me?" Did she have another man? Is that why she didn't want him here? The control he'd fought so hard for flew further away. He'd kill whatever bastard laid a hand on her.

"I can't tell you. Just trust me, you don't want to be here."

"Is it another man? Is that why you're so hell bent on stomping me down?" Fury faded to red. Then black. He couldn't see straight. Ranger had fought for so long against a ghost, he didn't know if he could deal with a real live person.

"Is that what you think, I'm sleeping around? You've lost it. I haven't ever been with anyone else!" Amy shouted and twisted in his grip.

"Why else won't you let me protect you?" Ranger roared in response to her outburst. His chest clenched so tight his ribs were near breaking. He didn't think he could take it. If she was in love with someone else. If she chose someone else again. He knew he couldn't take it.

Chapter Six

"Let go." Amy screamed so sharp the metal walls rattled. She lifted her arms, and then yanked them down, flinging Ranger's grip from her.

Rage. Fear. Heat. Was she losing her mind? Why did she crave the touch of a man who thought she slept around? How could she betray Shane so quickly. It hadn't even been a year since the funeral. What kind of woman could move past her husband's death like that? And for a man who thought she was a slut. "You asshole. You really think I'm seeing someone else?"

Ranger didn't look remorseful. In fact, he leaned down, his stupid-perfect chest glowed gold in the sunset. And her stupid-stupid heart did a flip-flop for joy.

"I don't know what to think. You've flown circles around me so long I can't see straight."

"So of course, big caveman, you assume it's about sex?" Amy balled up her fist, the blood pumping. Shane had never talked to her like that. Never.

But he'd never talked to her at all.

"Just tell me. End my misery." Ranger yelled right back. He didn't turn and walk away. He didn't go cold and distant, like she didn't matter. "Dammit Amy Ann, I've never loved another woman in my entire life. It's always been you.

Always."

Oh God. "Ranger..." What to say?

I love you?

She might as well close her business and hang the foreclosure sign in the window. And Chloe, what about her daughter? Could Mavis use her relationship with Ranger to take her daughter away? Make her look like an unfit mother?

Ranger stood tall then. Looked down at her. A look she'd seen before. The one right before the people in her life walked out the door.

Amy swallowed past the lump of cotton in her throat. Her father had given her that look. Seventeen years old, the week before prom. She hadn't seen him since.

Shane gave her the same look after their fight. He'd boarded a plane for Afghanistan without a backwards glance.

Now Ranger.

Tears threatened but she looked away and blinked hard. Not again. She didn't care. She didn't freaking care.

"I'm not leaving. You can scream and cuss all you want. I know you love me." Ranger grabbed her arms again. This time though he held her at arm's-length. Trapping her in his strong hands and strong gaze. "I'm. Not. Leaving."

The metal cage around her heart cracked. "What?" He wasn't giving up?

"Your temper might scare off a weaker man, but not me. Because deep down, I know you want me to stay. I know you've got some fucked up reason to tell yourself why you can't let me, but you want me too."

He wasn't leaving. Not Shane. Not her father.

"Tell me you don't want me. Tell me right now to my face that our kiss doesn't drive you wild. That you don't think about that night together. Tell me it didn't mean anything." Ranger didn't blink or break his gaze from hers. He didn't give her the chance to look away.

She couldn't speak. Her mouth went dry. She couldn't tell him that, because she'd dreamed about that night every single day since. She'd imagined his lips on hers. Imagined his mouth on her skin. Tasting. Taking. Torturing.

"I can't. Please, Ranger. I can't. Why are you doing this to me?"

"Because, you're worth fighting for. Every damn day for the rest of my life." Ranger's voice was harsh, deep, and caressed her skin like the softest silk. "Tell me you don't want me."

I don't want you. But her lips wouldn't form the words. He wanted her enough to see past her false anger. Past the front. He wanted her enough to stay. "I want you."

Ranger groaned and yanked her to him. "Dammit." Ranger crushed his mouth over hers in a kiss that communicated all the pent up need. All the longing. She parted her lips, welcomed his probing tongue. Met him head on and clutched his shoulders like a lifeline, because if he let her go, she'd collapse on the ground. He tilted his head, slanting his mouth over hers. The kiss was so intense she almost melted.

She couldn't help but notice every little detail. His day's beard growth scraping across her jaw. His tight lips, so tender and soft. His smell. The way a man should smell. All earth and musk and raw sex. Her stomach clenched, her thighs clenched, her entire body clenched, desperate for more of this man.

He drove her wild, past reason, past her a-good-girl-shouldn't-do-this thoughts. She wanted him so bad.

His hands moved from her shoulders, down to her elbows. Each inch of her skin burned. When his hands fell on her hips, she jerked forward. He cupped her ass, lifted and squeezed. Amy moaned, the intense sensations torturing her insides. Please don't stop.

Her cellphone buzzed in her back pocket. She ignored it, Ranger's lips trailed down her throat, in light fluttering whispers against her skin.

The buzzing in her pocket came to life in a loud ring, and AC/DC's "Highway to Hell" filled the hangar.

Holy. Crap. Amy jerked back and snatched the cell from her pocket. She'd pre-programmed the ringtone to warn her of impending disaster. Her mother-in-law had the sixth sense.

Ranger pulled her to him again, but Amy wriggled free. "You must really love that person."

Love? Sure, like the devil loved church.

"I gotta go." Mavis and her weekly calls of guilt to remind Amy that she'd stolen her only boy too early. Now she could add lusting after his best friend to her list.

"What? Wait a minute. Who was that? What's wrong?" Amy wanted to tell him it was Mavis. But no. That was her own cross to bear.

"Listen. I know you want to stay and help out. But you can't. Not tonight. Please, I promise to call Bo over if there is trouble."

"Tell me what is going on."

"I can't. Listen, I'll call you tomorrow afternoon. Okay?" Amy backed up a step. Then another.

Ranger's look of confusion and hurt and anger filling up her vision.

Her cell buzzed again, indicating a voice message from Mavis Carter. The mother-in-law to make Ursula the Sea Witch look like a guppy. Eighty percent of the reason Amy could never have a life or relationship past Shane Carter.

"Amy stop. Talk to me."

Amy backed up one more step. "I'm sorry."

Then she did what she did best. She ran. All the way to the house. She left a too perfect sculpted set of abs in her dust and high-tailed it to her back door. He'd said he didn't want her just one night. He wanted her forever. Wanted her enough to fight for her.

Amy went into the kitchen, slammed the door behind her and grabbed the back of her kitchen chair. Her heart hit so hard and fast it might as well have been the plane propeller whacking her chest.

Ranger. She closed her eyes. Want wandered down her body. His confusion was worse than his outrage. Damn Mavis and her call. Amy wouldn't be surprised if the woman hadn't set up cameras to spy on her. She had made it plain she never trusted Amy. And that she blamed Amy for Shane joining the military and therefore his death. That her mission in life was to make Amy miserable.

She never missed a photo op for the press. Mavis had cried on more news stations than Oprah. And then she'd dragged Amy to the cemetery every month to stare at Shane's grave. And to remember the guilt.

But Shane had been the one to walk away. Not Amy.

And now she had a flesh and blood God-given second chance all but beating down her door and threatening to drag her by her hair to his cave to be his little woman.

And she wanted that so bad.

Her body felt on fire. Maybe she was having heat stroke. Amy went to the cabinet, grabbed a glass and filled it with ice water, downing half the contents in one long gulp. She needed to cool off.

Needed the shock to remember who she was. She was Shane Carter's widow. She was loyal. She wasn't attracted to her dead husband's best friend.

Not attracted. Not attracted. Not attracted.

She didn't want him every second. She finished the water. Maybe if she told herself often enough she would start to believe it.

She'd done everything she could to warn Ranger away, and he kept coming. And thank God he did, otherwise she and Pedro would have been alone with Santos. Amy knew the man could have done anything to her, and no one would have been able to stop him.

Except Ranger.

She went to the living room, stopping in front of the fireplace mantle. Shane's military picture sat right there, in a black frame. His straight lips and serious eyes glared at her. Cold. Hard. Distant.

Remember, Amy, remember.

Chapter Seven

Ranger slammed into the newly finished log house he shared with his brother and new sister-in-law, barely keeping his rage in check.

No matter how much he wanted to turn and put his fist through the wall, this wasn't his house to destroy.

But if his commander kept him stateside, he'd build his own house. Then he could put a hole in any goddamn wall he wanted.

Amy blew so freaking hot one minute he thought he was in the Mohave Desert and so cold the next he might as well be in Ant-freaking-artica. He didn't know whether she'd given him heat stroke or frostbite, but either way his brain was fried.

Damn woman. No one had ever made him lose control like that. When they kissed, he felt like a king. But after, when she opened her mouth and spoke, he felt like a fool.

And now, all he felt was rage. Santos had sealed his fate. The man would die. It was just a matter of when. But Amy didn't want Ranger there, at her house, at night. Part of him realized she was running scared and needed time. Needed soothing.

But the other part. The caveman part, wanted to beat down her door and scream mine.

"What the hell?" Hunter walked into the kitchen.

"What?" Ranger half-growled the word.

"Where is your shirt? Why aren't you doing recon on the Lobellos? And what the fuck is that smell?" Hunter filled up the doorway from the living room to the kitchen. His brother, black hair, black eyes. And up until last year, Ranger had almost been convinced, a black soul.

But then Hunter found Evie. And the big grizzly bear tamed into a cub in her hands.

Ranger briefly considered lying, but there was no point. He'd not only completely neglected his mission, but he'd almost blown it.

"Grab me a beer." Ranger moved to the table, pulled out a hand carved wooden chair and sat.

"Sure." Hunter strode to the stainless steel fridge, pulled out a couple of beers, passed one to Ranger, and took a seat opposite. "Spill."

Ranger twisted the cap off his beer, downing half the bottle in one swallow. The cold liquid cooled his temper to about a half a degree below boiling. "I stopped on the way to McGehee."

"What was so important you detoured from the Lobello's home town?"

"Amy Carter."

"Jesus H. Christ. You do like your torture don't you?"

Ranger knew his brother thought he'd lost his mind. Hell, sometimes Ranger even thought he'd lost his mind. "Yep."

"And what, you thought if you showed her your muscles she'd change her mind and jump your bones?" Hunter leaned back in his chair, his amused grin growing wider, and crossed his hands behind his head.

"I had a shirt on when I saw her." Ranger took another swig, needing the liquid courage.

"And?"

"And I stopped by the field she was spraying, hoping to catch her for a minute, and she doused me in goddamn herbicide."

Hunter tipped back in his chair and roared with laughter. Ranger gave serious thought to kicking his brother's chair backwards. He planted a booted foot on the edge and gave Hunter a nudge. His brother stopped laughing. "Do it and die."

"I'm glad I can provide so much entertainment, brother." Ranger eased back, letting Hunter's chair back down flat on the kitchen tile.

"Just tell me the next time you plan to visit her. So I can provide back up. Evie's gonna be pissed you stank up the new house."

"Sure. Right after you help me over a cliff." Ranger paced to the trash, tossed the empty beer, and grabbed a new one. "She's driving me nuts."

"All the best ones do," Hunter said.

"Yeah easy for you to say, yours didn't twist you up into knots. Blow hot and cold."

"Were you here last year? Are we talking about the same woman? My wife? The one that ran from me at every opportunity?"

Ranger nodded and sat back down. "Yeah. That one. She's an amateur compared to Amy."

Hunter's stare probed too deep, his silence telling. Hunter had almost lost Evie to her own psychopath stalker. And Ranger knew, if his brother had lost Evie, Hunter wouldn't have made it. He would have lived, as is took oxygen in and out of his lungs, but Hunter would have shut down, and what little edge of peace he'd gained, would disappear.

"So quit then. Give her up."

"Okay. I'll give up when you give Evie up." Same thing. Ranger felt for Amy deep beyond his heart. Into his soul.

"You've got it bad, man. And no way Mavis is gonna let her move on, that woman will flay her alive and eat her for lunch." Hunter leaned forward, rested his arms on the matching heavy wood table.

Ranger cringed. Shane's mother moved beyond contentious to downright mean. The woman may lead the Baptist Church women's prayer group, but she belonged in hell with her father, the devil. Then realization dawned. The phone call. Highway to Hell. Mavis.

No wonder Amy went ghost white and ran off. This shit storm of small town drama was about to go FUBAR.

"The commander is gonna have your ass either way. We can't do the mission without the intel." Hunter reminded him in his calm big brother voice.

Shitballs. The mission. Ranger was the only team member yet to come face to face with Lobello and therefore the only one to do intel and a possible meet and greet without tipping their hat. Small town gossip wasn't the only thing about to go FUBAR. "Hunter. I ran into a Lobello named Santos at Amy's hangar this afternoon. He was there, threatening one of her workers."

Hunter stopped moving, his stare turned deadly. "The Santos Guillera who is in charge of new inductees?"

Arturo. Shit. "We need to call command. I think he was there to take Arturo away from his father. And I think Amy is in danger too."

Hunter had his phone in his hand punching in numbers when it rang. Hunter met Ranger's gaze. Command.

Hunter sat back and answered the cell. "Sir."

Ranger couldn't hear what was said, but whatever it was, it was loud. Cpt. Grey, it seemed, was pissed. Ranger made to grab the phone but Hunter held up a hand. "Yes, sir. Be there in five."

Hunter disconnected the call, downed his beer. "Well little bro, you started your own shit storm alright. Cpt. Grey wants us there five minutes ago. Oh, and in case you were wondering, he's gonna ream your ass for screwing up."

"I couldn't tell. Damn. I can't stay long. I have to set up at Amy's. That bastard might show up tonight for a snatch and grab." Ranger headed toward the spare bedroom and shower.

"You gotta take a shower and get to the meeting or the CO's gonna tag you AWOL. I'll call Bo Lawson, fill him in, have him sit tight on her property until we can get there later."

Ranger all but snarled. "Tell that sadist to keep his hands off my woman."

"Sure. Touch your woman and die. Got it. Now hurry the fuck up so we don't get reamed any more than necessary."

Ranger didn't bother to answer, he rushed through the shower, change of clothes. Black shirt. Black tactical pants. Boots. Better.

Hunter hung up the phone when Ranger got back to the kitchen. "Ready to go sunshine?"

"What did the sheriff say?" Ranger had no more play left.

"He's loading up the cruiser now and heading over to her house." Hunter threw some stuff in his tactical bag. Ranger shoved his 9 mm in his pants. His KBAR knife in his boot.

"He better call me if anything so much as twitches out of place." Ranger kept the killing rage down. He caressed his gun, imagined all the ways he could take out Santos with his favorite sniper rifle.

"You two need a room?" Hunter continued to pack up his bag then zip it closed.

"Yeah. On top of a tower is preferable. That way I can see all the mother fuckers coming."

Hunter rolled his eyes. "Come on, we can take your truck. Evie might need mine."

By the time the two brothers reached headquarters they were both pumped and primed for a tongue-lashing. Ranger had to fight to keep his hand off his cell and not check on Amy.

Ranger parked the truck, and Cpt. Grey opened the door to command. His eyes flat, his lips flatter. The killing rage banked just beyond his expression louder than a shout.

"Shit, bro. He's pissed." Hunter pulled his gear on.

"I know. Just let me do the talking, okay?" Ranger jumped down from his truck and strode to his commander.

"Inside, now."

Hunter and Ranger followed, the heavy metal biometric

door sliding shut behind them with a finality that belonged on a *Star Wars* movie.

"Have a nice afternoon drive? Enjoy spending some time with your sweetie?" Cpt. Grey's voice was cold, cold as his eyes. "While you two were playing patty feet with the ladies, the Lobellos started their new recruit hunt. A whole slew of young men have gone missing in the past ten hours. And thanks to you," the Cpt. Pointed directly at Ranger, "we have no intel. No idea where they're taking them. I hope that piece of ass was worth these boys lives."

Cpt. Grey threw out a handful of pictures. Ranger fought the bile rising into his mouth. Young boys. Boys that should be playing video games and eating mac-n-cheese, not learning how to shoot Uzi's.

"They're at a whole new level this year. Instead of going for the teenagers, they're after pre-teens. They want to get them in solid. Brainwash them African rebel style."

"Jesus. Santos is after Arturo. He's five. They are taking them that young?" A wild bullet of fear ricocheted through Ranger's body, taking out whatever organ got in its path.

"Yes. The younger the better. So far there have been five confirmed kidnappings, and who knows how many that were too scared to report it. But they're just getting started. Santos is head of recruitment. You met him? Did he know who you were?"

"No. We just ran into each other. He was there for him." Ranger's mouth went dry and he pointed to the picture of Arturo.

"So the mission may be salvageable. We still need to get someone inside and plant the monitoring device. We can record their conversations and track all movements that way."

"I can do it. Right now. I can get in and out before Santos has a chance to report back to his headquarters."

"Yeah, unless he's already there and tags you." Cpt. Grey paced the length of the end wall. The wall covered in monitors with multiple images. Images from satellites of the

Lobello's known locations. Pictures. Hierarchy.

Hunter met Ranger's gaze. They could do it. As a team, the James brothers were the best machine the military ever created. And it had all been started when the brothers witnessed their father murder their mother. They knew then they had the genes to kill. And the need. Because they wanted to kill their bastard father that night. But he was a grown man in an alcoholic rage against two children. Hunter and Ranger barely made it out alive that night.

"Okay. I don't have any other option right now. Pack up. Plant the device. That's it. We have to get info on these assholes before they kidnap more kids. If we can ID the leader, we can take out the whole gang." Cpt. Grey turned back to the James brothers. "But if you two fuck this up, your happy little vacation in America is over. I'll personally ship your asses back to Africa."

"Yes, sir." Ranger saluted, and so did Hunter. They had a mission to complete. Ranger just needed to figure out a way to trust Bo with protecting Amy for one night. One night. That's it. And maybe if Ranger got lucky, he'd run into Santos and let the bastard trip on his knife

Chapter Eight

Ranger and Hunter locked, loaded, and primed for the mission. Adrenaline pumped through Ranger's veins, pushing his feet faster. His steps harder. He had to see this task through. Had to stay focused. Failure meant innocent kids would become criminals. Killers. Failure meant Ranger gave up his only solid link to ISA. Meant he failed Shane Carter.

But more than that, he hurried because of Amy. Bo Lawson might be there, keeping watch over her, but Ranger needed to protect her.

The security door slid open. Bo Lawson stood there, blocking the exit, arms crossed over his chest.

Fear slammed into Ranger with the force of a freight train. The only man standing between Amy and a Mexican mafia wasn't between them at all. "Why the fuck aren't you at Amy's?"

"I knew you two were planning something." Bo Lawson, Sheriff of Mercy, stepped forward, finger pointing directly in Ranger's face. "You might be military, but this is my town. Everything and everyone goes through me. I warned you what would happen if you tried to run some spook mission behind my back."

Clouds slid across the sky, obscuring what little light

the moon provided. The darkness perfect for undercover work and sneaking into a drug compound.

Perfect for Santos to slip into Amy's house undetected.

"What is this place?" Bo stepped closer, his face a mask of fury.

"You left Amy alone." Ranger spoke soft, the fear and anger choking his windpipe. She could be hurt right now. If Santos was there... He was going to kill the bastard, fuck all if he was the sheriff. "I swear to God, if she is hurt, I'm going to kill you."

Bo didn't back down, he pushed his chest to Ranger's, nose to nose. "I warned you and your brother. Don't try to run ops behind my back in my town."

"If this is your town, why aren't you protecting it? Hunter told you about Santos, about Amy. That bastard could be there right now." Rage. Ranger saw red. He clenched his fist, ready to smash it into Bo's face.

"Then why aren't you there? I know you're spec ops. You could take care of her problem."

Ranger's lip curled and he slapped Bo's finger down. "You wonder why. Look at the last sheriff. For all I know, you're the criminal."

Veins popped on Bo's neck. His face flushed. "I warned you if you did this shit I'd throw your entire team in jail. Even if it's for twenty-four hours. I can still fuck up your mission."

"Try it." Ranger bit out.

Hunter's hand sliced between them, cutting the tension. "We don't really have time for this right now. We have something to do."

Bo turned to Hunter. "What exactly do you have to do?"

Hunter sighed and stepped back. Dammit, Ranger knew that sigh. Knew that look. His brother's eyes shadowed. "What branch of the service were you?"

Bo lifted his chin. "Marines."

"Ever do counter-intel in country?"

"Shit." Bo said.

"Yeah. You know what happened last year, with Evie. You know Sheldon got away with the weapons. We've been tracking them." Hunter turned, indicated for Bo to follow.

"We don't have time for this. They could already be at her ranch." Ranger interrupted, standing with one foot out the door. He had to get to her house. Now.

"You can make time now or you can explain it from jail. It's up to you," Bo said.

Ranger wanted to smash something. He couldn't afford to stand around explaining anything. Amy was alone with Chloe, and Santos was out there. Ranger could feel the bad karma in the chills needling up his spine.

Hunter's gaze slid to Ranger, communicating everything with a look. Bo wasn't going to let this go. He was going to either find out from them or from his own investigation, and if the local law enforcement started investigating, it would draw attention. The Lobellos would go underground. The missing children would disappear.

TF Scorpion's missing guns would disappear.

Al Seriq. Gone.

Ranger turned from the pair, punched in the code for the door panel, and then held his hand up for the biometric lock. The door slid open.

Bo let out a low whistle. "Uncle Sam is a hell of a lot nicer to you than the Sheriff's Office. I had to beg for a new patrol car. You got freaking 007 level shit."

Bo stood still, studying their building. He took everything in slow, his look not giving anything away. Ranger tried to see it through an outsiders eyes. A wall of monitors, high tech computers and tracking systems, tables full of maps and intel. The CIA spared no expense when it came to covering their tracks.

"Hunter, get on it. I'm giving you two minutes to explain. Then I'm gone." Ranger kept his back to the wall beside the door. Bo might arrest him, but he'd have to catch him first.

Cpt. Grey was studying the monitors on the back wall, his broad shoulders bunched beneath his grey shirt. He pressed a button on the table beside him and the monitors went black.

"Why are you studying my case files?" Bo's wide awestruck gaze morphed to pissed.

The Captain turned to the men, his face blank. The man was a machine. Able to shut off his emotions, if he had any, in a split second. Another reason their commander was the best interrogator in the military. "Sheriff."

"Who are you?"

Their commander walked across the room, held out his hand. "Captain Mack Grey."

"I would introduce myself, but I get the feeling you already know me. Especially seeing as how you got my private case files." Bo didn't extend a hand in return.

"Why are you in my compound?" Grey's eyes shifted to Ranger and Hunter.

Ranger found himself explaining, or trying to. "He followed us out here."

"I see. And why would the Sheriff be following you?"

Because he was a bastard. "I am trying to find that out myself."

"Look, Captain, I'm sure you're used to running your own show, without checking in. And I'm sure you usually get what you want. But this is my town. Not D.C. Not a third-world country. And if you want to run ops here, you go through me first," Bo said.

Cpt. Grey showed as much emotion as a broken grandfather clock. Hunter sighed, crossed his arms and propped a hip against the center table. Ranger barely banked the need to slam Bo into the wall. Fuck all. Today was turning into a disaster.

If Santos got to Amy's house before Ranger or Bo, she was dead. Or worse.

"We don't have to tell you shit. This is above your security clearance." Ranger said.

"You don't want to tell me? Fine." Bo shrugged his shoulders, the tan cop uniform pulling tight, his star gleamed in the fluorescent lighting. "I'll just call in my deputies.

Looks like I may have found a drug smuggling operation. It could take us weeks to comb through all this stuff. Hell, I know my tech guy will take at least a month to go through the computers."

Ranger took a step toward Bo, every intention of wrapping his hand around the man's neck. He'd killed before. More times than he could actually recall, adding another body to his list of sins wouldn't bother him in the least. Him and the devil were brothers.

"Stop." Cpt. Grey gave the command and Ranger froze.

"Good call." Bo smiled and Ranger barely kept from driving a fist into the man's face. Again.

"You served under General Blackstone. Four years in counter-intelligence." Grey said.

Bo's smile disappeared and his face hardened. "Yes."

"You were on SEAL Team Reaper." Grey didn't move anything except his lips. The man's expression might as well be granite.

"So." Bo bit out, his demeanor had gone from gleeful to deadly in less than a second. Ranger had heard of team Reaper They were a legend. Nearly the entire team had been taken out on a mission because one of their own turned traitor.

"You are the only one to survive. You were betrayed by one of your own men." Grey continued like he was talking about the weather.

"What is your fucking point old man." Bo bit out, the veins that stood out on his neck throbbed. Pulsed.

"You should understand, better than anyone, why we would be hesitant to let an outsider in. Especially one with your background. You were forcibly detained at Walter Reed for a year before you got right."

Bo blanched, his red face faded to pale. Ranger felt the first small measure of sympathy for the sheriff. He'd lost his entire team. Ranger had lost one man and barely dealt with the guilt. How Bo managed to not lose his mind was a measure of his strength. Conviction.

"How do you know that?"

"I know everything. Just like I know the military is forming a second Team Reaper right now."

"I would know if that happened. General Blackstone would tell me." Bo bit out.

"Sure. I guess that is why you're still hiding in Mercy instead of training at Coronado," Grey said.

Bo took a step, closed the gap between him and the commander, surprising Ranger. The man's face had gone from shock and pain to death and destruction. His lips slashed into a cruel smile. "That's right. I am Sheriff of Mercy. And I'm going to shut your operation down. You can talk about my past all you want. I don't care. The men I cared about are dead. All of them. I have nothing to lose. I will make it my personal mission to fuck up your life."

Grey smiled, crossed his arms over his chest. The silence stretched thin. Ranger was ready to snap. Hunter watched the two men face off, tense.

Ranger's shitty day turned into the shit beneath the shit. His plans to infiltrate the Lobello's compound were over. His mission to protect Amy and Chloe were in severe jeopardy

Grey studied Bo. Ranger wanted to pull out his hair. Storm out the door and take off.

"If you can answer my question, I'll fill you in." Grey waited for Bo to nod.

"What?" Bo said.

"Why are you the only survivor?"

Chapter Nine

Amy sat straight up in bed, ripped from sleep by a distant banging. She strained for alertness and listened, rubbing sleep from her eyes. Her imagination filled the silence in with creaks and groans from the old farmhouse, but she ignored those. Bang. There it was again. The sleep completely gone now, she jumped from the bed and pulled on her robe. Chloe.

Had she fallen out her crib? Oh god, what if she hit her head.

Bang.

The sound reverberated through the house. Not her baby. Not some small rap on a hard wood floor. That was her kitchen door.

Bang.

Something slammed into the back door. Her heart slammed hard in response, kicked over and spun out of control.

Amy grabbed her cellphone off the bed stand, her hands shaking so bad she could barely open it. The numbers wobbled. Call Ranger. He will come. No. Not Ranger. She'd told him to stay out of her life. Why couldn't she get him out of her head?

Come on. Call the sheriff. Call Bo. Only her hands trembled and she couldn't hit the right numbers. What was his number? She couldn't think.

Call for help. Get to Chloe.

Before she finished dialing, the silence caught her attention.

Silence.

Blood pounded in her ears, rushing and ripping through her body, but the silence was louder. Scarier.

Amy took a deep breath. Thank the lord for the metal bar she'd wedged beneath the doorknob. She'd run to the hardware store and bought the extra security device after Santos. It wasn't a high-tech security system, but it was enough to keep someone from simply kicking in her back door.

Something cracked. A loud tearing sound. Amy jerked. Dropped the phone. Wood splintered. Tears clogged her throat and her legs turned to rubber. Someone was trying to pry open her door.

Santos. The monster was back. All the warnings Ranger told her, everything he'd warned her about, came crashing into her mind.

Amy fell to her knees and scrambled in the dark for her phone. She couldn't see. Couldn't think. A light flashed beneath the bed, her phone beeped.

She heard another loud crack. The door wouldn't hold much longer. Amy fell to her stomach and stretched her fingers as far and long as she could, until she tipped the phone. It slipped further away.

She dropped her head to the floor. Come on, Amy. Get it. Get the damn phone.

Amy strained, her muscles protested. Finally she felt the phone, and carefully this time, touched it. Pulled it back. When she had it in her hand, she sat back against the bed, using the solid frame to steady herself.

She dialed.

Another loud crack. Sweat broke out across her neck, her shoulders, her arms. Chloe. She had to call Bo and get to Chloe.

The phone rang once. Twice. She swallowed. Please answer. Please answer.

"Amy?" Bo's smooth voice was a blessing and she nearly cried.

"Bo. Someone's trying to break in my back door." Afraid to speak loud, her voice came out in a whisper, filled with tears and fear.

"Do you have a gun? Where are you in the house?" Bo asked. Amy heard someone talking in the background through the phone. A door slammed. A car cranked.

"I'm in my bedroom." Amy took a deep breath, fought back the tears. Chloe was on the other side of the house. Her little baby, alone. Innocent. Amy scrambled for the baby monitor, pressed it to her ear. She heard Chloe's soft even breathing.

Another crack. Louder, longer. What if the metal rod was bending? She stood, holding the phone and baby monitor.

But her feet wouldn't move forward. She backed away from her door. Retreating until her back hit the wall.

"The gun, Amy. Where is your gun? Can you get it?"

Amy shook her head, no. Where was it?

Another bang, followed by more cracking.

"Amy, I need a verbal response. Can you get to your gun?" Bo's smooth voice ripped her thoughts from death and rape. Being sold into slavery.

"It's...It's, I can't think." She gripped the monitor harder, holding onto the device, like she could somehow anchor to Chloe.

Why hadn't she told Ranger about the strange sounds she'd heard in the past couple of weeks? The lights she swore she saw in her old barn at night? Maybe they weren't her imagination. Maybe it had been Santos all along.

"Amy, listen, I know you're scared, but I need you to take a deep breath. Focus," Bo said. Amy heard cursing through the phone in the background. Ranger. Her eyes squeezed tight.

Would she ever see Ranger again? Would she get the chance to tell him she really did care for him? That she wanted him in her life?

She heard a scraping sound through the phone, rough breathing, and a new voice. This one harsh. Dark. And sent from Heaven. "Amy, honey, I need you to listen to me, okay?"

The tears threatening her eyes spilled down her. "I'm scared."

"It's okay, honey. We're almost there. But I need you to get your pistol. Do you still keep it in your closet?"

Bang!

Amy jumped, flattened her back to the wall. That one sounded like the hinges broke loose from the door.

"Dammit, Bo, go faster. I can hear the bastard through the phone."

"Ranger," Amy whispered. Frozen in fear like a statue. Unable to run. To speak.

"Amy Ann Carter. Go to your closet right now." Ranger's harsh tone snapped her attention back to reality.

"I can't. I can't get my feet to move." They might as well be cement.

"Concentrate on my voice. I'm not going to let you go. I'm not going to let anyone hurt you. I want you to walk to your closet. Now."

Amy concentrated. Focused her energy on picking up her right foot and taking a step.

Bang. Metal crunched. Her back hit the wall again, that one small step getting her nowhere.

"I think...I think he's in the house."

"Dammit Amy, move your ass to the closet now." Ranger's voice rose.

The closet.

Her gun.

Her baby.

"Chloe." Amy breathed, her throat closed off. No oxygen, no air could get through. She hid in her room like a scared rabbit. Left her baby alone and unprotected.

"Don't go out there. I'm almost there." Ranger's voice was desperate.

Fear for her child obliterated the selfish terror for her

own life. Only a coward would be too scared to take care of her own flesh and blood. No. "I'm going to get Chloe." Amy ignored Ranger's shouts, and without looking at the screen, tapped the hang up button and shoved her cell into her robe pocket. She dropped the monitor on the bed and ran into the closet, ripped open the gun cabinet and pulled out her shotgun.

She flew back through her bedroom and grabbed the door handle.

Glass shattered.

Her heart skittered through her chest so fast she almost passed out. No. No fear. Protect her baby. She swallowed, clutched the gun, and slowly turned the knob and opened the door to her bedroom. So scared now she couldn't feel her fingers or feet.

She swallowed, but her throat didn't work. Her hands shook. Chloe. Chloe. Chloe. Amy repeated her daughter's name over and over. Stepping from her bedroom into the kitchen. Slow. Steady.

She caught a glimpse of a man through the small window in her kitchen door. Tall. Skinny. Dark ski mask. They made eye contact and the man stopped. Something familiar whispered through her mind.

He kicked the door. Her heart slammed into her throat. Not familiar. Just deadly. Amy took off running to the nursery.

Chloe slept, on her back, her tiny hands up above her head. So sweet. So perfect and innocent. Amy gripped the gun tighter. She would protect her daughter with her life.

Moving faster now, with purpose, Amy crossed to the nursery door and locked it. She backed up to the crib and took aim.

Chloe was the reason Amy kept living after Shane's death. Her baby had needed her mother. Amy didn't have a choice but to get out of bed in the morning. Keep going. Keep living. Keep the only part of Shane.

Amy primed her gun.

The kitchen door crashed in. Wood and glass shattered.

Amy steadied the butt of the shotgun to her shoulder.

Another crash, like someone kicked over a chair. The man had seen her run through the kitchen.

Amy felt behind her, smoothed a hand down the baby blanket. Touched Chloe's satiny cheek. Unable to resist, she leaned down and placed a kiss to her head, inhaling that scent, that special perfect scent that was specific to her baby.

"I won't let anyone hurt you. I promise." Amy braced herself, and lifted the gun once more. She took aim at the door. Let the bastard come. If he thought he would hurt her or her baby, he would have to do it with a hole in his chest.

Chapter Ten

"Dammit, floor this machine. I can hear the bastard trying to break in the back door." Sweat broke out across Rangers brow and dripped down into his shirt collar. Fucking Lobellos, he knew it. He knew it with every single fiber of his being.

"I've got the gas pedal on the floorboard. It won't go any faster." Bo leaned forward over the steering wheel, swerving to the right and left as the road curved.

Unable to resist, Ranger pressed the cellphone to his ear. Listening for every nuance of sound. He heard the door open. Heard her harsh intake of breath. The banging sounded like it was right there, in the phone. Then nothing. Silence. Had the bastard got inside the house?

Ranger slammed his fist into the dashboard. Bo cut him a look but held silent. Anything happened to her, or Chloe...

He wouldn't think like that. He had to keep his shit together for Amy. And for Chloe. He would protect them both with his life.

He knew the moment Amy entered Chloe's room, he heard her quiet sob and then the soothing sound of a mother with her baby. A silent baby. Please let her be okay. Please let Amy be okay. Please let Chloe be okay.

Ranger wanted to scream in the phone for Amy to pick up, but he knew that would just scare and distract her. Instead he leaned forward, put his forehead on the dashboard he just punched a dent in, and took a deep breath. "Come on baby. Come on, lock the door."

He heard an explosion and his heart plummeted to his stomach. The bastard was inside the house. Bo cut a sharp right, Ranger flew sideways and then righted himself. The police cruiser spun tires down Amy's driveway. He flipped on the overhead lights and siren.

"Maybe the siren will scare them off," Bo said.

Ranger didn't answer. He ripped his gun from its holster, cocked it, and exploded from the police cruiser before it stopped ten feet from Amy's front porch.

The front door was secure. Ranger ran straight up to it and threw his shoulder against the door, slamming inside, not even registering the pain from the blunt force.

"Amy!" Ranger shouted, plunging through the living room, barely catching a shadow of movement. The intruder. Man. Tall. Thin. Face covered. The man bolted out the back door.

"Bo. Out the back." Ranger kept running straight to Chloe's nursery. Cold sweat drenched his temples and dripped down his back.

"On it." Bo rushed past Ranger in pursuit.

Ranger stopped at the closed nursery door. "Amy, honey. It's Ranger. Are you okay?" Ranger put his hand on the lever style doorknob.

"Ranger?" Her voice was weak, faint.

"Yes. Open the door." He held his breath, waited what seem like an eternity before he heard the soft snick of a lock. She pulled open the door. Amy stood there, a huge shotgun clutched at her chest, pale, shaken. Her eyes wide with fright.

Ranger tucked his pistol in his pants, and then he gently cupped her face between his palms. "Are you okay?" Tears streamed down her lovely cheeks.

Ranger forced his chest to unlock and take in a breath. Another breath. She was okay. He was holding her in his arms right now.

"Chloe?"

Amy nodded and relief crushed him. He pulled Amy into his arms, unable to think beyond just holding her. She shook in his arms, her entire body dissolving into tremors and sobs. The soft heartbreaking noises stabbing him repeatedly like a knife in the chest.

"Hush. Hush baby. I'm here. I'm not going to let anything happen to you." Careful as his shaking hand would allow, he removed the shotgun from Amy's grip and leaned it against the wall. Then, unable to hold himself back a minute longer, he yanked her into his arms.

Her heart raced against his chest, her hands clenched and twisted his shirt. She cried harder. "Oh God. What if, what if something happened to Chloe. It's all I could think about."

Ranger soothed a hand down her hair and rubbed her back with his other. "Nothing did happen. You protected her."

He should be the one protecting both of them.

No, not his family. Not his wife. Not his baby.

But dammit, he wanted them so bad. He wanted Amy. Chloe. He wanted to protect. To love them both.

Ranger shuttered and ducked his head, nestling his nose against her neck, savoring the sweet smell special only to Amy.

If something had happened to her, to Amy or Chloe... He couldn't even finish that thought. Nothing was going to happen to them.

Because he would protect them. Whether he had the right or not, this aching driving need controlled him. Possessed him. Amy was in his every thought. The only way Ranger would get a future out of this life would be with her.

He knew he didn't deserve her, and he never would. And he knew he'd always have to deal with the memory of his best friend. But right now he didn't care. He wanted her too much, too deeply. All-consuming desire ripped through him.

Her sobs quieted to soft hiccups. Gently, he sifted his fingers into her hair and tilted her head back. Her tear-reddened eyes tore at his already raw emotions. Unable to wait, to fight the desire, Ranger lowered his head, pausing just above her lips.

"Tell me to stop." Ranger didn't even recognize the ragged whisper from his own lips.

He felt her tremble. A soft low moan tore from her lips a split second before she lifted on her toes and closed the distance between them. Her breath mingled with his.

Ranger's resistance evaporated. He groaned into her mouth, deepening the kiss, taking possession, slanting his head taking more. Her soft sounds of pleasure filled his ears like sweet heaven. Never had anything tasted this good, felt this right. This woman. His woman. Her fingers were on his cheeks, soothing down to his shoulders and then gripping his biceps. Ranger plunged deeper into her mouth and she met him head on. Not just taking but giving.

He cupped her ass and lifted her against him. Her soft breasts smashed against his chest and he nearly came undone. She fit against him so perfectly.

His conscience whispered somewhere in the far distant back of his mind, not yours.

Ranger crushed it into dust. Shane was dead. He wasn't coming back.

Ranger would make her his.

A soft cry interrupted his thoughts. He lifted his head, panting, out of breath, shaking with need. He tried to get his emotions under control. Amy's eyes met his and he realized she was just as affected as him.

Chloe cried out again from the crib and Amy rushed over, scooping her up into her arms. The sight of her lips swollen from his kisses, holding Chloe to her chest, filled his chest to the point that he thought it would burst. Ranger placed a hand on his sternum and rubbed the pressure.

"He got away." Bo approached, out of breath, his voice raspy from running.

Ranger couldn't break his gaze from Amy.

"Is everything okay in here?" Bo continued.

Don't scare her. Don't take too much, too fast. He had

to take it slow. Easy. He turned to see Bo bracing both hands in the doorframe, bent forward sucking in air.

"Everything is fine here, he didn't get into the nursery," Ranger said.

He sensed Amy's movement and she stepped next to him. Fuck taking it slow. Ranger wrapped his arm around her and pulled her into him.

"He was at the door." Amy's normally strong voice was weak and wobbly as a newborn colt.

"I had my gun aimed at the door."

"I'm so proud of you." Ranger kissed the top of her head. The call was too close. Way too close.

"Did either of you get a look at his face?" Bo said.

"He had on a ski mask." Her voice broke.

Rage ripped through his veins. Ranger knew exactly who had tried to break into her house. And that was one Mexican that was about to disappear from the planet. "I didn't get a look at his face, but we both know who it was."

Bo Lawson stood tall, his ice blue eyes as cold as pressed steel. "You don't know it for a fact. I have to collect evidence. Follow the law. You don't call the shots here."

"You want me to sit on my thumbs and wait for the locals while a sex trafficking murderer just tried to get my woman?"

Bo's steady gaze didn't flicker. "Don't you mean Shane's woman?"

After thirty minutes of arguing and talking and interviewing, Bo left. Amy fed Chloe and rocked her back to sleep, checked the baby monitor and pulled her door partially shut before walking into the kitchen. Part of her prayed Ranger would leave. The other part prayed he would stay.

Tonight's scare honed in just how truly alone she was out here. Her family farm was beautiful. Sprawling. Isolated.

Amy emerged from the hall, into the living room, and stopped cold. Ranger stood with his back to her, facing the fireplace. The mantle. Shane's picture and the folded flag from his casket.

The two men she loved in the same room.

At least in spirit.

"Ranger?" She forced herself to speak, the words dry and ashen on her tongue.

He turned then and the emotion in his eyes nearly floored her. "When you called Bo, when I heard your voice and knew you were in trouble, I couldn't think."

Amy approached him, tentative. She had scared him. Or Santos or whoever that had been in her house had scared them all. "It's okay. I'm okay. You made it in time."

His jaw clenched, his lips formed a hard line. The emotion in his blue eyes changed to anger. "Yes, I did. Barely." His voice wasn't ragged with pain anymore. Ranger stormed to her, grabbed her arms. "All because you are too stubborn to let me in."

Her own anger rose, but she forced it down. Amy knew he was reacting to the fear. Knew it deep in her heart. "You're right. I am afraid. I'm afraid of what people will say when they find out about us. I'm afraid of what Mavis will try to do when she finds out."

Ranger had refused to back down earlier. He said she was worth fighting for. Well, he was worth it too.

"When they find out? Find out what? You won't let me close enough to make anything worth finding." His words were harsh, but his hands gentled on her arms. His thumbs brushed up and down continuously, rubbing. Teasing.

"When they find out how I feel about you." The air left her lungs. She'd said it. She'd admitted it. Now she needed him to fight for her, because she didn't know if she was strong enough to take it all the way alone.

"And how do you feel about me?" He wasn't giving in, he was going to make her say it. "I need to hear the words Amy. I need you to come to me. To know that it's just you and me."

Her heart constricted. She tried to swallow, but her throat wouldn't work. Could she really say her feelings out loud? Amy glanced past Ranger, trying to center her emotions. Shane stared back at her. His gaze accusing.

Did she want to give up on her only chance at love

again because of her past? Because she was hung up on a marriage that had been falling apart?

"Look at me. Shane is dead. I know you love him. I'm not asking you to forget about him. I will never forget him. I will love him with you." Ranger's voice broke. Amy ripped her gaze from the picture. Ranger's eyes turned red, wet with unshed tears. Her heart cracked. This strong man cried for his best friend and for the first time, Amy let herself realize she wasn't the only one grieving.

Ranger continued, "I'm asking you to give us a chance. I'm here, right in front of you and I love you."

A tear slipped down his cheek. Amy reached up, her hand shaking with raw emotion. This man needed her. Loved her. Fought for her. Was she too scared to try?

She lifted up to her toes and pressed a kiss to his lips.

"No." Ranger grabbed her face and held her away. "I need you to say it. To know you want me."

Amy gazed into his eyes, searching for something, anything to make her stop. But all she saw was open love. "I want you."

Amy held her breath, waiting. Dying. Hoping. This would be so much easier if it was just lust. But her feelings for Ranger had never been simple. She always wanted more with him. They could have a life together. A happy life. Amy just had to shake the chains of Shane's memory.

"You have no idea how often I've dreamed of you saying that." Ranger slid his hands up her back and around her neck. "I dream about you every day."

* * *

Ranger's entire body tensed. She drove him crazy with her worries. Pulling away one minute and reaching for him the next. But now her liquid brown gaze stared up at him with vulnerability.

Then her eyes slid shut and she offered her lips to him. His hand trembled with raw desire as he threaded his fingers in her hair, locking her in his grip. Her lips parted. "Please, I need you."

That was it. Lust raged through his body and Ranger crushed his mouth to hers. He groaned against her lips, her taste sweet torture. That one wild night they'd had together had been enough to make him addicted.

Now he craved.

She whimpered in the back of her throat and he swallowed the sound whole. Her surrender even sweeter. But even he couldn't take her with Shane's picture at his back. Ranger lifted her, not breaking contact with her lips, and carried her through the open doorway to the kitchen. He backed her up to the table, sat her down on the edge and nestled his hips between her spread legs.

Not once did he take his mouth from hers. He couldn't. He didn't want to give her a chance to think. To change her mind. He needed her too much, and he didn't think he could stop even if a tornado ripped through the house right now. Ranger laid her down on the table, sliding a hand to her waist. Her hip, her thigh, his hand inching beneath the edge of her nightgown.

Amy's hand threaded in his hair, holding him to her. He eased his hand up her leg, stopping when the back of his fingers brushed her panties. Her heat radiated through the thin material.

"You're so beautiful. So soft." His cock was so hard it was about to explode. But he had to take his time, drive her beyond the point of control. Leave her needing and wanting until she was begging. Until she only wanted him.

His lips drifted down, caressing her throat, her collarbone. Her fingers tangled in his hair and he used his teeth to pull the thin strap of her gown down her shoulder, baring her breast. A perfect pink little nipple thrust up, hard and searching. Ranger suckled it into his mouth, groaning at her perfect taste.

"Ranger, yes." His name was a hiss on her lips, her hips rising. He ripped the remaining strap off her shoulder and lavished the same attention to her other breast until she was keening under his touch. Ranger had to fight for every ounce of control and his body not to rip her nightgown off and take her right there.

"You like when I kiss you here?" Ranger lifted his head, watching her. Her eyes were half closed in pleasure.

"Yes." She arched up from the table and pulled him down to her. Seeking more.

Ranger smiled, holding his head up. Slowly, he dipped his finger around the edge of her panties. Grazing her between the legs with the back of his finger. She gasped and lifted her hips. "What about here? Would you like me to kiss you here?"

He flicked his finger again, back and forth, her moans driving him wild. "Yes. Please." Her voice was barely a gasp. Ranger lowered his head and took her nipple back into his mouth, drawing hard. He found her entrance and thrust a finger inside, her tight sheath squeezing him. "Oh God, don't stop."

His cock longed to replace his finger, but he forced himself to go slow. He wanted more than a one-night stand and a lifetime of regret.

He wanted all of her body heart and soul.

Ranger kissed and licked his way down her stomach. He pulled her nightgown down, over her hips and tossed it on the floor. He stood then, needing to see all of her. Amy stared up at him, panting, her chest rising and falling in sharp breaths. Ranger hooked his fingers in her panties. "If you want to stop, tell me now. I'll leave. I'll walk out that door. This is your last chance."

He held his breath, her answer could rip him apart. Or make him whole. Amy sat up on her elbows, her long loose red hair falling in waves down her back. Ranger stood transfixed at the sight before him. She was breathtaking.

"I don't want you to go. Stay. Make love to me." Her words went beyond sweet and sent him soaring. He captured her lips once more in a fiery kiss meant to sear her soul, but he knew she was permanently imprinted on his.

Ranger broke long enough to rip his shirt off. Then he wrapped his arms around her, pressing her naked chest to his and groaning at the sensation of her soft skin and her hard nipples digging into his chest.

She was his. He pressed her back on the table and stood. Amy lay before him like a feast and he had every intention of devouring her, every last drop.

Chapter Eleven

She shouldn't be doing this. Shouldn't be letting him touch her like this. She shouldn't be touching him like this. But God the need was burning out of control. His mouth seared her body. Controlled her lips. And she was helpless to do anything but return his kiss, return his touch. She was on fire.

His mouth trailed down her neck, licking and sucking, stopping to nibble briefly on her breast until she arched and cried out. Then he went further south, tracing down to her navel and hooking his fingers into the top of her panties. He didn't stop and ask for permission. He yanked them down and threw them over his shoulder. Then he pushed her knees wide and pressed his lips to her sex. Her mouth opened but she couldn't scream, all the oxygen left her body in a rush. He licked her. Amy grabbed the sides of the table and held on for dear life.

"You're so wet for me baby. You taste so good." Ranger's words were rough with desire and so sexy she almost came. When his mouth returned to her, he started a long, slow torturous dance that had her hips bucking uncontrollably to the tune of his tongue.

It had been so long since she'd felt anything. Let alone the desire to have a man's hands on her body driving her wild. He increased his pace, flicking light and quick. Her desire rose high, pulled tight, she was so close. If he would press a little harder, she would shatter into a million pieces, but it was like he sensed how close she was and pulled back, slowing his movements. Just enough to hold her at the edge, but not push her over.

And then she felt his finger tracing her lips, easing inside her. She held her breath, hoping he wouldn't stop. Ranger pushed in, shallow and pulled back out, leaving her frustrating and wanting more. Again, he repeated, sliding his finger in only to pull out too soon. Her hands left the table and locked into his hair groaning in frustration. He chuckled against her skin. "Do you want more?"

"Yes. Please." Amy was beyond caring or thought. Her body craved him. If he didn't finish she would die.

He slid his finger in a third time, not stopping until he bottomed out inside her and she gasped and spasmed around his finger.

She'd been without a man for too long. Ranger flicked her clit with his tongue and worked her with his hand. Amy held on to him, riding him.

Her world narrowed to just Ranger. Just his torture. Her muscles tensed, her stomach heavy and tight. So close. So close.

Ranger stopped and pulled out. "I need you to tell me again. Tell me that you want me." Rangers voice broke through the haze of desire, but she couldn't comprehend his words. He'd turned her into a mindless mass of desire and need. She twisted her head from side to side.

"I want you so fucking bad I'm about to explode, but I need you to say it. Tell me that you want me." His tone was even darker, rasping over her sensitive skin. His tongue lashed her clit and she cried out, but couldn't say the words.

He growled, sensing her resistance and inserted a second finger, slamming into her hard and fast and deep driving her so close to the edge, only to pull out again and leave her sobbing with need.

He pushed her past logical thought, past sanity. She knew she shouldn't be doing this, but she wanted him more than she wanted to breathe. She wanted Ranger James. And she wanted him now. "I want you. Please, Ranger please I want you." Her voice was edged with desperation.

Ranger all but growled and ripped his jeans off. He stood before her one hundred percent drop dead sexy. His muscular chest expanding and contracting with deep breaths. Her gaze traveled down an abdomen chiseled from stone, his huge cock jutting up almost to his belly button. She swallowed.

"Last chance. I don't know if I can stop, but I will try." Ranger held her hostage with his intense gaze. She knew he was barely holding himself back. And she had never wanted anyone as bad as she wanted this man.

Amy was past the point of talking. She reached up and wrapped her fingers around him, thumbing his tip, spreading the small drop of pre-cum. He bucked, his cock swelled and throbbed in her palm.

Ranger fell on her, taking her lips in a searing kiss. His cock nestled at her entrance and she let her knees fall wide. He pressed inside her, stretching her, wider than she remembered. She gasped at the sudden sensation, he filled her. Going slow. Inching inside, knowing she needed time to adjust to his size.

Amy watched as he gritted his teeth and pushed forward, sweat dripping onto her as he leaned down and took her mouth. They touched everywhere, and she felt every millimeter of friction inside and outside. The sensation was too much and not enough. He was taking it easy on her, going slow, but she didn't want slow anymore.

"Honey, if you don't stop wiggling I won't be able to control myself." Ranger inched in a little more.

"Ranger, now. Please, don't go slow. I need you." Her nails dug into his butt, urging him forward.

And he obliged, driving in hard and deep, stealing her breath and filling her completely.

She gasped, skating the edge of pain and pleasure, her hips bucking to meet him, take him. He was so big she didn't know how they fit, but they did. Perfectly. And she wanted all of him. Every bit. He pulled out, leaving her empty, but just as she felt the keen absence, he filled her again. And again. He thrust, taking her in long, hard strokes, driving her beyond thought. Beyond anything but feeling. All she could do was hold on and trust Ranger to take her there.

Ranger stood, lifted her legs from around his waist and up over his shoulders, pushing her down until her knees were almost touching her shoulders. The new position allowed him to go deeper, to places she'd never been touched. He felt bigger, harder. He pulled out and thrust in, taking her so completely she shattered.

She heard herself crying out, but couldn't register anything but the ride of pleasure. And Ranger didn't stop, he didn't give her mercy, he slammed into her over and over, forcing her to ride that wave. Finally, he stiffened and groaned. He filled her with his heat. With all of him.

Her body went limp and he let her legs fall to the table. He wrapped his arms around her, crushing her to his chest.

Amy wasn't sure how much time passed before Ranger started to nuzzle her neck and place small kisses on her cheek. She smiled, high on her first climax in years. And if she were honest, her best climax ever. Without a word, Ranger lifted her up, keeping her legs wrapped around him and carried her into her bedroom. Once they settled on the bed, she laid her cheek against his chest.

Thoughts of the past few months, thoughts of shame and guilt couldn't punch past her consciousness. She refused to let go of this feeling. Tonight, tonight she would savor him. And tomorrow... She would think about tomorrow in the morning.

Chapter Twelve

Ranger came instantly awake. He blinked, trying to bring the strange surroundings into focus. Then Amy shifted in his arms and memories from earlier in the night flooded back. Contentment filled him and he pulled her tighter against his chest, every single inch of her skin pressed against him.

His dream had come true. Amy admitted she wanted him. Only him. And she'd shown him in ways he'd not even dreamed existed. He rubbed his chest again, that familiar ache forming. He'd told her he loved her. He'd given her all of him. Every piece.

She hadn't said she loved him, though. She said she wanted him. Ranger wanted more, he wanted all of her. Forever. But he knew he had to go slow. Amy wasn't immature and rash. She thought about decisions and she took her time. And she needed time to accept him in her life.

Ranger glanced around the dark bedroom, taking in the four-poster bed. Shane's bed. His memory hung over Ranger's head like a freaking ghost. Got to stop thinking about him. Shane isn't here. He would want someone who really loved Amy to take care of her. Of the child he'd never met.

He forced himself to shake off the eerie sense of being watched. It was just his mind, his guilt. He looked around, taking in his surroundings, studying the concrete. The here and now. The wall to the right was nothing but windows and French doors leading out onto the back porch. To the left was the door, and toward the end of the bed on the far wall was the door to the bathroom. Something fluttered, snapped, and Ranger's gaze jerked back to the right. A curtain billowed out from the window.

His breathing slowed. He reached for his gun, and then he remembered it was in the kitchen. In his pants on the floor. The curtain lifted again, but no one stepped from it. No shadow emerged. He watched, waiting, unable to really shake the feeling of someone else's presence. Great, he was turning into one of those pussies that freaked out over every little shadow. Had to be the crazy night. Had to be Amy scaring the ever-loving shit out of him. And Shane's picture on the mantle as Ranger kissed his wife.

Stop. Stop now. Ranger wasn't scared of shadows or ghosts. He was the fucking shadow in the night.

Amy's thigh shifted across his own, and his cock hardened instantly. He knew without a doubt that having her once would never be enough. He planned to take her until she couldn't think. Couldn't form reasons for them not to be together. Until all she could think of was him.

He would fuck the past right out of them both.

He flipped her onto her back and nestled between her legs. Her body was still hot and wet. He was at home with her. He pressed a reverent kiss to her parted lips. She was completely bare for his perusal and he took his time exploring the curves and depths of her body. Her breasts were big and heavy for such a petite woman, but fit her perfectly. Her hips flared out provocatively, drawing him down. Pressing kisses across her flat tummy and hipbones. And still she slept.

Ranger continued lower until he was nestled between her legs. She was completely bare here. He inhaled, her scent filled his nostrils and his cock swelled. She smelled of sex and spice and him. And he fucking loved it. Wanted more. Ranger dipped down and kissed her there. That first taste hadn't been enough. He continued at his leisure, exploring her depths until her hips were lifting. Soft moans came from her mouth and her fingers tangled in the sheets beside him. He knew she'd wakened. But he wasn't about to give in yet. He continued tasting her, learning what she needed. Intending to drive her crazy with lust. As crazy as he felt.

He licked her, from bottom to top. She screamed his name and lifted her hips completely off the bed. His cock was so hard, he could feel the pre-come dripping from him. He couldn't hold out any longer. Quickly, he rose on his elbows and slammed into her, enjoying her gasp. She wrapped around him like a tight hot fist, squeezing his cock. Milking him. Made just for him.

"Ranger, don't stop. Please." Her voice was raspy with sex and sleep. Her sweet begging drove him beyond sanity. He couldn't take it slow. Couldn't hold back.

He flipped her over and lifted her hips until she was on her knees and elbows. The most perfect ass he'd ever seen lifted for his pleasure. Before she got her balance, he slammed into her from behind. Her fist clenched into the sheets and she screamed.

"Fuck, you feel so good." He almost growled the words. "You're mine." They came out rough and uneven, his need to possess her bordering animalistic. And still it wasn't enough. He needed all of her. He dipped his thumb into her sweet juices and spread her wetness from her pussy to the tight little pink hole between her butt cheeks. She squirmed, but he continued to spread her juices up, coating her other entrance, while he fucked her. Sliding in and out, her pussy so tight he couldn't stand it. Each time he pulled out, he slid more of her juices, coating her until she was slick enough for him to slip his thumb inside.

"Ranger. What are you doing?" She gasped, but continued to ride him.

"Shhh. Trust me. Relax." Ranger worked his thumb, eased it inside, until she clenched around him. Amy moaned and dropped her head to the mattress, her fingers tangling in the sheets. Yanking and fisting the material. Her hair matted to her back with sweat. She was gorgeous.

And he was so close to breaking.

Ranger forced himself to slow down, to go easy. He knew she hadn't been with a man in a while, and suspected, from her tight little anus strangling his thumb, she'd never been taken there. The thought that he would be her first had his balls tightening and his cock swelling rock hard. He leaned down and kissed her shoulder, bit down, then licked the pain away.

Her fingers twisted and tangled the sheets, her eyes were closed, her mouth open and gasping. Ranger pushed his thumb all the way in, watching as her brows drew together and she bit her lip. Fuck she was so sexy. "I need you. I need to hear you say it again, Amy. Tell me you need me."

There's no hesitation on her part this time her words came out sobbing, "Ranger. Please Ranger I need you."

"Do you trust me?" He held his breath, held his body still inside her.

She jerked, clenched around him. "Yes. I trust you." Amy buried her head in the mattress and thrust her hips back, impaling herself this time. Ranger threw his head back, barely holding on to the need to scream.

His hands locked onto her hips and he pulled out, lining himself up with her back entrance. Sweat beaded and dripped down his face. He pushed forward, her tight entrance strangling the tip of his cock. He inched further, pushing past her resistance, past her tight ring until his head popped inside. She squeezed him. Hard. Her ass clenched around him and it was all he could do to keep from shooting his load right there.

"Oh God." Amy yanked on the sheets again, so hard she pulled them off the mattress. Tigress.

"Are you okay?" He forced himself to ask.

"God, yes." Her cry drove him beyond reason. Ranger gripped her hips and pushed inside, grinding his teeth together, vowing he would hold on to his control. He rubbed a shaking hand down her back and pushed forward another inch. Each time he moved, she gasped and her soft whimpers drove him wild. This is what he needed from her. What she needed from him. Unable to stop himself or hold back another second he thrust forward.

Amy cried out and his own cry matched hers. She was so tight, she was strangling his cock. Warm. Hot. His eyes nearly rolled back in his head with pleasure. He knew no matter how much control he practiced he wouldn't be able to last long. So he spread her knees until her chest rested on the bed, her arm stretched out above her head and the only thing sticking up in the air was her glorious ass with him buried deep inside.

He reached between her legs and stroked her clit. Amy writhed against him. Ranger slammed into her, over and over, rubbing her. Taking her. Fucking her with long strokes until they fused together as one.

He raked his finger hard across her and she screamed. Her already tight ass spasmed around his cock, her climax so strong it ripped his own free. He grabbed her hips with both hands and slammed to the hilt, releasing himself completely.

Unable to break the tender bond between them yet, Ranger stayed planted firmly inside, and rolled to the side, taking her with him. His chest to her back, enjoying the small spasming aftershocks of pleasure. He wrapped his arms around her, moved her hair from her neck and nuzzled her there.

They lay there together, both of them panting and out of breath. His cock was still hard, but he knew she couldn't take more tonight. No matter how much he wanted it. Careful not to hurt her, Ranger eased from her body and carried her to the shower. Then he sat her on her feet and placed a tender kiss on her swollen lips. The look of sleepy satisfaction was evident in her flushed cheeks and lowered eyelids.

Ranger turned on the shower and guided her inside, washing her body first, then himself and drying them both off. Amy didn't protest his ministrations and Ranger felt a small measure of satisfaction. He carried her back to the bed and snuggled in with her. She fell asleep almost instantly but his brain kicked into overdrive.

Would tonight be enough to break down the rest of her barriers? Would she give in and let him into her life? He kissed her cheek again, finding it more and more impossible to keep his hands from her. He hoped he'd managed to anchor her to him. He prayed for it.

Because tonight he'd gone all in, he'd given her his body and heart. He didn't know what he would do if she denied him in the light of the rising sun.

Chapter Thirteen

Amy woke to sunlight streaming through windows and luxurious warmth cocooning her body. Ranger's arm draped across her waist, the weight heavy and heavenly at the same time. His warm chest swelled against her back with each breath, his skin smooth. She wiggled, needing to feel a little friction of skin on skin.

He made a sweet sound in his sleep and pulled her tight against him. Her butt snuggled against his growing hardness and heat flooded her cheeks.

He'd consumed her last night and she'd let him. Begged him. He'd taken her. Hard. And in places she'd never imagined. He'd given her more pleasure than she'd ever dreamed. Unable to hold still, Amy glided her fingers down his forearm, tickling the growth of blond hair. Images from last night pinging her brain. Ranger pounding into her, crushing her resistance with every thrust. Soothing her aching body with soft languid kisses.

It was like he knew what she needed, when she needed it. When she needed him to demand she give herself to him and when she needed a slow hand.

Last night hadn't been about just sex. He claimed her, body and soul. Ranger made it perfectly clear that he wasn't after just one night from her. He wasn't after a quick lay. No, that would be easier. What he wanted wasn't just her body.

He wanted her heart, mind and soul.

And he didn't want to replace her dead husband. He wanted to share his memory with her. He wanted them to heal together. He wanted to raise her daughter.

Ranger James had taken one giant wrecking ball to the walls of protection around her heart and demolished them. Leaving her chest aching. Feeling. Since the news of Shane's death she'd gone unemotional, unfeeling and unresponsive. Living to take care of Chloe and earn a dollar. That's it. She'd shut down and perfected her gut response of 'I'm fine' whenever anyone asked how she was doing.

When in reality she'd been anything but fine. She'd been a robot. A machine. Her emotions laid to rest with her husband.

And she'd been fine.

But Ranger didn't accept her self-imposed isolation. He wouldn't let her go it alone. He drove her crazy calling, stopping by to check in. And every time he showed up unannounced she felt.

But she didn't want to feel. Feeling hurt. Feeling reminded her she was alone.

Amy grabbed Ranger's hand and pressed it to her aching chest, needing his healing touch.

Something changed last night. Emotions overtook her. Tears threatened her eyes. How could what they did be alright? Her with Shane's best friend? His teammate's wife?

Would the rest of the world understand?

He was her emotional bloodhound - sensing when to go easy on her and when to push her. If it were left up to her, Amy would still be that wooden statue imitating her former self. A single parent. Single business owner. Single.

Could she open her heart to Ranger James? He was Special Forces. SF's didn't get to stay and play happy family. They got called out, sometimes with no warning. They were gone a lot. And sometimes, they didn't come home. Could she handle another loss?

Could Chloe?

Someone knocked on her door. Amy's body went ice

cold. The sound still gave her chills, haunted her dreams. Her nightmares. What time was it? Who would be knocking this early? Maybe it was Bo Lawson with news about Santos.

They knocked again. Amy jerked upright. Someone was at her door and she was lazing in bed, naked, with Ranger James, thoroughly satisfied.

Her discarded clothes lay in the kitchen, right beside Ranger's. Careful not to wake him, she eased from the bed and slipped into her closet. With speed born of desperation, Amy yanked on a cotton sundress and raced into the kitchen, easing the bedroom door shut behind her.

She passed by the folded flag and picture of Shane on the mantle, ignoring the small flash of guilt. No. She'd mourned long enough. She wouldn't feel guilty. She had a flesh and blood man wanting her heart. Wanting to be part of her life. Her daughter's life.

Amy grabbed the doorknob and turned, eager for news. Only the person standing there wasn't Bo Lawson. An iceberg of dread slammed into her with the force of the freaking Titanic.

Mavis Carter. Her worst nightmare.

Her stomach dropped to the floor and Mavis stomped on it with polished leather pumps.

Saturday. How could she forget about today? The third Saturday of the month.

"Are you going to just stand there like an idiot or invite me inside?" Her mother-in-law's voice laced with annoyance, pierced her chest.

"I...I overslept." Amy tried to sound calm, but she sounded like she swallowed a frog with the flu.

"I can see that." Mavis stood there, swollen face resembling an over-ripe grape about to bust in her perfectly pressed purple suit. Had her second neck fold increased to three?

"I'm sorry, can you give me a minute to get ready?" Amy gripped the doorknob, trying to think of any excuse to keep Mavis out of her house. Forget southern hospitality. If her mother-in-law found another man in her bed it wouldn't be the Titanic sinking. Her house would turn into Pearl Harbor.

Mavis huffed and pushed into the house. "And you expect me to stand there on your front porch in this heat? I told my Shane you weren't a lady."

Amy checked the urge to plant a foot up her mother-in-law's flabby ass and shut the front door. Keep Mavis contained. Keep her out of the kitchen and as far from Amy's bedroom as possible. "Why don't you have a seat on the couch and I'll put on some coffee for you while I get dressed?"

"That lumpy old couch? No thank you, I'll sit right here. You should have let my son buy that nice leather one over at King's Furniture when he wanted it. Now he will never get the chance to have nice furniture." Mavis plopped back into Shane's recliner, or what used to be his recliner, and dabbed at the corner of her eyes.

The zipper holding Amy's repressed anger came undone. It wasn't like she'd told Shane no out of spite or some sort of control grab. She'd told him no because they flat out didn't have the money to pay for a new couch. They'd been too busy trying to cover their existing bills after Shane bought that shiny new jacked up four by four. His military pay coupled with her earnings from waiting tables at the Wharf covered the basics. Not leather couches and King Ranches with air-conditioned seats.

But as much as Amy wanted to tell Mavis where to shove her comment, she had a matter altogether more pressing. She had to get Mavis out of her house before Ranger woke.

The thought gave her fear of discovery a shot of steroids and left her hands shaking and cold sweat dripping down her neck. "I'll start the coffee."

"Make sure you put three teaspoons of sugar in my cup. And not that fake stuff either. And bring me the picture of my baby so I can hold him close." Guilt trip? More like guilt voyage around the planet.

Amy grabbed Shane's photo from the mantle, trying to

steady her hand and pass it to Mavis. Whatever it took to keep the woman corralled and quiet. "Be right back."

She bolted from the room, hit the brew button on the coffee maker and rushed into her bedroom, locking the door behind her. Today of all freaking days. What had Amy done to piss off fate?

***

Ranger lay sprawled on the bed, his massive chest taking up over half of the mattress. His blond hair mussed with sleep. His expression peaceful. Relaxed. And so heartbreakingly handsome it took every ounce of her willpower not to dive back in there with him.

But fate was a twisted bitch insistent on carving out her pound of flesh. Mavis would only sit still for so long before she started snooping around. And the two-by-fours nailed over her kitchen door could catch a blind man's attention.

Amy rushed back into the bathroom, washed her face and brushed her teeth at warp speed. She yanked a brush through her hair and didn't even attempt makeup.

She ran back through the bedroom, pausing for one last look. As if sensing she were near, Ranger rolled to his side, one arm reaching out in his sleep to the empty space where she had slept. Her heart tugged at the gesture. He'd been so open and honest with her. He wanted her, he wanted all of her.

Amy trembled and took a step back, unsure if she had anything left to give.

She exited the bedroom and shut the door behind her. The coffee should be done by now. Mavis could have a cup while Amy got Chloe dressed and ready.

"What on earth?" Mavis stood in the kitchen, staring at the fragments of broken doorframe and glass still lying on the kitchen floor.

Amy's heart stopped beating all together. Ranger's clothes lay just out of sight, but if Mavis came in the room any further...

"Stop. There's glass. I haven't cleaned it up yet." Amy moved to stand between her mother-in-law and the clothing.

"Amy Carter, what did you do?" Mavis propped a hand on her more than generous hip, glaring at the mess.

"I tried to break into my own house." Amy immediately slapped a hand over her mouth but her smart-ass comment was out and she couldn't pull it back in. She knew better than to poke a hornet's nest.

"Excuse me?"

"What, you don't like the way I redecorated?" She poked alright, and the hornets flew out with a venom.

"You little hussy. I don't need your smart mouth. You can go to the cemetery by yourself. I'm sick and tired of wasting my time on a piece of trash like you."

Amy's first instinct was to turn tail and run. Mavis with her full venom unleashed was as pretty as rotting cow manure. But the calm control she'd perfected over the past year didn't rise to the forefront. No, Amy lifted her foot and stepped right in the big pile of shit.

"Good, cause this piece of trash is sick and tired of listening to your big fat mouth."

Mavis jerked back as if slapped. Good. Amy would be willing to bet no one in the state had had the guts to talk back to her. Her already bulging eyeballs seemed to swell, and Amy prayed they didn't pop out of her head. "You-you-"

"Listen, why don't you just go? You can stop coming out here for your monthly guilt trips and I can get on with my life. You can pretend like you never had a daughter-in-law."

Mavis made a full recover. "You can go on with your life while my son lays rotting in the ground? I don't think so. I'll be out here every third Saturday for the rest of your miserable life."

"Why? Why can't you just leave me in peace?" Amy had blown her top and now had no reserve fuel left to carry the fight.

"Because, if you hadn't made him so miserable, he never would have joined the military in the first place."

"Are you serious? Are we talking about the same

person? Because Shane Carter was never made to do anything."

"He didn't have a choice."

"If he was so damn miserable he should have asked for a divorce."

Mavis gasped-and oh unholy mother of Jesus-divorce. What a blot on the family name. "Divorce? You know how I feel about divorce."

"So maybe Shane was too scared of you to ask for a divorce. Maybe it was your fault." Amy hurled the accusation.

"I can't believe you said that. A sinner like you, daring to question my good judgment about my boy." Mavis pointed a long fingernail in her face. "I've tried to be good. I've prayed for your soul and prayed for the patience to deal with you, but no more."

"While you're doing all this praying, maybe you should pray for yourself, cause you're the most rotten evil person I've ever met."

"Well I never!"

Amy held up a hand. This was going nowhere. "Please just go. I have to clean up my kitchen and call the sheriff with my official report. Someone tried to break in last night. The last thing I need is more drama."

"Someone broke in?" Mavis put a hand to her neck.

"Yes. Not that you care. But I am tired. I was up all night. I really don't have the energy for this."

Mavis seemed to deflate, her shoulders sagging for a brief instant. Concern maybe? "I told you to sell this place didn't I? Shane never wanted to live out here on this run down farm. You should have listened to us."

Had she thought Mavis was capable of concern? As much as Dahmar had for the human race.

"Shane agreed we would live out here." Amy couldn't hold in her annoyance.

Mavis huffed, her heavy jowls jiggling. She reminded Amy of that giant evil marshmallow man on *Ghostbusters* - too bad Amy didn't have a laser gun.

"Well, this place is filthy."

"I would have cleaned it, but someone showed up at the ass crack of dawn uninvited." Amy's tolerance for hateful ex-mother-in-laws had reached the limit.

"Unplanned? It's the third Saturday. You know what happens today. It's not my fault you lazed in bed all morning," Mavis said.

Amy forced her voice to drip with sweetness and resisted the urge to grab a shard of glass off the floor and stab Mavis. She had to get her out of the house. "You're right. Now, please go."

Mavis's eyes all but disappeared in her swollen face, but she turned and walked back into the living room. "Make sure you clean up all that glass before you let my grand baby crawl around in this pigsty."

Amy waited until Mavis disappeared and let out one long breath. She'd done it. She'd gotten Mavis out of her house and bypassed the nuclear bomb in her bedroom.

Now she had time to grab her broom, sweep up the glass and maybe make breakfast. Or she could crawl back in bed with Ranger...

"I'm sorry. I shouldn't say those mean things to you. It's just that...I miss him so much."

Amy froze, broom in hand on a half-sweep. Mavis stood inside the kitchen door, Shane's photo clutched to her generous chest. Tears. Real live tears dragging her black eyeliner down her cheeks. "I know I've been hard on you. And it's not right for me to blame you."

Mavis took a step forward, her hand covering Amy's own. The broomstick the only solid object holding her upright.

"What?" Not the most poetic response, but her mother-in-law had shocked the brainpower right out of her.

"I'm going to try harder to be nice. To be a mother to you. Lord knows you need one." The small sliver of hope inside Amy cracked a little. Mavis's version of nice still had vinegar.

But part of Amy understood. The woman had lost her

only child. Her reason for living. If anything ever happened to Chloe...she couldn't even finish the thought. She covered Mavis's hand with her own. "I know it's hard. It's been so hard for me. I can't imagine how much you hurt."

They'd both lost someone. Amy had lost her husband. Mavis lost her only son.

"You really are a good and true wife. You've been there every month, putting fresh flowers on his grave." Mavis wiped her pudgy hand down her pressed pleated pants leg. She looked away, the first time Amy had ever seen her avoid her gaze. "I was wrong. About you. You really did love my son."

Her mattress creaked in the bedroom, Ranger made some kind of cough snore sound and the quiet settled back down. Amy froze and her heart clawed up her throat.

"What was that?" Mavis peered around her shoulder.

Not now. Please stay asleep. Please stay asleep. "Nothing." Amy's voice came out higher than normal and she cringed.

"That didn't sound like nothing." Mavis pulled her hand from Amy's and her hawk like gaze zeroed in on her bedroom door.

Amy needed to think of something. Fast. Before Mavis stormed into her bedroom and found Ranger in her bed. Amy swallowed and glanced around, but for what? What would be her excuse? Her brain blanked.

"I know I heard..." Mavis's voice trailed off and Amy closed her eyes in resignation. She knew without turning around that her bedroom door was no longer empty.

"No wonder you didn't want to tell me."

Amy opened her eyes, steeling herself for the explosion about to take place. But Mavis didn't scream or rant or rave.

Unable to stand to torture a moment longer, Amy whipped around and had to grab onto the counter to keep from falling to the kitchen floor.

"I had a feeling you were hiding something. Thank goodness my son isn't here to see this. You know how he felt about animals indoors."

Jesus Christ almighty. A stray cat, she'd nicknamed Bodacious, strolled through the kitchen, curling his long black and grey tail up her leg. He must have come in last night. He normally preferred the old barn and it's plethora of fat mice. Amy didn't have to pretend to care, she dropped to her knees and grabbed Bodacious to her chest, relief robbing her of breath and muscle strength.

"I hope you had him wormed. He shouldn't be around Chloe unless the vet cleared him," Mavis said.

Amy still couldn't get her mouth to work. Her heart was too busy trying to hammer through her chest.

Mavis took a step forward held her hand out to pet the cat, but he recoiled and leapt to the chair.

"I thought a pet would help cheer the place up some." Amy rediscovered her voice and stood.

"I can't blame you for that. Why, I was walking past the pet store the other day and stopped to look at one of Mr. Tom's kittens for sale."

Amy suppressed a cringe and quickly crossed her arms over her chest, silently thanking Bodi for saving her ass. "You should really give it a try one day Mavis. I think you'd be surprised at how easy it is to fall in love with a pet." Just as easy as Amy had fallen into Ranger's arms.

Chapter Fourteen

Ranger rolled over in bed and grabbed nothing but cold sheets. The only proof Amy had been in his arms was the indentation in her pillow and the lingering smell of flowers and heaven. He rolled to his stomach and gathered her pillow to his face, inhaling her scent.

His chest tightened and he felt the loss of her presence. He needed to touch her. To talk to her and make sure she was okay with last night. He'd taken her so thoroughly, his every intention to replace her thoughts with nothing but him. What if he'd been too rough? What if he scared her?

His heart skittered and he pushed up from the bed, uncaring he was naked. If she ran, he might not get her back. She had his heart.

And he wanted hers.

Ranger ripped open the bedroom door, ready to run through the house to find her. To apologize, grovel, whatever it took to make her happy.

But when he opened the door, he froze. The deep down knowledge that this was one of those moments that could forever change his life settled in his gut. And he'd royally fucked up.

Mavis Carter, stood in the kitchen, her perfectly coiffed hair and tailored suit had no hope of restraining the unbridled rage growing with the ferocity of an atomic bomb. And he knew without a doubt the explosion of anger she was about to unleash would be on Amy, not him. Not the one who deserved it. Ranger grabbed for the sheet and wrapped it around his waist, ready to tell Mavis his thoughts.

But Mavis beat him to the punch. "You little slut. How dare you desecrate this house with your filth. After I came over, ready to accept you."

Amy paled to a shade he'd never seen and her bleak eyes turned to him. Ranger cringed, knowing he was the reason behind her please kill me look. His own anger rose and he clutched the sheet tight to keep from throttling Mavis. "Don't talk to her like that."

Mavis straightened her shoulders and glared at him. "I always knew you'd be trouble. I tried to warn Shane to stay away from you. From both of you. And look, both of you standing in his house. Naked. Cavorting in sin. And my son is cold in the ground because of both of you."

Mavis might be spiteful but she aimed true, her arrow of guilt shot straight to his soul. But no matter how much Ranger regretted not saving Shane, he'd come to realize he wasn't totally at fault either. "A terrorist killed Shane. I tried to save him."

Mavis stepped toward him, her body visibly shaking. "The terrorist might have killed him, but you left him. You left him behind. And I hope it haunts you for the rest of your rotten days."

Ranger straightened from the doorway, his own fury rising to match that of Mavis's. "You better watch what you say to me woman. You being my best friend's mother will only protect you for so long."

But Mavis didn't back up. And she didn't shut up. "You think I worry about your threats? I died the day my boy died. You can't do anything else to hurt me. But by God, I can hurt you." Mavis turned towards Amy. "And I can destroy her. Your slut."

"Mavis, please. It's not like that. Ranger and I... We never..." Amy trailed off and Ranger knew she was struggling to find the words.

He wanted to stride to her, take her trembling body in his arms and tell her it would be okay. Everything would be okay.

"You mean to tell me you and Ranger never slept together? Never cavorted in my son's bed?" Mavis bit out.

"We, please..." Amy paled even more.

Rage rolled through Ranger. He'd be damned if last night was their last.

Mavis cut Amy's words off with a slice of her hand through the air. "No. I see that it isn't. So, when did you start betraying my son? Was it when you were still with him? While you were still married?" She seemed to swell. Her rage palpable.

"It's none of your business. We don't owe you any explanation. You know that Amy is an honorable woman, just like you know she would never betray your son. And you know, deep down, that she was too good for Shane." Ranger's chest constricted. His heart swelled. He met Amy's broken gaze. "Just like I know she's too good for me." But he loved her anyway. He had loved her since he first met her. He didn't know why she ended up marrying Shane, and he didn't know why they'd been given a second chance, but he wasn't going to waste it. Not one minute.

Ranger strode across the room and took Amy's hands. Her pulse beat wildly at the base of her throat. Her gorgeous chocolate eyes, the color of spring in full bloom, watered.

"I know you're scared. I'm scared too." Ranger tucked a strand of hair behind her ear, wanting to touch her more. "I loved Shane like a brother. I will always love him and miss him. And I know you will too. But I love you too. I've always loved you Amy."

She shook harder and he cupped her face. His stomach tight, knotting and twisting.

"I cannot believe what I'm hearing. Traitors, both of you." Any façade of calm completely disappeared from Mavis Carter's face. Her voice rose sharp and grating. "I'll make sure everyone knows. You're ruined Amy. If it takes the rest of my life, I'm going to make sure you suffer."

Ranger held Amy's face between his palms, attempting to shield her from the gross fury. The need to protect her strong and righteous. His woman. His heart. He turned to face Shane's mother, restraining his violence by a steadily fraying thread. "Get out. Get out of this house and don't ever come back."

Mavis didn't move. Ranger let go of Amy and grabbed Mavis's arm and pulled her to the door. She yanked back. "You can't kick me out of my son's house."

He grabbed her arm again, pulling her hard and yanked open the door, "I can. And I did. Don't come back. And if you do anything to hurt this woman I'm going to make you regret it." Ranger slammed the door in the older woman's face and turned to Amy.

Her pale face turned parchment white, all the color completely leeched away. His heart twisted at her pain. Ranger took her in his arms, wrapping her close and tucking her head against his chest. "It's okay. She's not going to do anything."

The possession. The growing need to protect her rose. She was his. And he would take care of her. Love her. And destroy anyone who threatened.

"She will tell everyone. No one will want to hire me." Amy shook in his arms. Hard jerks rocking her entire frame. Damn Mavis. She hurt Amy, the girl who'd never done anything wrong to anybody.

"I won't let her. I promise."

Amy's breath was hot against his bare chest, her palms searing the skin on his ribcage. She pushed away from him and felt the loss immediately.

Her eyes were wild with unshed tears. "I'm ruined. You ruined everything."

Ranger rocked back on his heels in shock. He'd been expecting her to cry, to worry, to need him to calm her. "What? What are you saying?"

Ranger reached for her, but she yanked back out of his reach. "This is a mistake"

"No, it's not. We are not a mistake. Last night was the

best night of my life." Ranger struggled to hold on to her, to find the right words.

Amy flinched. "I can't do this. I thought I could, but I was wrong. Mavis will tell everyone that I betrayed my husband."

The tightness knotting Ranger's chest grew. Amy took another step back, pulling away from him. "No. You didn't. We were never together when Shane was alive." Ranger closed the gap between them and took Amy's shoulders in his hands, anchoring her in place. "Shane is dead. He's gone and not coming back. You are alive and have every right to move on. He would want you to be happy."

Amy shook her head, tears running down her cheeks. "I can't believe we did this. I can't... You need to leave. Now." Her words ripped through him, sharp and ragged.

"You don't mean that. We didn't do anything wrong."

"Mavis doesn't care. She'll make it look like we've been having an affair."

"I won't let her." Ranger wanted to shake the wild look of panic off Amy's face.

"You can't stop her. I can't stop her. I can't believe I let you stay here when I knew she'd be here this morning. I'm so stupid." Her words came out broken.

Ranger felt fear ripping at his insides. She was pulling away from him. He could see her visibly withdrawing. The progress he'd made last night slipping away. "I promise I will make things right. No one will blame you for moving on. For us."

Amy yanked back, pulling her arms free from his grasp. Her sobs breaking his heart. "There is no us. There can never be an 'us.' I was stupid to think we had a chance."

He couldn't live without this woman. He wouldn't. "You don't mean that."

Amy hugged herself and closed her eyes. He needed her. Loved her.

When Amy opened her eyes again, Ranger sucked in a breath. Her gaze was...empty. "Please. I want you to go."

"Amy..." Ranger reached for her one last time, but she

kept her distance and shook her head.

"Please, Ranger. If you really care about me and Chloe, you will leave."

The perfection of last night shattered inside him. He'd gotten close enough to touch her. Hold her. And now, because Amy was ruled by fear, they would never find that happiness. "You will regret this, Amy. Don't let her win."

"I can't fight this."

"You're too scared to fight. Stand up for yourself. For your family. For what you want." Ranger didn't try to hide the edge of anger in his voice.

But Amy held silent, unwilling to take that step forward. He might love her more than his next breath, but he sure as hell wasn't going to stand here, naked and begging. Ranger grabbed his clothes off the floor and let the sheet drop. Amy averted her gaze as he pulled on his jeans. Misery crawled up his body from her rejection. Misery and anger.

"I know you're scared and confused right now. Dammit, I'm confused too. But at least I'm willing to give the future a chance. You're spending all your energy focused on the past." Ranger grabbed his shirt from the floor and pulled it on. "When are you going to wake up and realize you can't live in the past?"

Chapter Fifteen

How could a door opening destroy her life so many times? Amy leaned her head against the front door, listening as Ranger roared down her driveway. Tears burned hot trails down her cheeks. She balled her fist and punched the door, rattling it on its frame.

Stupid. Stupid. Stupid. She'd let Mavis in to her house. Her life. And let her destroy the fragile thread of happiness Ranger had created. Instead of fighting for him, Amy blamed him. Yelled at him. And even worse, she'd hurt him.

Ranger wasn't some playboy looking for an easy lay. He wanted her and he hadn't been bashful about the fact. He told her he'd fight for her, but she was too scared to let him.

He gave her his heart and she stomped on it.

Her own heart twisted in response, the pain bowed her forward and sent her to her knees. Sobs wracked her body. Why did it have to be so hard?

She had to live with the repercussions of her choices. Shane's choices. Amy had made the decision to get drunk all those years ago. She'd seen Ranger kiss Tonya Lee Swopes and gotten jealous. She'd made out with Shane in an effort to make Ranger notice her. But they'd both had too much to drink. They went beyond kissing and petting to pregnant and married.

The miscarriage came after the vows. But Amy had

made a promise before God to honor Shane. She'd made her bed and she wouldn't just lie in it. She would live in it.

Her tears fell faster and she curled into a ball on the floor. The pain, the grief, the anguish so much she could no longer support her own weight.

Amy had just ensured that Mavis's persistent nicks and pinches to her emotional state would transform into an all-out assault, intent on total annihilation.

Mavis hated her, always had. Shane abandoned her, always had. And then the one man who came back for her - she pushed him away.

Amy had gone from letting others hurt her to hurting herself. But wasn't hurting herself better than letting Ranger get too close and losing her business? Losing him?

Who was she kidding? She didn't let Ranger James do anything. He was as unstoppable as the mighty Mississippi. Driving forward, slowly and surely eroding her battered shores of defense, chinking away at her dams of resistance. He didn't accept anything. He fought for what he wanted, and he'd made it more than clear he wanted her.

And her daughter.

Amy was the weak one in the equation. She'd never been indecisive a day in her life, but now...now her decisions didn't just affect herself.

Chloe cried out from the nursery and Amy forced herself to stand. To wipe away her tears. Her baby needed her. Needed her mother.

What Amy needed didn't matter where her daughter was concerned. She would do what it took to ensure Chloe had a roof over her head and food on the table. If that meant Amy couldn't have Ranger, so be it. She'd made tough decisions before, she would do it again. Alone.

So why did the walk to the nursery feel like death row?

A few hours later, Amy had changed and fed Chloe, swept the kitchen floor and cleaned up as best she could, considering her back door was held up by two-by-fours. She'd just sat down for a glass of tea on the couch, watching Chloe play on the living room floor.

"Amy, open up. It's Evie." Her best friend, called from the front door.

Amy got up and unlocked it, allowing Evie, followed by Hayden James, inside. Hayden was Ranger's much younger adopted sister and had babysat for Amy in the summer.

"I heard what happened. Are you okay? Are you hurt? Chloe?" Evie didn't pause but pulled Amy into a tight hug.

The action caught Amy off guard and unexpected tears pricked her eyes.

"I was so scared. What if something happened to Chloe?"

"Hush, it's okay. Chloe is just fine."

As if to signal her agreement, Chloe squealed from her mat on the floor and kicked her toy puppy. Amy laughed and stepped back, wiping her eyes. "Yeah, you're right. I am trying to block it out. I mean, they kicked down my back door. I even went to the hardware store and had new locks put on."

Evie scooped Chloe off the floor and went into the kitchen, Amy followed. The sight of the boards nailed across her door looked even worse.

"Geez, you weren't kidding," Evie said.

"Yeah, how crazy is that? Why would someone try to break into your house?" Hayden hovered near the door, shifting her weight from foot to foot.

"I don't know for sure, but I am so tired. We were up half the night."

"We?" Evie arched a brow before returning to the living room and plopping down onto the couch.

Amy could have kicked herself. Of course Evie would pick up on that one little slip. "Um, yeah, I called Bo. He brought his deputies out."

"I know. Ranger told me." Evie dropped that grenade and let it sit for a minute before continuing. "He also said he was out here all night too."

A blush heated Amy's chest and cheeks. "Ranger has a big mouth."

"Spill. Now."

No way, no how. Especially with his little sister hovering near the front door. "He slept on the couch. Said no way was he leaving us here alone after a break-in."

Amy glared at her friend, silently telling her to shut her big fat trap. Evie smiled in response, the kind of smile that said there was no way she was letting this drop.

Before Evie could open her mouth, Amy said, "Hayden, you okay? Need something to drink? Some food? I haven't made lunch yet, but I've got some cold turkey for a sandwich." Hayden didn't move from her stance at the door, avoiding looking directly at anyone in particular.

"Um, no thank you. I'm fine." Hayden's reply was awkward, like they were strangers.

"Well, you're acting weird. Do you need to talk? Something I can help you with?" Amy said.

Hayden stared at the floor. The wall. The furniture. "No. I'm sure."

"So give me the dish girl. What the hell happened?" Evie asked.

"The damn Mexican cartel is what happened."

Silence. Her living room went completely quiet.

"The cartel?" Hayden asked, her voice more of a squeak.

"And they want to break into your house because?" Evie said.

"One of their thugs was threatening Pedro. In my airplane hangar. Then he threatened Artie."

"And…" Evie juggled Chloe over to her other arm and gestured at Amy to continue.

"And I told him to get the hell off my land."

"So you showed your usual sweet southern charm and told a Lobello to kiss off?"

Amy froze, staring at her friend in surprise. "I never said anything about the Lobellos."

Evie met her gaze, her clear blue eyes widening. "Yes, you did."

"Nope. Your turn to spill."

"Hunter will kill me."

"I will kill you if you don't tell me what the heck is going on. Ranger knew the Mexican was Lobello right away."

Evie made an almost imperceptible nod toward Hayden, clearly unable to talk around the girl. Amy caught on and said, "Hayden, would you mind making Chloe a bottle of formula? She hasn't eaten in a few hours."

Hayden startled from the door, as if lost in thought. "Yeah, um, sure. Of course."

Amy waited on her to leave the living room before talking. "What is wrong with her?"

Evie shrugged. "No idea. She's been weird all morning. Probably boy trouble or something."

Amy let that go for now, she had more important things on her mind. Such as how Evie seemed to know exactly what was going on, as did Amy and Hunter and Bo Lawson. "Spill. Now."

"You know last year, when I was helping C.W. with the MRG?" Evie had gotten roped into working with her grandpa's old militia, the Mississippi Revolutionary Group. The MRG was the entire reason that Hunter and his team had returned to Mississippi last year.

"You mean when you took your little walk on the criminal side and nearly died?" Apparently, the CIA had suspected the MRG of gunrunning for the very terrorist they'd been tracking overseas. Hunter's unit discovered the MRG, and Evie, was actually innocent, and it had been Evie's crazy ex-fiancée, Marcus Carvant that had ties to the terrorist. But not before Marcus kidnapped Evie and her mother, holding them hostage and nearly killing them.

Evie glared at her. "Yeah, thanks for the reminder. Anyway, Marcus's lackey, Sheriff Brown, escaped with the weapons before Hunter and his team could get them. They've been tracking them ever since."

Mercy's ex-sheriff, Lee Brown, had been as dirty as Marcus. He'd not only tried to kill Evie, but set up the MRG as the fall guy and stolen the weapons. "You mean Brown is still here? In Mercy?"

"Hunter thinks so. And he thinks Brown contacted the Lobellos to move the weapons out of the U.S."

"Oh my God."

Evie nodded, "Exactly. Now, I've told you everything, and you cannot tell my husband-got it?"

"Of course."

"Your turn."

"What do you mean?" Amy hedged. She knew exactly what Evie was talking about, but that didn't mean she was ready to tell her everything. Like Amy and Ranger's insanely explosive bout of mind blowing sex.

Or the fact that Amy was falling for Evie's brother-in-law.

Except she'd kicked him out. Nope. Not going there.

"Here you go. Sorry it took so long, but I over heated the first bottle." Hayden came back into the living room and held out the bottle of formula to Evie.

Evie peered at her with way too muck knowledge and Amy, unable to handle her best friend's soul-searching gaze, turned away. Her gaze collided with Shane's.

Guilt slammed into her like a heart attack. Her feelings for Ranger were too raw. Too fresh. She needed a minute to consolidate and compartmentalize.

"Okay, so Hunter sent you out here to check on us? We're fine. I'll call the hardware store on Monday and have them replace the back door. I think the two-by-fours will hold until then."

Evie glared at her but accepted the change in subject and moved on. "No, Hunter sent me out here to get you. He and Ranger have to leave for a couple of days. They think you should come stay with us until they get back."

To Evie's house? Ranger lived with Evie and Hunter. That meant his things would surround her. How was she supposed to forget about having the best sex of her entire life with Ranger if she was in his house?

"They are going on a mission?"

Evie nodded.

Another mission. Amy's stomach clenched and she looked away. This was just another reason she couldn't be with Ranger. She knew, without a doubt, she was falling for him and falling harder than a damn avalanche. As the former wife of a Special Forces operative, she knew the risks. Knew the call outs didn't get put on hold because of family. And Ranger's team wasn't just normal SF. They were part of a special Task Force, a fact Amy only knew from one of Shane's drunk nights when he admitted that fact. Even obliterated as he had been, he'd quickly shut up when she'd questioned him further.

"No way. I'm not intruding on ya'll."

"I thought you'd say that. Ranger said for me to tell you if you didn't come stay with me, he would come drag you out of here himself." Evie cut Amy an I'm-not-kidding look and then nuzzled Chloe. Her daughter wholeheartedly loved the attention, latched on to Evie's long hair, yanking and pulling.

Crap. Ranger didn't make empty threats.

"Ranger can't tell me what to do." Just saying his name brought heat to Amy's cheeks. She turned quickly, trying to hide the blush and physical and emotional reaction. Up until now she'd been able to tamp it down, to keep her distance. But last night had opened up a deep and gaping chasm inside her. One she had no hope of closing anytime soon.

"You're right, he can't." Evie said from right behind her. "But he can still worry, so will I, and I know I won't be able to sleep knowing you are out here. Alone. With a psycho Mexican after your ass."

The shattered glass and wood gave testament to that fact. Her door smashed in. Her bed sheets rumpled. Her life was falling apart. Again. "Okay, you're right. I need to get out of this house. Mind watching her while I throw some things together?" Amy turned back to Evie.

"Not at all. I'll finish feeding her the bottle and take her outside to swing for a minute. Get everything you need for the rest of the weekend."

Amy shot Evie a grateful smile, sparing a glance for

Hayden who still held close to the exit. Maybe the break-in freaked her out. Amy didn't have time to study Hayden's behavior right now.

The seed had been planted. Now she wanted to break out of this house like breaking out of a prison. She rushed into the bedroom and started packing. By the time she finished packing and lugging the pack-and-play out of the nursery, Evie was outside with Chloe. Amy dragged everything into the living room. Hayden stood facing the fireplace.

"Mind helping a girl out?" Amy said.

Hayden jumped and spun around, her tan skin pale, her blue eyes huge. Shane's photograph fell from her fingers and crashed onto the stone hearth. Hayden's hands flew up to her mouth. "Oh, my God. Amy, I'm so sorry." Tears formed in the girl's eyes.

Amy sat the luggage down and walked over to Hayden, needing to comfort the younger girl. "It's okay, it's only a picture frame. I can get a new one."

Hayden shook her head wildly. "I didn't mean to. I swear I didn't mean to."

An inkling of unease trickled down her spine. Hayden's reaction was a little bit too severe for simply breaking a picture. "What's going on? You've been acting weird ever since you stepped into my house. Is there something wrong? Boy trouble?" The drama of young love was a roller coaster of emotions. Maybe Hayden had a recent break up.

Hayden started to shake. She took a step back, away from Amy. Her shoe cracked and crinkled the broken glass into the floor. "You know?"

Amy kept her voice calm and eased forward. "Listen, I know this past year I've been distant, dealing with my own stuff. But really, you can talk to me. I know I'm old to you, but I do remember how much it hurts when you're dealing with a break up."

"Oh… I...yes. You're right. But I'm not ready to talk about it yet. I'm so stupid and clumsy right now. I'll buy you a new frame. A better one."

Amy tried to grab Hayden's hand, but she took another step back. "I'll get the broom, clean this mess up and load up your bags. You go outside with your daughter."
Everything Hayden said made sense, but the panic in her gaze didn't mesh. Amy wanted to push, to get the girl to open up, but right now was not the time. She promised herself she would talk to her later, after she and Chloe settled in at Evie's new place. And as soon as Amy found out what boy was responsible for the awful heartache on Hayden's face, she would rain down punishment he'd never forget. "Tell you what, I'll get the broom. You get the bags."

Chapter Sixteen

The truck door didn't slam hard enough behind Ranger as he disembarked from the jacked-up four-by-four. Dust swirled around him from the daredevil brake job he'd pulled, congealing on the sweat beading his brow. But he didn't bother wiping the grime off his face. Why should he?

Amy wasn't here to see it, and by her own words, she wouldn't want to see him any time soon. Or ever.

Ranger slapped his palm on the scanner at the door of the war room, a huge metal pole barn on his father's property that Team Scorpion had commandeered last summer. What looked like an innocent metal door slid to the right, the hydraulics hissing as it opened and slid shut behind him.

Fucking empty. Perfect. Just like his life.

Before their last mission together, Shane had made Ranger promise to look after Amy if he died. And Ranger had agreed, wholeheartedly, even knowing he'd once been attracted to her. But he'd been so sure his training and years of separation from Amy would ensure he could carry out that mission without a snag. He hadn't counted on the absolute and overwhelming need. The dreams. The cravings. He was fucking addicted to her.

And she rejected him like a Baptist rejected alcohol. Taking small sips in the dark to satisfy her craving, then tossing him in the trash the next morning.

Ranger grabbed the nearest stack of papers, and flung

them across the room. It wouldn't hurt so bad if he hadn't had a taste. If he didn't know exactly what he would be missing without her.

His training taught him to withstand the extremes. Torture. Days without food. Without water. But Amy was like air. He needed her to breathe.

"Rearranging?"

Ranger whipped around to see Riser, his teammate, standing with his arms crossed.

"When the fuck did you get back from Pakistan?" Ranger tried to get his breathing under control.

"Last night. Like the new digs." Riser stood a couple inches shorter than Ranger, but was more muscular. His dark brown hair was long, as was his beard, but it didn't disguise the look of amusement on his face.

"Beats the FOB overseas." Their forward operating base had been in the middle of bum-fucking-Egypt. Surrounded by desert, not amenities. Just sand. Sand. And Sand.

"Yeah. Grey called us back after we wrapped up." Riser went to the long table in the center of the room, pulled out a chair, and sat.

Ranger ignored the steel band tightening around his gut. The unspoken words as loud as if Riser had shouted them. They'd wrapped up the search for Shane's body and his killer. Striking out on both counts.

"Where is everyone else?" Ranger said.

"Right behind me, so if you don't want to hear shit about your little hissy fit, I'd suggest you clean up." Riser crossed his arms, not bothering to help, and leaned back in his chair.

"Dammit." Ranger immediately went to the scattered paper, gathered it and placed it back on the desk. The last thing he needed was ribbing and questions.

Questions he wasn't ready or able to answer.

Mostly because the answer was being as fickle as a freaking teenager picking out her prom dress.

"Want to tell me what's up?" Riser joined their team at

its inception a few years ago. He'd had Ranger's back on multiple occasions. But no fucking way was he going to spill his emotional guts.

"Just some shit. No biggie." Ranger went to the small fridge at the side of the room, swiped a bottle of water and downed half, before returning to the oval table and taking a seat across from Riser.

The door slid open and most of the rest of the team walked in. Hunter. Aaron. Merc. Ethan. Cord Carter, the newest member. Shane's cousin and replacement.

"The Brady Bunch, late, as usual," Riser said.

Hunter's gaze cut straight to Ranger. "Where the fuck were you? I've been trying to get in touch with you all morning."

Ranger shrugged, unwilling to say anything, and rose to greet his teammates. Aaron had been almost as close to Shane as Ranger. The tall Texan spoke slow and easy, but killed fast and proficient. Ethan had come from the streets, a troubled teen who'd turned to the military for guidance. Merc. Who the fuck knew where Merc came from? The man towered over everyone. His expression always constant, always lethal. He spoke as little as possible. But he'd saved the group on more than one occasion. Cord, their newest member, was still in the beta stage and kept separate from the group, missing the easy blending of men who'd fought and nearly died together.

Hunter shot Ranger a questioning look, but kept his mouth shut.

Everyone took their seats, leaving two empty. "Where are the Crowe's?"

"Gone to the mountain." Ethan was the smallest of the crew, but just as corded with muscle.

The mountain. The Crowe's home in the Tennessee hills. A place of trouble and nightmares that the brothers had barely escaped. But their parents were buried there, and every year, the two took leave for a weeklong trip to pay their respects. And every year they came back different. Dark. The memories taking their toll.

Memories probably similar to Ranger's own not-so-fairytale childhood.

"Only five minutes late." Grey appeared on the wall of monitors at the back of the room. His angular face even more sharp. His steel grey eyes deadly calm.

"Had to wait on some cows to cross the road." Hunter said.

"I'm glad you felt at liberty to take your time. At least someone does." Grey's scathing reply was met with silence. "While you were pissing off, the Lobellos were busy."

The Captain didn't waste time. The bottom screens transformed into satellite images of the Lobello compound twenty miles away. "The first are pictures we took last week. As you can see the place is pretty empty."

The grainy image showed mostly buildings with a few guards along the compound's wall. "The next is from yesterday, the final from this morning."

The team sat forward in their chairs studying the images. They may joke and rib each other, but each of them took their missions serious. They knew lack of intel could mean their deaths. Or their teammate's death.

"I sent Cord in last night to get some intel up close," Grey said. Everyone turned to Cord Carter, their gazes assessing.

"I set up right outside the compound, in an abandoned warehouse. The trucks arrived around midnight. Three of them. Big rigs capable of carrying anything from kidnap victims to weapons or both. I never got eyes on the contents. But I did see the drivers, and from the way they moved, they weren't amateurs. And they definitely weren't Lobello," Cord said.

"My people are running their pictures through our database to get names and backgrounds. We should have that intel within the hour." Grey nodded for Cord to continue.

"A few minutes later, a black Land Rover pulled in. The passenger kept his head down and covered with a hat so I couldn't get a clear shot of his features. Pull it up."

Grey turned to someone off screen and a new image

popped up on the far right. The man was in a grey suit, small in stature. His features completely obscured. "We didn't get a positive ID, but the size and clothing match up perfectly with Lee Brown."

Hunter stood so fast his chair rolled back six feet. Ranger grabbed his brother's forearm to restrain him, but Hunter shook it off. Brown had nearly killed Hunter's wife, Evie. Ranger could imagine the killing rage his brother must feel and had every intention of making sure Hunter got his revenge.

But more importantly, he'd made off with the weapons before the team could get to him.

"Where is he now?" Hunter's commanding tone boomed across the metal building. He leaned forward and planted his fists on the table.

"Sit down Chief. I understand your anger, but you need to hear the rest." Grey stared Hunter down, his deadly gaze glued to Hunter until he finally resumed his seat. "While Carter was pulling recon he saw something even more interesting."

Cord started again, "After the man went inside, I saw someone trying to climb over the compound's wall. Only he wasn't trying to get in, he was trying to escape. I went to investigate and caught one of the Lobello's prisoners." Cord got up and exited the building, only to return a minute later with a small boy.

The boy had a large blindfold on, obscuring a lot of his face, but he had dark skin, dark hair and was as scrawny as a bean pole. He looked to be about six or seven. Mexican for sure.

Ranger froze. This boy was all legs and arms and clumsy. Just like another young boy he'd recently been around. Shit.

Cord pushed the boy into a chair at the table and worked on the knot at the back of the blindfold. Ranger held his breath. No fucking way could it be Pedro's boy.

When Cord finally got the blindfold off, Ranger's heart plummeted. Arturo sat directly across from him, his eyes red and watery, his gaze frightened. "What the fuck is the meaning of this?"

Ranger shot to his feet and strode around the table. Anger fueled his movements, his fists clenched. When he stood next to Artie, he spun the boy's chair around to face him. Artie cringed and held up his hands, shielding his face, but not before Ranger saw the large purple bruise on the boy's right eye.

Rage ramped up inside him and Ranger spun around, his vision tunneling on Cord. "You're going to pay for that."

Maybe Ranger still had some residual anger from this morning, and maybe that clouded his judgment, but it didn't stop him from diving for Cord and wrapping his hands around the man's neck. Cord pushed back, dropped his chin, grabbed Ranger's arm and spun around. He used the momentum to throw Ranger to the ground. Cord followed him down, slamming his forearm into Ranger's windpipe. "Stop. I know you don't know me that well, but I do not hurt kids. Ever."

Cord punctuated each word and held Ranger to the floor. Ranger stared into the man's eyes, trying to get a read if he was telling the truth. He saw nothing but straight forward honesty and determination. And the exact same shade of green as Shane's eyes.

"I'm going to let you up. But know I'm more than capable of defending myself if you attack." Cord pushed off and stood.

Ranger shot to his feet, his fists balled. His chest expanding and contracting with the force of a five hundred pound compressor. Cord didn't back away, but stood ready.

Men with something to hide didn't stand tall. Cord told the truth. Ranger forced his fingers to uncurl, one at a time. "Sorry. I have a problem with grown men hitting kids."

Everyone in the room was standing by now, the tension thick as the August humidity. They were all ready to launch in for the attack. Pulled tight like a bomb.

Cord was the one who diffused it. He smiled then and nodded at Ranger. "I feel the same way."

Ranger took the offering of peace and turned back to Artie, who cowered in a ball in the chair. His knees pulled up to his chest, his arms wrapped around his legs, holding on tight.

Ranger sighed and dropped into a squat right in front of Artie. "I'm sorry, little man. I didn't mean to scare you like that. I thought he had hurt you."

Artie gave a cry and launched from the chair, wrapping his arms and legs around Ranger, nearly knocking them both to the floor. Thanks to his quick reflexes, Ranger caught the boy and grabbed onto the table to keep from toppling backwards. Artie's body shook with sobs.

Ranger's chest tightened in a vise of regret and sorrow and fury. Fucking Santos must have hit Pedro's house before trying to break into Amy's. Ranger eased into the newly vacated chair and held onto the young boy, rubbing soothing circles on his back. The gesture felt awkward, but he'd seen Amy comfort Chloe that way.

"You know this boy?" Grey spoke from the wall of monitors.

Ranger spun around to face his commander, but held tight to Artie. "Yes, his father works for Amy Carter. Shane's widow."

The room fell silent except for Artie, who'd only started to cry harder.

"Good. Maybe you can get him to talk. I tried but he refused to speak." Cord said.

"Ranger, I need to know what that boy knows." Grey's face might as well be carved from granite. His high-and-tight grey hair was just as stiff as his expression.

Ranger nodded, knowing someone had to question the boy, and it would be better if it were someone he knew. "Give me a minute to calm him down. I'll call back as soon as I get some intel."

Grey nodded and the monitor went black. Ranger turned to his brother. "Get me some water and something to clean up his face."

After Hunter left to gather the supplies, Ranger looked

to the rest of the team. "Ya'll take thirty, give the boy some space. I'll bring you back in ASAP."

Everyone gave their agreement and left, the door sliding shut behind them. Hunter returned right after with a fresh bottle of water, a wet washcloth and a first aid kit, and a Hershey's chocolate bar.

Ranger reached back and peeled Artie's fingers from his shoulders, forcing the boy to release his death grip. When Ranger saw the dark bruise on Artie's face up close, he clenched his teeth, reining in the fury. After Ranger's own abusive past, the sight of another injured child made him boil.

Artie fought to grab onto Ranger again, but the boy was too weak. "I need to clean you up, little man." Ranger knew his voice was gruff, but didn't care.

Hunter had the exact same expression of explosive rage.

Artie still cried and shook, but not as hard as a few minutes ago. Ranger took the washcloth and gently wiped the boy's face, flinching when Artie flinched.

He felt big and clumsy with the child. Once he finished wiping all the dirt off, Ranger inspected Artie for more wounds. Aside from a few more bruises on his arms and some skinned knees, the boy seemed healthy.

Hunter opened the candy bar and extended it forward, crouching down a safe distance away. Artie wiped his eyes and tentatively took the bar, diving back against Ranger's chest as soon as Hunter let go.

Hunter met Ranger's gaze over the boy's head, his black eyes communicating silently. Grey wouldn't give them all day to question the boy. They needed the intel now, before the Lobellos moved whatever was in those trucks.

Ranger cleared his throat, his mouth feeling dry, his jaw tight. The last thing he wanted to do was upset him when he'd already been through so much, but if he'd seen anything inside the compound that could aid their team, Ranger needed to know. "Artie, you like the chocolate bar?"

Artie didn't speak, but nodded against Ranger's chest

and his body relaxed a little.

"You want some water?"

Again, no words, but another nod. Hunter uncapped the bottle and handed it to him, waiting on Artie to finish before setting the bottle back on the table.

"Cord was the man who rescued you. He said you were so brave climbing over that wall all by yourself." Ranger searched his mind for a way to ease into the questions, without upsetting him all over again. Artie's sobs had turned into quiet sniffles and an occasional hiccup.

"He said he'd never seen anyone climb a wall that fast. You must be really strong to do that. And you must have been really strong to have gotten away from those men."

Artie stiffened immediately, but Ranger kept rubbing small circles on the boy's back, trying to keep him calm. "I need you to be strong for me right now and answer a few questions. My team and I, we're trying to get the bad men and lock them up so they can never hurt anyone again. But we need your help. You saw the inside of their compound. Maybe you saw something that could help us."

Artie kept his head down and handed the half-eaten candy bar back to Hunter. Ranger stiffened, afraid he'd asked too much too soon. But then Artie sat up straighter and faced the brothers, Ranger still siting holding him in his lap, Hunter crouched right beside them.

"The man, Santos, he-he came to my house. He fought with Papa and took me away. I tried to fight him. I tried to stay with Papa, but he was too strong."

"So he took you but left your papa at home?" Ranger asked.

"Si. He hit him and Papa didn't get back up." Artie's voice cracked, a sob escaped. Ranger tightened his arms around the boy and tilted his head to Hunter. His brother stood and walked outside. Ranger wished with all his might Pedro was simply unconscious, but he hadn't alerted the authorities and it had been over twenty four hours. The most likely scenario was gloomy, but they would confirm and hope for the best. Even if the Lobellos weren't known for leaving witnesses.

"I'm sending my brother to check on your dad right now. He will take care of your dad."

Artie nodded and stayed against Ranger's chest. "Artie, I need to know what you saw at their compound. Where did they keep you?"

"Santos throw me in the trunk. When we stop, we already inside. There were big buildings. He took me to the last one. He hit me and threatened me. Then he throw me inside and locked the door. There were a whole lot of kids there, like me. Mexican. And there were white kids, too. All of them were quiet. They were scared."

Artie took a shuddering breath and Ranger squeezed him tight. "Keep going. You're doing so good."

"I talk to a boy. He been there a while, he didn't know how long. He say the men come in and bring food once a day. They keep two men inside all the time, to watch us and make sure we stay quiet. But the men drink and they talk and yell.

If anyone cries or screams, the men hurt them. At night, when everyone slept, the men talk and drink. I listen."

Ranger felt the first leap of hope. "What did you hear?"

Artie sniffled and wiped his nose. "They say they have big deal happening soon. They going to be rich, like the cartel."

"Did they say what the big deal was?"

"No. They just talk and talk. They talk about selling us kids in Mexico. About how much more the white kids will make them."

"Did they say any names? Anything about guns?" Ranger tried to keep calm, but his heart was pounding against his sternum.

Artie held silent for a minute. Then he spoke. "The night I escaped, I hear loud trucks. The men say they getting lots of guns. They kept drinking."

"Did they say a name? Who had the guns?" Ranger said.

Artie sucked in a breath and sobbed. "I no remember,

senor. Please, I want my papa. Please don't give me back to them."

Artie grabbed onto Ranger's shirt, his little nails digging into his ribcage. The fear in the boy was a real, living thing.

"Shhh, it's okay. I will never let them hurt you again. I swear it." Ranger hugged the boy to him, the surge of protectiveness taking control.

"P-p-please. I want my papa. I don't know anything else." Artie sobbed harder.

Ranger clenched his jaw and tilted his head back, every muscle in his body tightening to the point of snapping. The Lobellos had done this. They had terrorized this child, and no telling how many others were still locked up.

"Artie. I will get your papa. And I will get all of those kids back to their families. I promise you. You were so brave. I am so proud of you." Ranger rocked the boy back and forth, making soothing sounds and rubbing his back, at a loss of what else to do to give comfort.

He'd never been around kids. Except Chloe, and that was only briefly and when she started fussing Amy had always been there to take charge. Ranger couldn't remember the last time he felt so helpless.

"I swear to you. I will protect you."

That was one promise he could keep, even if he had to take the kid himself.

Chapter Seventeen

"You know, the true sign of an alcoholic is drinking alone. This is screwed up." Amy took another sip of one very large glass of Chardonnay and placed it back on the coffee table. She sat cross legged on Evie's living room floor, Chloe playing with her toys a foot away.

"Well, thank God you've got a friend like me." Evie leaned back on the couch and propped her feet up on the ottoman.

Chloe crawled into her lap and gave her a goofy toothless grin. "You know, I think we should make this a thing. Every Saturday."

"Ooh, I know. Sippin' Saturdays" Amy said as she picked her baby up and placed a big fat kiss on her chubby little cheek.

"So, are you gonna fill me in on Ranger or do I have to entertain myself with imagining what happened?"

Amy sighed and set Chloe back on the floor. Her baby immediately went after the cloth blocks, playing and giggling without a care.

Amy's insides churned. She wanted so badly to tell Evie everything. About the insanely awesome sex she'd had last night. About the undeniable feelings developing for Ranger.

Hunter and Ranger and Shane were all part of the same team. Evie married Hunter. And Amy bed hopped from

Shane to Ranger. Wives didn't sleep with their husband's teammates, dead or not.

"He was that good, huh?" Evie lifted a blonde brow, her look pretty much saying she already suspected the truth.

"I don't know what to do. I mean, how messed up is it that I'm screwing Shane's teammate? His best friend, for chrissake." Amy grabbed her glass and took a gulp, finding she needed a gulp to cleanse her mouth. "Everyone will hate me."

Her last words were whispered and Amy clutched the glass, staring into its contents. She could lose everything, even her friends.

Evie sat forward. "Are you kidding me? I've sat back and watched you withdraw, watched you completely stop living. Stop smiling. Stop everything since Shane died."

Amy swallowed and looked away. She knew Evie told the truth. She'd been on autopilot since the funeral. Effectively moving from point A to point B. But she'd never asked for help, for anything. She'd taken care of her family.

Evie slid down to the floor on her knees. "I tried to get you to laugh, to come out to the house, the bar. I tried everything I could think of to help." Evie's voice cracked, forcing Amy to look at her. "But I never made you smile. I mean really smile. I couldn't even get you angry. It was like you shut me out."

Tears formed in Evie's eyes and Amy's chest ached for her friend. "I didn't mean to. I didn't know how to...to move on."

"But I was always the one who helped you. Only this time I couldn't help." Evie's voice broke again and Amy felt her own tears gather.

"You did help me. If it wasn't for you, I don't know how I would have survived." Amy sat her wine down and grabbed Evie's hand.

"You stopped feeling. But with Ranger, you're different. He makes you mad. He makes you smile. I've seen it. I don't care if he is part of the Team, he's good for you."

"He can't be good for me. He just can't. What will his

team think? I know they have a code."

"Who gives a rats ass what they think as long as you're happy."

"I do. I can't be that person who asks him to give up his life for me." His father lived here. His brother. His base was here. In or near Mercy.

Evie squeezed her hand. "Ranger James isn't some scared little boy. He's a full-grown man capable of owning up to his choices. His Team will understand, I know Hunter already does. Who else do you think Shane would want for you?"

Amy searched Evie's expression, looking for something. Anything to make this decision for her. But all she saw was fierce determination and loyalty. "What about everyone else? Don't you think I'll be shunned? Rand Carter controls my supply. Mavis will do anything to shut me down. I could lose my business. Then what? How will I support Chloe?"

"No one in this town will shun you for moving on. Are you supposed to be a lonely widow with no hope for happiness for the rest of your life? They will understand. I promise you."

"What if they don't?" Amy's words came out a whisper. Her truest fear choking her words.

"Mavis threatened to tell everyone that me and Ranger had an affair when Shane was alive. That Chloe isn't Shane's daughter."

"That bitch."

"I know, but you know her cronies will listen. She's the matriarch of the Baptist church for God sake."

"She's crazy."

"She will ruin my reputation. None of the reputable farmers will hire me."

"Then screw them all. Ranger loves you. I can see it every time he talks about you, and yes, he does talk about you. All the time. He will take care of you. The question is, can you let him?"

Amy bit her lip and glanced at Chloe, playing happily

without a care. If she chose Ranger, she'd be risking everything. Her life. Her business. Her heart.

But if she didn't that would make her a coward.

"Come on Amy. Do you want to be a lonely old spinster like Ms. Buela, or do you want to live a full and happy life? Give Chloe a father she can be proud of?"

Evie didn't pull any punches, but then again, that was part of the reason Amy loved her so much. Amy had to make a decision. She had to make the right decision. Should she listen to her mind or her heart?

"You're right. I don't want to be alone. I want him." The same words she'd told Ranger. Only then, she'd been holding back, still scared. She was still afraid, but admitting it out loud somehow freed her. Amy's lungs expanded and she sucked in a breath, like some huge tumor had been removed from her chest and she could breathe again.

"That's my girl. Now, we need to celebrate. Go change clothes, let's go to town." Evie grabbed the couch and pulled herself to her feet.

"Town? Celebrate? For what?" Amy stayed put, staring up at her friend in confusion.

"To mark this day. You made your decision, you want him.

It's time to show him."

***

An hour later Evie and Amy pulled up to the Stellar Star Salon, with Chloe strapped in the backseat. "What are we doing here?"

Evie unbuckled her seatbelt. "When's the last time you had your hair done? I can look at your nails and clearly see you couldn't give a crap about them."

Amy glanced down at her short and cracked nails, spying some oil beneath one and quickly hiding the evidence. She honestly couldn't remember the last time she'd been to a salon.

"That's what I thought. I called, they've got a chair

waiting." Evie climbed out and shut the door, leaving Amy with no choice but to scramble out after her.

"But...but...what about Chloe? I can't possibly spend all afternoon in the salon with a baby." Amy searched for any excuse. The door to the studio loomed large and foreign. What would she talk about in there? Airplanes and engine oil? It'd been so long since she'd done anything else.

"That's why I am here. If she gets fussy, I'll take her down to the ice cream parlor. Now, quit arguing and get Chloe out of the car." Evie propped a hand on her hip and waited.

She was being stupid really. Why on earth should she be scared of a salon? It wasn't like she hadn't been in one before. She'd had her hair cut. She'd even had a few highlights put in for her wedding.

"You're making me stand out in the heat," Evie said.

Amy opened the back door and pulled Chloe, still in her infant carrier, out. "I work outside. Don't try to play on my sympathy."

"Yeah, well, I don't. Now get your butt up here so I can get some a/c."

Before Amy knew it, she followed Evie into the salon, their doorbell chime a death knell. Mrs. Trudy Van Meter and Mrs. Oralee Bates sat with magazines in the hair setting chairs to the right. Amber Atkins stood behind a salon chair, fixing her lipstick in the full-length mirror. Lori Videl, Evie's cousin, standing off to the side, removing the black salon apron. Everyone stopped what they were doing and stared.

Amy had to fight to stand her ground and not back up a step. The two older ladies were about as sweet as lemon juice with acid tongues to match. Their reputation for scorching reputations was a well-known fact for nearly the whole state. Evie cleared her throat and said, "Amber, I've brought your subject. As you can see, she has seriously neglected herself."

Amy shot Evie a killing glance, but all she did was smile and take Chloe over to the row of chairs along the wall. Then she turned and enfolded Lori in a big hug. "I've missed you, Tim and Miley must be keeping you really busy."

Amy remembered when Tim and Miley, Lori's children, were born. Now they had to be what, eight or ten years old?

Lori sniffed and then smiled. "Yeah, just normal mom stuff."

Evie, in the process of turning back to Chloe, stopped and faced her cousin with crossed arms. *Uh oh, Amy recognized that look.*

"What's going on? You and David used to come to the bar at least one Friday a month. I haven't seen ya'll in forever. And no bullshit," Evie's tone brooked no argument.

Lori wiped her eyes. "I know. We've just been having some trouble you know? I'm sure it's normal for all marriages."

"What? Is he cheating on you or something?"

Lori paused, a little too long. Her gaze skittered sideways and she grabbed up her purse. "Listen, we're fine. David just works a lot, you know? I'm being silly."

"Wait-"

Lori lifted a hand and cut Evie off mid-sentence. "I told you. It's fine. It was great to see you again. I'll see if our babysitter can't come over one weekend so we can go out together, okay?"

Lori bolted for the door, leaving Evie, mouth open, staring after her. Amy approached her friend, "You can call her later. She looked pretty upset."

"I knew something was up when they cancelled the last two times I invited them over," Evie said.

"I hope she's okay," Amy said.

"Well, I'll find out." Evie walked over to Chloe and sat down.

Amber approached, her pace quick and efficient. Her dark brown hair pulled back in a no-nonsense bun. Amy had always gotten along with Amber in high school, but that was years ago. She'd changed. Amber could have changed, too. Nervous energy zipped down Amy's arms, into her hands and she clenched her fingers almost in reflex.

Amber gave her a once over, and Amy felt every oil

and dirt stain on her jeans grow. Ellie Mae meet Grace Kelly.

And then Amber smiled, and her whole face transformed. "While I can't say you've taken the best care of yourself, you have, and always have had, a natural beauty I've envied."

"What?" Okay, so not the best response, but Amber's words had taken her for a loop. Amy finally allowed a quick glance down, just to make sure she was talking about the same person.

Amber surprised her and pulled Amy into a hug, whispering in her ear, "And still the sweet personality to match." Amber stood back, holding on to Amy's hands. "I'm so sorry about Shane. How have you been doing?"

Amy cleared her throat, "Fine."

"I'm glad you finally decided to pay me a visit. I've been dying to get my hands back on your hair since your wedding."

Her wedding. And here she was, getting fixed up for another man. Not her husband. Amy's gaze dropped to her boots like quicksand, her stomach sinking with it. "Um, thanks."

"Oh Lordy, my mouth has got me in trouble again. How can I be so callous to talk about that after what happened? I am so sorry."

Amy glanced up to see Amber, red faced and mortified. "It's okay, you're right. I've been neglecting myself. Do you really think you can fix this?" Amy swept a hand down her torso, trying to put her at ease.

The doorbell chimed before Amber could answer. "She's not a miracle worker."

Mrs. Oralee choked on her sweet tea and Mrs. Trudy set up to pounding her best-friend's back. Amber spun around, her mouth open. The blood leeched from Amy's extremities.

Mavis Carter sauntered in, her voice as venomous as a rattle snake. As easy as she pleased, she went to the mirror and primped hair so over-sprayed a high wind wouldn't knock it loose. That is, if the wind dared to mess with her in the first place. Amy met Mavis's gaze in the mirror reflection.

Mother of God. Evie rose from the waiting chairs next to the window, Chloe on her hip. Amy signaled for her to stay back. If she was going down, she was doing it alone.

"Mavis."

"Amy, I thought that was your truck. Or should I say, my son's truck." Mavis spun around slow, like in a movie. Amy straightened her legs and squeezed her fists at her side.

Amy felt the heat rise and spared a glance to the gossip queens in their thrones. Oralee and Trudy were sucking back their tea like they needed it to survive, their gazes locked on Amy and Mavis. Her plan to fly under the radar came crashing down like an earthquake in Cali.

"Mrs. Carter, can I help you?" Amber spoke tentatively, the tension in the air thicker than Mississippi mud.

"Yes, as a matter of fact you can. You can throw this piece of cheating white trash out of your salon."

A chorus of gasps sounded and Amy barely suppressed a cringe. The gleam in Mavis's eyes was already triumphant. And why shouldn't it be? She had the perfect audience for Amy's social execution. She could practically feel the noose slide around her neck.

"Cheating?" Mrs. Trudy said.

"Caught her myself." Mavis's chin lifted another degree.

"That's a lie." Evie was at Amy's side. Bless her for her defense but Amy wanted to crawl into a hole.

"Of course you would say that. But you weren't there. I caught her red handed."

Mrs. Oralee approached the small circle and cleared her throat, "Maybe I'm missing something, but when exactly did you catch her?"

"Saturday morning. In Shane's own house, with Ranger James."

"Mavis honey, I don't know how to put this delicately, so I'll just say it. Shane is dead. How is it that Amy cheated on him two days ago?" Mrs. Trudy asked that question.

Amy felt a small measure of relief. A very, very small measure.

"You always were a bit thick Trudy. What do you think? Her and Ranger started sleeping together before Shane died."

Amy gasped this time. "That's not true. I never cheated on Shane."

"Like anyone in this town will believe you." Mavis turned to Amber and said, "If you want to keep half of your customers you better kick this hussy out. Otherwise, I'll have to make sure all my acquaintances take their hair elsewhere."

Amber stiffened beside her and Amy felt the first twitch of anger rise. Mavis didn't care who got caught in the explosion as long as she took Amy down. "Don't you dare threaten her. This is between you and me."

"That's right. I'll make sure the whole town knows how toxic you are too," Mavis said.

"I'm sorry you feel that way."

"It ain't got anything to do with feelings girl. You never deserved my son."

"That may be true, but Shane wasn't perfect. He had his faults too. But I didn't betray him. Ranger would never betray him. He was Shane's best friend."

Mavis snorted, "Yeah, despite my attempts to keep them apart. Those James boys are trash, just like you. My Shane should have had better. But no, you sunk your claws in deep and then he had to join the military to get away from you."

"Mavis Carter." Mrs. Trudy threw a hand over her chest and sucked in a breath.

"Don't you pull that high and mighty act with me. You and Oralee might head up the Methodist church, but I got every Baptist in town on my side."

"You're evil. I'm surprised God lets you walk through the church doors," Evie said.

"So says the bar junkie. Serving alcohol is a sin."

"Then it must really get in your craw that your husband

is in my bar every Friday night."

"Liar." Mavis's eyes practically bulged from her round face.

Evie smirked, "I don't have to lie. You can ask anybody who comes out on a Friday night."

Mavis sputtered, for once unable to deny the facts.

"The girl is right. Rand is one of C.W.'s best customers," Mrs. Trudy said. C.W., Evie's grandpa, co-owned the Wharf with his granddaughter.

"You can lie all you want, but it doesn't negate the fact that Amy cheated on Shane." Mavis was fast turning a dark shade of red. She pointed her finger at Evie and Chloe. "Chloe isn't even Shane's daughter."

Amy felt the noose cinch so tight around her neck the air couldn't get to her lungs. Was she going to stand here and let Mavis talk about her daughter?

Amy ripped the noose off. "That's a lie. The fact that you can say something so malicious about your own granddaughter speaks to the kind of person you are. Hate festers in you. It sure is a good thing you're in church so much, cause you need to be on your knees every day, praying for your soul."

"You can't talk to me like that."

"I damn well can."

"You just wait. I'll make sure Rand cuts you off today. No more business. You're ruined."

"I don't care. I don't need anything from your family."

"Now wait a minute. Mavis are you trying to say that girl ain't Shane's?" Mrs. Oralee pointed at Chloe.

"Exactly."

"Then how come her eyes are the same green as every Carter in this county?" Mrs. Trudy said.

"You don't know what you're talking about."

Trudy stood her ground. "Oh, I think I know exactly what I'm talking about. Ever since your first husband ran off with that waitress you turned into a spiteful witch."

Mavis gasped but Mrs. Trudy continued on, "You use people, that's the only reason you have any power in this town. Everyone is afraid of you. I'm gonna tell you something though. I know this girl didn't cheat on your son. Just like I can see plain as day Chloe is his."

"Clear as a damn picture," Oralee chimed in.

"And in case you missed roll call last Sunday, we got twice the members in our church as yours. If you pull this girl's credit from Rand's store, I will make sure every soul in this town knows your husband keeps the liquor store in business. Even if I have to personally go door to door."

"You wouldn't dare."

"Try me." Trudy crossed her arms over her chest.

"I'll help," Oralee cackled and clapped her hands together.

Mavis took a step back, her composure slipping. "You can't threaten me."

"Oh, that's no threat. That's a promise."

Mavis's eyes bounced from woman to woman. She took another step back. If word got out about Rand to the church crowd, Mavis's position of power would sink faster than a brick in water.

"You did this," Mavis pointed at Amy.

"I did nothing but try to live my life. You're spite did this. You never wanted Shane to have anyone but yourself."

"I'll make you regret this, Amy." Mavis backed all the way to the door.

Amy lifted her chin and gave Mavis a small smile. "I'll pray for you."

After a strangled growl, Mavis fled, the doorbell chiming behind her. Amy let out a breath she hadn't even realized she'd been hiding.

"Holy mother, that felt good."

Amy turned to see Oralee and Trudy giving each other a high five. "That woman has needed a put down for years."

"About time we stood up to her. She isn't anything but trouble," Mrs. Trudy said.

Amy grabbed Chloe off Evie's hip, needing a distraction from the close call. That situation could have gone so much worse.

"Can you believe it Trudy? I said a curse word."

"I'm sure the lord will forgive you for it, if anyone in this town deserved it, it was her." Mrs. Trudy hugged Amy. "And if I may say so, it's about time you started dating again. And a man as good looking and good hearted as Ranger James too."

Amy grabbed onto the older lady's arm, tears prickling her eyes. "Thank you."

"That's right, girl. Don't want to end up pining after your man for fifty years like this one." Mrs. Oralee elbowed Trudy, and then checked her perfectly permed grey hair in the mirror.

"If you recall, I am not pining anymore." Mrs. Trudy huffed then turned to Evie. "What's your grandpa up to today?"

"He's fishing, I believe, with Mr. Smith," Evie said.

"And this sweet girl." Trudy kissed Chloe on the cheek. "Why haven't I seen her in church?"

Amy's face heated. She hadn't been to church since Shane's death.

"Leave her alone, can't you see she's trying to get ready for a date?" Mrs. Oralee patted Amy on the shoulder.

"Tell Cyprien I'll be expecting his phone call at five o'clock sharp," Trudy said.

Evie stifled a laugh and agreed to convey the message. A more odd couple Amy couldn't fathom, but for some reason, Mrs. Trudy set her hat after C.W. Videl, Evie's grandpa, and the two had been courting for months.

"Sinful." Mrs. Oralee muttered.

"Now, Oralee, I've caught you staring at James Harlow in church for the past three months," Mrs. Trudy said.

"You're getting the dementia. Come on, let's let these young girls get dolled up. I want to catch Rhetta before she stops making her fried pies for the afternoon."

"If you can forgive the drama, I'm ready." Amber stood behind the swivel chair.

"Fried pies it is. Can't hurt to add a few more curves to my girlish figure. C.W. swears he likes curves."

Amy grabbed Trudy before she could leave and pulled her into a swift hug. "Thank you for that."

Mrs. Trudy patted her and stepped back, "She's been needin' a set down for quite some time. The good Lord just presented me the opportunity with which to do it."

With a wave goodbye, Trudy and Oralee left, and Amy headed to the chair. "Is this going to hurt?"

Amber spun her around to face the mirror, "Not if you hold still."

Chapter Eighteen

Amy wiggled her freshly painted toes in her brand new sandals and placed her muddy boots in the back of Hunter's borrowed truck. Her feet felt...lighter. After a highlight, cut, mani and pedi, Evie in all her good wisdom, had brought Rosalee over for a new wardrobe. Rosalee Cosas owned Swank, the newest trendiest boutique in town. Amy bought not one but two new outfits, one of which she wore right now, along with matching shoes and accessories. And, on the side, she'd purchased a certain special outfit for Ranger's eyes only.

She was now refreshed and rejuvenated. She'd been dreading the confrontation with Mavis, letting her fear hold her back for so long, but now she was free. Trudy and Oralee had her back. If there was one thing guaranteed to keep Mavis's fat mouth shut, it was her husband's closet alcoholism.

Amy buckled a sleeping Chloe into the car and climbed behind the wheel, ready to take on the world and all the Mavis Carters in it.

Ready to take on the one task she had avoided more than her monster-in-law. "I think I'm ready to go through Shane's belongings."

Evie reached across the console and grabbed her hand. "Are you sure? After all this excitement?"

"Yes, you've helped me see that I've not only been

hiding from myself, but I've been avoiding moving on. I think I have to do this before I can completely close the lid on that box, and move past Shane without baggage. Without reservation. I want to give me and Ranger a real chance."

"Let's get to it then. Where are we headed?"

"U-Store-It." Amy had been so shell-shocked after the funeral, she let Ranger handle moving all of Shane's belongings back home. He stored them in the heated and cooled storage sheds in town, safe and secure for her when she was ready. Amy pulled out onto the highway, biting her lip. Even then Ranger had anticipated her needs.

A few minutes later they pulled into the storage parking lot, the lines of orange and tan metal units lined up five rows deep. Amy reached into her purse and pulled the key from one of the inside pockets. Thirteen. Shane's football jersey number. She turned right, in between the first and second row, and parked at the third unit down. Thirteen. The number glared down at her from above a large orange garage type door.

Another door she had to open. Would this one change her life for the better?

"You sure about this? His stuff isn't going anywhere, we can always come back another day," Evie said.

Amy steeled herself, straightened her spine. "No. It has to be today. If I don't find a way to move on I'll be stuck in this... this... I don't know what to call it. I'm ready to move on with an open heart and open mind. It's not fair to Ranger that I keep holding back."

Amy grabbed the door handle.

"How about I stay in the car with Chloe and let her sleep and give you a minute alone?" Evie said.

Amy nodded, unable to talk around her knotted up throat, and exited the truck, shutting the door quietly behind her. She stood before the shed, key in hand, feeling like David ready to face Goliath.

I can do this. I can do this. I can do this.

Amy repeated the mantra over and over as she knelt on the asphalt and unlocked the door. The door snapped up, rolling with efficiency, and Amy almost fell backward. Instead, she gathered her willpower, stood and took the first step inside. The room was small, no bigger than eight by ten feet, and empty except for one black box.

Amy took another step, her legs as wobbly as a loose tire on a gravel road. All that remained of her husband's belongings from overseas were packed into a box the size of a trunk.

She approached with caution born of fear and grabbed the lock. A lock for which she had no key. The walls shrunk, the ceiling lowered. Cold metal walls. Cold concrete floors. Sterile. Unfeeling. Uncaring.

The lock clattered from her shaking fingers. Not here. She couldn't go through his private belongings here. Amy spun and ran to the truck, yanking the door open. "I can't do this here. It's not right. Can we take it back to your house, let me open it there?"

"You okay?" Evie peered at her like she was losing it, and maybe she was, all her bravado from earlier dissipating in the afternoon sun.

"Yes, I don't want to do it here."

"Well of course you can. The guys won't be home anytime soon. We'll have the house to ourselves."

"Thanks." Amy closed the door, went back to the box, and started to drag it to the truck. Sweat dripped down between her breasts by the time she'd pulled the heavy trunk the twenty feet to the truck and lowered the tailgate. She stood and fanned her new shirt out from her chest, attempting to circulate some air.

Evie hopped out, took one look at Amy and shook her head. "We need help."

"Yeah, I'm not leaving without it. Not now."

"Wait here." Evie went off in the direction of the office, reemerging a few minutes later with a familiar face in tow.

"Now Ms. Amy, you can't lift that thing by yourself. You shoulda come got me from the get go." Steve Jones, lifelong resident of Mercy, towered over the women in his

Big Smith overalls and sleeveless t-shirt.

"Thank you so much. I tried, but I just can't pick it up. I had no idea it was so heavy," Amy said.

"No bother at all." He bent down and picked the trunk up with ease and placed it in the back of the truck. "I know I should have come by sooner, but I'm sorry for your loss. Shane was a good man. Served his country. Wish we had more like him."

"Thank you. That means a lot to me and I know it would mean a lot to him," Amy said.

"Anytime, ma'am. Let me know if I can help you out in any way." Steve said and then turned and went back in the office. Amy slammed the tailgate shut, locked up the shed and hopped back in the car.

"I need to see what's inside. I want to know what his life was like all those months away." Amy pulled back out on the highway and sped toward Evie's turn off. They'd built the log cabin on Hank's property, out in the woods, but not far from the river. Not far from the Wharf.

"I can't even imagine. To know if something happened to Hunter and that's all I had left." Evie stared out the window and Amy felt the need to comfort her friend.

"You know as well as I you can't think like that. Hunter is a strong man. And now he has something to fight for. Don't let my life make you worry." Amy turned left on the newly asphalted road to Evie's house. After Hunter's team set up permanent residence in Mercy, they'd paved the road and cleared sights for new buildings back off in the woods.

"Listen to me. I have my family and I'm whining over a possibility. I'm sorry," Evie started tearing up.

"Stop apologizing. That's all everyone does anymore. I'm sorry. I'm sorry your husband is dead. I'm sorry you're having to be a single mom. Well, you know what, I'm not sorry. I'm thankful. I'm thankful for the time I had with him. I'm thankful for the blessing he gave me." Amy swiped at the tears trailing from the corners of her eyes and glanced in the rearview mirror at her baby. A blessing Shane would never get the chance to see. To touch. To hold.

Evie cried harder and grabbed Amy's free hand. Thelma and Louise. Best friends forever. "I love you. And I'm happy you've gotten your second chance."

"Me too." Amy whispered, unable to get the strength in her stomach to push the words out. Her second chance. Ranger. A man that vowed to fight for her. Without apology.

A man she was close to losing unless she got over her past and Mavis's threats.

Amy pulled the truck into the drive, parked and got out, meeting Evie in front for a fierce hug. "Thank you for not giving up."

Evie stepped back and wiped her face. "Well, I know how stubborn you are."

"And you didn't give up."

"I will never give up on you."

"Dammit, we gotta stop this or all my new makeup is going to run," Amy attempted a laugh, almost hit it.

"I hate to tell you this honey, but you're a little closer to raccoon than supermodel right now," Evie said. "Okay, enough waterworks, we have a mission and I happen to have a dolly to lug that heavy thing in the house."

"Great." Amy went about unlocking Chloe's car seat, careful not to wake her, and Evie returned with the dolly. A few grunts and curse words later, she'd managed to get Shane's trunk in the living room, Chloe still asleep and all.

"Okay, go wash your face. I'll pour us a couple of glasses of wine."

Amy ran down the hall and turned into the first door on the left. Ranger's room. His stuff. His bed.

She swallowed the warm shiver running down her tummy. Focus. Wash your face. Deal with your baggage. Then you can bag your new man and show him what a real woman wants.

Amy went in his bathroom, grabbed a bar of soap and quickly washed all the makeup off her face. Her new shirt would need to be washed before the sweat stains set in, but later. That could be dealt with later. She went back to the living room. Evie had resumed position on the dark leather couch, feet up. Amy grabbed her glass and downed half in one swallow. Forget alcoholic. She needed the courage.

Amy faced off with Shane's trunk. Big. Cold. Impenetrable. She lifted the lock and realization struck. No key. Ranger had given her one key. Not two. The lock fell from her fingers and clattered against the trunk with a sonic boom.

"I don't have the key." The wail of despair was real this time.

"Don't panic. Wait right here." Evie jumped up from the couch and ran from the room, returning a few minutes later with a large tool in her hands. "Bolt cutters."

"Do I even want to know why you have bolt cutters?" Amy accepted the tool, almost dropping it. The cutters had handles at least two feet long and a beak made of steel.

"You can thank C.W. and the MRG." Evie plopped back on the couch.

"You mean I can thank your near criminal background and your crazy grandpa who got you in that mess?" Evie had been inducted into the Mississippi Revolutionary Group last year, at the insistence of her grandpa. The move had not only made Evie skate the law but nearly get killed in the process.

"Exactly. Now stop yapping and get to work. I can't handle all this suspense."

Amy placed the bolt cutters and squeezed the handles together. The lock clipped in half with surprising ease and fell to the rug. "This is some serious equipment."

"Told ya," Evie said.

Amy knelt before the trunk, a wave of dread following her down, feeling like Pandora about to open her box. She swallowed and looked to Evie, who gave her a nod of encouragement. Pandora or not, Amy was doing this. Right here. Right now.

Chapter Nineteen

Shane's trunk lay open before her filled with...video games? Amy reached in and pulled them out. *Halo. Modern Warfare. Medal of Honor.*

What the hell?

Next came a PlayStation. Socks. Army shirts. His pillow.

His pillow. Amy pulled the soft cushion to her face and inhaled. Shane filled her senses. Memories flooded her mind. His smile. His laugh. Times of happiness. When she could move again, Amy placed the pillow to the side. A stack of metal picture frames lay in the bottom next to a shoe box that looked like an emotional atomic bomb.

Amy went for the pictures first. Lifting them one at a time, surprised at their size and weight. He must have bought them overseas. The frames were some sort of grey metal, heavy and thick, like nothing she'd ever seen before. The first held a picture of her in her wedding gown. She carefully sat it to the side and inspected the rest. Each frame held a memory. A picture of Amy in their old tire swing. Amy and Shane at the sandbar on the river. One of Amy sleeping...she didn't even know he'd taken it. Fresh tears formed and dripped onto the glass. He'd taken all of her with him.

Shaking and sobbing and needing something else, Amy reached for the last photo. Ranger and Shane. Teenagers. A string of catfish and the river. Their smiles genuine and huge, arms around each other.

Oh God. His best friend. His wife. Together.

"Amy. Amy. Look at me." Somehow Evie was beside her, grabbing her shoulders, shaking her. Her voice seemed to come from some far away tunnel.

"I can't do that to him." Amy sobbed and clutched the picture to her chest, her world cracking open again. The pain and betrayal fresh acid on an open wound.

"Yes. You. Can. Look at that picture. Look at those men."

Amy pulled the frame from her chest and stared down through guilt colored glasses.

"Who else would Shane trust with your heart? With your life?" Evie forced Amy to focus. "With Chloe's?"

Amy's heart stopped all together, like God himself had reached his hand in her chest and closed his fist around it.

"Are you listening? Think. Use your brain, not just your heart. Do you think Shane would rather you be with a stranger, or the man he trusted like a brother?" Evie kept talking, her words starting to sink in.

Amy shifted her focus to her friend, the picture cutting into her palms. "Do you really believe that?"

"Of course I believe it. It makes sense. He gave his life for Ranger and their team. Ranger nearly gave his life for Shane. And I know he would gladly give his life for you and Chloe."

Amy sucked in a shuddering breath, trying to make sense of her words. Of the past. Of the future. Her future.

Her heart kicked hard against her chest.

Her and Chloe's future with Ranger.

"He would," Amy said.

"He's crazy about you Amy. It's time you accepted that Shane isn't coming home. And deep down, you know he wanted you to be happy."

Happiness and a chance at a real family. She took a deep breath and nodded, Evie let go of her shoulders and Amy set the photo to the side. "I'm ready. I'm ready to move forward."

Evie searched her face, her own eyes full of moisture.

"I'm serious. Now quit looking at me like that before I start sobbing again." Amy forced a laugh, broken but real, and faced the last item in the trunk. A shoe box.

Surely its contents couldn't be as hard as the pictures.

She pulled it out and sat it on the floor in front of her. Amy glanced at Chloe, still sleeping, before prying the lid off. Letters.

The box was full of letters. He'd kept all her letters.

Amy placed a hand against her chest and pulled the first one free. Her first letter to him. She pulled each one out of the box, smoothing them flat then placing them in a pile. She didn't want to read them, she remembered every word. But touching them seemed to heal something inside her.

Three left. Amy pulled one and smoothed it out flat, not looking as she stacked it with the others. The next, same thing. Only one left. Amy unfolded it, almost reverently, and looked at it. Her last letter.

She paused.

Not her letter.

She looked again, taking time to study the script.

Not her handwriting.

Her hands started shaking, the paper crinkled and crumpled in her fingers.

A love letter from another woman.

Amy, her vision blurry, her world tilting, scanned the letter. The words love, hot night, sex....punched her in the gut. Bile rose and she ran to the bathroom, puking up the meager breakfast in the toilet. When the food was gone, she dry heaved. Distantly she felt Evie holding her hair back, placing a cold cloth on her neck. "What is it? Amy, talk to me."

At some point the dry heaves subsided and Amy sat back on the cold tile floor, the letter still clutched in her hand. "Water."

She could only manage one word. Her throat dry and raw, but not nearly as burned as her heart.

Evie quickly handed over a bottle of water and Amy took a sip. She grabbed the toilet and pulled herself to her feet. In a daze, Amy stumbled from the bathroom and into the living room.

"Talk to me," Evie commanded.

But Amy couldn't make her throat work, couldn't make her lips form a sound. She thrust the letter to Evie, who snatched and read it. The look of shock that overtook her friend's features was a mere shadow of Amy's own pain.

Then Evie's dread morphed into anger.

"Who the fuck is H.J.?"

Evie's emotion breathed a little life into Amy and she snatched the letter, studying the signature, the handwriting, the string of hearts, x's and o's. Familiar. She'd seen this before.

Evie bent over, reached into the box and pulled out a phone.

"Shane's sat phone. Oh, my God. Is there a charger? Plug it up. I can see what numbers he called." Amy made a wild grab, snatching the grey phone from Evie's hand. Flipping it open in desperation, knowing it was dead.

"Amy, maybe we should slow down. Talk to Hunter first."

"Get me the damn charger." Amy might regret her tone later, but now she was beyond caring. Evie stood, unbending and blocking Amy's path. "Come on. I have to know. What if it was Hunter, wouldn't you have to know?"

Evie didn't move for a full minute, but finally sighed and handed over the power cord. Amy rushed to the wall, fumbled with the cord before finally getting the phone plugged up. The minutes it took before the phone charged enough to power on stretched for decades.

"It's on." Amy all but shouted and scrolled the last dialed numbers. Most were foreign. She passed them quickly. But then Mercy's area code popped up. Not her number.

Amy hit dial and held the phone up to her ear.

A phone rang in Evie's house. Amy's gaze collided with her friend. "That's not my ringtone."

Amy dropped Shane's phone to the floor and raced in the direction of the sound. She ran down the hall and slammed open the last door on the right. Hayden James sat on the bed, her face pale, her eyes filled with tears. Her cell clutched in her grip.

***

Evie was behind her, pulling her back, but Amy couldn't feel. Couldn't hear. Couldn't breathe.

No air. She couldn't get in any air. The hallway closed in on her. Had to get outside. Open spaces. Amy ran out the back door, barely making it off the porch before she was gagging again. There was nothing to hold on to in the back yard and she fell to her hands and knees, gasping. Hayden. Amy had babysat Hayden. She'd been her friend. Her confidant.

Hayden was just a little girl.

Pain twisted and wrenched her insides.

No. Not a little girl. A woman full grown, sleeping with Amy's husband.

Amy doubled over again, unable to move, the knife of betrayal cutting and shredding her insides like a meat grinder.

"Amy. Honey, what happened? Are you okay?" Deep voice. Not female.

Amy lifted her head enough to see Ranger standing there, his face a mask of worry. But what could she say, the news would rip him in two. Amy sobbed and hit the ground with her fist. Hard.

"You're scaring me, dammit. Is Chloe okay? Did something happen to Evie?" Ranger bent down and lifted her by the arms.

"Do I need to call in for back up?" Hoyt appeared behind Ranger and she ducked her head against Ranger's chest, wanting to crawl up in a hole and hide. Her humiliation wasn't personal, not with an audience.

"Go check the house." Ranger ordered.

Amy heard his footsteps pounding across the yard as he ran to the house. Ranger got her attention again. "Amy, tell me what's wrong."

How? How could she tell him? She shook her head. No. She couldn't tell him.

"I can't fix it if you don't tell me."

She couldn't, but he did have a right to know. She had to tell him.

"Shane. Hayden." Amy croaked, her voice hoarse, raw from puking.

"What? That doesn't make any sense," Ranger said.

"Amy, stop." Evie burst from the house and stumbled to a stop, holding Chloe on her hip. She was panting from running.

Ranger looked at Evie. "Is Chloe hurt?"

"No."

"Are you okay?"

"Yes."

"Where's Hoyt?"

"I'm right here, man. House is clear." Hoyt eased out the back door and stepped to the side.

"What the hell has you two looking like you've seen a goddamn ghost then?" Ranger's questions grew louder and in rapid fire succession.

"I don't know if I should say." Evie hesitated, looking at Amy for answers.

Amy dragged her broken soul out of the gutter and sucked in a breath, trying to find the words. The bitter betrayal burning up her insides too scorching to contain, but she didn't want to hurt him. To hurt this man who'd done so much to protect her. "I just...I just went through Shane's trunk. I got upset."

Amy shook her head at Evie, giving her the order to keep her mouth shut.

"Then why did you say my sister's name?" Ranger stooped down, got eye level. His gaze cutting through her resolve like a hot knife through butter.

"I...I don't know. I don't know what I was saying."

"You're not telling me the truth."

"What she isn't telling you is that I slept with Shane." Hayden stood on the back porch, clutching a post, her eyes blank. Her face chalk white. Her long honey colored hair hanging in wild waves around her small shoulders making her appear young. Too young to be so damaged.

"You did what?" Ranger's skin flushed red and his fingers cut into Amy's arms.

"I slept with Shane." Her breathing hitched. "I was drinking with some friends. He showed up with some guys. I don't know how it happened."

"I'll tell you how it happened, you spread your legs for a married man. My best-fucking-friend." Ranger's hoarse voice rose with each word, whipping through the air with a crack.

Hayden jerked back, as though physically struck. The tears swimming in her eyes fell in straight lines down her cheeks. Her chin trembled. "I didn't mean to. I'd never. . .I was drunk. I would never hurt you like that. I swear."

Amy's heart reached out to the broken girl. She wanted to comfort her, despite her anger.

"You didn't mean to? How exactly do you not mean to have sex with someone?" Ranger's voice boomed across the yard.

Hayden shook her head wildly, sobbing. Ranger made to advance, but Amy pulled him back. Her instincts firing on full-blast. If he got to Hayden, in his current state of mind, he'd regret it for the rest of his life.

"Please. Please, I'm so sorry," Hayden pleaded, clutching the porch post like she was on a sinking ship.

Ranger stopped fighting, his muscles went slack, but Amy didn't relax. She watched the man in her grip transform from a wild rage into the cold blooded soldier he'd been trained to be. "Get out of my sight. You disgust me."

Hayden jerked and pressed the back of her hand to her mouth. The only sound in the yard was the keening moan that escaped from her lips. Her gaze flickered right, then left, and then she turned and ran back in the house. Gone from sight, but her presence hung heavy in her wake.

Amy's heart ached for Hayden in the same beat with her anger. How could she betray them like that? How could Shane?

How could Amy blame Hayden, barely out of being a teenager?

Anguish flooded Ranger's expression and Amy wanted so bad to take that away from him. His best friend's betrayal. How could Shane have taken advantage of an innocent?

"He slept with my sister." Ranger stared at the now empty spot where his sister had stood, no question in his voice. He turned back to her. Her heart stopped. His expression, his body language. His essence was cold. Empty. Deadly.

No. She would not allow it. Ranger was worth fighting for. He was worth it. No way in hell her dead husband would make this hard shell on Ranger permanent.

He needed her as much as she needed him. The only way they would survive this was together. Alone they were broken and bloodied. But together they could be solid and strong.

"Yes." Deep down she knew Shane was the one at fault. Hayden had been wild and spoiled by her family, but she wasn't a slut. Unbidden, the memory of her first time with Shane rose. Head spinning, too much to drink, she didn't really want him to touch her like that. . .Amy had been young and innocent herself. "Don't go after her. It's not her fault."

"Not her fault?" Ranger all but screamed. "She slept with your husband. How is that not her fucking fault?"

"Because she's just a kid. If she got drunk and didn't know what she was doing, I can't just blame her." But she could damn sure blame Shane. A man fully grown. Married. Having sex with a twenty year old who'd never been out of Mercy, Mississippi. Disgust crept up the walls of her stomach, burned bitter holes in her heart. All this time she'd felt so guilty for fighting with Shane before he deployed. Even more guilty now, desiring Ranger.

The whole time Shane had been with someone else.

He'd not only broken Amy. Hayden, Hunter and Ranger would be destroyed.

Devastated.

"You can't let this ruin your relationship with Hayden. You can be mad, but be mad at the right person." Amy took a deep breath. As bad as she wanted to crawl in a hole and hide, she couldn't. She couldn't let this rip apart a brother and sister. She couldn't only think of herself. She would help repair the huge fissure of pain growing in Ranger's gaze.

The sound of tires peeling out of the drive filled the back yard. Amy met Evie's gaze, "That's Hayden."

"Shit. She shouldn't be driving." Ranger's expression was a torn mask of fury and hurt and worry.

"I got her, bro. Evie, can I borrow your car?" Hoyt said.

"Of course, come on," Evie and Hoyt disappeared into the house.

Ranger's gaze was locked onto the now empty porch, his jaw clenched and ticking. Amy gently turned his head back to her. "Hoyt will make sure she's safe, okay? Don't worry."

"How can I be so damn worried and mad at the same time?" His voice dropped to a whisper and he lowered his forehead to hers. Anguish drawing new lines around his mouth.

"Be mad at him. Be mad at Shane. Not her. You know as well as I how innocent Hayden is. She might not think she's still a child-but she is. She's never even been outside of this town." Each word cinched the belt of grief tighter. She'd mourned Shane, she'd grieved, moved through the guilt, the loneliness. And she'd just started to emerge from the dark side into the light. Now his betrayal cast a shadow darker than a full eclipse.

Then Ranger's words came back to her. I will always fight for you.

This man who hadn't given up, who'd fought for her, this strong man stood before her now. Broad shoulder's stooped. Defeat circling his blue eyes. Leaning on her.

She'd mourned a man not worth her tears. She'd hidden herself from the world, keeping his picture on the mantle like a shrine, letting the guilt over her feelings for Ranger eat her alive.

And for what?

"How could he do that to you?" Ranger said.

Amy fought the urge to rub her fist over her aching chest and instead cupped his cheek with her palm. "I don't know. I never will. But I won't waste any more time on him. He's dead. Buried."

Ranger didn't move. Didn't even acknowledge that she'd spoke.

Amy foraged on, determined to pull him back from the edge.

Knowing he was her only hope of happiness. "Don't look

behind you. Don't look at the past. Look at me."

Chapter Twenty

Ranger blinked, like he was coming back from a daze. The warmth from Amy's palm seeped into his cold skin. The chaos in his mind whirled in a violent tornado of images of his best friend and his little sister. The happy memories tainted by the ugly ones. Sucking him into a vortex of pain.

"Ranger. Look at me."

Amy. Her soft words flung a life line and he grabbed on, fighting his way back. Focusing on her golden eyes, glowing bright in the darkness of his soul, her freckles, a gift from the kiss of the sun.

"Hoyt will take care of Hayden. If he brings her back here, I will talk to her. I don't blame her."

"How can you be so forgiving of what she did?" Ranger said, confused. Yes, Shane had violated Ranger's trust. But Amy had been his wife. Shane didn't only violate her trust, he violated the entire foundation of their marriage.

"Because he's gone. He's been gone for a long time. And because now I don't have to feel guilty for caring about you."

Her words detonated in his chest, expanding his ribcage to near bursting. "What did you say?"

"He's gone."

"Not that. The last part. Say it again." Ranger held his

breath, not daring to hope.

Amy cupped his face between both her palms. "I care about you."

The storm of pain dissipated beneath the power of her words. To know she wanted him. Needed him like he needed her. Ranger groaned and crushed his lips to hers, her sweet essence a balm to his soul. Amy returned his kiss, just as passionate. Just as hungry. Heat, hot and fast, scorched through him and he wrapped his arms around her waist, lifting her.

When they pulled apart, minutes later, they were both panting. Ranger allowed her to slide slowly down his body, savoring every inch of her skin against his. What he saw in her gaze took his breath away. Open desire burned in those depths. Desire painted with love.

"No more running," Ranger said.

Amy shook her head, smiling.

"No more hiding."

She shook her head again.

"No more guilt."

"No. I want to be with you and I don't care if they put it on the five o'clock news."

"God woman, you're killing me. I want to take you in that house and make love to you until we can't walk." That was putting it mildly. He wanted to chain her to his bed and never let her go.

She blushed, but instead of ducking her head, she raised up on her tippy toes. "What are you waiting for?"

He searched and couldn't come up with a single reason. Except the reason he was here in the first place. Arturo.

As much as he wanted to take her home right this minute, he couldn't. He had to focus on the mission. And find a way to break the news. Amy had one giant ton of crap dumped on her today and he was about to drop the next brick.

"I need to tell you something."

She smiled and did that tickle thing on the back of his neck that drove him crazy. "Talk? How about kiss?"

He grabbed her hand and pulled it between them,

watching with resignation as her smile faded. "What?"

Worry gripped him, his back tightened. God, he didn't want to do this to her. Not now. But he had a mission to complete and a little heartbroken boy sitting in his truck. "I am so proud of you. You're so strong."

She snorted. "Yeah, that's why I was puking my guts up a few minutes ago."

"Yeah, well you're human. But you're standing on your own two feet. Comforting me for Christ sake." What kind of man did that make him?

Her gaze softened. "You needed me."

"Damn right I needed you. I will always need you." The truth hammered home. She was his heart, his future, his existence. "God, you're sexy."

She laughed outright then, the sound music to his ears. "Yeah, no makeup. My new clothes ruined. You're crazy."

"Crazy for you."

Her laughter doubled and he couldn't suppress his own grin in response. "Does that pick-up line really work for you?"

"Not yet, but I'm hoping."

Her laughter faded, but a small smile lingered on her lips. Lips he'd kissed and wanted to again. If he had to give her cheesy pick-up lines for the rest of his life, he would. The image of them together, forever, popped in his mind. He would be her husband. Chloe's father. Their family.

A family that might grow by one sooner than she expected. Ranger took a deep breath and expelled. As much as he loved the sparkle in her eyes, he had to tell her the truth.

"I have to leave for a couple of days." He held her to him, wanting to savor every minute.

"I'm not new to this game. I get it."

"That's not all." Shit. Why now? Why the boy?

She pulled back and stared up at him. "You're starting to scare me. What is it?"

"We've been doing surveillance on the Lobellos. My teammate had watch last night." Ranger paused, finding it harder and harder to break the bad news. "He saw a little boy escape the compound. He helped rescue him."

Amy sucked in a breath, her pulse pattering at the base of her neck. "Is he okay?"

Ranger nodded. "He wasn't wounded. But we don't know what happened to his father."

"Who is it? Can I help?"

Ranger took her hand and led her to the truck. She would have to see the boy unharmed to believe it. He grabbed the door handle and pulled the door open. Arturo huddled in the front seat, his knees tucked to his chest, his head down. Dirt smudges and bruises still dotted his arms.

Amy's fingers tightened in his grip. Arturo lifted his head, his big brown eyes red from crying. He saw Amy and, with a cry, launched from the truck and wrapped around her. Ranger stepped back in time to avoid being kicked.

"Arturo?" Amy said. Artie started crying in earnest and she wrapped her arms around him, hugging him to her.

"He said the Lobellos came to his house and took him. Bo is searching for Pedro right now, but we don't know anything yet." Ranger rubbed a hand over his head, exhausted mentally. He'd never been able to stand seeing children hurt or scared. Not after his childhood. Now he was up close and personal with a boy whose father might not be missing, but murdered.

And the only other person on this planet who could care for him was the woman he loved. He had a brief worry about taking on two kids - but squashed it. He would, and he would do it with pride. But a part of him still held out hope that Pedro was alive.

"Are you hurt? Let me look at you." Amy tried to pull Artie from her, but the boy doubled down on his cling effort.

"I've already checked him over, and tended to the few scrapes. He's okay," Ranger reassured her.

"Thank you," she mouthed and cupped her hand to the back of Arturo's head, tucking him into the curve of her neck.

Ranger shifted, unsure what to do. Give him a gun and

he could take it apart, clean it and reassemble in under a minute. But kids. . .he might as well try to figure out wallpaper and curtains. His phone buzzed in his back pocket, saving him from too much contemplation. Ranger snapped it open and lifted it to his ear, walking a few feet away to give Amy and Arturo some privacy. "What?"

"Where are you?" Bo Lawson's unmistakable no-bullshit voice came through the phone.

"I'm at Evie's. Amy is here. Just gave her the boy." Ranger peeked over his shoulder to see her rocking side to side, trying to comfort Arturo. Her stance, her grip, her expression pure fierce protectiveness. Just like he expected.

Some unfamiliar ache started in his chest. His mother had never held him like that, her own flesh and blood. She hadn't been allowed to. His father was jealous of everyone and everything that took attention away from him, even his children. Ranger turned back from the sight, too many painful memories attached. Memories he'd long thought buried.

"I need you here ASAP," Bo said, pulling him back to the present. "I'm at Pedro's."

Bo hung up before Ranger could speak, giving his command without a doubt it would be followed. Ranger suppressed a curse and shoved his phone in his pocket. He wasn't through here. He needed more time.

Ranger strode back to Amy, steeling himself. "I need to talk to you. In private."

She nodded. "Let me take him in to Evie and I'll be right back."

Amy walked to the house, talking the whole time. "How about some ice cream and a soda? I bet that will make you feel a little better?" Her words faded and she disappeared in the house, reappearing a few minutes later. Alone.

It had taken her less than half a second to go total momma-bear-protective over the boy. If Pedro turned up dead, she'd take Arturo as her own, Ranger had no doubt.

She came back outside, glancing over her shoulder every couple of feet. Despite the worry and exhaustion painting her face, Ranger reacted to her like she'd walked out in lingerie. No matter what she wore or how she did her hair, she was the most beautiful creature he'd ever seen.

"Is he okay?" Ranger said.

"For now. We've got about five minutes before the ice cream disappears and Chloe wakes up. Who was that on the phone?"

Ranger couldn't stand the shadows of fatigue lining her eyes, but he had every bit of faith she could shoulder the burden. "Bo. He's at Pedro's. I don't know anything yet, but I will call as soon as I have some info, okay?"

Tears brimmed in her eyes and Ranger cursed, hating the pain he caused, and pulling her back into his arms where she belonged.

"Can this day get any worse?" Her voice was muffled against his shirt.

"I don't know, but I will do everything in my power to find his father." Ranger clenched his jaw, mentally going through the list of items he would need for the upcoming mission. Now he not only had to complete the Op on the Lobellos, but find and rescue Pedro.

"I know you will. Please be careful. I don't know if I can handle it if something happens to you, too." Amy stared up at him, her tear stained cheeks ripping him apart.

"I can't promise you I won't get hurt. You know the risks involved in my job." Ranger wanted to lie and tell her everything would be butterflies and rainbows, but she deserved better. He got down eye level with her. "But I can promise I will fight to get back to you. I will fight with every single breath in my body."

Damn, if she wasn't the sexiest woman on the planet. His every instinct screamed for him to carry her inside and love her. Comfort her. Never leave her. But that wasn't his job. And he wasn't alone. His team depended on him. They were a unit. They moved as one. And right now, his unit was waiting on him to move in on the Lobellos.

"I shouldn't be gone for more than a couple of days. And hopefully, when I get back, you and Arturo will never have to worry about the Lobellos again." Even if he had to take them all out himself.

"I'll be okay. Please be careful." Amy lifted up and pressed her lips to his. Desire exploded at that brief touch and Ranger held her to him, deepening the kiss in a desperate need to imprint on her his possession. She belonged to him now.

And he belonged to her.

Ranger pulled back, catching his breath. "Promise me you will stay here until I get back."

She was breathing just as hard as him, her hard nipples pressing into his chest, evidence that she wanted him just as much. "I will. Don't worry."

Ranger placed one more kiss to her lips. Her nose. Her forehead. Inhaling her scent. "I will be back soon."

Chapter Twenty-one

"Jesus Christ." Ranger stopped inside Pedro's front door. The small white ranch style farmhouse looked innocent enough. A porch stretched across the front, the bright blue front door friendly and inviting. Everything about the house seemed welcoming, everything but the giant pool of blood staining the living room carpet.

"Yeah, I've got my team on the way over to start the forensics. Hopefully, they can get what we need before the DEA and ATF show up." Bo, in his tan Sheriff uniform, minus the hat, stood off to the right, snapping pictures with his phone.

The sheer amount of blood spelled death. Shit. Ranger had hoped to bring good news to Amy, but no way Pedro, or any living being, could lose that much blood and walk out of here. "Where's the body?"

What must have been a coffee table lay in bits and pieces on the living room floor. Pictures hung at odd angles. A lamp lay on its side. Blood spray dotted the couch. Arturo's toys mixed in with the destruction.

"Haven't found it yet, but there is a drag pattern towards the kitchen. I'm thinking they dragged him out back. Possibly took him with them."

Ranger circled left, towards the kitchen door and Bo followed. The blood smear started a few feet from the kitchen and continued all the way to the back door. The kitchen table and chairs were in perfect condition. It was obvious the fight had taken place in the living room. "Any tracks?"

"Look out back." Bo handed Ranger a handkerchief to open the kitchen door. Ranger moved with caution, careful not to disturb the crime scene. Bloody footprints appeared halfway across the small concrete patio leading into the back yard.

"Someone walked out," Ranger said.

"Yeah, but the question is, who? Did they carry him out? Just walk through the blood, throw him in a truck and drive off?" Bo stood in the doorway, his large frame equal to Ranger's, filling up the door.

"Could have been they left Pedro for dead, but he managed to get out. Or it could be one of the gang members." Fucking shit day. No way Pedro survived this attack. Every instinct in Ranger told him the man was dead, it was just a matter of finding the body. His death would tear Amy apart. And what would happen to Arturo? He had no idea what the deportation laws were or if they even applied, but he did know without a doubt Amy would fight tooth and nail for the boy, and he'd be right there beside her.

The steel reflection in Bo's grey eyes mirrored Ranger's. There was minimal likelihood of a poor immigrant farmer getting the jump on a trained bloodthirsty murderer. "When forensics' gets here we'll run samples, check the DNA."

Ranger had already spent more time than he had to spare. He had to get to headquarters, report and gear up. "I need you to set a man on Evie's house. Keep watch on the girls until we complete the mission." There was no doubt the Lobellos would come for Arturo. No one left the gang. Especially a witness to their crimes.

"Already on it." Bo Lawson was an ex-Marine, been in multiple deployments and done some serious combat time, but unlike Ranger, he'd gotten out. Elected to move to Mercy and run for sheriff. In part, Ranger was glad. The man was a badass not many would fuck with and he didn't take shit from anyone. The bad part was he didn't back down from Ranger or TF-S either. "I've got my K-9 unit coming to track in the woods out back and Haskell is headed to Evie's."

"You sent freaking Haskell?" The old man fancied himself as a John Wayne, but had to be well into his seventies. "You think he can protect them?"

Bo stared him down, muscles bunching underneath his uniform. "I'm not funded by the federal government. I have to work with what I have." His voice was harsh, daring Ranger to counter him. "So if you want a damn guard on your women, he's all I've got. My other option is a trainee fresh out of the police academy, would you rather I send him?"

Ranger clamped his teeth together, barely holding back a retort. If he had one extra man to spare he would, but all of TF-S was needed for tonight's op. "Shit."

"Haskell it is. When I finish up here, I'll head over there myself, but that's the best I can offer."

Ranger wanted to punch something. Hard. Like the sheriff's jaw, but he held tight. The man was an ass, but he knew what he was doing. If anything happened to Amy...No. Nothing would happen to her because he was going to kill the fucking leaders of the Mexican gang. He would take every single one of them down if that's what it took. And then they would never have to worry about the Lobellos again.

And maybe then, when people stopped trying to kill him and kidnap her, they would have a chance at starting a normal life together.

"Fine. But if anything happens to her or Evie on your watch I'll put a bullet in your head." Ranger harnessed the anger, the frustration. He would need it.

"If I let something happen to them, I'll put the bullet there myself." Rumor had it that Bo had come close to suicide once before. A lone wolf terrorist had discovered his identity, found Bo's wife and child, and killed them. Bo had been overseas on a mission at the time and unable to protect his family.

Ranger felt a small pang of guilt for him. Now that he

had Amy and Chloe, now that he had someone to come home to, he couldn't imagine his life without them.

He needed to make sure he removed all threats from them. And he would start tonight. Captain Gray had called in ATF and ICE to coordinate the takedown. But stage one of the attack was all still TF-Scorpion. And Ranger would be the first one through that door. He had a bullet saved especially for Santos.

***

Amy tucked the sheet around Arturo's shoulders, the full size bed making him appear even smaller. More vulnerable. The past hour of crying without a break had worn them both out. An occasional hiccup still shook him every few seconds, but sleep had claimed him for the night, and she prayed he would be safe in the cocoon of sweet dreams. Innocent dreams. Dreams a young boy should have.

Not the nightmare of losing his father.

Amy bent forward, guilt gripping her stomach and pulling her down. All this time she'd only thought of herself and her misery, when Arturo had been suffering. Hurting.

And she hadn't even realized he was missing.

How could she be so selfish? Why hadn't she gone to check on them after her break-in?

Stupid selfish girl. Of course the Lobellos would go after Pedro. Wasn't he the reason they'd showed up in the first place? From what Pedro said, they'd been the ones to transport him and Arturo from Mexico. Now they wanted more. Amy and Chloe were just collateral damage to their destruction. She'd taken in the father and son. She'd given them a home. A job. And then she'd abandoned them at the first sign of trouble.

Her own tears slipped free and she dropped her head to her hands, resting her elbows on her knees, needing the support to stay sitting upright and not curl into a ball on the floor. She caught the first sob, forcing herself to be quiet and not wake Arturo. The second sob hit, then the third. Wave after relentless wave crashed over her, the emotions forcing themselves from her body.

Why was she being punished?

She deserved it. Her conscious whispered the ugly truth. What kind of wife sent her husband off to war with a fight? Even if he was cheating, she hadn't known at the time. So what did that make her? Selfish.

Selfish. Selfish. Selfish. She should have kept up the house and yard without complaint. She should have done so many things. And now what did she have? A post-mortem broken marriage. A daughter without a father. And possibly Arturo, who she hadn't even thought about in the last twenty four hours.

"What are you doing? Come here." Evie stood before her, arms crossed over her chest. She must have snuck in while Amy was distracted with her abject misery.

Amy shook her head and buried her face in her hands, uncontrollable sobs wracking her frame. She felt Evie pull her from the bed beside Arturo. Was dimly aware of leaving the bedroom and entering the kitchen. Away from the sleeping boy, her emotions ripped free of the frayed rope barely holding them in check.

"Talk to me." Evie pulled Amy into a hug.

"I...I...I didn't even...think about him." She grabbed onto her friend and held tight, needing her support.

"Who?"

"Arturo. Pedro. I didn't even check. What kind of a person am I?"

"Um, the kind who'd barely saved herself and her baby from an attack? Or the kind who'd found out her dead husband was a cheating dirt bag. Take your pick. You're human. No one expects you to carry the burden for everyone." Evie set Amy from her, pushing her down into a chair at the table and grabbed a tissue from the counter.

Amy took it, wiped her face, blew her nose and started crying again. Her ability to hold it all in, her control, had disappeared. "No. I should have known, I should have checked on him."

Amy watched Evie squat in front of her through a fog of tears. "I'm calling bullshit."

The coarse words gave Amy pause. "What?"

"I said bullshit. You were trying to survive and protect your baby. It's not your job to protect everyone in this town." Evie held her gaze, her blue eyes determined.

"I picked a huge fight with Shane right before he was deployed. And then he died. What kind of wife does that?" She ended her question with a loud cry and grabbed another Kleenex. The water works had turned to full blast.

"A fight about what?" Evie countered.

"I don't know. About the house, the yard. I wanted him to help out more." *I was a lousy wife.*

"So you asked your husband to help out around the house and he got pissed?"

"But he worked so much. He was tired. He needed to rest when he was home." Evie fought, trying to make her understand. She knew how wrong she'd been.

"Bullshit." Evie's blue eyes flashed bright with anger. "That is bullshit, Amy Carter. That man was home plenty and he didn't do crap to help you around the house. If I recall correctly you were working, too. And I'm pretty damn sure I'm right, since you were working in my bar. I was the one cutting you the paycheck."

True. "But I didn't risk my life serving drinks at the Wharf."

"Oh, boo-hoo. Shane signed up for that job. Just like Hunter. Just like Ranger. And I'll tell you something-Hunter James helps me fold laundry, clean the kitchen and still does all the yard work himself."

Amy sniffed her tears back and searched for another excuse, another reason to hold on to the blame. She came up empty. If Hunter did it without complaint, why couldn't Shane have?

"You're forgetting one giant ass thing, too," Evie said.

Amy sat up straight, stared down at her friend. "What?"

"That dirt bag was out screwing a teenage girl while you were cleaning the house and mowing the yard and working your ass off. So I'm sorry, but this self-blame line of crap doesn't hold water. Have you really been thinking this about yourself?"

Amy bit her lip and thought hard. Evie's words made too much sense. If Hunter did that, voluntarily, what excuse did she have? Her guilt had dug in deep and taken root.

Shane had been sent on deployments, fairly often, gone for a few weeks at a time. Sometimes a few months. But he'd been home just as much. He'd sit on the couch and watch T.V. Drink beer. And go out, without her.

When she'd griped, he'd always gotten so angry. "Do you know I risk my life every time I go out? Do you have any idea what kind of stress that puts on me? You think I should come home and not relax, but work my ass off for this shitty little farm? The other wives don't bitch and nag like this. They have supper waiting. A clean house. And a fucking smile on their face. But me-I get a nag who does nothing but whine about doing her job."

"No. I swear, that's not it. I just wanted you to mow the yard, bush hog the pasture. It's so much I can't keep up."

"Can't or won't? I know how much you're on your phone. Probably laid up in that bed, texting and talking to God knows who. Maybe you're trying to get me to do all the work so you can talk to your boyfriend online."

Amy remembered the argument like it was yesterday. He had accused her of cheating.

Her face flushed and she crushed the tissue in her hand. "You're right. The fight. He'd accused me of cheating."

Evie stood abruptly and marched over to the kitchen cabinet. Her polished hardwood floors gleaming, the new granite counter tops and modern appliances lending chic appeal to the rustic log home. She returned, wine glasses in hand.

"You already put Chloe to bed?" Amy asked and accepted the glass.

"She went down in under a minute. We've all had a

long day. I put the pac-and-play in the spare bedroom with you. Now drink." Evie tipped Amy's glass up and she took a sip. The cool white wine was straight up muscadine heaven down her throat.

"Thank you for doing that for me. For taking care of her."

"No thanks needed. I fully expect you to babysit when I have kids - one day. Not booking anytime soon, but in the future." Evie winked and downed half her glass. "And freaking hell, after a day like today, I don't think I want anything more than me and my man. Lord, you attract drama like flies on a carcass."

Amy cringed, but took another sip of wine. "Wow. Thanks."

Evie smiled and sat back in her chair. "What are friends for?"

Friends. Men. Husbands. She remembered then her anger and sat straight up, slamming her wine glass on the wood table. "He accused me of cheating. Can you believe that? After what he did?"

"Asshole. He was making you feel guilty so you wouldn't notice his own guilt. And over a kid! Granted, she wasn't really a kid, but barely nineteen is still a freaking kid."

A shudder of disgust moved through Amy. What kind of man targeted someone like that? And Amy had been sleeping with him too, albeit, not the best sex, but they'd still been husband and wife. Then another thought, one more horrifying than the rest, popped in her head. "Could he have given me an STD?"

Her mind quickly ran through all the diseases she remembered from sex-ed and which ones were communicable through child birth. She might have given Chloe some lifelong disease. Amy slapped a hand over her mouth, the thought so insane she couldn't process.

"No way. First off, do you remember how many tests and blood work they did while you were pregnant? I promise, you would know if you had anything. I've never seen a doctor take so much blood." Evie shuddered, her face going pale.

At that point, Shane had been on deployment and refusing to communicate with her, then he'd gone MIA, missing in action. And poor Evie had stuck by her, despite her fear of all things medical-especially needles. Right now her friend turned from pale white to pale green, and that was from only talking about shots.

"You know, I didn't even feel the shots," Amy offered, trying to help Evie past her unreasonable fear.

"Sure, okay. Anyway, secondly," Evie paused and gulped down her entire glass. Geez, this must be big. "Secondly, and don't freak out when I tell you this, I think Hayden was a virgin."

Amy shot to her feet, some unknown mix of anger and disgust and fury driving her. "What!?"

"Sit down. I told you not to freak. I know she acts tough, but I've watched her around guys. She flirts, but she never leaves with them. Never lets them touch her too much. And as much as she acts like the wild child, Hank says she comes home every night."

Amy choked, "You're telling me my cheating husband deflowered a teenager?" Bile shot up her throat, hot and burning, clawing and fighting to get out. How could he? How could he sleep with his wife and pursue Hayden at the same time? Revulsion crawled across her skin and she wanted more than anything to run to the shower and scrub her skin raw.

Evie seemed to mirror Amy's disgust, her skin shading even greener. Suddenly, Evie slapped a hand over her mouth and ran to the sink and vomited.

"Holy crap. I'll get a wet wash cloth." Amy went to her friend, turned the faucet to the side and wet a washcloth. She pulled Evie's hair back from her face and blotted her neck until she stopped puking.

When Evie could stand up, Amy passed her the washcloth and made her a glass of water. Evie accepted it and took a small sip, then wiped her mouth. "Thanks. I don't know what happened. Must have been the wine mixed with the bullshit."

"I hope so. Our luck, it's a stomach virus and we'll all be down."

Evie shook her head. "Nope. No way. You're streak of bad shit is done. I've been feeling queasy all day. Probably the sausage I had for breakfast. It was a couple days past expiration."

Amy shook her head. "You need to clean out your refrigerator. That's gross."

"Ya'll don't know the meaning of gross."

The deep crackly voice made Amy jump and spin around. C.W. Videl stood right behind her, his normal uniform of camouflage pants and black shirt in place, only now he had a huge rifle propped up under his arm like a crutch.

"What are you doing here?" Evie went to her grandpa and gave him a hug. Amy offered a little wave, still trying to get her heart rhythm down from its rabbit race.

"Hunter called earlier, said he wanted me to stay while he was away. Something 'bout some damn Mexicans." C.W. leaned the rifle against the wall. "Evie girl, make me some sweet tea will ya?" C.W. pulled out a chair across from Amy. Evie went into the kitchen and poured some tea. He took a sip, leaned back in the chair, and stroked his long grey beard. "Ya'll wanna fill me in?"

Evie sat, met Amy's gaze, then quickly filled C.W. in about Mavis and the Lobellos. The old man's dark eyes narrowed beneath his busy grey brows and small reading glasses. "Good thing I'm here then. Hated to miss my date, but Trudy understood. Family first."

"Oh no, C.W., go on and see Mrs. Trudy. I don't want to interfere with your plans," Amy said.

C.W. and Mrs. Trudy Van Meter were about as likely a couple as a grizzly bear and a house cat. Ever since Vietnam, C.W. had been different - as in borderline crazy. Mrs. Trudy, on the other hand, was head of the First United Methodist church, wore pressed dress outfits daily and never missed a Sunday in church.

"Ain't no question. You're family too. I'm stayin'."
C.W. said.

Amy bit back her argument knowing she wouldn't win
this fight and said, "Thank you."

"Besides, I seen Deputy Haskell sitting out front. That
man is blind as a bat." C.W. pulled a bag of chewing tobacco
out of his front shirt pocket and put a wad in his lower lip.
"So, I'm here til' Hunter gets back. Now - you're telling me
that someone broke into your house and then into that
Mexican's house you got workin' for ya? And you all don't
know if he's dead, but you got his boy in there?" C.W.
indicated the spare bedroom down the hall behind him.

Evie sighed and leaned forward, still a little pale.
"That's right. And the guys are keeping their whereabouts all
hush but I know they're going after the gang."

Amy resisted the urge to tell her friend to go lie down
and get some sleep. Dark shadows formed under her eyes,
making her look like a wrung out washcloth.

"What about the boy? If his pa is dead, you gonna ship
him back to Mexico?" C.W. asked.

Amy sat up straight, her muscles tense. Send him back?
"Hell no. He's going to stay with me."

"You let old C.W. know if someone tries to take him.
The government thinks it knows what's best for everyone
whether you like it or not. I still got friends all over, they
won't ever find that boy." His weathered face reflected
straight conviction and Amy felt a measure of relief for his
support. If someone tried to force Arturo away she would
fight, and fight to the bloody end. Already she was thinking
of him as her own child, while silently praying Pedro was
alive and well.

"Me, too. I'll help out." Evie nodded at the two.

Amy's emotional roller coaster kicked in and tears
pricked her eyes. She hastily wiped them back and said,
"Thank you."

"Now you start them waterworks girl and I'm gonna sit
outside. Ain't never been able to stand women's tears." C.W.
stood and went to the kitchen, as if being close to Amy

crying meant he'd catch some sort of disease.

"I'm sorry," she sniffed and sucked it up, "it's been a really long day."

"Don't apologize. You got every right to be upset. Make sure and let me know so I can get out of here." He winked at her.

Amy smiled, his old gruff exterior held a good man. One who protected his family with a cutthroat viciousness unrivaled by anything she'd ever seen. Last year, C.W. lead Hunter's group to rescue Evie from her psycho ex-fiancée. Before that he'd defended his daughter and granddaughter with unrelenting determination.

Amy hoped she could be half as fierce guarding her own family. Makeshift or not - Chloe and Arturo were hers.

Chapter Twenty-two

"I'm in." Ranger squatted low behind a stack of crates, held his weapon to his chest and scanned the area. He'd managed to infiltrate the Lobello's compound through a drainage gate in the south wall.

"Report." Hunter grated through their hidden com system. The rest of the team remained outside the walls, waiting on Ranger to secure the west entrance.

"Two guards with machine guns on the ground. One on each roof. Two at the front gate. Heading west." Ranger eased from behind the crates, his weapon raised, careful to stick to the shadows. Night had fallen, but the area was lined with flood lights that provided a warm glow regardless of the moon's absence. The compound had three buildings side by side, all of them constructed with painted cinder blocks, bars on the windows and metal doors.

"Copy," Hunter replied.

Ranger ran in a crouch along the south wall, barely ducking down before a walking guard on the west wall spotted him. He held his breath, tucked his M-4 over his shoulder and pulled his K-BAR knife from his pants. The guard lit a cigarette and gave Ranger his back, the only opening he needed. Ranger crept forward on silent feet, covered the man's mouth with his free hand, and then slit his throat.

The guard dropped and Ranger dragged his dead

weight to the corner, covering him with a discarded tarp. "One down."

Ranger tucked his knife back in its case and pulled his 9mm, holding it high as he approached the west entrance. The small back door was located dead center in the wall. One guard remained, machine gun held ready, scanning his surroundings.

It wouldn't be long before the guard noticed his partner's absence, all Ranger had to do was wait him out. He crouched behind a metal drum, waiting, knife in hand. A few minutes later he heard footsteps approaching. Ranger tensed, ready to spring. The guard appeared and before the man could raise an alarm, Ranger drove his knife straight through his windpipe, cutting off his air.

He dragged him to the same corner as his dead comrade and covered them both with the tarp. Pausing, listening for any alert. The only sound was cars speeding down the highway in the distance outside the walls.

Ranger quickly secured the west wall and unlocked the door. Hunter, Riser and Merc stood waiting. Ranger spared a quick glance up at the buildings across the street where Aaron and Ethan had set up with their rifles.

"Secure. We've got the two at the front gate, two more in front of the buildings and the three guards on the roof." Ranger tucked his knife back into his pants once more and checked his M-4.

"ATF and ICE are waiting for our signal. As soon as we've secured the hostages, they'll move in." Hunter said. The CIA took authority over the other government agencies in this instance. Normally, ATF would breach first, but TF-S's new handler wasn't willing to risk losing the intel. A stray bullet from an over eager newbie could take out the leaders of the Lobellos, which meant no intel.

Merc, without a question the deadliest member of their team, nodded to the east wall, where the front entrance was located. "Me and Riser will take the front. You two take the buildings. Aaron and Ethan can take out the rooftop."

Hunter lifted his com and said, "Aaron, Ethan, you get

that?"

"Roger, Top. On your signal."

"Okay. Two minutes. Take out the rooftop." Hunter dropped the com back to his neck and surveyed the area. His brother had more interest in this op than anyone else on the team. Ranger could feel the anticipation rolling off him in waves. "Move out."

The four men moved as one, splitting up when they reached the back of the row of buildings. The James brothers moved left. Riser and Merc moved right. They had to strike at the same time or risk alerting whatever guards remained inside the buildings.

Hunter held up a fist and then flattened his hand. Ranger dropped. Merc spoke through the com, "Ready."

Hunter answered, "Three count. One. Two. Three."

Ranger exploded from behind the wall, slipping behind the first guard and silencing him with his knife. The second guard turned, weapon raised, and Ranger held the now dead man up as body armor.

But before the guard could fire, Hunter shot him, the silencer on his 9 mm muffling the sound. The man dropped and Hunter dragged him between the buildings, Ranger following suit. Four down. Five to go.

Ranger ducked back into the shadow of the building and watched as a shadow flew across the open ground. One of the guards fell to his knees, clutching his throat. The second turned and Merc slipped up behind him, wrapped his hands around the man's head and snapped his neck like a twig.

Ranger heard a grunt above him, then another.

"Roof top secure."

"Front gate secure," Riser said.

"Building secure," Ranger said.

Hunter walked to Ranger's spot, waiting on the other two team members to join. Neither of them had broken a sweat, or even raised their heart rate. The job was simple. Take out the Lobellos. Secure the weapons and hostages. And if the fucker was here, take Lee Brown alive. Riser and

Merc joined the group a few seconds later.

"Cord, ready," Hunter said.

Cord waited outside with ATF. He'd protested when they'd told him to stay out of the main mission, but Grey hadn't fucking cared. The man had to be vetted fully before he could have a brother's back. His history with the Marine's as an elite scout sniper was great, but it didn't mean he was Task Force material.

"It looks like the women and children are being held in the north building. The men in the left. I couldn't get much intel on the central building, but I think that's where Santos is set up. Where Brown would be, too."

"You think?" Hunter's harsh question would've sent a full grown man running.

"Yeah, I think. Since last night, only two men have entered and left the building, I'm not a freaking magician who can see through walls." Cord's retort was just as deadly.

Hunter's chest swelled, his veins popped on his arms, and rage rolled out of his pores as straight and burning as eighty proof rot gut whiskey. Lee Brown had nearly killed Hunter's wife. The man's time on earth was limited.

Ranger spoke up, knowing his brother needed a sec to gather his fury and regain perspective for the mission. "Okay. We'll take the women and kids first. Then the men. Once we've secured all hostages, we can take the central building. Cut the head off the snake."

Riser and Merc nodded. Hunter paced away, rubbing his hands over his head. "Fuck. Okay." He approached the group again. "But you fuckers better get something straight. Brown is mine."

"Got it, Top," Merc said.

"Okay, let's move." Hunter led the team, the four men resuming their unit as one. They moved fluidly through the dark, winding around debris, ducking beneath the barred windows and then lined up beside the only entrance into the north building. Ranger checked his pistol. Hunter tried the door knob and shook his head, locked.

Riser slipped around and pressed the small explosive

clay into the doors hinges. The material was small enough not to cause a loud blast, but strong enough to get the job done. Ranger and his team ducked, the bombs went off with a small bang and hiss, and the door caved in.

A few people cried out from inside. Ranger heard men cursing in Spanish, then heavy footsteps toward the door. Hunter stood back, raised a booted foot and kicked the door in. The team moved, sweeping right, left and center. Easily taking out the unprepared guards, dropping them like flies.

A woman screamed, near the back. One guard remained. Fat. Dirty. His long hair stringy. But he had a pistol to the female's head. "You let me pass or the woman dies."

The men stood, pistols raised. "Let her go. Now."

"No. Put your guns down. I'll let her go when you let me pass." Spit dribbled down the man's chin.

"Not gonna happen," Hunter said.

"Then she dies."

He pressed his gun tighter into the woman's temple. Hunter nodded at Merc, who took aim and fired, planting a bullet in the center of the Mexican's forehead.

"Damn, look at this," Riser said.

Ranger scanned the room, finally able to take in the sheer amount of women and children packed into the room. Most of them stared silently up at the group of armed men.

Riser stepped forward, the only one in the group halfway fluent in Spanish. "We are here to free you, but we have to secure the other buildings first. I need you to stay here and keep quiet. Can you do that?"

One woman, older and calm stood. "Si, senor. The women will keep the children silent."

Riser nodded to her. TF-S waited at the door. "Women and children secure. What's it look like out there?"

"Good to go."

"Moving to breach the south building."

Hunter led, Ranger behind, Riser and Merc bringing up the rear. Riser planted the explosives on the hinges again, not bothering to check the door. The hinges dropped and they breached the building, taking out the two guards inside. Men sat on the floor, knees to their chests, not even standing for the invasion.

Riser delivered the same message as he had to the others.

"Second building secure. Cord, ready ATF and ICE. We are moving to breach central in one minute." Hunter, leader of TF-S, said.

"Got it, Top."

"Okay, we don't know what or who they have inside so we need to be ready for anything." Hunter said and the group circled around him.

"Could be five, ten, fifteen guys."

"Excuse me, senor. You want know what Santos have?" One man approached, shirtless, his torn pants hanging on a gaunt frame.

"Yes. Do you have any information?" Hunter said.

"Si. Santos like to pretend he big man. He keep lots of guards. Lots of the women on hand. He have two with him all time. I see five more go in and out."

"Gracias, mi amigo," Riser said.

"Please, senor. My wife, she one of the women." The man grabbed Ranger's arm. Ranger looked down at the point of contact and the man let go. "Please, no harm the women. They no part of this."

Ranger's cold blooded armor shifted a little, understanding the man's plea. How he might feel if it were Amy. Instead of scoffing he gave the man a reassuring smile, or the best semblance of a smile. "We've already secured most of the women. We won't harm any of them."

"Gracias. Gracias. Bless you," the man said, dropping his head and hands as if the men were some kind of gods.

"Okay, let's move before they realize we're here. Cord, is ATF ready?"

"Lined up at the gate, waiting on your orders."

"Count of ten, we move." Ranger exited the building with his team and backed up to the central door. Riser planted the last of the explosives, uncaring if the blast was heard.

Hunter lifted five fingers. Four. Three. Two. One. The bomb detonated. Ranger moved in lead, breaching the door before the smoke cleared. Gunfire erupted in the dark interior. Men screamed. A bullet hissed past his ear and embedded in the concrete wall behind him. Ranger returned fire, aiming in the general direction of the shot. A thick thud sounded, followed by a groan. Target hit.

"Hold."

The men stopped firing but held their guns ready. Merc flipped on the lights. Precisely five men lay in their own blood. Just like the man had said.

One door remained locked at the back of the room. "He knows we're here." Ranger stepped over the nearest body, still scanning the room just in case.

"Well, let's go say hello." Hunter was the first one at the door. He smiled, his grin closer to the grim reaper than a real man. "Santos, we know you're in there. Come out now."

"Fuck you," came the muffled response.

"No, Santos. We've taken out all your guards. ICE is escorting your captives as we speak. It's over."

No answer.

"Let's finish this." Ranger was ready for the mission to be over. Ready to get home. To Amy.

"Remember, if Brown is in there, he's mine." Hunter's smile disappeared and in its wake was nothing but the cold promise of death.

Hunter kicked the door in and Ranger moved past, first to enter. A man, not Santos stood, a half-naked woman held in front of him.

"Where is Santos?"

"Right here."

Ranger felt the press of cold steel to his temple. Realized his eagerness to get back to Amy may result in his doom. He swallowed, lifted his hands and dropped his gun. Images of Amy's stark grief stricken face at Shane's funeral flashed in his mind. Only this time, it would be Ranger in that casket

Chapter Twenty-three

Ex-Sheriff Lee Brown paced the confines of the large barge anchored just up river from Coldwater Paper Mill. He'd heard last year from his buddy in Game and Fish that the barge was out-of-commission. It had run aground and the company that owned it had come into some financial problems and hadn't been able to come free it. After finding Marcus's weapons last year, weapons he'd intended to sell to an international terrorist, Brown had quickly set about moving them to a new, hidden location. This barge was the only place big enough and far enough from land to hide a weapon like he'd acquired.

What Brown had assumed all along was a cache of AK's and grenades was in fact only five weapons. But these weapons weren't ordinary handguns. After doing his fair share of research, and a little help from a few old friends in law enforcement, he'd discovered what a treasure he now possessed.

But he'd balked at handing over such power to terrorists. So he'd made contact with some bad guys a little more local, if he could call Mexican's local. They hadn't agreed to his price at first. But when Brown had threatened to go elsewhere with his business, they'd quickly capitulated to his demands.

If it hadn't been for pure luck, Brown would have been at the Lobello compound a few days ago, and he'd be in custody right now. Or dead. He'd been on his way to the meeting, with proof of his weapons, when he'd hit a deer coming up Red Fork Road.

The damn thing had taken out his front bumper and drove a dent deep enough to kill his radiator. Brown got the truck off the road, then put it in neutral and let it roll into Bayou Bartholomew. He'd cursed and ranted and raved that night. Until he heard about the raid on the Lobellos.

Santos, his contact, was now dead, as was most of his gang. Now Brown was left with a boatload of weapons and no buyer.

He stared at his sat phone again, his hands shaking as he contemplated his future. He'd killed before and honestly hadn't felt much remorse for it. He'd committed his fair share of crimes. But he'd never considered himself a traitor.

If he made this phone call he would betray his country.

Probably be responsible for thousands of deaths around the world.

Brown's finger hovered over the dial button. He might be a traitor, but he would be a filthy rich one.

He hit dial.

"Who is this?" The man's accent was definitely foreign.

"This is your new best friend."

By the time he disconnected the call, Brown had a new outlook on life, and it was good. The man had been extremely interested in his deal and had in fact, already sent his own man to Mercy in search of the weapons. All Brown had to do was wait for the contact's phone call and he'd be set. He wouldn't have to worry about purchasing a plane ticket out of the country and getting flagged by the FBI. He could buy his own plane.

* * *

Amy stood at her island, chopping vegetables for supper. Zucchini, squash and carrots colors were bright and happy, the total opposite of her mood for the past few days. She hadn't heard from Ranger in two days. Two whole days and she was a freaking train wreck.

Sunlight filtered in through the kitchen window, gleaming on the island countertop and lighting the kitchen.

She hadn't bothered to turn on any lights in the house, preferring natural light. The oven dinged behind her and she jumped. Every time something clicked in her house she startled. Every time her phone rang her heart raced. The memory of Shane's death whispering through her mind, constantly reminding her how easy it was to lose the ones you love.

The logical part of her knew Ranger was fine. He was strong. Capable. Damn good at what he did. But the other part of her, the part that finally opened up and admitted her feelings for him – that part throbbed like a raw and aching wound.

The pot of purple-hulled peas was already on the stove boiling. The aroma of cinnamon and fresh vegetables filled the house, their delicious scent helping sooth her frayed nerves. Amy grabbed the fresh okra and started chopping. She sliced down and cut the tip of her finger. Instant sharp pain flooded her senses and she dropped the butcher knife. She ran to the sink and ran water over the cut, cursing herself for her clumsiness. For her distraction. For letting herself care so much that it hurt.

The cut on her finger wasn't anything compared to the pain in her chest.

Amy grabbed a paper towel and wrapped her finger, squeezing it tight to stem the blood flow. She glanced at the clock on the oven, six o'clock. The local news would be on. She found the remote and clicked on the TV.

A reporter stood off to the left, federal officials escorting women and children and men through an open door behind her. The scene looked like controlled chaos.

The reporter said, "The Mexican gang known as the Lobellos was taken down last night due to the coordinated efforts of multiple government agencies. Behind me you see ICE officials escorting the hostages out of their prison where they have been held for over two weeks. Initial reports say there are fifteen dead, five wounded. We just arrived on the scene, but will keep you updated as more information becomes available." The remote control clattered to the floor.

Amy forgot about her finger. Forgot about the blood. Forgot about everything.

That nagging sensation of worry that had been growing like a fungus in the pit of her stomach consumed her. It hadn't been worry, it had been instinct. Instinct telling her something bad had happened to Ranger.

Her knees gave out and she sank onto the barstool at the island. Don't be stupid. Don't jump to conclusions. The reporter hadn't said who had been killed or injured. It could've been anyone. It could've been the bad guys. Wasn't good supposed to triumph over evil?

Her cell phone rang and she snatched it to her ear, adrenaline giving her superhuman speed. "Hello?"

She held her breath silently praying and begging she would hear Rangers deep rich voice on the other end of the line.

"Amy? Are you home?" Evie said.

Amy expelled a breath and fought the disappointment. "Yes, why?"

"Hunter is on his way over."

Why would Hunter come to her house? Her subconscious whispered why do you think?

Her mouth was dry as a desert. "Did he say why? What about Ranger?"

"He didn't say, he sounded like he was in a hurry. I just wanted to give you a heads up."

Hunter was headed to her house. He was rushing. Something Hunter never did. He needed to talk to her. And he hadn't said anything about Ranger.

She walked into the living room, with Evie on the phone, and pulled her linen curtains to the side. Two vehicles were pulling down her driveway. Hunter James' truck and the sheriff's cruiser.

Her fingers went numb and she dropped the phone, vaguely aware of Evie still talking, she stumbled a few steps back, tripped and landed on the couch.

Please God, please, please let Ranger be okay.

And some other part of her mind scrambled furiously

for another excuse, any other reason that Ranger's brother and the sheriff would be coming to her house after a mission, without her man.

Her experience slapped her hard. Knocked her down and left her gasping for breath. There was no other reason.

One of them knocked on her front door but she couldn't make her feet move. She couldn't coordinate her legs to straighten and simply walk across the floor and turn a doorknob. She couldn't even breathe.

A vise tightened around her chest, each knock cinching it tighter, inch by inch, until her ribs threatened to crack and her heart to shatter.

"I'll get it." Arturo rushed into the living room, all knobby knees and elbows.

Amy's throat worked convulsively, trying to scream at him no, but her lips refused to move and no sound escaped. Arturo turned the handle and the door swung open and there stood Hunter James. Black pants. Black shirt. Black bottomless eyes filled with some awful expression she didn't even have a name for.

The vise cinched another notch tighter.

Arturo looked between Amy and Hunter, and then he ran to Amy and sat on the couch beside her, taking her hand. Hunter's gaze flickered for the briefest instant to the boy at her side and she found herself praying – praying he was here because of Pedro not Ranger.

Shame filled her. How could she wish for Pedro's death when it would leave Arturo an orphan?

And then Bo was there, standing beside Hunter, his tan sheriff's uniform a death knell.

The vise cinched the last notch around her chest and her heart collapsed under the pressure. She felt herself falling into a deep dark bottomless hole of grief. Because Bo's expression wasn't as guarded as Hunter's, and she could clearly see the emotion in his grey eyes.

Regret.

The only sound she heard was the buzzing in her ears, her hands were cold and numb. She was distantly aware of

Arturo squeezing her arm.

How could fate be so cruel to give and take from her twice? She'd fought so hard to deny Ranger, her instinct to guard her heart, to protect herself, had been right all along.

Her subconscious had known she would shatter. She'd survived Shane's death – barely. But now she was expected to survive Ranger?

"Amy, maybe we could talk alone?" Hunter's voice scraped across her raw and bleeding heart, jerking her back into the here and now. And then she felt Arturo's little fingers digging painfully into her skin. She swallowed back the bile and the tears and the horror and pried his little fingers from her arm.

Think of the children, don't think of yourself. "Hey Artie, why don't you go watch cartoons for a little while in the playroom?"

Artie looked at her, his gaze filled with worry and indecision but he nodded as if sensing how close Amy was to breaking. After he left the room, she turned to Hunter and forced herself to stand and lock her knees tight. Her voice was harsh when she spoke, "Just tell me."

Amy sucked in a deep breath and held it, waiting on the words that would destroy her forever.

Amy's heart slammed against her chest, fracturing her sternum with the force. She clutched at her neck, her throat bobbing furiously in an attempt to swallow her tears. "Ranger?"

Hunter's unreadable expression cracked and a small smile played at his lips. Then he stepped to the side, allowing Amy to see through the open door.

Ranger limped up her front porch steps on crutches, his left eye black. "Thanks for the help, bro."

Amy's eyes widened. Her mind must be playing tricks on her in some foolish attempt to hold onto her sanity.

And then Ranger was elbowing his way into her house. She'd never seen anything so beautiful in her entire life. Amy launched herself at Ranger with a cry. "I thought you were dead. I thought they were telling me you were dead."

She sobbed, uncontrolled and a little unhinged, but she didn't care. Ranger had come home. Her prayers had been answered.

One of his arms wrapped around her and she clutched him tighter, needing to anchor him to her.

"Shhh, honey, I'm okay. Hunter had to drive me over here. Doc said no driving for a full week." His slow southern drawl soothed across her soul and filled her with warmth.

Her sobs eased a little, but didn't stop. Two days of torture needed their release. "I'm sorry, I can't stop crying."

"I promised you, didn't I? I promised you I'd come back to you, I'd fight for you."

Chapter Twenty-four

Ranger had never felt anything as right as Amy in his arms. She had a death grip on him, but dammit, he liked it. He liked it so much he completely ignored the throbbing pain in his thigh from taking on her extra weight. If he could hold her like this forever, they could cut his damn leg off for all he cared.

Ranger locked onto Amy's deep brown eyes, and the worry reflected in her gaze sent a wave of euphoria rushing through him like he'd hit the lottery. When he lowered his head to hers, unable to resist brushing a kiss across her trembling lips, he knew he had won.

Those tears in her eyes were for him. Those blubbering sobs were for him. Her arms were around him. If he'd been a caveman, he would pound on his chest and yell out, Mine. But Ranger subdued that primal instinct and instead squeezed her against him tighter.

When Santos had held that gun to his head on the mission he'd thought he would be coming back to Amy in a casket. If it hadn't been for his brother's quick thinking and even better aim with his gun, Ranger would be dead. And Amy would be alone. Again.

Because of that, though, Hunter had to take out Santos, thereby killing their chance at finding solid intel. TF-S had taken as many of the Lobellos alive as possible, but Santos had been the key.

Ranger heard another vehicle coming down the drive at high speed. The pipes and skidding stop proclaimed the driver without him having to look. Only one female in Mercy drove like she belonged in NASCAR.

"Slow down before you bust your ass." Cheri, owner of the vehicle in question, said.

"Amy!"

Ranger sighed and didn't bother turning around. He knew Evie's voice like he knew his sidearm.

"Hunter James, you tell me what is going on right now. Where is Amy?" Evie was right behind him now and Ranger knew he should step to the side, but Amy felt too damn good. And every time he looked down at her he got lost. Someone could walk up and fire off a missile right now and he'd die happy.

"Ranger if you don't let my wife see that her friend is okay I'm going to kick your ass. And we both know that I can do it." Hunter stood a few feet away, his arms crossed, glaring at Ranger.

"The last time you kicked my ass, I was ten years old and you'd just hit a growth spurt," Ranger said.

Hunter relaxed and leaned against the wall, one ankle crossed over the other. "You know, I don't think I'll be the one kicking your ass. I believe I'll let my wife do the job."

"Let me see her before she has a panic attack," Amy's voice trembled but a smile played at her lips.

"They're going to have to pry me off you with a crowbar, honey. I haven't seen you in two days."

"How about a tire iron?" Evie did not sound happy at all.

Ranger knew he should move, but for some reason his arm wouldn't unbend from around her.

Then Amy cupped his cheek with her incredibly soft palm and he knew he'd found his heaven. "How about we resume this conversation later tonight?"

Her whispered words struck a match inside him, setting off a forest fire of desire. Unable to make his brain coordinate his lips to respond, he simply nodded, stepped to the side and adjusted his pants to hide the instant hard on her words had caused.

He barely cleared the way when Evie flew past, swooping in like a hawk on her prey, pulling Amy into a fierce hug. Cheri, the final tip of the triangle of friends, stood behind the two, studying her deep red nails as if she didn't have a care in the world.

"Don't you ever, ever, ever, scare me like that again. I was worried sick about you." Evie held Amy at arm's length, giving her a once over.

"And when she says sick, she means literally. We would've been here five minutes ago if I didn't have to stop and clean out the front seat of my Charger." Cheri's drawl drew everyone's attention.

"You threw up again?" Amy said.

"What do you mean, again?" Hunter stepped in crowding his wife.

Evie reached over and patted Hunter's arm as if trying to soothe a wild beast. "Nothing to worry about. Just a little stomach bug. I feel better already." Evie turned and glared at Cheri. "And if you didn't drive like a blind woman on crack, I wouldn't have gotten carsick in the first place."

Cheri lifted a dark brow. "Please. Why don't you just admit you're pregnant?"

Forget a missile, Cheri dropped a bomb. The room went post-apocalypse silent.

"Pregnant?" Hunter turned the most amazing color of red. More like crimson.

As deep red as Hunter had turned, Evie turned just as white. "I'm not pregnant. I have a stomach bug."

Glad to have the attention off himself, Ranger yanked Amy back to his chest.

Cheri snorted and propped a hand on her hip. "Yeah. Tell that to the baby growing in your belly."

"You're pregnant?" Amy echoed.

"I am not pregnant! I would freaking know if I was pregnant for Christ sake. I can't have a baby." Her words trailed off, ending thin and broken like one-ply toilet paper.

"So you started abstaining, have you?" Cherri said.

Hunter's gaze ping ponged from Cherri, to his wife and back again.

"No, but, but."

Cheri cut in. "So you started using protection?"

"Oh. My. God." Evie's hand fell to her belly.

"You forget that I'm the youngest of four girls. I know the second a woman gets pregnant. And honey, you're most definitely pregnant."

"I'm going to be a father?" Hunter said.

"Yep. I mean, I'd stop at the drugstore and get a pregnancy test and everything, but my preggo radar is pretty damn good," Cherri said.

Ranger leaned on a crutch and extended a hand to his brother, "Congratulations."

Hunter took his hand, his eyes glassy, his face slack. Ranger almost felt sorry for him. Almost.

Evie looked like she was going to hyperventilate. Or puke. And Ranger sincerely hoped it was the previous. The only thing he could handle less than crying was puking.

"But I don't know what to do with a kid," Evie said.

"That's not true. Look how much you've helped me with Chloe. You're going to be a wonderful mother," Amy said.

Bo Lawson butted in, "And hopefully it'll be a girl just as pretty as you."

The vein in Hunter's temple popped and throbbed. "Shut your mouth before I shut it for you."

"Think about it. Hunter James with a teenage girl. Oh the poetic justice is just too perfect." Bo kept going, either completely unafraid or insane. Either way, the outcome would be the same.

"Don't listen to him, he's just trying to get a rise out of you." Evie pulled her husband close. "Besides, we both know with your genes we're going to have a boy."

Ranger met Hunter's gaze over the top of Evie's blonde head. He knew what Hunter was thinking without him having to say a word. It would be the same thought that

Ranger would have. He couldn't have a boy. Too much risk of him turning out to be like their biological father. A man who would rather murder his own wife than let her leave. A man that tried to beat his children to death.

Not many children had the luxury of escaping such a monster. But Ranger and Hunter had. And they'd been lucky enough to find Hank James, a man unafraid to adopt two homeless boys off the street and raise them as his own. But no matter how well raised, they would never forget their past. The risk of repeating their father's mistake was too real.

Ranger sent up a silent prayer right then and there that it would be a girl.

"Let's go." Hunter grabbed Evie's hand and started dragging her from the room.

"Go where?"

"To the drugstore. We're getting a pregnancy test. No. We're getting ten pregnancy tests."

"I'm pretty sure one does the trick." Cheri deftly stepped to the side as Hunter plowed out the front door.

Hunter growled and Cheri threw her hands up in the air. "Okay buddy, buy 'em all. See if I'm wrong."

Evie managed a quick glance back, even as Hunter pulled her faster. "Sorry about your car, but thanks for the ride over."

"You got it, babe."

"Call me and let me know what the test says," Amy called out.

Hunter didn't give his wife time to respond. He opened the door to his truck, and put her inside, buckling her like a child and then climbing into the driver side and spun out in a hurry.

"There ain't no way I'm wrong. She's been downright moody. Hell, when you dropped her call earlier she started crying. When's the last time you knew that girl to cry? And the puking. You don't have to call me Dr. Oz, but I know pregnant," Cheri said.

"Seems like you were the only one." Ranger took a deep breath and inhaled Amy's shampoo. Her hair hung loose between them, the soft strands like silk as he rubbed his cheek against the top of her head.

"I almost feel sorry for your brother. But then again, I think this child will be a good thing for them," Cheri said.

"Why?" Ranger knew he shouldn't keep the conversation going, especially if he wanted to get some alone time with Amy, but he couldn't help but ask.

"Cause, no matter how much they love each other and how lucky they are to have found that kind of love, there is still a darkness in Hunter. Something I sense lurking inside. Something that needs more than a good woman to drive it out."

"Don't you think that could be a side effect of his job?" Bo arched a blond brow.

"No. I think there's more to it than that, not that I expect someone like you to understand," Cheri said.

"Someone like me? What the hell does that mean?" Bo spread out his arms, his eyes wide and waiting.

"A stick-in-the-mud. You know. Charlie Brown. You see only what you want to see. I can't help it if you're unenlightened."

"Woman, I've seen more in my life than you could ever dream. Just because I don't believe in psychobabble doesn't mean I'm a freaking stick."

"No, it just means you're boring." Cheri poked her nail in the sheriff's chest, all but daring him to a challenge.

"Do something," Amy whispered to Ranger.

"Sorry, honey, but this is just getting good." Ranger had been waiting way too long for someone to put Sheriff Lawson in his place. Now it appeared a redhead was about to unleash on his ass.

"Who the hell do you think you are? You know nothing about me. Absolutely nothing." Bo puffed out his chest, stretching the tan uniform taught.

"I know you're too scared to take chances." Cheri leaned in, unrelenting. Her head barely reached Bo's chest, but she didn't back down. Not one inch.

"Do you know what I do for a living? I take a chance

with my life every day I go out on patrol." The ever calm and cool Bo Lawson had disappeared, in his place was a man on a ledge, jaw clenched. Hands clenched. The tension between the two was practically sparking.

"Not your life. Your relationships. You keep those quiet little mouse girls around just long enough, then you cut ties. Why? Aren't you bored with doormats for girlfriends?"

"If you're so damn worried about my love life, why don't you offer a suggestion?" Bo leaned down, getting nearly nose to nose with Cheri.

Ranger wanted to ask Amy to place a bet on the winner, but he didn't want to break the two apart.

"I have. You're just too blind to see." Cheri turned on her heel and stormed from the room.

"What the hell does that mean?" Bo threw up his hands.

"Don't you worry your sweet little head about it, sugar." Cheri walked to her car, blew Bo a kiss and got inside. Her engine cranked with a loud growl.

"Your friend is freaking nuts," Bo said.

Amy bit her lip, her obvious attempt to hold back a grin failing miserably. "Not nuts, just a little different. More like a raw uncut diamond."

"Yeah, right, and I'm a precious ruby."

Chapter Twenty-five

"So what's for supper?" Bo's lack of compunction had Ranger's teeth on edge. No way was he staying for supper and interrupting their alone time.

Ranger opened his mouth to tell him to fuck off, but Amy beat him to the punch. "Meatloaf. I've got plenty. Why don't ya'll go sit in the kitchen and I'll finish up after I check on the kids."

Bo lead, Ranger following on his crutches. Ranger took a seat at the table, directly across from the sheriff. Bo took off his cowboy-style sheriff's hat and hung it on the back of the chair. The setting sun turned the white tables and chairs a bright yellow. Cheery multi-colored place mats and napkins littered the small round table. If it weren't for an uninvited guest and a broken back door, the room would be downright cheery.

Amy came into the kitchen a minute later and placed a hand on Ranger's shoulder. "Arturo's locked into the Kids Channel and Chloe's still asleep."

Ranger covered her hand with his own.

"Can I help with anything?" Bo asked.

"No, ya'll just relax. I'm almost done. Can I get you something to drink?" Amy said.

"Tea, if you've got it," Bo said.

Ranger gnashed his teeth, barely holding back the need to pick Bo up and toss him bodily out of the house. "Same here."

Ranger had to turn partially in his chair to watch her. Her movements were unhurried, graceful. She was obviously comfortable. She poured the tea and brought it over, dropping a quick kiss on Ranger's brow before walking back to the stove. He kept a relaxed smile in place until she turned away, and then let his expression go full disclosure.

Bo leaned back, hands raised. "Hey, I need to talk to her for a sec."

"You need to make it short and sweet. Got it?" Ranger had every intention of spending some time at the table with his family and then a hot and heavy night, bum leg or not. On his mission he'd been unable to get her out of his head. She'd told him she loved him. And her reaction when she'd thought he was hurt...

Fuck manners. "Forget what I said. Make your excuses and leave. You can come back tomorrow after she's had time to rest."

"Rest? Ha, I'm sure that's exactly what you plan on letting her do." Bo took a sip of his tea, studying Ranger over the brim.

"It's none of your business what we do. Whatever you have to say can wait." Until he'd had a night with Amy to show her exactly how much he cherished her, and always would.

Amy pulled the meatloaf out of the stove and stood, wiping a hand across her brow. The cotton dress she wore pulled tight across her chest and Ranger went hot. "I'm going to check on the kids, be back in a sec."

"Hold on. Come here and sit for a minute. I need to talk to you about Arturo."

The heat turned into an all-together different kind. The kind that lead to him punching Bo for ignoring Ranger's order. Dammit. Whatever he had to say couldn't be good; otherwise Pedro would be standing here right now. The grim turn to Bo's gaze didn't bode well either.

Amy hesitated, then squared her shoulders and marched back into the dining area. Pride rose in him at her bravery. She stood beside him and he wanted to pull her down into his lap and wrap his arms around her, but he had to settle for holding her hand as she sat in the chair right beside him.

Bo cleared his throat. "I haven't found the boy's father yet. I'm still tracking, but it's been over three days and no sign of him."

Amy squeezed his hand, but her expression remained calm. Controlled. Except for her eyes, which mirrored her pain. Thoughts of himself and a long night with his woman faded. She would need more than that from him after this. She needed his support emotionally. The weird thing was, he looked forward to holding her as much as loving her.

Bo hesitated and glanced at Ranger. Oh now he wanted support? What did he expect? Ranger knew the odds-Pedro had been missing for over forty-eight hours. The likelihood of finding him alive shrunk with each minute past that time frame. But he sure as hell wasn't going to be the one to tell her that. "We captured some of the Lobello gang members. I've told the interrogators to find out all that they can about Pedro."

Bo finally continued, "Hopefully they will turn up some new info, but if Pedro is no longer with us, there will be the issue of the boy's care taking. Finding next of kin."

Amy paled. "But he doesn't have anyone else."

"That you know of. I started making some inquiries, and it seems the boy has a distant cousin in Mexico. I haven't contacted her yet, but she is the next of kin."

"But Pedro fought so hard to get here, he wanted Artie to be in the US. He's already started kindergarten," Amy said.

"Let's not get ahead of ourselves. There's still the possibility he's alive. No reason to start worrying a lot about that part yet, I only thought you should be prepared for all possibilities."

The pain in Rangers leg was nothing compared to what he felt when he saw Amy's worry.

He told her he would fight for her.

"What if he had a family here, willing to adopt him? Foster him. Hell, whatever the freaking system will allow,"

Ranger said.

"I'm afraid the system doesn't look too favorably on single parents that already have children to raise." What Bo didn't say was single mothers struggling to eke out a living.

Ranger glanced at Amy and his chest tightened, not liking the bleak lines forming around her mouth. Dammit, he loved her so much it hurt. What if it wasn't just her asking? Was he ready for a turn-key family?

Could he marry her and take on two children when his longest relationship was three months and he'd never spent more than five minutes with a kid?

The answer came to him faster than a bullet. Marrying Amy wasn't a sacrifice, it was a blessing. And getting the opportunity to raise two great kids like Chloe and Arturo was icing on the cake. He leaned forward, placing his free arm on the table and stared at Bo, leaving him no doubt that his next statement was serious. More serious than anything he'd ever done in his entire life.

And Ranger was not afraid.

"What about a married couple? Two incomes. Stable home life."

The sheriff glanced at Amy then back to Ranger. Ranger didn't move.

"Well now, that definitely tips the scales in your favor. And with a little support from the local law-enforcement, I can almost guarantee that would work."

Amy froze, but she had a death grip on his hand. His revelation about his feelings for her had driven him forward with-out thought. After all these months of chasing her, coaxing her just to talk to him, and he drops the M word like an RPG. The surety of his decision started wavering. Maybe she didn't want to marry him. She'd been married to his best friend.

How could he let his sick and twisted mind jump the Grand Canyon and think she'd be happy he wanted to marry her?

He'd never been scared a day in his life, but right now he couldn't make himself turn to Amy and watch the horror spreading across her features.

And the sheriff, damn him, stood, his chair scraping loud across the floor. "Let's not be hasty. We haven't found Pedro yet. I'll keep you posted."

* * *

Amy sat there, stunned and shaken, her hand cold and sweaty in Rangers warm grip. Marriage? Marriage to her?

Her ears started ringing. Had Ranger really said that?

He was willing to sacrifice his freedom as a single man for her and an undocumented little boy he'd met only a few times? And what about Chloe?

A single sexy man like Ranger James taking on a widow with baggage and a baby and possibly a foster son?

The idea was crazy. Just plain crazy.

It had to be a hazard of his occupation, always saving people. She swallowed, barely able to make her throat work. Was that what she was to him, a damsel in distress? Someone to stroke his alpha male ego? Or did he really think about her that way? Ranger held her hand, but didn't look at her. He stared straight ahead, a statue of regret.

The sheriff was gone. They were alone in the room together, Ranger's words hanging over their heads like a herd of elephants in the Sahara.

Amy knew she should say something, but for some reason she couldn't coordinate her lips and tongue.

Who was this man that was willing to give up everything for her?

Chloe cried out from the nursery, signaling she'd woken from her nap and Amy had never been so relieved to hear her cry. She dropped Ranger's hand without a word and ran from the room, escaping his presence and his words and the thoughts and the hope they brought up inside her. She passed Arturo, coming out ofthe guest bedroom. "Supper's almost ready. Mr. Ranger is in the kitchen, why don't you hang out with him while I change Chloe? Then we can eat."

"Miss Amy? Did the sheriff man, did he find my

papa?" His little voice wobbled, his chin trembled. Then he sucked in a breath and straightened his spine.

She wanted to drop to her knees and take him into her arms. Tell him everything would be okay. But she didn't know that. She didn't know if anything would be okay. But she knew she was on the verge of hysterics. So she sucked in her own trembling lip and offered him a smile, "Not yet little man, but he's still looking and so are a whole bunch of other people. He's gonna let me know as soon as he knows anything."

Arturo nodded, he didn't move. He needed more than words from her and she fought hard to push past her own problems and act like a grown up. She knelt down and brushed a stray lock of dark silky hair behind his little ear, marveling at how a boy so small could take on so much.

Over the past couple of days, he'd held it together so well. Helping around the house, playing with Chloe and not breaking into hysterics the whole time. But she could see the strain now, a strain no child should ever have to face. "I want you to know something. No matter what happens, I will be here for you. Do you understand?"

He nodded again and said, "Why did those men want to take all those kids?"

Such a big question and one he had the right to know the answer to. But how was she supposed to tell a five-year-old about child slavery?

"There are bad people in this world, Arturo. Bad people who hurt others, even if they don't deserve it. The Lobellos were bad people. We might not ever understand why they do those things, but all that matters is that you're safe now. Those kids are safe now, too. And you know why? It's because there are a lot more good people than bad out there."

"Good people, you mean like Senor Ranger?"

Amy jerked at his name. Ranger was a good man. "Yes, baby. Like Ranger. He's one of those special people who saves others, even if it's dangerous."

"I'm glad Mr. Ranger is your friend."

Her friend, her lover, her would-be-hero in waiting.

Chapter Twenty-six

The next couple of days passed in a blur. Ranger stayed busy finishing up from the raid and filling out paperwork. He'd spent the majority of his days away, but each night he'd been drawn to Amy's. Each night, he slept on the couch, careful to give her space, but not too much. He couldn't take the chance that she'd run again.

Bo still hadn't located Pedro. The ATF, FBI and his own team had been unable to locate him either. None of the Lobellos knew what happened to him. The more time went by, the worse it boded for Pedro. And the more he and Amy fell into a routine of talking but not talking, and touching but not feeling.

Ranger wanted to get back out in the field and assist in the search, but his damn leg was healing slower than Christmas. At headquarters, every one avoided him and those few that didn't got a terse response. The fear of being a burden was grinding his nerves to dust. He'd never been an indoors kind of guy. And now he was stuck sitting at a desk during the day while his team was out searching.

By the time he left work, his tension was about as tight as a tourniquet. But each night, when he pulled into Amy's driveway, the tightness in his chest eased a little. But tonight, the tension hadn't eased. It had pulled even tighter. And he was on the verge of snapping. He had to do something to break this system of avoidance before they both detonated.

After supper, Ranger helped Amy put the kids to bed. A wholly domesticated process that he'd never imagined himself doing. Not until Amy.

If it hadn't been for the kids, supper would have been a ghost town. Ranger had caught her staring at him repeatedly, but hadn't been able to coax more than a sentence or two from her lips. Not that he expected her to gush or anything, but her silence killed him.

His half-assed proposal sat large in both their minds. But he hadn't regretted it. Not one bit. The more he thought about making a family with Amy, the more he became convinced they were meant to be. Not that he waxed poetic or what the hell ever that meant, but how could he not feel like fate played a role?

His childhood had been full of darkness and abuse. His father murdered his mother and then tried to kill him and Hunter. If it hadn't been for luck they wouldn't be alive today. After roaming the roads, scavenging for food and whatever they could get their grubby hands on, the boys had stumbled on Hank James' Broken River Ranch. Hank had given up his bachelor lifestyle and became an immediate father to two rough boys off the street. He'd taught them respect. He'd taught them loyalty. He'd taught them sacrifice. But more importantly, he'd taught them the importance of family.

And now Ranger had a chance at a real family of his own. He could take Arturo under his wing, and help him grow into a good man. Just like Hank.

"Would you mind tucking Arturo in while I rock Chloe to sleep?" Amy said, juggling a fussy Chloe on her hip. Arturo had already gone to the bedroom to change into his pajamas.

At least she hadn't asked him to leave, something he'd been half expecting and half dreading. "Sure thing."

She grabbed his hand and the gesture sent a flare of hope to his heart. "Thank you."

Ranger had to clear his throat to get it to work again.

The woman was driving him nuts. He wanted to drag her to bed and make love until they were both too exhausted to sleep, but he knew she needed time. Needed to process. "Anytime, honey. Go on now, I've got this."

Amy took Chloe to the nursery and Ranger went to tuck Arturo in. The quilt on the full-size bed swallowed the boy. Ranger felt clumsy and unsure of himself, but he lowered down to sit on the edge of the bed and propped his crutches on the night stand. He didn't know what to say or do, so he sat there, silent. It was Arturo that led the way.

Ranger watched in the lamp glow as Arturo grabbed his hand. Ranger marveled at how tiny his fingers appeared wrapped through his own. Interwoven. "Will you stay here until I fall asleep?"

At that moment, any doubt that Ranger would be this boy's father was completely erased from his mind. "For sure, little man. I'm not going anywhere."

He nodded, held onto his hand and closed his eyes. Anger at the Lobellos for hurting the boy filled him. Arturo was too young to have suffered such a loss. To have been kidnapped and scared out of his mind and his father possibly murdered. But he was resilient and he had a shot at a bright future.

A bright future with Ranger and Amy as his parents. As long as Amy would accept him into her family.

At that moment Amy peeked her head around the door and Ranger lifted a hand to his lips for her to be quiet. Arturo's breathing had fallen deep and even, his fingers slack. Ranger picked his crutches up and left the room, letting Amy softly shut the door behind him.

They went into the living room, and he sat on the couch, patting the cushion beside him. Amy hesitated a second, and then sat. The few inches between them like miles. Unable to stand the distance any longer, Ranger wrapped his arm around her shoulders and pulled her close. Amy tucked her head against his chest, fitting him perfectly. But more importantly, she didn't fight him or push away. And damn it felt good. Really good. Her head lying against his chest, the smell of her shampoo filling his senses. Her breasts pressed against his side. Blood filled his cock, giving him an instant hard on. Whenever the woman was around he responded like a teenager. No longer a full-grown man in control of his own body.

Distraction. He promised himself that he would take it slow. "How about a movie?"

She wrinkled her nose, and that smattering of freckles was so cute. "A movie?"

"Yeah, like a normal couple that's dating would do." Because Lord knows they hadn't had anything close to normal. From the intruder, to the Lobellos, to finding out about Shane's infidelity. Normal would be heaven.

"That sounds nice."

"And because I'm such a gentleman, I'll let you pick it out. As long as it's not *The Notebook* or something like that."

"Darn, that's my favorite movie," Amy said.

He cringed, wondering if he could make it through the sob fest without gagging. But if it would make her happy, he'd do it.

Her soft laughter interrupted his thoughts. "You should see the look on your face right now."

"You're laughing at me and I was seriously contemplating sitting through that?" Ranger was outraged. Damn female was driving him crazy.

"No, I'm laughing because I'm happy." She placed her palm against his cheek and rose up, searing his lips with a scorching kiss. When they broke apart they were both breathing hard.

Distraction. He needed a distraction before he lost his resolve and laid her down on the couch right now. "So what movie do you feel like?"

She sighed and he could tell she was thinking the same thing. Forget the movie let's go to bed. But he pulled on every ounce of willpower he possessed and resisted the urge. She needed time. And he would give it to her, whether she wanted it or not.

"How about *Super Troopers*?"

"Are you serious?" He couldn't believe what she just said. One of his all-time favorite comedies. "I thought you females hated that kind of stuff."

"Listen, if we're going to get serious about this relationship, you've got to cut the sexist crap out. Just because I'm a woman doesn't mean I can't like movies like that." Amy sent him a narrowed glance.

His heart slammed in his chest. She wanted to give it a try? "A serious relationship?"

"You're the one who brought it up."

And you ran from me scared out of your mind. "Of course."

"So no more sexist stuff?" The small smile teasing her lips begged to be kissed.

"Not sexist, babe. You just rose another notch in my estimation. The guys won't believe me when I tell them." Ranger could see the look on their faces, especially after hearing them whine about dates and having to put up with chick-flicks to get laid.

"Good." Her grin was huge and full of laughter and he tensed, knowing he wouldn't like what was coming next. He'd learned to read her expressions and her smiles. And she was definitely giving her mischievous smile right now. "Because we're going to watch *Titanic* after this."

He groaned and fell back on the couch. He didn't know which one was worse. But then again, *Titanic* was three hours long. That meant three more hours he could hold her. And just because he was going to be hands off with the sex didn't mean they couldn't do some heavy petting on the couch. "Deal."

* * *

Amy woke the next morning, stretched out on the couch, with Ranger's arms wrapped around her. Sunlight streamed in through the semitransparent curtains in the living room. *Titanic* played on the TV, they'd fallen asleep in the middle of the movie. The second time around.

Heat filled her cheeks when she thought about everything they'd done on the couch last night. They'd acted like lovesick teenagers. Going all the way to third-base but too scared to hit a home run. But Lord how she wanted to. Her nipples grew heavy and tight thinking about his callous roughened hands on her skin. If it hadn't been for Ranger's restraint, they most definitely would've gone all the way. It certainly wasn't for her lack of trying. But he refused, stopping her every time her hand traveled too far south.

In all honesty, Ranger's insistence on holding back was working. Each day he remained sweet and sincere, he dug deeper, planting roots in her heart. Her thoughts about him mentioning marriage just to rescue a modern day damsel in distress had completely gone away. A man with a false sense of justice wouldn't sacrifice his whole life for a women he didn't love and respect.

Amy studied him, so content, so peaceful in his slumber. He was so handsome it hurt. And hearing him talking to Arturo last night had obliterated her defenses. She knew she was a lucky woman to have a man like him.

But was she ready to take that lifelong leap of marriage? Not only marriage, but marriage to a Special Operations soldier who put his life on the line constantly. Ready to go through that insane worry every time he walked out the door. Was she really ready to deal with reality if he didn't make it back?

Amy got up and went to the kitchen and put on a pot of coffee. Ranger's profession was the same as Shane's. What if he didn't come back on his own two feet, but laid out in a coffin?

A thought almost as bad flittered through her mind - what if he cheated too? She'd trusted Shane and look what he'd done. He betrayed not only his wife, but his best friend and he'd taken advantage of a girl barely out of her teens. Amy poured a cup of coffee and took a cautious sip, daring the tongue burning to try and get rid of the bitter taste Shane's betrayal left in her mouth.

How could he have done that? How could he be

so...callous. So unforgiving? How could he make her feel so damn guilty when he'd been the one to screw up in the first place? Had he sensed her hidden feelings for Ranger? She'd ignored them after her and Ranger's break up all those years ago. She'd forced those thoughts for him down as far as they would go and remained true to Shane.

Maybe that had been his plan all along, to pick a fight and ignore her until she had no hope but divorce. Only instead of divorce he'd gotten death.

The early days of their marriage had been filled with lots of laughter and fun. Then he started leaving, more and more. And when he was home, he'd started drinking, more and more.

And apparently he started screwing another woman.

"Damn you, Shane Carter. Damn you for doing this to me." Tears welled and spilled over. His death was a heavy enough burden, but his betrayal made her feel emotion so ugly it didn't even have a name. She wiped her tears with a trembling hand. He didn't deserve her tears. He didn't deserve her thoughts. So why couldn't she stop crying?

"Amy?"

She spun around to see Ranger standing with his crutches, shirt just as wrinkled as his hair.

"What's wrong, baby?"

She couldn't speak, couldn't tell him the truth. He didn't want to hear that she was thinking about another man, even if it was her ex-husband. No man was that big of a saint. She steeled her nerve and forced a smile, even though it felt dead on her face. "Nothing."

Ranger hobbled over to her until she was trapped between his crutches and the counter, with no way to escape. "I know when you're lying. Tell me the truth." His voice was gentle and that only pulled more tears free. He should be stony, suspicious. Not caring.

She held firm and squashed her thoughts back into the coffin they belonged in. "I swear, I'm being silly."

He cupped her cheek and held her hostage with the most startling blue eyes. "When are you going to learn I know you. I know your really happy smiles, because they reach all the way to your eyes. And I know your sad smiles, because your lips barely pull up. And I know your fake smiles – like the one you're giving me right now. Because your whole face freezes. There's no emotion."

His words stabbed sharp in her chest, causing her to react like a wounded animal, striking to avoid more pain. "Dammit Ranger, why can't you just leave it alone? You don't want to know what I'm thinking about right now." She slapped his hand away.

He didn't move an inch. Amy wanted so bad to run away, but she was afraid she might kick one of his crutches and hurt his leg. He had her trapped. And that only made it worse.

"I told you, I'm not scared of you. I'm not going to walk away."

"Fine. You want me to tell you why I'm crying? I'm thinking about another man. I'm thinking about Shane. There, are you happy now? Is that what you wanted to hear?"

Ranger stilled and her heart dropped to the floor. "See. Why couldn't you leave it alone?"

"You think I'd be angry at you for thinking about Shane?" Ranger sounded incredulous, but she knew better.

"Aren't you?"

"I think about Shane every day. I think about how much I miss him. And I think about how, if he was standing here right now, I'd beat his ass into a bloody pulp for what he did to you. I don't expect you to forget him. He was your husband, cheater or not, you can't forget that."

Now it was her turn to freeze. His words shocked her, freezing the loneliness starting to climb back through her body. What kind of man would say something like that? He couldn't be real. No way. "You mean you're not jealous that I'm thinking about him?"

"No. I want you to understand something right here and right now. I'm here for you. And that means physically and emotionally. If you want to talk about him, who else better to talk to than his best friend? And whatever you say, it doesn't matter. Because I love you. I love you and everything that has made you into the incredibly strong and capable woman you are today.".

Chapter Twenty-seven

The phone rang, drawing her attention from Ranger. He leaned back, giving her space to grab it and she used the opportunity to take a much needed breath. "Hello."

"Amy? This is Doyle Murdock. Been waiting on your flyby, figured you'd have started by now, but I heard you've had some trouble at your place and I wanted to check and make sure you were okay."

Oh crap. Amy glanced at the clock. Eight a.m. Two hours overdue. Which meant she'd be working until the last rays of light disappeared tonight. "Thank you for your concern, Mr. Murdock. I have had a few issues that put me a tad behind, but I'm still starting today. I'll be over in the next couple of hours. Sorry for the delay."

Amy met Ranger's gaze, reading the question in his blue eyes. She held up a finger to wait a minute as her brain rapidly worked out what to do. She needed a babysitter, and she needed one lickety-split. The sad thing was, Hayden had been sitting for her up until now. Amy's stomach knotted. Had Hayden been thinking about Shane the whole time she was babysitting Chloe?

"No apology needed. I can get some clean up done in the meantime. I'll see you soon." Mr. Murdock disconnected the call and Amy sat her phone on the counter.

"Stay here with me," Ranger said.

He had no idea how much she would love to stay in and steal some hours with him, but no work meant no money.

"I have to. I'd completely forgotten what day of the week it is."

"Come on, you've had a really long weekend. You should take a day off and rest."

Amy could have gotten pissed that he wouldn't let it drop, but she knew he was speaking from concern for her well-being. "I am, but I don't have a choice. My only problem is I'm without a babysitter. Maybe Evie can come over?" She cringed thinking about asking her, though. Amy was sure the shock of pregnancy hadn't worn off in a few days, and the last time Evie had called, she'd confirmed she was indeed pregnant and promptly burst into tears.

Amy briefly toyed with the idea of asking Cheri, but just as quickly threw that one out. Her other best friend would be here in a heartbeat, but Amy didn't want to come home to a destroyed house and no telling what else.

"You have a baby sitter right here." Ranger puffed up his chest.

"You? Have you ever looked after a baby before?"

"I've helped you with Chloe." He seemed offended, but Amy pressed on.

"Helping and being all alone is another matter entirely." Maybe she could call Mrs. Trudy. She'd be more than glad to help out.

"Woman, I've fought in wars. I've taken out terrorists way scarier than you could ever imagine." Yep, he was very offended.

"Terrorists don't have anything on a pissed off baby." She was exaggerating a tad, but only a tad. Chloe could scream with the best of them. She could picture Ranger holding her, confused and freaking out when she wouldn't calm down.

"Listen, if we're going to have a serious relationship, you've got to quit pulling that sexist crap on me." Ranger's words mocked her, repeating what she'd said to him last night.

"I'm not joking. Babies are hard work." Amy felt her will slipping. How bad could it be?

"You don't have a choice, either stay home or go to work and let me babysit." Ranger lifted one blond brow and waited.

No work, no food, no stability. That meant no Arturo. Her back was against the wall. Not that she didn't trust him to keep them safe and fed, but she didn't think he really understood how hard it was to keep up with a mobile baby and a five-year-old at the same time.

Then again, this might be a good dose of real family life for him. He would get the chance to see what being a father meant. "Okay. Chloe's oatmeal is in the pantry. She drinks milk or water. I have some vegetables prepared in the green containers in the refrigerator for her lunch. There are corn dogs and chicken nuggets in the freezer for Arturo."

"Go. To. Work. I've watched you all weekend. I know what she eats and drinks. Don't worry, we'll have a blast."

* * *

The sun had set by the time Amy walked through her yard to the back door. Cicadas and crickets chirped all around signaling the coming night. At least the temperature dropped a few degrees to a tolerable ninety-five degrees. Not bad considering the summer in Mercy usually meant triple digit days.

Right now, the heat was the last of her worries. Having to refuel the plane and mix the chemicals, on top of flying, added up to three times the work. Which meant it took her three times longer to get the job done and she was using precious time she didn't have. Time that meant money lost to her already nearly non-existent budget.

If Amy couldn't fill all her orders, she would lose the farm. Literally. A farm that had been in her family for generations. Quarterly taxes were coming due, and she didn't even want to think about how much she was short on cash.

It seemed like she was short on everything these days. Short on money. Short on work. Short on time.

Her shoulders were on fire, her back felt like someone

had taken a sledgehammer to it. Her stomach grumbled and rolled like thunder reminding her she hadn't eaten since breakfast. She didn't even want to see a mirror. She knew what she must look like-road kill after a rainstorm.

Amy stopped at the door and rested her head against the doorframe, sending up a silent prayer for Pedro. She'd missed him today and not just because of the extra workload. He'd made for her only company, talking to her through the radio in the plane, offering her a bottle of water when she landed. Today she realized how much she relied on him for friendship.

Now she had to rely totally on herself. Liar. She had Ranger, a man ready and willing to provide companionship and a whole lot more if she was willing.

The silence grew, interrupted only by an occasional bullfrog croaking over the insects. Amy lifted her head and stared at the door. No sound came from inside either. Dread sprouted inside her and she grabbed the handle and froze, actually taking in the door before her. A new door. A new kind of warmth spread through her. Ranger fixed her door- and cared for her children.

She turned the knob with a renewed eagerness. The door swung in on silent, well-oiled hinges. A single light over the oven seeped through the dark kitchen, highlighting the clean counters. Amy wandered over to the sink. Empty. No dirty plates to wash up and put away. No trash sitting on the counter to clean.

The oven was empty of dirty pots and pans. The only thing out of place was a plate covered in tin foil. Amy peeled the edge of the foil back. The most delicious smell wafted to her. A plate of food sat there like an offering to the gods. To the side of the stove sat a tall glass of tea, a napkin and a fork. Sweat dripped off the glass, and only a few small cubes of ice remained. Ranger had not only cooked dinner, but cleaned up and left her supper.

Exhaustion hit her at high speed and tears misted her eyes. She'd been so relieved that Ranger volunteered to keep the kids, but she'd also been secretly dreading the state of her house. Even when it had been just her and Shane, her house was always a wreck. She would often have to work late into the night at the Wharf, leaving Shane to cook his own supper and when she got home from work the kitchen would be a mess of dirty dishes and trash and scraps of food left sitting out. Ranger, a single man, was here all day, alone with two kids and he'd left her house spotless.

Amy blinked back her tears. She'd cried enough in the past year to last forever. Crying over frozen pizza was ridiculous.

She grabbed the fork, waffling for a moment between her choices. The chicken won. Amy took a bite of the chicken and her eyes drifted shut on the wave of pleasure taking root in her mouth. She wanted to savor each and every bite of food on her plate, but her stomach growled in protest, demanding more. Helpless, she dug in and finished the entire plate, silently vowing to show Ranger just how much she appreciated his help.

Amy rinsed the plate, put it in the washer and went to the living room. She rounded the corner and stopped dead in her tracks. Her heart did a little flip flop. Ranger lay back in her recliner with Chloe asleep on his chest.

As if sensing her presence, Ranger cracked open his eyes and turned to her. A slow and sweet smile drifted across his lips, leaving her with the feeling of warm sunny days and the taste of sweetness on her tongue.

Her heart did that little flip-flop thing again, only this time it felt more like a full-blown kick to her sternum. Ranger didn't just give her bubbles and butterflies; he filled her with a sense of contentment she'd never known existed. She wanted to crawl in the chair with him and Chloe, and never get up.

"Go take a shower, we'll be right here." Ranger whispered.

She nodded, not able to speak past the lump in her throat. A few minutes later she stripped out of her dirty clothes and stepped into a blissful shower. The hot water beat down on her shoulders and back, working some of the tension and soreness out. She popped open a bottle of body wash and the fresh sweet smell filled up the bathroom. Hopefully, it would get rid of her current perfume of grease and sweat. After shampooing and washing her hair, she got out and dried off, slipping on some pajama shorts and a tank. She let her hair hang dry and went back into the living room. True to his word Ranger, hadn't moved.

Carefully, she lifted Chloe, studiously avoiding direct contact with Ranger. Her willpower was pretty much depleted, if she touched him too much she might not be able to leave. Amy carried Chloe to the nursery and laid her down. Chloe stirred a little but settled quickly. Amy pulled a sheet up over her shoulders and took a second to enjoy watching Chloe sleep. Being a working mother was fulfilling, and she loved being able to support herself and her baby, but at the same time, she hated being gone from Chloe all day.

Next, Amy peeked in on Artie, fast asleep in the guest room. He lay curled on his side, too small in that large bed. She'd had Ranger bring some of Artie's toys and clothes from his house, hoping to make him feel more comfortable. But the room screamed guest, not family. And even though he technically wasn't family yet, she intended to make sure he felt at home. A fresh pang of sadness hit her and she teared up again. Get it together girl. Pedro would be fine. Bo would find him safe and sound and their lives could pick up like before.

Only Pedro had been missing over a week now. She knew enough from the crime drama TV shows that once a person was missing over forty-eight hours, the likelihood of them being found safe was slim to none.

"Everything okay?" Ranger appeared behind her and put his hands on her shoulders. Amy leaned back into his body, needing to borrow some of his strength.

"I'm worried about Pedro." And Artie. And her job. Without Pedro's help, they might all be homeless in a few months.

"Come with me." Ranger's hand slid down her bare arm and his fingers tangled in hers. She let him pull her from the bedroom and into the living room, where he pulled her down on his lap in the recliner.

She curled up and rested her head in the curve of his shoulder. He felt so right. She wanted to wrap her arms around his neck and kiss him until she forgot about all her worries.

"Talk to me, baby." His chest rumbled beneath her cheek, sending a delicious vibration through her body.

"It's been almost a week and still nothing. How much longer will Bo look before he has to call off the search?"

Ranger sighed and wrapped his arm around her, pulling her tighter against him. "I don't know. But I've got my team looking, too. I really expected to find him at the Lobello's place. Something isn't adding up."

"What do you mean?"

"I mean, if Santos took him, he would either have dumped the body nearby or kept him alive to sell on the black market. So far, neither of those possibilities have panned out."

"There's a lot of woods around here, is it possible he escaped and is out there somewhere hurt?" She was reaching but she couldn't wrap her head around Pedro being dead.

"Maybe."

"You don't believe that?" His voice held too much doubt for her to miss.

"Bo has one of the best blood hounds in the south. That dog can track a tick from a mile. I think that if Pedro, injured and bloody, were out there, Bo's dog would have found him by now. Or someone on the force would have found him. Injured men leave lots of trails."

Would they ever catch a break? "I know you're right, but I'm not ready to give up. Maybe Santos had another location he was keeping people."

"If he does, we'll find him. Hoyt handles all of our techy stuff. He's been keeping an eye on all their known hideouts through the satellites from headquarters. My team, and the ATF, have been questioning all the hostages to see if they remember him. If he's out there, we'll find him."

"Thank you. I know you don't have to do all this, help so much. I want you to know how much I appreciate it." That bone weary tiredness started to return and Amy yawned.

Ranger slipped a finger under her chin and tipped her head up. "I do it because I care about you."

He pressed a kiss to her lips. More of a gentle caress. Not asking for anything. A simple and sweet kiss. "And because my happiness is tied to you."

Ranger let go and she dropped her head back to his shoulder, lifting her fingers to trace her lips. He didn't ask more than she could give.

"How was work today?"

She shut her eyes and enjoyed the way he felt beneath her. "Awful. I didn't realize how much Pedro did for me. Having to refuel and reload the plane myself is cutting my time in half."

Ranger stroked her hair, the soft tickle as he pulled the strands lulling her eyes to half-mast. "You should've called me. I would've helped."

"No way." He was already doing way too much. She didn't feel right, having to ask him to help out so much. She snuggled deeper, burying her face in the crook of his neck. The man smelled divine.

"Hard headed woman. You should let people help out. You know that saying, no woman is an island." Every time he spoke, her senses purred with pleasure. Ranger started massaging her scalp and Amy didn't even try to fight the groan. "Artie helped out a lot around here. He's a good kid."

"Mmm."

"Chloe too, but you should have warned me how fast she can crawl."

"Tried to warn you," Amy mumbled, unable to keep her eyes open another second.

Chapter Twenty-eight

Amy fell asleep in his arms. Ranger knew he should get up and put her in bed, but he wanted to hold her. Feel her body against him. The wash of contentment that came over him surprised him. He'd never sat and held a woman before. In the past, with the few women he'd been intimate with, he'd had a goal. Get his pleasure, give her hers and get out. He'd never stayed and slept with a woman. Never played with her hair, thinking about how silky it felt. Never studied a splash of cute freckles across her nose.

He'd never loved a woman before now.

Ranger knew he would never find this complete package with anyone else. Someone who could light his blood on fire in an instant and cool him down in the next second. This woman didn't need him to take care of her, she was more than capable of taking care of herself, but that didn't stop him from wanting to give her the world.

He respected her tough side. She got the job done, no matter how tired she was. And Lord was she hard headed. Determined to earn her place. She was a fighter. And fucking sexy as hell when she was mad.

As much as he loved her strength, he yearned for her softer side. For those moments like tonight, when she was vulnerable and sweet. He wanted to hold her and promise her that he would always be here for her. No matter what.

Amy Carter was an enigma of sugar and spice. She fought with every fiber in her body for her home and her life.

And he knew she would love just as fierce.

She let out a soft snore against his neck. Ranger sighed. He recognized that kind of snore. He'd bunked with enough military guys over his life to recognize exhaustion.

She needed a bed and a good night's sleep. Ranger eyed the crutches leaning against the wall next to him. He'd been able to carry Chloe around all day today without too much pain in his leg. But Chloe was a baby. Amy, although small, was a full-grown woman.

The bum leg was a damn nuisance. There was no way he could pick her up and carry her the few feet to her bedroom. If he was honest, he was happy with her right here, snuggled against him.

Ranger grabbed the recliner pull and leaned the chair back. He didn't have a choice. He wasn't willing to wake her. And he couldn't carry her. Looks like the chair was it for the night.

She'd worked too hard today. He had no intention of letting her do it alone again tomorrow. The woman thought she had to do it all by herself. But Ranger knew better. A good soldier knew how to support himself, but an even better soldier knew when to call in reinforcements.

If it wasn't for his bum leg, he'd be out there in a heartbeat, even if he had to strap Chloe on his back in one of those baby carrier thingies. But as it was, crutches and all, he would probably get in the way more than help. So he settled for the next best thing.

Out of their entire team, either Aaron or Riser had to have some experience in this arena. And those two were usually together. So he called Aaron.

"Don't tell me the door screwed up?" Aaron said without a greeting. Thanks to Ranger's bum leg, he'd had to call in reinforcements to help hang Amy's new door. Aaron, Riser and Merc had all shown up to do the task.

"Come on, how can you screw up a perfectly good door?" Ranger said.

"Just checkin'. What's up, man?" Aaron's drawl was definitely longer, more southern, with a distinct Texas twine.

"Riser there?"

"Yep."

"Either of y'all know your way around a crop-duster?"

"Not me, if it don't have hooves and horns and go moo, I can't help. Hold on, I'll ask the rest of the team." Ranger heard Aaron pull the phone away and repeat his question. A few seconds later, he got back on the phone. "You're in luck, brother. I happen to have one big son of a bitch right here that can help you out."

Ranger sagged in relief, he knew either Aaron or Riser could handle the situation. "Great. Tell Riser to be out here at sunrise."

"Well, I can tell him, but he doesn't know shit about crop-duster's."

Ranger stilled and lifted his head. "Who then?"

Ethan grew up in the city, on the streets. Merc grew up who the hell knew where. The man spoke only when necessary and even then it was mainly grunts or one-word responses. He killed as easy in hand-to-hand combat as with a weapon. Aaron and Riser were the only ones who had grown up in the country.

Ranger heard the phone shuffle. "Aaron?" If that asshole hung up on him...

"I'll be there." The line went dead. Holy mother of God. Merc. The man scared the shit out of assassins and terrorists. Ranger sure as hell didn't want him around Amy.

* * *

Ranger woke to the beeping of his watch alarm. Five a.m. The sun didn't even shine at this ungodly hour. This before sunrise stuff sucked.

But it would suck a whole lot worse if he wasn't sleeping next to Amy. He'd kept his touches to G rated, knowing how exhausted she was, and lain awake half the night with the most painful raging hard on of his life. Her scent surrounded him. Her soft skin caressed him. He bit back a groan and gently nudged her awake.

"Rise and shine." For the past week, they'd gone no further than some heavy petting. He reacted worse than a horny teenager. His every waking thought was about her. How her hair felt like silk sifting through his fingers. The exquisite taste of her lips.

Amy grumbled and rubbed her eyes. "Morning."

"Go get dressed, I'll make you some breakfast."

"Okay." She got up and walked out of the room, still half asleep. Ranger grabbed his crutches and used them to help him stand.

He went to the kitchen, put on some coffee, and pulled out some bacon and eggs and pancake mix, determined to make her a big breakfast to get her through most of the day. He grabbed some sliced turkey and bread too. He'd be danged if he'd let her work all day with no food again.

A little while later Amy appeared in the doorway, dressed in blue jeans and the formfitting muscle shirt. Her heavy breasts strained against the gray material. His mouth watered, remembering the taste of her nipples in his mouth. He couldn't tear his gaze away, watching in fascination as those very nipples beaded and hardened.

"Ranger." The huskiness in her voice hit him with another bolt of desire. Shit. Get it together man. Merc would be here anytime and she had to get to work, but all he could think about was lifting up that shirt and devouring her pretty nipples.

Ranger cleared his throat and turned away, flipping the last batch of bacon in the skillet, and briefly contemplating grabbing a cup of ice water to pour down his pants. She touched him, feather light on his arm, and he jerked.

He quickly removed the bacon from the pan, set it to the side and turned off the heat. Then he faced her and immediately had to stop himself from groaning. Desire glowed in her brown eyes. Her plump lips parted and begged for him to taste. "Amy, you've got to quit looking at me like that."

She smiled an impish up to no good smile. "Why is that exactly?"

Ranger wrapped an arm around her waist and pulled her against him, pressing himself against her belly. Her eyes widened in shock. Good. "That's why. If you don't stop looking at me like you want to devour me, I'm going to lose control."

"Now, why don't you quit poking the bear and make yourself a cup of coffee?"

"Sure thing."

Amy's words were followed by a knock on the kitchen door. Her brows swooped down, "What on earth?"

"I got it." Ranger hobbled past her, cursing the fact that he hadn't put on a shirt yet and there was nothing to disguise the aching bulge in his shorts. He yanked open the door anyway. Merc, the big son of a bitch, stood on the concrete patio, both feet planted on the ground. Hands clasped behind his back. Elbows out in a classic call to attention. Only Ranger would be damned if the man ever took orders from anybody.

Ranger stood tall at six foot four, but Merc had at least another inch on him. He let his dark hair grow a little past a buzz cut, blending in with a thick beard. Heavy muscles bulged from beneath his T-shirt, pulling the material taut. "You're early."

Merc glanced down. "Am I interrupting something?"

Hell, yes you're interrupting something. Ranger felt Amy's presence behind him and took a breath. His friend was here because Ranger had asked for his help. His dick would have to wait. Ranger stepped to the side. "Merc, this is Amy."

"Ma'am."

"Nice to meet you." Her gaze cut to Ranger. "Everything okay?"

"I knew you needed some help and Merc here knows his way around a hangar. He volunteered to help you out."

Amy's gaze traveled up the entire length of Merc. Ranger saw her visibly swallow. "How nice of you, but I don't need help, really. I could never ask you to do something like that."

"It's done," Merc said and stepped inside. They both watched as he pulled out a seat at the kitchen table and sat down, stretching his long legs out in front of him. The man made the entire kitchen seem too small.

"Well then, looks like you're in time for breakfast." Amy went to the kitchen, leaving the two men at the table.

"Smile or something. You're scaring her."

Merc turned his black eyes to Ranger, and he repressed a shudder. Asshole. He knew exactly what kind of effect he had on people.

"Want some coffee?" Amy asked from the other side of the island.

"Yes, ma'am." Merc answered, still staring at Ranger.

"Cream and sugar?" Amy said.

Ranger bit the inside of his cheek. No way Merc put anything in his coffee, except maybe some battery acid.

Then Merc surprised the ever loving shit out of Ranger. The man smiled, not that small side smirk he was so good at, but a real one that showed all of his teeth. "Sounds wonderful, thank you."

Holy crap.

"Ranger, don't just stand there, fix your friend a plate."

Chapter Twenty-nine

Saturday morning Amy woke and rolled over in an otherwise empty bed. Ranger still refused to do more than kiss and touch. He slept on the couch every night, giving her time and space. And she'd had enough. She wanted more from him. She wanted all of him.

She sat up and grabbed her phone. Ten a.m.? She jumped up from the bed in alarm. She'd never slept this late. Never.

Amy raced from the room. Chloe never slept this late. What kind of mother doesn't hear her child cry? Surely she had cried out this morning.

She flew down the hall in record time only to hear a choking sound coming from the nursery. Her heart raced in her chest like a thoroughbred racehorse. Amy skidded to a stop in the nursery doorway.

Ranger had Chloe at the changing table. The choking sound wasn't coming from her daughter, but from the six foot four Special Forces operative bending over Chloe as she cooed and giggled and squealed.

The lower half of Ranger's face was hidden beneath a dishtowel that he had somehow secured around his nose and mouth with clothespins. Amy's elbow length pink cleaning gloves were on his hands.

Ranger gagged, his frame bending. Then he lifted a dirty diaper, toed open the wastebasket nearby and dropped the diaper, making sure to hold it out as far from him as possible.

Once that part was over, he grabbed a wipe from the warmer and gently swabbed Chloe's bottom, managing to finish the task with only a few more coughs. At this point, Amy could no longer hold it in. She grabbed the frame of the door and doubled over in laughter. Ranger turned, and all she could see was the surprised expression in his gorgeous blue eyes

"I thought you military guys were supposed to be tough. How on earth did you do this all day yesterday?" Amy could barely get the words to her lips without shaking. She couldn't stop laughing. She clutched her chest and tried to suck in a breath.

She couldn't see the lower half of his face, but she knew he was glaring. "I can handle explosives and guns and killing. But this... this is just wrong. How can such a cute little baby produce something so awful." His voice was slightly muffled by the dishtowel.

Amy approached him, lifted the towel and pressed a quick kiss to his lips. "Thank you for letting me sleep in."

His eyes darkened with pleasure. "You were exhausted. Apparently Artie is too, cause he's still sleeping. I figured me and Chloe could hang out. But she needs to come with a warning label."

He knocked a chink into the concrete surrounding her heart, but instead of a crack, it opened up one giant pothole. And not a regular pothole either, the potholes that knock a car completely out of alignment.

Ranger staying here every day, taking care of the kids and the house wore on her. And not in a bad way either. She thought it had started out as a sense of obligation, but now when he looked at Chloe there was real love in his eyes.

Love Shane never got the chance to experience. Her heart clenched, choked and restarted. No. She wouldn't cry. Not again. Look forward, Amy. Move forward. Chloe didn't need a mother locked in the past.

She needed laughter. She needed love.

And she needed a father.

Amy reached behind his head, popped the clothespins

open and gently pulled the dishcloth from around his face. His handsome features hit her hard, stealing her breath. Would she ever get over how good looking this man was? Everything about him was appealing.

Blond hair cut close to his head. An incredibly square jaw. Freaking chiseled from stone kind of square jaw. But that jaw was softened by a gorgeous grin just for her.

Ranger lifted Chloe, the pink rubber gloves stark against her naked belly. Chloe grabbed for his mouth, yanked his lower lip down and giggled when he nipped at her. The man was not only knocking holes in her resistance, he was laying explosives at the foundation and blowing the wall completely away.

Mavis had stayed away from them since the hair salon and her husband hadn't slammed the door in Amy's face when she ordered more chemical supplies. The threat of Mavis wasn't completely gone, but it was no longer scoping Amy for annihilation down the end of a barrel.

Ranger proved how much he cared not only for her, but for her children. In one week, he'd fixed her old barn door out back after he'd heard it creaking open in the wind. He'd replaced her broken kitchen door. He took out the trash when it got full and even changed the oil in her truck. He'd made her supper.

And he did it all without her having to ask.

"You okay?" Ranger seemed to sense her moods.

Amy wanted to tell him how she felt. Let him know she was ready to move on. But not now. She would save that for tonight. "You keep my child and she'll turn out rotten."

Ranger gave Chloe a big kiss on the cheek and Amy felt it all the way to her soul. She kicked and squealed and then her newly placed diaper popped free and dropped to the floor. Ranger's eyes widened and his arms shot straight out. "Here, take her before she goes off again."

"Such a sissy." Amy grabbed Chloe and swooped down to grab the diaper. She put her back on the changing table and snapped the diaper in place in under five seconds. All the while, Ranger leaned over her shoulder, studying her movements intently. "It really helps if you don't put the diaper on backwards."

"What I want to know is what kind of idiot sells diapers without instructions?" Ranger grumbled. Amy wanted to poke him some more, to tease him, but she didn't want to wound his already injured pride. But then again...

"Look." Amy pointed to the front of Chloe's diaper. "See right there it says front." She had to drive the point home, so she bit her lip to try to keep the laughter inside and rolled Chloe over to her belly. She squealed and slapped her hands down on the bed, enjoying the attention. Amy pointed to the back of her diaper. "See there, it says back."

Amy lifted Chloe and snuggled her belly up to her nose, savoring her soft sweet skin, and also hiding the huge grin she could no longer contain.

Ranger stepped back and crossed his arms, his big manly chest poking out, but the effect was totally ruined by the long pink rubber gloves. "Are you making fun of me, woman?"

"Never. I would never make fun of you." But her laughter erupted once more and she felt the need to clutch her side.

Chloe joined in on the fun and popped Amy in the nose, cutting her laughter off abruptly. Amy straightened and grabbed her face.

This time it was Ranger's turn to laugh and he didn't hold back. "That girl's got my back. Better watch what you say about me."

Amy rubbed her nose and tickled Chloe's ribs, pulling forth another peal of giggles. She was so sweet, Amy could never get mad. "Have y'all had breakfast?"

"Oh yeah, hours ago. As a matter of fact, we might be ready for lunch soon." Amy let her gaze travel down that flat washboard stomach, secretly wishing he wasn't wearing a shirt.

"How about I make us a light lunch, and then I can cook a big meal for supper. All of us together."

Ranger shook his head and Amy had to catch her heart

from sinking. Did he plan on leaving now that the work week was over? Did she want him to leave? She'd avoided the whole marriage thing so much, maybe she'd pushed him away.

But ever since that night when he made that crazy declaration to Sheriff Lawson, a declaration that she was finding more and more appealing every day, he'd been careful to keep his distance.

"Look, I know I've been avoiding talking to you about the other night."

His intense blue eyes held hers and he trailed a finger down her cheek. The small contact sent sparks of electricity shooting through her body. "Yes, you have. And I've let this go on long enough.

"I don't want you to leave." She blurted out the declaration, her stomach tight.

"I'm not leaving. We are going to talk. Today. What I wanted to say was I have to go out for a couple of hours, but I'll be back before supper."

Her body went limp with relief. "Good. I'm ready to discuss it."

"Tonight." Ranger brushed a kiss across her lips.

"Tonight," she agreed.

"Aaron and Riser are going to come pick me up. Do you care if I take Arturo with me? I figure the boy needs some man time before he turns into an all-out girl."

"What's that supposed to mean?"

Ranger lifted his hand and swept it over his head, gesturing to the room. "This nursery is pink. You got him sleeping in a purple guest room. If I'm not careful, he'll be playing with Barbie dolls next. He needs tractors. Dirt. Monster trucks."

"So you're saying you don't like my house decorations?"

"I couldn't care less about the color of your house, as long as you're in it."

Amy started feeling generous, despite his sexist comments. "Okay, since you let me sleep then why don't you tell me what you'd like for supper. I'll make it."

"Woman, you make me happy." Ranger pulled her to him, with Chloe squished between them. "I'm a meat and potatoes kind of guy. I will leave the details up to you."

Chapter Thirty

"Now this is what I call a homecoming."

Amy's heart slammed into her sternum at high speed and her eyes flew open. Ranger stood in the doorway, a duffle bag in hand, black shirt and tactical pants practically painted on. His bulging biceps rippled. Her mouth watered.

"Where are your crutches?"

He let the bag drop to the kitchen floor and leaned against the doorjamb, crossing his arms over his massive chest. Her breath quickened and her stomach fluttered like a teenager. Ranger's gaze drifted down her body then back to her face, locking on her eyes, communicating his desire with a scorching look. Her nipples beaded instantly.

"Doc said I didn't need 'em anymore."

He pushed off from the wall, stalking around the island like a true predator. She couldn't help but devour his wide shoulders and lean hips. The man was walking sex on a stick. Amy tensed, waiting for the familiar guilt to slam into her, but all she felt was a keen yearning.

"Where's Artie?" Was that her voice all raspy and weak?

Ranger leaned in, his low deep voice sending chill bumps racing across her skin. "He's spending the night with Evie and Hunter."

Her mouth went dry and she grabbed her wine, tossing back the liquid in a desperate attempt to calm her nerves.

"Why?"

"The same reason Evie is here to pick up Chloe. To

give us a night all to ourselves."

"Hey girl, don't worry about us. I got her bag and her formula." Evie popped into the kitchen holding Chloe and gave her a quick wave.

"But...but..."

"No buts. You need this." Evie cast Amy a look that clearly stated she better take advantage of the hot man standing in her kitchen. Amy offered her a weak smile.

"Now, little missy. It looks like I'm going to need to practice being a mommy with you." Evie's voice drifted away and then Amy heard the front door shut.

"You've been planning this."

"Absolutely." Ranger's answer was swift and solid, leaving no doubt in her mind that he wanted her.

It was now or never. Amy carefully placed her glass on the counter. Her hands tingled and shook.

Was she really ready to jump off that cliff?

The answer flooded her immediately. Of course she was ready. She'd been ready. Amy took a small step back and Ranger frowned. "What's wrong? Did you change your mind about us?"

She didn't answer, couldn't make her lips work. She wanted to show him how much he meant to her. They'd been talking and dancing around the subject long enough. Amy reached up and snapped open the top button on the front of her dress. Ranger's gaze dropped to her finger and his nostrils flared. A white hot heat set up in her belly. Amy unbuttoned the next one down.

Ranger grabbed the counter beside him.

Her fingers shook so bad she almost couldn't get the third one undone.

Ranger closed the gap between them. He didn't give her a chance to talk. To think. His lips closed over hers and she gave herself to him. His mouth was hot, sweet and dominating. He took control of the kiss, slanting his head for better access. Nerve endings she didn't even know existed lit up. The rasp of his tongue over hers sent heat flooding her core.

He didn't stop. He lifted her onto the counter, wedging himself between her legs. He smelled of sweat and sex and pure man.

He broke the kiss and finished the task she'd started a moment ago, his large fingers surprisingly nimble as he swiftly unbuttoned her dress all the way down to her waist. His gaze lifted to hers, trapping her in those blue depths, as he slowly lowered the straps off her shoulders.

Amy sent up a silent thanks to Saline for helping her pick out new lingerie last week. The pale blue lace bra was completely see through, and the sexiest frilliest thing she'd ever owned. But if the look of worship on Ranger's face was any indication-it was worth it.

"You're the most beautiful woman I've ever seen."

Amy felt a flush creep up her chest. "Ranger, I'm nervous."

"Me, too." Ranger cupped her face between his large hands. "Do you trust me?"

Amy bit her lip, thinking hard and fast, but the answer was right there. "Of course I trust you."

Ranger let his fingers trail down her shoulder, her chest. He tickled the skin just above her bra. Her nipples hardened almost painfully, seeking his touch. She wanted him to take her. To rip her bra off. But he kept his touch feather light, grazing her nipple through the thin lace with the back of his finger. Electric heat shot through her and she groaned, leaned back on her hands and let her head fall back.

Ranger continued his sweet torture, gently rasping over her nipples until she couldn't sit still another second. Her hips lifted and he pulled her to the edge of the counter, her core coming in contact with him. His pants held him in, but she felt him. Hard. Big.

"Look at me," Ranger commanded and she lifted her head, opening her eyes. His expression was dark with barely restrained lust. He slid her bra straps off her shoulder, the soft material abrading her sensitive skin.

Ranger pulled her bra down, baring her breasts. "You're so beautiful." He lowered his head, keeping his gaze locked with hers until his lips closed over her nipple, suckling her into the hot depths of his mouth. Lightening zinged down her body and she arched up, crying out at the sweet torture.

Never had she felt anything so intense. So consuming. Her entire body reacting to his touch. Amy threaded her fingers in his blond hair and held him to her, needing more. Wanting him to take more. Ranger cupped her breasts to his mouth and lavished his attention on her aching nipples until she was a ball of unrestrained lust.

With shaking hands she reached behind and unsnapped her bra, tossing it behind her. She was completely bare from the waist up and Ranger took full advantage.

"I want to touch you." Amy said, her voice a throaty whisper. She'd always been so passive with Shane. The chemistry from early in their marriage had quickly fizzled out. Shane had started putting sex with her on the back burner, choosing instead to go out and drink. Something Ranger would never do.

Amy wanted to drive Ranger as crazy as he drove her. She wanted to give him the same pleasure. She'd never felt this consuming edge of need.

Ranger bit down on her nipple and she cried out, arching into his touch. Then he stood and tore off his shirt, his abs rippling and rolling with the movement. God he was gorgeous. But he didn't give her enough time to savor the sight of him, instead he yanked her to him again, crushing her breasts against his bare chest and taking possession of her mouth again. And she was helpless to do anything but respond. His touch turned her to liquid.

She rubbed her hands down his arms, around his chest and back, learning his contours. Needing to drive him as crazy, she broke free of his lips and trailed kisses down his thick neck, stopping to nibble the curve of his shoulder. Ranger groaned and heady pleasure filled her. The skin of his chest was so soft, a contrast to the granite hard muscles beneath. Amy flicked her tongue lightly over his nipple, enjoying how he jerked at her caress.

His taste filled her. His scent invaded her. She wanted all of him. Amy leaned back, letting her legs fall further apart and grabbed his belt. She ripped it free in seconds, despite her trembling hands. His pants buttons followed, but before she could reach inside and grab him he shackled her wrist and held her away. "It's my turn now."

Ranger placed a hand on her chest and pushed her down. The cold granite came in contact with her bare back and she arched up, sure she was about to go up in flames.

* * *

Ranger stared down at the goddess before him, laid out for his pleasure. Her heavy breasts bare. Perfect pink nipples begging for his touch. Long red hair spread out around her. His chest ached with love for this woman.

He'd been so scared she would change her mind. Knowing if she did it would shatter him. But she gave herself freely and fully to him. Spread out before him like a feast. Her chest rising and falling, tapering into a flat tummy and small waist. The yellow sundress pooled around her hips, hiding her core, but still so sexy he couldn't speak.

She trusted him. The thought made his chest expand, his heart near burst with pride. She chose him. And dammit he wanted her more than he wanted his next breath.

Ranger grabbed the dress and Amy lifted her hips, helping him slide it down her legs, revealing matching baby blue panties. He let the dress fall from his fingers. His mouth completely dry, his cock ready to explode. Ranger hooked a finger in her panties and slid them down, baring her completely.

His heart stopped beating all together. Never in his life could he have imagined anything so perfect. So sexy. Her hips flared out, the curve generous and heavenly. Ranger gave in with a groan and dropped to his knees. She was completely bare. Her pussy wet and glistening. He lifted a shaking hand and grazed the small nub nestled in her folds. "When did you do this?"

Amy cried out and his cock jerked in reaction. He

wanted to bury himself so deep inside her she'd never forget him, but he promised himself he would take it slow this time. Woo her. Love her. Cherish her.

"Today. I-I shaved today."

Amy's scent pulled him in, dying to taste her, he leaned forward and flicked his tongue over her clit. She jerked, her legs closing around his head. Ranger grabbed her thighs and pushed her legs apart. "Open."

He held her that way and resumed tasting her. One long slow lick and his eyes rolled back in his head. She was heaven, pure unadulterated heaven. Ranger devoured her, teased her, driving her forward until she was riding his tongue and clutching his hair, pulling him to her.

"Oh God, don't stop. I'm so close." Her plea was music to his ears. Ranger felt the pre cum drip from his cock, knew he couldn't hold out any longer. He rose, ripped his pants down and lined his shaft up with her entrance. Amy's head was back, her eyes closed, her lips parted as she gasped and panted.

"Look at me," Ranger commanded, his tone harsh with need. He wanted to see her eyes when he took her. To know she was thinking only of him.

She complied immediately, her normally dark brown eyes a dark honey drenched with desire. Desire for him. He reaffirmed his need for control and clenched his teeth. He had a mission to complete. He held on to his cock and fed it to her entrance. He had to grit his teeth and force himself to go slow. She clenched around him, nearly his undoing.

Sweat broke along his forehead and neck, but still he held himself back, easing inside her inch by torturous inch. She was so fucking wet. So fucking perfect. So fucking his. "You're mine. Say it."

Amy nodded and lifted her hips. Ranger held back. "No. Give me the words."

She groaned then, her lips parted. "I'm yours, Ranger James. Yours. Please."

Her words destroyed his control. He grabbed her hips and rammed forward, bottoming out inside her tight depths.

Amy's scream mixed with his own yell of pleasure. She spasmed around him, squeezing him until he almost came right there. Ranger called on every single ounce of training he possessed and forced himself to take his time. Drive her crazy.

He pulled out, savoring the feel of her around him, slow and easy. Then he rammed back in, hard and fast. He kept that pace up, until she cried out, clawing at his chest, grabbing his arms. "Ranger, I'm about to come."

"Yes, baby. Let go. I've got you." He drove forward again, slamming into her, faster now. She screamed, her entire body arched off the counter. Ranger threw his head back, her response pulling his own release free. The entire world shattered around him, there was nothing left. Just Amy. Just his woman.

He fell forward, spent, and braced on his elbows, unwilling and unable to pull out. The small aftershocks from her orgasm still rocked him. He wanted to spend the rest of his life right here. Right now. "I love you."

Chapter Thirty-one

Her breath caught at the look of complete adoration in his gaze. She caressed his cheek, lifting up enough to gently kiss his lips. "I love you, too."

"Say it again."

"I love you, Ranger James." Amy's heart caught up in her throat. Saying the words out loud seemed to free her. "I'm ready."

Ranger swept a sweat soaked strand of hair off her forehead. "I want to spend the rest of my life with you. I want to take care of you. I want to take care of Chloe and Artie."

Tears stung her eyes, his words piercing her heart with their sweet sincerity. He brushed away the tears tracking out of the corner of her eyes. "Why are you crying?"

"Because I'm happy. I don't deserve you." She didn't. He was too good to be real. And she was scared to death she would wake up and discover this was only a dream.

"I think you have that backwards. I don't deserve you. But I promise to try to make you happy. I will never hurt you. Never lie to you."

"You won't ever leave me?"

"Never."

Amy pulled him down to her, needing his mouth on hers. Her body was limp and useless, but still she wanted him. Her satisfied repletion morphed into frantic desire and she deepened the kiss, pulling on his hair. As if sensing her desperation, Ranger wrapped her legs around him and lifted her, never breaking contact with her lips. He carried her to the bedroom and laid her gently back on the bed.

"I want to make love to you," Amy's entire body trembled. She pushed him over to his back and quickly straddled him. His eyes flared and his hands went immediately to her breasts.

Amy nearly got lost in his touch, but pushed his hands away, determined to give, not take.

She started at his neck, nibbling and licking and learning his taste. His skin was salty with sweat and when she felt his racing pulse, she smiled against his flesh. Emboldened by his reaction, Amy worked her way down his body, laving at his flat nipples until he shuddered beneath her touch.

Never had she ever felt such sensuous power. She could trace the hard lines mapping his abs with her eyes closed. Every part of him was contoured. Ripped. Practically begging her fingers to trace each groove.

She traveled lower, flicking his navel, and loving his sharp intake of breath. She reached his cock, already hard and ready for her, and paused. Ranger groaned and grabbed the sheets, bowing up. He was so big. So perfect. She wanted to savor this moment.

Amy flicked him with her tongue and Ranger jerked completely off the bed. Again she repeated that, barely making contact. Ranger was sweating and shaking. She wrapped her hand around his base and took him fully in her mouth, loving the way he stretched her lips wide. He felt like hot satin sliding over her tongue. Ranger's hands buried in her hair and he thrust up to meet her mouth.

Exquisite power flooded her. She closed her eyes and groaned around him. She'd never received such pleasure by simply giving. Ranger's fingers tangled in her hair, forcing her mouth from him. Before she could utter a protest, he lifted and settled her on his length, impaling her fully in one stroke. Amy cried out, the intense sensation stealing her breath.

"God, yes. You're perfect. So damn good." Ranger's voice was thick and raspy with pleasure, scraping across her sensitive flesh.

Full. He filled her so full she felt ready to burst. Her heart. Her soul. Her body. Though she was on top, he stole her control. "Ranger."

"That's it baby. Love me."

His words spurred her into action, driving her into a frenzy of need. Amy rode him hard and fast, the need to take it slow completely obliterated. Ranger grabbed onto her hips, helping her move, connecting them in every way possible, until the pleasure became unbearable and she came, screaming out his name.

Ranger's yell mixed with hers and she felt him swell even more inside her, filling her. She collapsed onto him, breathing hard and sweating from her exertion. Her only consolation was Ranger's harsh breathing matched her own.

Never had she felt so much pleasure. Such a connection, as if their souls merged into one. Lying on top of him felt...right. Like he was the missing piece to the puzzle of her life.

* * *

Ranger had never felt anything as perfect as Amy sleeping on top of him. Her body curved to his perfectly. She was so small, but so vibrant and full of life. And she trusted him. He knew that now. He'd waited for what seemed like eternity for her to love him. He'd almost given up hope, but he'd soldiered on, never stopping. Always fighting for her. In the end, it had paid off. Amy Carter was his.

As if sensing his thoughts, she snuggled deeper into the curve of his shoulder. Ranger squeezed her to him like a man possessed. He was hers, had always been hers, and now, finally, she was his.

Ranger slept that night, uninterrupted with nightmares. He slept and dreamed. Dreamed of his new family, dreamed of his bright future, dreamed of growing old with Amy at his side.

Chapter Thirty-two

Ranger woke in an instant, grabbed for his gun on the nightstand, and came up empty. Dream. He'd been dreaming. The sun was just starting to chase away the dark shadows of night. Ranger sat up and dug his palms into his eyes, rubbing the sleep away. Amy lay curled on her side, her features soft with peace and sleep, a small smile on her lips.

"Good morning, brother."

That voice.

"Shane." Ranger's gaze shot up from his woman to the man in the corner chair past the foot of the bed. Then he stopped thinking. He stopped breathing.

The ghost of his best friend taunted him. Only he wasn't a ghost. He was there, flesh and blood, staring at Ranger in bed with his wife.

"How did you get here?"

Shane's reddish-brown hair was long and tangled, like the beard covering his narrow face. He'd lost weight, his arms and shoulders smaller, but corded. His green eyes held a hard glint that went beyond the typical post-deployment shell.

"Not exactly the homecoming I imagined." Shane remained leaning forward, elbows propped on his knees, his gaze unwavering.

Ranger had never felt threatened around his friend, but

his fingers itched for his pistol.

"I thought you were dead. We all thought you were dead." A spike of shock lined with guilt buried in Ranger's back. Shane was alive. Alive.

Which meant Amy was still married.

"Apparently you were mistaken." Why was Shane just sitting there?

"You were dead. Your casket is in Mercy Cemetery. I lowered it into the ground myself." Not dead, alive. Ranger tried to swallow past the huge lump of emotion growing in his throat, choking off his air. His ability to think. To act.

His worst nightmare was his dream come true. The never-ending cycle of blame for leaving Shane behind, the aching crawling guilt for his death, could end. But a new nightmare, worse than any other, would begin.

That's when he felt it. The fear. Fear of losing Amy.

"Funny thing about coffins that don't have bodies in them," Shane said.

A wave of anger mixed with the fear, exploding before Ranger could leash it in. "Where the fuck have you been?" His voice boomed through the room.

Amy shot straight awake, turning bewildered eyes his way. "What's wrong?"

Only he couldn't speak, the lump of emotion had grown into a mountain of guilt and rage. Ranger's shoulders heaved, his heart slamming against his ribs like he'd climbed that mountain only to tumble down the other side.

The man he'd prayed for. Cried for. Pleaded for. The man he'd left behind sat ten feet away. His very presence threatening Ranger's sanity.

Amy stiffened and he closed his eyes, unwilling or unable, to watch the love of his life slip through his fingers.

"Shane?" Her voice was thin, reedy. Trembling from the inside out.

Ranger clenched the sheets, fighting not to touch her. His every instinct screamed for him to hold her, shield her from her husband.

"Good morning, wife."

Horror crept down Ranger's spine, and his eyes opened, staring at Shane back from the dead. This couldn't be real. Not now. Not when he'd given his heart away.

Amy paled, her deep brown eyes going stark with shock. "Shane, is that really you?"

Ranger's heart skyrocketed into his throat when Amy's gaze cut to his own. He saw it all there. The confusion. The question. The shock. But under all that he saw something that gave him hope. He saw her love.

Ranger took a deep breath and forced himself to think. He grabbed Amy's free hand. Shane had been gone for over a year now. He wasn't going to give up Amy to a fucking ghost.

"How touching. My wife and my best friend. How long did you wait? Or did you even wait?" Ranger watched as Shane finally showed some emotion. His deadened responses had reminded him of a corpse. Now his calm façade cracked. "Were you fucking before we even went on deployment?"

Anger. That, he could deal with. He knew how to fight that. "Don't you dare talk to her like that."

"I'll talk to her any damn way I please. She's my wife." Shane's words whiplashed through the room.

"Was your wife. You were declared dead."

"Something I intend to rectify."

"Over my dead fucking body." Ranger couldn't stop the fury rolling through him. He'd fought so long for her, just to lose her? No way. Not now.

"I can arrange that." Shane rose from the chair, his lean physique even more obvious. His clothes were clean, pressed, but his hair and face dirty with grit.

"Stop it." Amy rose up on her knees, clutching the sheet to her nakedness. "Both of you."

Tears streamed down her parchment white cheeks. Ranger's heart clenched in the noose of her obvious pain. He forced the vehement response back. She was hurting. They were all hurting. Amy held up a hand and took a shaky breath. "Shane, please, give me a minute to think and get dressed. Then we can all sit down and have a conversation."

Shane didn't move a muscle. His eyes hardened and his lips twisted into some sort of sardonic smile. "Are you telling me to leave my best friend alone in bed with my naked wife?"

Every muscle in Ranger's body went tense, ready to spring. "I warned you."

Amy's ice cold hand squeezed his, pulling his attention. She needed his support right now. Needed him to be her rock.

How could he be her rock when his foundation was crumbling? He tried to imagine what kind of shock it must be for Shane to come home to this. No one thought he was coming home ever again.

Ranger had buried him. Cried over him. Mourned him. And now here he was, sitting at the end of the bed as if he still owned the place. How was it possible for him to show up, alive and in one piece?

Ranger had been there when the box containing two of Shane's fingers was delivered to Captain Grey. He'd seen the DNA test results confirming Shane's identity.

"We'll settle what's between us later. I'm not asking you to do anything but give Amy a minute of privacy. You can do that for her can't you?"

Murderous rage flashed across Shane's features. His eyes bloodshot, his cheeks hollowed out. Ranger waited on the attack, but Shane didn't move, his normally quick temper hadn't reared its ugly head. That was one of the reasons they had been best friends. Ranger was the slow burner, a joker and a good time guy. He balanced out Shane's quick temper nicely and was usually able to talk him down from fights.

Ranger knew he wouldn't be able to talk him down from this.

Small sniffles interrupted his thoughts. Both men turned to Amy. Ranger watched as Shane's gaze softened a fraction. Amy cried silently, tears streaming down her face.

Shane nodded once, and abruptly strode from the room. Ranger didn't take his gaze from the dead man walking until the door shut behind him. Something was off here.

Something not quite right.

Shane had been ambushed and taken hostage before Ranger's very eyes on their last mission. Then he'd been confirmed dead. Killed by the terrorist Al Seriq. So how was he here now?

Amy dove into his arms, her silent tears turning into broken sobs. He clutched her tight, part of him wondering- would this be the last time he held her?

He couldn't sit back and lose her. He leaned back and brushed the strands of hair from her face. "We'll figure this out."

"Ranger..."

He didn't know what else to say. He couldn't lie to her. He couldn't tell her everything would be okay. He didn't know that himself. So he did the only thing he could. He kissed her. Kissed her with every ounce of love and support he possessed.

Amy returned his kiss with desperation, digging her nails into his shoulders, and then she ripped away from him. Her hand flew to her mouth. "We can't do this now."

His shaky foundation shifted. No. He wouldn't let her go. "What do you mean?"

She shuddered, each of her teardrops taking a chunk out of him. Helpless fear took root. What would he do if she chose Shane?

"I...I don't know. I can't think. I need to get dressed. Oh, my God. He's alive. What am I going to do? He saw us." Her words tumbled out in jagged uneven shards, cutting through his heart. Ranger watched, powerless to do anything to fix her pain, as she stumbled from the bed.

Choose me. Please, choose me.

"Amy, calm down." Ranger stood and approached her, careful to go slow. She looked ready to fall apart.

"I. Can't. Breathe." Amy doubled over, catching her hands on her knees. Ranger dove for her, lifting her upright before she fell.

"Easy. Breath with me. That's it. Slow." Ranger wrapped his arms around her, fighting the urgent shudders working through him. He wanted to cry. To scream. To rage. But more than any of those things, he wanted to comfort Amy. "I love you."

He would do what it took to make her happy. Even if it meant his doom.

When her shaking subsided to a tremble, he took a step back and wiped the tears from her face. "I know you're shocked. Me too. But I'm not going anywhere unless you ask me to, okay?"

She held onto him, nodding after a minute that felt like an hour.

"Good. Now, go get dressed. I'll be right here." When Amy disappeared into her closet, Ranger yanked on his jeans. She returned a minute later, covered in a pink sundress. She looked beautiful. Beautiful and shell shocked.

Ranger held out a hand, waited on her to take it, and pulled her down to his lap. He couldn't shake the niggling sensation that something was off with Shane. "Amy, I'm not leaving you. I meant what I said. Promise me you will stick by my side, at least until you know he's...okay."

A fresh wave of tears immediately tumbled from her eyes. "What do you mean?"

"If he's been held prisoner this long, he could have been tortured. Men don't just reappear a year after their disappearance, the same as they were when they left."

"Do you think he's not safe?"

"I don't know what to think. But I want to be cautious until we do know."

"And what if nothing is wrong? What if he escaped and has been alone all this time, thinking about me."

"We'll find a way. I promise. I love you." Tears threatened his own eyes and he tucked her head against him, needing to hold her. He took a minute and got his emotions under control. She needed him to be strong.

He would be her warrior.

They entered the living room together. Shane sat on the couch staring out the window, lost in his thoughts. A love seat and recliner separated by a coffee table faced the couch.

Ranger stared at the man he considered as close as a brother. So many emotions overwhelmed him. The sense of joy that his friend was not dead. And the sudden shock of having his future plans possibly ripped out from beneath him.

Amy drew attention when she squeezed his hand and let go. He felt proud of her bravery. Amy took the first step forward, leaving Ranger with his feet glued in place.

"Shane?" She said his name softly, as if testing her ability to speak.

Shane stood and Amy approached him, stopping when she stood right next to him. Ranger couldn't help when his muscles tensed. Shane, although much leaner than before, still towered over her.

Shane reached a hand out and gently touched his wife's face and then Ranger saw it. Saw tears on his friend's face and his anger and tension drowned under a wave of guilt. He'd been so busy thinking about himself and his needs that he'd purposely ignored Shane's.

Ranger took a step back, the outsider intruding on a reunion between husband and wife, a moment that should be private. Not shared. He watched helplessly as Shane took Amy in his arms, hugging her as a shudder worked down his mangy frame. Doubt assailed Ranger. How could he expect their relationship to just...continue?

How could he try to keep Amy? Not from his best friend, not from Shane. How could he ask her to choose between her husband and himself? That he deserved her? But seeing them embrace, jealousy ate at him, burning in his gut. Mine. Just as that thought hit, another trailed on its heels. His.

Unable to stand there and watch his plans unravel, Ranger crept silently to the kitchen and gave them a moment of privacy. Staying close enough to hear everything.

Amy's sniffles passed through the open doorway. Ranger paced the kitchen, restless. He should be holding her. She needed time. He didn't want to give it to her. He stopped by the counter and put his head in his hands, trying to hold himself together. Pain. Anger. Jealousy. Love. Hurt. He didn't know what to feel first.

Jealousy won. It destroyed his altruism. He wanted her. He knew he had no right to want her. No right to feel this way. She wasn't his wife. It was eating him alive the jealousy he knew he had no right to feel. She wasn't his wife. But God he wanted her more than he wanted to breathe.

Images of her pleading beneath him. Her nails digging into his back. Her skin. Her sweet smell. The taste of her lips driving him crazy. Then the image twisted into one of Shane kissing Amy and he nearly lost control.

Ranger stalked back. Shane pressed his mouth to hers. Ranger's world shattered.

Ranger's feet carried him to the couple, standing behind Amy. She broke the embrace and stepped back. Ranger couldn't see her face, see if she enjoyed that kiss. But he saw Shane's.

He saw the fury.

"We need to talk." Ranger grabbed Amy's hand and attempted to pull her away.

"Let go of my wife." Shane took a menacing step forward.

"She's not yours anymore." Ranger advanced.

"Stop it!" Amy pushed her hands out, keeping herself bodily between them.

Ranger's composure slipped, his ability to separate his emotions from logic disappeared. He balled his hand into a fist, ready to attack his friend for touching her.

Shane leaned forward, crowding her between them. His nostrils flared and his lips fell into a tight line. "Are you deaf?"

"You can't expect her to jump back into a relationship with you after you've been dead for so long."

"Newsflash asshole, I wasn't dead. So technically she's still mine. She's always been mine."

"Please, I can't take it if you fight, please stop." Amy pleaded trying to keep them apart. Ranger glanced down, saw her distress, and backed off slightly.

"I always knew you had the hots for her. Every time

you came over you were sniffing around her. You couldn't wait to get in her pants." Shane spewed his venom, spit flying from his lips.

"You son of a bitch, I never touched her. I would never disrespect you or her like that." Ranger knew he was shouting now but he couldn't stop.

Shane sneered, "Yeah, you had enough respect to wait until I was gone before you fucked my wife."

Ranger threw a punch, landing a solid blow to Shane's unguarded jaw. He flew backwards to land in a heap in front of the fireplace. Shane scrambled to his feet and Ranger shoved Amy behind him. "Stay behind me."

Amy tried to sidestep, but Ranger countered her move, keeping himself between her and Shane. She pounded on his back. "Stop it Ranger. Don't do this. If you love me, you'll stop."

Amy's words were a bucket of ice water, freezing him in place. Ranger shook his head, clearing the red haze that had slid over his vision. The man standing before him was broken. His friend. His narrowed chest rising and falling with the force of his heavy breathing. Fists clenched at his sides.

"You come into my house, screw my wife and have the nerve to punch me?"

Ranger backed up a step, unease trickled down his spine. He herded Amy behind him as Shane advanced. "Amy, get out of here, now."

"I'm not going anywhere." She dodged his heels, not giving an inch.

Shane threw a punch and Ranger took it, staggering back a step, unable to defend himself without risking hurting her.

"Amy, for the love of God, get out of here."

Ranger lifted his fists in front of his face, elbows down, shielding his body. He felt her move back, chanced a quick look over his shoulder to see her edge to the side. Not out of the room, but out of the way.

Ranger refocused on his friend. "Shane, stop. I don't want to fight you. I shouldn't have done that."

Shane kicked the coffee table over out of the way and advanced, as if he hadn't heard a word Ranger had said. The man advancing on him wasn't his best friend. He was hard. Wild. Unpredictable.

"Brother, listen..."

Shane leapt forward, threw a punch. Ranger ducked down and came up with an upper cut to Shane's stomach. He doubled over at the waist and then fell to his knees, gasping for air. Ranger quickly stepped back, keeping on his toes, fists up. Ready for the next attack.

Amy ran past him, her dark red hair flying behind her and knelt on the ground next to Shane. She touched his shoulder and looked up at Ranger, her face flushed. "Please stop this now."

Tears continued to stream down her face and Ranger lowered his fists, remorse settled heavy on his shoulders. He wanted to defend himself, tell her he tried not to fight. He had more control than this. He was acting like a lovesick, horny teenager, fighting with his best friend over a girl.

But not just any girl, Amy was his girl. They were meant to be together. He knew that with the certainty the sun would rise in the morning. He also knew with a certainty he couldn't go on living without her.

"Get out." Shane rose on his knees, his voice harsh with finality.

Ranger lifted his chin and looked at Amy. He'd made her a promise. He wouldn't leave her unless she asked him to go.

Her gaze wavered with indecision. "Ranger." She took a breath. "Maybe you should go."

It was as if a 50-caliber bullet lodged in his chest. He took an involuntary step back.

"I'm not leaving here alone." Shane might have been a friend since childhood, but Ranger knew somewhere down deep inside that something fundamental inside him had changed.

Amy rose and tucked her hair behind her ears, her eyes still moist from crying. She walked toward him, and he reached for her. Rubbing a thumb over her soft cheek. "I can't leave you. Not until I know you're safe."

Amy grabbed his hand and kissed his palm. He felt it all the way to his heart.

"We will sort this out." She glanced over her shoulder as Shane got to his feet. "But I think it would be better if you left. At least until everyone calms down some."

"I won't fight anymore, I promise, but I can't leave you here with him." Not when his eyes were edged with madness.

As if summoned from hell, Shane spoke from behind her, "I'm her husband. This is our house. The only one who doesn't belong here is you."

Ranger kept his gaze locked on Amy, hoping she would say something different. Pleading with his eyes. She bit her plump lower lip and took a small step back.

"Amy, he started cheating on you before the deployment. He betrayed you. Betrayed us both." The affair with Ranger's sister was a blow not likely to ease anytime soon. Regardless of that fact, he had to make Amy see. Had to make her realize her husband wasn't the man either of them thought.

"Ranger…"

Shane placed his hand on Amy's shoulder.

He had to try one more time. "Please Amy, you don't know this man anymore. Come with me."

"I promise I will call you in a little while. Please try to understand. Just give us some time to talk."

The pain was too much. The .50 cal in his chest exploded. His body went numb. He remained standing, but he was empty. Dead.

"You heard her, she asked you to leave," Shane said.

"If you hurt her you son of a bitch, I'll put you right back in the hole you crawled out of. Only this time, you won't come back from the dead."

Chapter Thirty-three

Amy watched Ranger walk to the door, trying to distance herself from her ground up emotions. She stood on the threshold of something momentous. A decision that could alter her. Alter the two men now in her life.

Shane's hand on her shoulder felt...heavy. Not right. *What are you doing?*

Was she really going to stand there and watch the man she loved walk out of her life? Sacrifice her heart for a promise made to someone that had been dead to her for so long? Someone who had clearly not honored their marriage vows?

Shane had not only disappeared, he'd screwed her. And he'd screwed Ranger.

Shane's grip tightened and she flinched. She'd asked the wrong man to leave. Ranger grabbed the door handle. No.

Amy tore from her husband and ran after Ranger, ready to scream out his name. He yanked the front door open and turned back for one last look. His face glazed with pain. Her heart broke straight down the middle. She was the reason for his pain. And she was wrong. "Ranger-"

A bright light flashed. Then another. And other. "Get in there girl, I told you. Told you she was a slut. We're going to get this on the news."

Ranger slammed to a stop and Amy rammed into his back. She peered around Ranger, knowing who stood there before she actually saw her. Mavis Carter stood beside her niece, the evil little witch Darla.

A white van with the logo, *Channel 11 News* sat parked in her drive. Darla was an intern at the local news station. Obviously, she hoped to get the position of news anchor with this stunt.

"Get in there closer, girl. He doesn't have a shirt on. They've obviously been cavorting in sin. You got your headline. Army spouse cheats on veteran with his friend. Think of the headlines it'll make." Mavis practically salivated. Her whole countenance had turned from mean to maniacal. She lifted her chin, the double-roll beneath quivering from the movement. "See girl. I told you I'd make you regret this."

"Mavis, I warned you." Ranger's fists clenched. His muscles pulled tight. Amy wanted to comfort him and tell him she didn't care. They could take all the pictures they wanted. She loved him. She loved Ranger.

She didn't care if the entire country knew.

"You get that, Darla? He threatened me. I think that's a lawsuit right there"

A vehicle turned down her drive. Amy recognized the truck and groaned. Cord Carter. Great the entire Carter family here to punish her. Cord parked and jumped out of his truck. He approached, his red hair and green eyes so much like Shane's it was eerie. He had the look of pure menace etched on his features. But his gaze was not locked on Amy. It was locked on Mavis Carter.

"Dammit, Mavis, what the hell are you doing? Have you lost your mind?" Cord bit out and then turned to Amy, his expression softened. "I overheard Rand talking to his brother about what she planned. I'm sorry I didn't get here sooner. But don't worry I'll take care of this."

A few shades of relief washed over Amy, but her reality stonewalled it. There was a much bigger shock waiting. Like life changer shock.

Then she felt him. Shane stood right behind her. She closed her eyes, heavy with dread.

"Mother?"

Mavis froze. Her eyes bulged and the blood drained from her face. For once Mavis was speechless.

"Jesus, Steve get your ass over here. Get the camera rolling." An overweight man lugged a huge camera from the van and came running. Darla pulled a microphone from her purse and shoved it in their faces. "Shane Carter, back from the dead. An honored veteran, purple heart recipient, thought dead for this past year. Where have you been Shane? How did you get home?"

Mavis's entire body wobbled. She took a hesitant step forward, but the now eager Darla blocked her path. "The world wants to know where you've been. Was this all some sort of hoax to garner sympathy?"

Amy gasped. "How dare you?"

Ranger took a menacing step and snatched the mic from her hand. He pulled back and threw it across the yard. "Leech."

"Shane? Is it really you?" Mavis's whisper thin voice broke through the chaos. She moved forward and again Darla blocked her path.

The next sound they heard was Darla's squeal. Mavis grabbed a handful of the girl's bun and yanked her backward, shoving her to the ground. A now red-faced Mavis turned her attention back to her son. She moved forward as if in a trance and Amy side stepped, bumping into Ranger. They were all crowded on her small front porch, except for Darla who now lay on the ground.

Shane stiffened as Mavis reached a hand towards him. "Is it really you?"

Shane grabbed her wrist and twisted "What are you doing here?"

"Honey, I..."

"You were trying to shame my wife on TV? How do you think that makes me look?"

"But, but, you saw. She's a whore. She doesn't deserve you or your name. I've been trying to tell you that all along."

"My wife. My name. Mine. You do this and you ruin

MY name." Shane's grip tightened and Mavis cried out.

"Honey, please. I'm your mother. You're hurting me."

Shane bared his teeth, lips pulled back. "Get off my property."

"But, I love you. I was trying to show everyone who she really is. A slut." Even frantic and in pain, Mavis managed to land another blow.

Amy tried to back away from them, but bumped into Ranger. He put his hand on her arm and steadied her. "Do you want me to take care of her?"

Shane's attention ripped to Ranger. "This is my property. My wife. My fucking mother. I will take care of it."

Mavis managed a smug look just before Shane flung her backwards to land on top of a still stunned Darla. Amy stared at her husband in shock. She'd never seen him this violent.

Cord stood right behind the two women on the ground, arms crossed, watching the drama. He looked relaxed enough, but Amy got the feeling he was ready to spring if necessary.

"You have shamed me. Get out of here. Now." Shane strode to the edge of the porch, glaring down at the two women.

Darla pushed and pushed, but couldn't budge Mavis. Amy didn't make a move to help. She wanted both of them to suffer. And she couldn't manage to tear herself from Ranger's touch. He'd begun caressing her arm with his thumb, rubbing soothing strokes. She wanted to close her eyes and let the rest of the world disappear. Just she and Ranger. Just them. Alone.

She'd fought her feelings long and hard. Now that she'd let them out, she knew she would never be able to put them back in. She needed Ranger.

She loved him.

And she would find a way.

Cord grabbed the women, lifting each of them up by the arm. "I'll take out the trash."

Amy offered him a small smile, glad for his presence.

Steve, the cameraman, snapped a few more shots and scrambled after them. Darla hopped into the driver side of her news van and Mavis in the passenger seat. Cord shut the door on her. She stared out the window, her gaze filled with longing.

Shane ignored his mother and faced Amy and Ranger. "You can say goodbye. I'll wait inside. But Amy, I won't wait long."

Shane didn't give her a chance to respond. He strode in through the front door and shut it behind him.

Ranger yanked her into his arms and she went to him, needing to feel him surrounding her. Amy buried her nose in his chest and inhaled deep and long, trying to memorize his scent. How his hard muscles felt beneath her cheek. So strong. Her support. Her love.

"I love you, Amy. Come with me. We can sort this out together." Ranger's fingers combed through her hair. She wanted to go with him so bad. More than anything. But Amy knew, if she wanted any hope of harmony with Shane in the future, she couldn't leave now. Shane would never forgive her, despite his own infidelity. He was Chloe's father. He had a right to know about her and be a part of her life. Even if they were divorced, Amy needed to maintain a peaceful relationship with Shane.

"I love you, too." Amy buried her face against him. He had to go. Please don't leave.

"Come with me. Please." Ranger's voice was ragged. And it was her fault. Can't help it.

She took a breath and stepped back. Ranger followed, holding her. "I can't. Not until I tell Shane about Chloe. He has a right to know."

"You can. Give him some time to assimilate. Think of how much shock he has to be in. We can all sit down and work it out later. Together." Ranger cupped her face between his hands.

Tears pricked her eyes. Ranger's sincerity tugging forth her emotions with the ease of a small southern breeze. "I can't leave him like this. Not now. You saw him." Shane had appeared...broken. And she was still technically his wife.

"Yes, I saw him. He's not the same man he used to be. I don't want to, but I'm getting this bad feeling about him."

She did too. "I have to talk to him. He doesn't even know he's a father. He doesn't deserve to hear about Chloe from someone else."

Ranger clenched his teeth, his jaw ticking and she could literally feel the tension rolling off him. But his hands remained gentle on her face. "Do you think it's a good idea to tell him about her right now? If he's been held prisoner for all this time and tortured, that might push him over the edge."

Amy shook her head. Shane might never forgive her for Ranger, but he would love his daughter. He would. She knew it. "Or it may be what pulls him back home."

Ranger closed his eyes and she couldn't help but reach up and caress him. Trace his blond brows, skim his cheeks and square jaw. This man was hers. But she had to take care of her husband and family first. "Ranger, I'm not asking you to leave forever. I am asking you to leave for now. Give us some time."

His eyes opened and Amy's stomach clenched at the hardness there. A hardness that had never been there before today. His hands dropped from her and her heart followed them down. "I can't ask you to choose between us."

He stepped back. She followed. "I'm not choosing. I've made my choice. I chose you."

"Amy." Shane spoke from the door, his tone not asking. Amy looked back.

She was between her husband and her lover. The magic carpet ride to happily ever after slid from beneath her feet. "Just a minute."

Amy turned back to Ranger, intending to finish her sentence, but he wasn't looking at her any more. He was staring at Shane, or through him. She couldn't tell. All she could see was his misery.

"You've had long enough," Shane said.

"Ranger, I love you."

"You damn well better call me in one hour. If I don't

hear from you, I'm coming back and I'm taking you with me. Whether you want to go or not."

Chapter Thirty-four

Amy stared at the door in shock, not knowing what to do. What to say. Unsure of herself without Ranger by her side. Alone with her husband. *Shouldn't she be elated?*

She wrapped her arms around her middle and turned back to Shane. He looked terrible. His cheeks carved in sharply beneath his cheekbones, leaving his face gaunt. Almost skeletal. Dark purple shadows smudged beneath sunken eyes. His normally clean-cut hair and smooth face a menagerie of long uneven hanks.

The house suddenly felt cavernous and empty.

Shane was home. After all this time of wondering and worrying about him. The self-condemnation over their fight and his death. She'd moved past her guilt and allowed herself to love, really love, and like a scythe Shane appeared from the grave, severing her tender new feelings.

She should be happy, crying tears of joy after his return, but all she felt was a malignant knot of despair. Amy forced her mind from those thoughts, knowing she needed time to sort it all out. Think about him. About Chloe. Oh Christ, if he'd been shocked about Ranger, she was about to blow his freaking shoes off.

"Shane-"

"You filthy whore. I'm out risking my life. Held hostage, tortured, starved, and what are you doing?" Shane's upper lip curled, a bulldog ready to bite. "Did you even wait for them to put the coffin in the ground before you started fucking him?"

Her heart tha-thunked at his deadly accurate bombs of guilt. Targeting her conscious with precision. The effect was like a percussion grenade had gone off in her body. Amy jerked. Unable to contain the physical reaction of his accusations. "Whore? You were screwing Hayden, a damn teenager, while you were home! At least I never cheated on you. I didn't get with Ranger until long after I saw the DNA evidence that you were dead."

Shane emitted a wild and animalistic snarl that sent her pulse skittering. He looked at her like a starved rabid wolf who'd spotted a wounded doe. And just like a predator, he advanced, pushing her bodily against the wall and pinning her there with an arm at her throat.

She choked, barely able to breathe beneath the painful pressure. Shane lifted his free hand, his spit splattered on her face when he spoke. "You mean this DNA evidence? The evidence they sent using a pair of dull wire cutters?"

Amy stared at the missing pinky and ring fingers on Shane's left hand and in their place a jagged scar. Nausea erupted on the tail of horror at his torture. "Oh, my God. What did they do to you?"

Shane leaned in, his face not even an inch from hers. "I don't think you really care what they did. Not since you've been so busy spreading your legs. I won't be able to walk through the streets of my own home town now that you have defiled my name."

Shane threw her across the room and she landed in the middle of the living room on her hands and knees. Her shoulder slammed into the overturned coffee table. Pain shot up her legs and arms. She lay there, stunned at his violence.

Who was this man?

He advanced and she scrambled away on all fours, unable to get her feet under her. The couch could provide an obstacle between them. It wouldn't keep her safe, but it would give her precious seconds. The foreboding she'd felt, the intuition something was wrong, came rolling in fast.

Shane wasn't just mad. He was unstable.

She'd hoped to talk to him, explain her feelings. Introduce him to his daughter. But this wasn't Shane resurrected like he was before. He'd come back…wrong.

She heard his heavy footsteps and practically stumbled behind the couch, jumped to her feet and held on to the piece of furniture for support and armor. Shane's shoulders heaved, his shirt hanging loose on his body.

"You're going to pay for betraying me. And then when I'm done with you, I'll finish him." Shane dove over the couch and Amy screamed. She ran blind, trying to get away. She should have listened to Ranger.

Shane grabbed her hair and ripped her back. She clutched her scalp, the burning pain, but he just pulled harder. Winding her hair around his fist until she was forced next to him, her head yanked backwards. "Shane, you're hurting me."

"You have no idea what pain is." He jerked her down to her knees. "You have no idea what it feels like to watch someone cut your fingers off while you beg for them to stop."

His slap caught her unprepared. Stinging pain radiated across her face and the taste of blood filled her mouth.

"You have no idea what it's like to go with no food for so long you forget what things taste like. Locked in a hole. You forget your own name."

Amy braced for another blow, but it didn't come. Shane seemed to shake himself. "No one survives that." He looked down at her again, this time his eyes weren't full of hate. They were empty.

"Shane. Please stop." Amy trembled, knowing deep down the blank look was far worse than the anger.

"Don't call me that. Never again. Shane is dead."

"What? I thought you were dead, but you're not. You're right here." He was crazy. Ranger had been right. She had to escape. Now. If she could distract him, maybe, somehow, she could run. Get to her truck.

Shane started walking, dragging her by the hair across

the floor. She tried to get up from her knees but he kept going. Her scalp was on fire. "Shane, stop!"

Amy did her best to catch up with him, but she was no match for his speed or power. His smaller size had done nothing to diminish his strength. "I am no longer Shane. I am Abdullah Asad Nassar. And you are an adulterer who must be punished."

He wasn't wrong. He wasn't broken. He was insane.

Amy screamed again but it didn't affect him in the least. He continued dragging her through the living room and when she realized his destination, their bedroom, dread filled her stomach. What kind of punishment did he intend? "Please, you can't do this. I'm your wife."

She kicked, scrambled, anything to get a foothold and rise, but he already crossed the threshold into their bedroom. He threw her near the foot of the bed. Her shoulder hit the hardwood floor, her skull cracked against the bedpost. Agony exploded through her head. Dazed, she lay there, unable to make her body work. The room seemed to flicker dark then light. Amy groaned and rolled onto her back.

Not her husband.

Shane squatted beside her and gently brushed her hair from her face. She longed to turn away from him, but her head hurt too much.

"You are my wife. But you are a sinner who must be punished and when I'm sure you have been cleansed, then we can start anew. In my new home." Shane spoke to her calm and collected, as if he hadn't just thrown her around like a rag doll.

"This is my home." Amy managed to croak out.

Shane smiled, for the first time, and she cringed. "No. Your home is with your husband. You will return with me to my true country."

"You're insane." There would be no reasoning with him. No anything.

His crazed smile disappeared and was quickly replaced with an impenetrable mask. "You will not speak to me this way."

He slapped her again. "You will realize that as a woman you must bow to your husband. You cannot help but do so. I know it is different than you are used to, but I will teach you."

She licked the trickle of blood from the corner of her mouth. "Screw you."

"You will, wife. You will."

Shane stood and she had the brief thought that maybe she was the insane one. She watched, transfixed as he pulled a booted foot back. Time seemed to slow. Her heart pounded hard and she clenched her muscles tight. His foot flew forward and buried in her side. Agony unlike any she'd felt before exploded through her ribs.

She couldn't breathe. Couldn't move. Couldn't do anything but ball up on the floor and fight for breath.

Shane knelt at her side again, sweeping the backs of his fingers across her cheek. "This is Allah's will. We must obey Him. My master taught me the true path to righteousness is through pain, and so, as your master, I shall teach you."

Chapter Thirty-five

"Dammit!" Ranger slammed into his brother's house, ready to destroy anything in sight.

"Come on, tell me how you really feel." Hunter appeared in the kitchen, his stance relaxed.

"I'll fucking tell you. Shane Carter. Is. Alive."

Hunter's relaxed pose disappeared. "What?"

"I can't fucking believe it. I just can't believe it." Ranger paced to the refrigerator, grabbed a beer and downed the whole thing. He silently prayed the day would rewind, and he would wake up, surrounded by Amy's soft scent.

"You wanna run that one by me again? 'Cause I swear you said Shane was alive."

"You heard me. I woke up this morning in his bed. Naked with his fucking wife." Ranger threw the empty beer bottle, watching with no satisfaction as the glass shattered against the kitchen wall.

Hunter got in his face and grabbed his arms. "Have you lost it? Shane Carter is dead. D.E.A.D. Dead. You saw the DNA evidence."

Ranger snorted and jerked away, immediately going for another beer. Maybe the alcohol could numb some of the pain. Ranger popped the top. Maybe if he drank enough he could pass out. "Apparently, our intelligent CIA isn't so intelligent. They checked the fingers alright. And they were his. Want to know how I know? Cause the fist the fucker punched me in the face with was missing two fingers."

"Jesus Christ." Hunter reached past him and grabbed a beer.

"Exactly. Amy is at home with Shane. Alone." Ranger suddenly realized how quiet the house was. "Where's Chloe and Arturo?"

"Evie took 'em over to Hank's to play. Maxine was there and wanted to see the kids."

"Good. I don't want Chloe going near Shane until I know he's okay."

"How the hell did he get here? And after all this time?" Hunter asked.

"I don't know, but something isn't right." Ranger shook his head, trying to clear the all-consuming rage from his mind so he could think straight.

"You bet your sweet ass it isn't. Why the hell aren't you at headquarters having Hoyt pull surveillance?"

Shit. *Because he'd been so wrapped up in jealousy he'd forgotten about the danger.*

"I'm going now. I'll clean the glass up later."

"Forget the glass. Get in the truck, I'm going with you."

A few minutes later, Ranger and Hunter parked in front of the pole barn that housed their current headquarters.

"No one answered their phone, I'll try again once we're inside." Hunter slapped a palm over the hand scanner and unlocked the steel entry door.

"Don't bother." Ranger stepped inside and nodded to their team.

"Dude, glad you two are here. I've been getting all kinds of traffic on Al Seriq's network. Something big is up." Hoyt spun around in his chair, putting his back to the computer screens.

"We think he's made contact somehow with Brown and has sent someone to pick up the weapons." Merc straightened from his bent over perch at the table. Multiple maps and profiles lay scattered all over its surface.

"Right. Grey is on the way from Ft. Grenada. ETA is about ten minutes," Hoyt said.

Riser, Aaron and Jared strode out of the weapons locker in the back, big black duffle bags in each of their hands. Jared said, "Just in time for the gun show, boys. Looks like Brown's gonna have to move the weapons and when he does…"

"I'll be there with my M32," Riser finished.

"You're gonna bring a grenade launcher?" Aaron asked.

"Shit yeah, bro. Been waiting over a year to use this baby." Riser lifted the M32 grenade launcher from the duffle bag, and held it in the upright position, nozzle pointed at the ceiling.

"Put it away. That thing has a kill radius of ten yards." Jared backed up a step, putting himself behind Riser and the huge weapon.

"Don't worry, I'm saving the rounds for my favorite sheriff."

"Wait, Hoyt, show me what video you've got of the movement at Al Seriq's camp." Ranger strode up to Hoyt's computer center. It looked like a miniaturized version of NASA.

"How far back?"

"Give me footage from eight months ago."

Hoyt cast him a quizzical look but did as Ranger asked. "Hunter, come here."

Ranger leaned over Hoyt's shoulder, studying the images. Most were taken from a distance. A few of Al Seriq talking to different men already known to be in his command. Hoyt started scrolling forward. "There wasn't much from this time frame."

"Stop," Ranger commanded. "Right there." He pointed at the last monitor. A grainy photo of Al Seriq, standing on a concrete balcony overlooking his court yard. Multiple combatants trained below, but it was the man standing next to Seriq that held Ranger's interest. "Who is that?"

Hoyt clicked and zoomed in. "Can't tell, he's covered

too much for our facial recognition to get a good read."

Dammit. "Okay, keep going."

There were too many coincidences to discount. Ranger fully expected to see something, anything.

"Wanna tell me who exactly you're looking for? If it's Mr. J, don't waste your time. I already ran every possible image against his and came up empty. If he is still alive, and that is a big fucking if, he ain't showing up near Seriq or his followers."

"Not Mr. J."

Hoyt crossed his arms and turned to Ranger. "I'm not budging until you tell me who."

Ranger squeezed the table, crushing it under the force of his grip. *The man threatening my woman.*

"Shane."

All eyes turned to Hunter.

Ranger stood, shoved a hand through his hair and sighed. "He's alive. He showed up this morning."

"What?"

"Where? How?"

"At his house," Ranger said.

"Were you there?" Aaron asked.

"I was in bed with Amy." Ranger dropped the info and waited for the atomic bomb to explode.

"Holy shit, dude," Hoyt said.

"Are you sure it was him?" Merc stepped forward and the rest fell silent, all eyes turning on Ranger.

"Yes, I'm as certain as the black eye he gave me."

Jared let out a whistle. "Talk about a cluster fuck."

Ranger resisted the urge to scream and instead said, "We had been together, the night before, when I woke up he was just sitting at the foot of the bed. Staring at me."

The moment replayed over and over in Ranger's mind, the worst movie he'd ever had the misfortune to see. That sinking sensation that the world he'd come to know with Amy was over.

"What did you do?" Hoyt asked.

"I tried to keep it together. For her. But I kept getting

this bad vibe from Shane. Something was way off."

The door slid open and the whole group turned to see Grey stride in. A call sound trilled from Hoyt's computer. Gray kept striding forward and said, "Answer it."

Hoyt spun around, clicked some keys and took the video call on the back wall of monitors for the whole team to see. Grey strode to the meeting table in the middle of the room and hit the speaker in the center. "Go ahead."

Mr. K, Team Scorpion's new handler appeared on the screens. His normally expressionless face was haggard. "Hoyt, I just had my man send you the intel. Pull it up so you can all see it."

"What is going on?" Grey demanded and crossed his arms.

"You won't believe me until I show you the picture. Hell, I didn't believe it myself until our cyber forensics team confirmed it."

A huge ball of dread formed in the pit of Ranger's stomach. Somehow, he knew. He knew before the picture even appeared on the screen. Too many coincidences. Too many surprises. "Fucking hell."

No one paid him any attention. All gazes were riveted on the blown up black and white surveillance image of a man in an airport. The image was grainy and way less than high definition, but the man was as clear as a cloudless sky.

"No way," Riser said.

"Meet Seriq's newest right hand man. Abdullah Asad Nassar, otherwise known as, Shane Carter." Mr. K's voice came over the comm and the room fell silent. "We lost track of him after that, but I know he's in the U.S. I need your team to find him."

"Already done. I know exactly where he is." Ranger felt every single nerve fire. He'd been so wrong to leave Amy alone with him. With her husband. A terrorist.

"How?" Mr. K asked.

"I saw him this morning."

"When the hell were you going to inform me?" Grey turned stunned eyes on Ranger.

"Now. That is why I'm here. He came to his house. I knew something was off, so I came here, looking for answers."

"Well you've damn well got them. You need to move. Now. He's more than likely been tortured and turned. And if that is true, anyone close to him is in danger," Mr. K said.

"Amy," Ranger breathed her name out.

His pulse skyrocketed. He'd fucking left her with a psycho.

"Easy, bro. We know where he is. We know exactly who is with him. How much easier can it get?" Hunter pulled Ranger's attention from his self-recrimination.

"If anything happens to her." Ranger couldn't finish the sentence. The thought was too painful.

"I know. That's why we go in together, and we go in prepared. He won't be expecting an assault this early."

"My team here has been tracking all footage from your area. Heat signals. Nuclear. Anything we can find. If our estimates are correct, you better find Shane soon, cause if Brown has what we think he has, this isn't just a shipment of automatic rifles," Mr. K said. Another image replaced that of Shane, Abdullah, walking into the airport. This image was taken from a satellite. There were five very large, very obvious heat signatures.

"We randomly stumbled on this around the time Marcus Carvant was killed. He'd kept it at your local paper mill, hidden in with the barges."

Ranger stepped closer to the screens. "What is it?"

"Long range missiles, capable of taking out an entire city. And capable of reaching the U.S. from another country."

"Son of a bitch." Ranger couldn't believe it. No way. This whole time, they'd been under the inclination that Marcus and Brown had guns. But not bombs.

"I don't need to tell you what will happen if Seriq gets his hands on these," Mr. K said.

"No, sir. We will recover the weapons, and we will recover Shane Carter." Grey turned to face the team. Each man there nodded his agreement.

"Do whatever it takes to keep these bombs out of their hands." Mr. K signed off. The bank of screens on the back wall flashed, the bomb signatures seemed to glow.

"You heard him. Gear up, get the fuck out of here and get me those damn weapons." Grey walked over to the table and rifled through the papers.

"Right, I think Ranger should take lead," Hunter said.

"I agree, he knows the lay out of the house better than any of us. He knows Shane the best. And Amy." Merc pulled a black duffle over his shoulder.

"Okay, me and Ranger in the lead. We can take my truck. It's quiet. Ya'll follow in the SUV."

"Roger."

Hunter made to stride past him, but Ranger threw out an arm, stopping his brother in his tracks. "Amy."

Hunter placed a hand over Ranger's. "Don't worry. We'll all do our best to keep her safe. The traitor is who we are after."

The traitor, Ranger's best friend.

And the bombs.

Chapter Thirty-six

Cold. The floor was cold and hard and digging into her back. Her body felt like a hollow shell of throbbing agony. Amy cracked open one eye, holding as still as possible in case he was still in the room. The lamp cast a glow over her body, but offered no warmth in the otherwise empty room.

Amy tilted her head back, and saw the night sky through her window. A scraping sound from her closet drew her attention. Shane. Where was he? She stiffened and the small movement sent burning pain through her ribs.

She forced herself to still and take stock. She gingerly moved her feet and legs first. She moved her arms and felt a twinge of pain in her right shoulder. The shoulder that had taken the brunt of her fall. Careful to keep that side still, she lifted her left hand to her face and cringed. Her eye was swollen shut and dried blood was on her chin. Those were pains she could recover from. But the constant grueling pain in her side was the worst. Every breath, every movement sent a fresh wave of agony shooting through her.

Shane had always had a quick temper. She'd watched him go into a full blown rampage over things she would have considered inconsequential. But he'd never gotten violent. Ever. That first blow had shocked her to her core.

Some innocent part of her had honestly believed he would never hurt her. But she hadn't realized who she'd been facing. Not Shane. He'd called himself Abdullah.

He might have been held captive at first, but it was glaringly obvious the man went to the other side. What side that was she didn't know, but his mind was as warped and twisted as his hand.

If he really thought of himself as Abdullah, why come home? Why not start a new life in his new country?

Why ruin hers?

She closed her eyes again, the effort to keep her lids raised drained too much energy. The air conditioner kicked on. Everything around her looked and felt normal. Everything but Shane.

She heard him curse, and then a loud crash, and realized he was in the master closet through the bathroom. A scraping sound followed the crash, and then another and another after that. He was going through her drawers.

This was her chance. If she could get up from the floor she could make a run for it. Amy planted one hand on the polished hardwood and wrapped the other around her ribs. Inch by inch, she rose from the floor. A wave of dizziness assailed her and she grabbed the bed post for support

She had to fight through the haze. She had to call Ranger. Warn him. Make sure Evie kept the kids safe. Amy focused on putting one foot in front of the other. After a few seconds, she chanced a look over her shoulder. Shane was still in the closet.

Her phone was in her purse, she remembered that much, but where had she left it? The answer came in a flash. She'd left it on top of the dryer in the laundry room. All she had to do was cross through the living room and kitchen to get to it. A feat that she'd done a million times before, only now she had to do it without her husband killing her.

Focus, Amy. Think of the kids. Of Ranger.

Amy took a small steadying breath and began her journey. She had to stop halfway and hold onto the doorframe. Her side screamed with every step, every breath. Her mind fogged. Nausea rolled in her stomach. *Keep going.*

Amy made it through the living room. She got to the kitchen table and held there, mapping out the rest of the way.

If she could get to the island, she could use it to help along. She took another step forward, blacked out a second, and then grabbed the counter with her free hand. She twisted and barely kept herself from falling. Agony exploded from her ribs, wrapping around her torso. Lights flickered around her periphery and the room grew fuzzy.

She fought through the pull of unconsciousness. The laundry. Just get to the laundry. The next few steps felt like miles.

Amy kept moving. Kept going forward. Then she was standing in the laundry room and her purse was laying right where she'd left it. She stumbled forward, dug in her purse and came up with her cell. She hit the first number that popped up.

"Evie, is that you?"

"Amy? What's wrong?" Evie answered.

Relief hit her so hard she almost crumbled. "No time. Shane's alive. He came back. He-He's not right. You have to keep the kids there. Keep them safe."

"What are you talking about? Shane's been gone for a long time, honey. Where is Ranger? I thought he was with you?"

The sound of Ranger's name brought a wave of tears to her, but Amy forced it back. "No. Shane came home. He's here right now. But he's crazy. Mental. Keeps calling himself Abdullah something."

"Oh, my God, you're serious."

"Listen, you have to keep my kids safe, okay? Do not let him near Chloe. No matter what. He wants to take me back overseas. If he finds out about her, he will take her too." Her voice broke on a sob she couldn't hold in, and Amy slapped a hand over her mouth.

"Is he with you now? Did he hurt you?" Evie's voice took on a frantic edge.

"Yes. Yes. Please, find Ranger. Tell him he needs to be careful. Shane will kill him." Amy kept her voice as quiet as possible and glanced over her shoulder.

"I will. What about you?"

"I'll figure something out. Just keep Chloe safe."

"Who is Chloe?"

Amy gasped and spun around. Shane stood in the doorway, blocking her only exit. She wouldn't survive him alone. She needed help. She needed Ranger.

"I have to go now. Just do what I said." She forced her voice to stay calm.

"Give me the phone." Shane held out his hand.

"Amy, hold on. Don't hang up." Evie's voice was frantic, but Amy was focused on the stranger in her house.

"I'll talk to you later."

Amy hung up. Shane walked forward, shirtless now, his hand held out. Amy bit her lip, knowing she would be handing over her only communication with the outside.

"Now." Shane commanded, whiplashing her back to reality.

She could try to fight him, caged in this tiny room and barely able to breath from the pain, or she could cooperate. Maybe lull him into believing he had her beat. Amy ducked her head and held out the phone.

He swiped it from her palm and she peeked up to see him slide it into his pocket. Without his shirt, she could see every single sinew of muscle. He was lean, but she knew from experience, incredibly strong.

"What are you going to do?" She held her breath, waiting on his answer. Or the next blow.

"You mean, we. What are we going to do." Shane backed her into the dryer, her side hit the corner and she cried out. Shane's gaze dropped to where she clutched her side. He reached out and moved her hand away. Amy sucked in a breath. Shane lifted her shirt and tsked. "You'll have to learn to listen to your husband. I do not like seeing you in such pain."

Amy chanced a glance down and immediately wished she hadn't. Her side was one large black and purple bruise.

"I will tend to your injury, then we're going to talk. You have something to tell me." Shane didn't wait for her response, and she honestly didn't know what to say. He lifted her into his arms and cradled her against his chest. Every movement hurt. Shane had carried her like this before, when they'd gotten married. She'd thought him so romantic.

Now her skin crawled with revulsion.

Breathe. Just breathe. She had to stay calm. Diffuse the situation. But when they walked past the kitchen counter, her hand gravitated toward the meat tenderizer hanging on the wall. The old timey kitchen utensil was shaped like a mallet and heavier than a hammer.

"Where is my box from overseas?"

Shane's question startled her from her plan for a moment. She sure as heck couldn't tell him the truth. She'd trashed the box and burned the letters. The only thing she'd kept had been the picture frames. She figured one day, when she'd moved past his betrayal, she might give them to Chloe. "In the U-Store-It in town. After the news of your death, I couldn't handle having it in the house."

His arms tightened around her momentarily. "We'll go there after I tend to you."

Amy nodded and squeezed the tenderizer behind his back.

"Are you ready to tell me about Chloe?"

Her throat closed off. No. She would never tell him about his daughter. He might kidnap her and disappear overseas. Force them to live like savages at his mercy in some desert dwelling. Or worse, he might decide he didn't need Amy anymore and take Chloe.

Amy clenched her teeth and forced herself to breathe past the fear. Over her dead body.

"Are you ready to tell me about Hayden." She raised the hammer high behind his head.

"She told you?"

"I found the letters. I confronted her. How could you?"

Shane shrugged. "I didn't love her. You are my wife. She was just entertainment."

"You don't care in the least? I never cheated on you. I never even touched another man." Amy trembled.

"Except Ranger." He tightened his hold and she cried

out. "Now, who is Chloe?"

"You'll never know." Amy brought the hammer down with all her strength. Shane sensed her movement at the last minute and turned his head. The tenderizer slammed into his temple.

Amy watched in horror as his eyes rolled back. Unconscious, he dropped to the floor and she followed him down. She tensed and tried to twist away from her bad side, but she was trapped in his arms. She landed directly on her injured ribs. Pain. Incredible torturous pain.

She couldn't move. Couldn't suck in a breath. Stars sprinkled across her vision.

Fight. Have to stay awake. Get to Chloe.

Somehow, Amy managed to combat the darkness. She made it to the back door.

Have to escape.

Chapter Thirty-seven

Amy clutched her side and ran to her truck. She slid into the driver side and reached for the keys. Empty. She flipped down the sun visor. Checked under the seat. On the floorboard. Her keys were gone.

Her head fell forward, and she let it rest there on the steering wheel. Shane must have taken her keys. If she took off walking down the highway, she might be able to flag down a vehicle. Or he might wake up and drive right to her.

Her phone. Stupid. Why hadn't she grabbed her phone? Amy steeled herself and slowly sat upright. She had to go back in the house. The truck door seemed to weigh a thousand pounds, so she left the door open and limped back to the house. The kitchen door stood ajar, just as she'd left it minutes before. Amy peered around the corner, Shane lay passed out on the floor, blood seeping from the wound on his head.

Her entire body shook with fear. He'd tucked her cell in his pocket. She'd have to touch him. Amy crept forward on leaden feet, each step an agonizing shot of pain and terror. Shane twitched and she froze, waiting on him to wake up, but he stayed out cold. Phone. Focus. She got down on a knee and dug in his pocket. Dang it. Wrong side. She would have to reach across him. Her skin crawled. Her heart pounded so hard she thought she might pass out.

She leaned over and dug into the other pocket, her fingertip brushed her phone. Shane moaned. *Oh Lord.* Amy forgot about being careful and shoved her hand in as deep as it would go, grabbed her phone and ripped it out of his pocket.

"Amy…" Shane's gravelly voice drew her attention. He was waking, his eyelids fluttering.

With her heart shoved up into her throat, Amy rose and ran from the house. Directly ahead of her was the old barn, a hundred yards beyond that was the hangar, with nothing but open ground between. No trees or bushes to hide behind. A soy bean field spread out to her left, a corn field to her right. Amy made a split second decision and darted right, running into the maze of fourteen foot tall corn stalks. Leaves crackled and crunched, her breaths sawed loud and heavy in and out of her chest. If she could keep a straight path through the next two fields, she'd be at her neighbor's house.

If only she weren't running perpendicular to the rows. Amy angled her body to slice between the stalks, her journey a valley of up and down over the hills of the rows.

"Amy!"

She stopped. He'd sounded like he was right behind her. Amy struggled to listen, but all she could hear was her breathing. Focus. Listen. The full moon provided too much light. He'd see her if he got close enough.

He crashed into the field and Amy took off running, unable to stand there any longer. Now she ran without thought or direction, just the need to get away. The crashing got louder, like he was gaining on her. Amy held onto her side and kept going. Huge green leaves slapped her in the face and cut her arms as she ran through the razor sharp blades. She held up her hand to protect her face. After what seemed like hours, and had to be only minutes, she chanced a look over her shoulder. Her foot caught the dirt and she tripped, slamming into the ground with enough force to paralyze her.

The pain from her ribs stole her ability to think. To breathe. So she lay there, her face in the dirt, listening as Shane's footfalls got closer and closer.

He moved slow, she knew, listening for her. Stalking her.

Amy tried to calm her racing heart, but her fight or

flight response had gone into hyper drive.

"I know you're out here. How far do you think you'll get injured like you are? Did I ever tell you what I did overseas? I led our reconnaissance for the team. They called me in to hunt down the men no one else could find." He paused and Amy held her breath.

"You have no hope of escape. If you come back now, I promise, I won't punish you for this." He was closer now. His voice growing louder. She heard his clothes rustle through the leaves. A whisper of sound, really, but if she could hear that, he was close. Too close.

The towering stalks disoriented her and she couldn't tell where he was. She let her head fall back to the dirt, a trickle of blood hit the ground, reminding her of his brutality and what he would do if he got his hands on her again.

"Come on honey, give up. You know I will find you. And I promise you won't like what happens when I do." His voice was so smooth, so sincere. Like he was talking sweet nothings.

She heard a whoosh as he brushed against the stiff cornstalks to her left.

"You can hide all you want, but I will find you." His voice changed back into the deranged monster. Amy buried herself further into the dirt, as if she could burrow and hide from his evil.

Please, please don't let him hear me.

Then she heard it.

A stalk crackled right next to her. A heavy footfall in the row beside hers.

Ever so slowly, she turned her head in the direction of the sound. A dark figure eased down the row not one foot away.

Her breathing hitched, the sound too loud. She couldn't get it under control, her heart raced. Shane was six inches away now, separated by one row of stalks.

Amy stopped. Stopped breathing. Stopped thinking. Her eyes were glued to his feet. If he turned, he would step right on top of her.

"Amy!" Shane roared and she nearly screamed in response. She bit her lips to keep from crying out.

Something crashed through the field in the distance and he took off running. Amy jumped to her feet, ignoring the stitch in her side, and ran in the opposite direction. She had no idea which way she was going, but she ran nonetheless. She ran, mindless, the corn stalks seeming to grow taller. More menacing.

She was going to die out here. She knew it.

Chloe would never know her mother.

Hell no. She wasn't giving up. Amy intended to fight for her life. She burst out of the corn field and stared in horror at her front yard. She'd come full circle from her back yard. A movement to her right drew her attention. Shane stepped from the field and disappeared behind her house.

Amy covered her face with her hands. What was she going to do? She was exhausted and her battered body couldn't move another inch, let alone run back into the field.

"You can stay in there all night long if you want. But I'll find you." Shane's voice carried across the area.

Could she make it to the highway? Maybe she'd get lucky and someone would drive by.

But before she could take a step in that direction, Shane's voice rang out again, stopping her in her tracks. "If you don't come out of that cornfield right now, I'm going to call Ranger and tell him we need to talk, all of us. I saw the way he looked at you. He's in love with you. The fool has been in love with you since high school. You know he'll come."

Amy stopped moving all together. Ranger had always loved her? Why the hell had he broke up with her all those years ago?

"Five," Shane paused.

Ranger could take Shane, she had no doubt about it, but he couldn't do anything if Shane shot him. She wouldn't survive without Ranger. He held her heart. The only future she wanted was with him and now that they'd finally found each other, she couldn't let him go.

"Four." His nonchalant tone belied his true purpose.

Could she do it? Could she surrender herself into the hands of a monster to save the man she loved?

"Three."

Would Ranger sense that something was wrong? Would you be able to escape? Thoughts raced through her mind at light speed, her blood pounding through her veins at the same rate.

"Two."

She stepped in his direction, her numb feet carrying her toward her husband. She made it to the corner of the house, just out of sight, and halted. If she took another step, it was over.

"You want to know what else I did for the military? I was a sniper. One of the best. I'll put a bullet between Ranger's eyes as soon as he turns down our driveway."

The truth of his words smashed through her like a wrecking ball. She'd survived Shane's supposed death. She wouldn't survive Rangers.

Amy stepped out of the shadow of her house. Shane stood at her back door, waiting patiently for her to come to him. His satisfied smile nearly made her turn and run, but she kept going until she stood right in front of him.

"I knew that would do the trick. The way you two looked at each other this morning was sickening."

"I love him." Amy lifted her chin. She was dead anyway.

His slap didn't surprise her this time. She touched the corner of her mouth where a fresh trickle of blood started and stood proudly before him. He could hurt her all he wanted, but Ranger would protect Chloe. And in the end, Shane would die.

"You're going to die." Amy smiled, knowing she was half-crazy for taunting him.

Shane grabbed her chin, forcing her to look at him. "No, wife. Not me."

Shane dragged her into the kitchen and pushed her into a chair. She watched him, no longer as scared as before. She was willing to die if it meant saving her family. He stopped and started every few seconds, as if his brain was shorting out and restarting.

Without a word, he grabbed her hand and pulled her behind him. She didn't try to fight this time. She followed, stooped over and holding her ribs, through her living room and down the hall. He stopped before Chloe's door.

"I was here that night. You were locked in there weren't you?"

His statement rocked her. "You? That was you that broke into the house?"

"I didn't have a key anymore." Shane answered as if that should explain why he battered down her kitchen door.

"Are you kidding me? You scared me to death. Why didn't you just knock? Or come home like a normal person - in the light of day?"

"I didn't know that you were home that night." He shrugged, like oh-freaking-well, and turned to open the nursery door.

"Why would you break into my house anyway?" She dodged his heels, sick and tired of his blithe responses.

Shane was on her in a flash, reminding her why she should learn to keep her mouth shut. "My house. Remember that."

Amy nodded, she couldn't talk. His hand squeezed her throat, strangling any attempt at speech. He held her like that, suspended on her toes. After a few seconds, Amy's bravado deserted her and she clawed at his hands. Tearing his skin beneath her nails.

He gave her a look that would make a grown man pale.

Shane used his hold to maneuver her around him, until she was in the center of the room. He forced her to her knees on Chloe's white faux fur rug, right beneath the tiny white chandelier she'd had installed after Chloe's birth.

Shane brought a picture from her hutch cabinet and held it in Amy's face. "Is this Chloe? Is she my daughter?"

Amy clawed frantically at Shane's hands. She went along willingly enough, but if he didn't let go soon, she'd lose consciousness. She tried to get a sound out, but nothing would make it past his grip.

Shane's face turned red, his green eyes glowing with insanity. When she was on the edge of passing out, he let go. Amy fell to her hands, choking and coughing, her throat a raw mass of burning fire. The picture he'd held was of Amy holding Chloe in the hospital, a few hours after her birth.

She remembered that day like it was yesterday. The torture of child birth and the sweet, sweet baby that followed. Amy had denied the epidural, thinking she should suffer through the pain as punishment for sending her husband off to war with a fight. Punishment, because, deep down she felt responsible for his death.

Not anymore.

"Screw you."

Amy braced for the next slap, ready this time, but he held back. Instead, he paced the room, doing that short-circuit thing again. Then he started talking, only it wasn't in English. Amy paled when she realized where she'd heard that before. On TV. The news show airing Shane's murder. The men standing behind him, with black hoods covering their faces. They'd been speaking in Arabic.

A new kind of terror traced down her spine.

"Shane…"

He roared, "Not Shane!"

Amy cringed back. "I'm sorry. I-forgot. Abdullah, isn't that right?"

"Yes."

What now? What to do? Could she calm him? "When you left, I tried to contact you."

Shane's nostrils flared. He clutched the picture in his hand. The glass crinkled and cracked and he didn't notice. "Um, your hand." Amy pointed as blood dripped down onto the pure white carpet.

Shane followed her finger, staring at his hand as if he didn't recognize it. Amy approached, on her knees, and gently extracted the photo, laying it to the side. "You're bleeding. I should clean your wound."

Please, please she wanted out of this room.

"I have a child?"

Amy stared at him. His voice had been almost reverent. The wild look dissipating. Was her husband returning? "Yes."

Shane fell to his knees before her. "I didn't know."

"I tried to call, but you'd gone black. I had no way to tell you. I kept waiting on you to contact me." Could she coax him back to normal? Make him realize he'd been brainwashed by the enemy?

"We fought." Shane spoke slowly, like an amnesiac starting to recall his past.

"Yes. We fought. You left on deployment. I found out I was pregnant soon after." A little lie. She'd known before, but had withheld the info after their argument. She didn't want to tell him her joyous news in such a bad situation. A fact she'd regretted-until now.

"The team. Al Seriq. The compound. We went in after Mr. J." Shane stared past her shoulder.

"Who is Mr. J?"

"He was dead. Or I thought he was dead. I was shot, taken hostage. They left me behind."

"What are you saying, honey?" Amy kept her voice soothing and calm, fearing any sudden sound or movement might set off the bomb that was Shane Abdullah Carter, and she might not be able to diffuse him again.

"Al Seriq. We went after him. To capture him for the government. But I didn't make it out."

"Where were you? Did he take you?" She had to know what happened to him. What had kept him from his family so long, and why he'd come back with a new identity.

"He did. He nursed me back to health. He showed me the true way. The path to Allah."

"Allah? Shane-"

He grabbed her throat so fast she couldn't finish the sentence. "Abdullah."

Amy gave a hysterical nod and he let go. "I'm sorry. Abdullah. You have to understand, I have always known you as your previous name."

"Not allowed to say that word. He'll punish me." Shane's words became distant, almost childlike, and Amy realized this Al Seriq had done a number on her husband's mind.

"I'm sorry I interrupted you. If Al Seriq nursed you back to health, what happened to your hand?"

"He needed it." His sentences were becoming shorter now, and she had the feeling she was losing him.

"For what?"

"For our true purpose. To destroy the infidel."

Amy let go of his bleeding hand and fell back on the rug. "Infidel?"

Only terrorists spoke that way.

Shane kept staring at the same spot on the wall behind her.

Amy started to crawl backwards, restricting her movements so she didn't alert him. Shane had gone somewhere else. Somewhere she never, ever, wanted to visit.

A phone trilled from his pocket, the shrill sound making them both jerk. Amy's bottom hit the floor and her heart bounced up in her chest. Shane answered immediately, but his face was pale and his expression shaken. "As-salam alaykom."

Amy inched back another degree. She had to get the hell out of here. She might have reasoned with Shane Carter. Abdullah what-the-hell-ever was another matter entirely. He had no connection to her. No marriage. No memories. No life.

And if Amy stayed, she'd have none either.

"Ana faahim. I understand." Shane wasn't staring at the wall anymore, but he wasn't looking at her either. Whoever was on the phone had his full attention.

She kept inching back, denying the urge to scramble to her feet and run. She was willing to sacrifice her life, but not willing to be kidnapped and taken to Afghanistan. The thought sent her heart skittering. Women over there had no rights. They weren't allowed to even show their face. Completely at her husband's mercy. Never to see Chloe again.

Not her. No way. Amy turned onto her knees and jumped to her feet. Shane's hand wrapped around her ankle and she hit the ground. Her ribcage screamed in protest, paralyzing her with pain. Shane rolled her onto her back. "Such a liar."

Amy cringed away, but he pinned her down.

"Where is my box? I know you didn't leave it to rot in some storage unit." Shane pulled a knife from his pocket with is bleeding hand and held it at her cheek. "It's time you started telling the truth."

Amy swallowed. What was it with his box? He had something in there, something she must have missed. Could it have been some kind of secret code on the letters? Would he kill her when she told him the truth? "I-I really don't have your box anymore. I threw it away when I found out about Hayden."

"You threw it away? Everything?" His scream made her ears ring and she turned her head to try and avoid the spit flying from his lips. Amy felt the first sting of the knife pressing into her flesh.

"No. Not everything." He stopped, but a trickle of blood dripped down her cheek and into her hair.

"What then?" He pressed deep again and the blade slid across her flesh.

"T-t-the pictures. I kept the pictures." She longed to close her eyes and block out the man on top of her. Block out the knife slicing into her cheek. The hot blood trailing to the carpet.

Shane expelled a breath and lifted the knife. "Good girl. Take me to them."

Amy nodded. She couldn't talk. Nothing. She was too scared to move.

"I said to take me to them." Shane's roar snapped her out of her paralyzed state.

"Okay. Okay."

Shane yanked her to her feet and propelled her in front of him. Amy stumbled but caught herself. She needed to find out what he was up to. If he was working for a terrorist, then he had malicious intent. What if he'd been turned into a suicide bomber? He wouldn't just kill her, he'd kill everyone around him. Including her family.

She had to stop him. But her ribs hurt so bad she couldn't see straight. What to do?

No solution came before she reached the bedroom. Maybe she could distract him with the pictures and grab her gun. She'd never shot anyone before.

"Under the bed. I put them away to give to your daughter when she was grown."

Shane seemed not to hear her. "Pull them out."

She clutched her side. "I can't. I think you broke my ribs."

"Stupid woman." Shane shoved her to the side and she sucked in a breath at the wrenching agony. Shane fell to his knees and pulled the clear tub containing the picture frames from beneath the bed. He picked up the tub, sat it on the mattress and lifted the lid. Inside lay the heavy black frames, carefully wrapped in cloth to protect them from getting scratched.

Shane unfolded the cloth on one of them and then slammed the butt of his knife down, cracking the first frame.

What the hell?

Amy watched as he flipped shards away with the tip of his knife. Light glinted off what was beneath, and when she saw what was hidden inside, she gasped.

"I will let you live because of this." Shane seemed as mesmerized as she.

"Where did you get that?" The pain forgotten momentarily, she eased forward for a better look. Gold inlaid with a multitude of gems glittered in the light. Red rubies. Emeralds. Diamonds. Others she didn't have a name for.

"A foolish villager who thought to hide them from me."

"What did you do to him?"

Shane sneered, "What do you think?"

Amy paled. "You killed him."

"And his family." The way he said it, like it was just another day, like he hadn't destroyed innocent lives for his own gain.

"Murderer." Amy whispered the word, recoiling from the very thought.

Shane got in her face, not one single drop of regret lining his eyes. "They sacrificed themselves in the name of Allah. They have been well rewarded."

She took a step back. There was no coming back from that kind of crazy. Or escaping it.

Chapter Thirty-eight

"Did that look like Amy in the passenger seat?" Ranger bore holes in the back window of her pickup. Ranger and Hunter had pulled down her road, lights off, intending to approach her house on foot, only to have them leave before the two men could get out.

"Yep." Hunter cranked the truck and put it in drive, lights off.

"Copy that, team two?" Ranger spoke in the comm at his throat.

"Roger. We're on your tail." Aaron, Riser and Merc followed in a jeep. Ranger glanced in his rearview, but couldn't see them. Both teams were operating dark tonight. No lights. No signals. Nothing that would alert their former team member to their presence.

"Where are they going?" Hunter kept a steady foot on the gas, maintaining enough distance not to spot them, but close enough to follow.

"Hell if I know, but I'm sure it's not good." Ranger answered.

"Do you think he knows about Chloe and is headed to the house?" Hunter leaned forward on the wheel and Ranger felt the truck accelerate.

"He's headed the wrong direction if that's the case." Amy and Shane turned right off her gravel road and onto

Highway sixty-five.

"Could you see her? Did she look okay?"

"Shit, I couldn't tell if she was injured though."

"Are you sure it was her?" Hunter said.

As sure as the bugs splattering their windshield. "Yes."

He didn't get a good look at the second person in the truck, but he felt her. Knew it was her without a doubt.

Hunter didn't respond, he focused forward and tailed her old Dodge. The truck had to be pushing eighty, which was asking a lot from the rust bucket.

"Sure are in a hurry."

"Yep." Hunter increased speed, keeping close.

The truck hung a hard right onto Cypress Bend road. The only thing down that way was Coldwater Papermill and the levee.

"Where the heck are they headed?" Hunter said.

"I have no idea. Night shift is on at the mill. Shane didn't hang out with anyone there. No one lives on this end of the levee anymore, not since the flood last year." The flood that had nearly taken both Hunter and Evie's lives.

Which left absolutely nothing for them to do. So why did they turn off down the back road beside the paper mill? Hunter followed at a more distant pace. The truck hung a right and headed up the levee, and then their lights disappeared.

"Go faster. We're losing them." Ranger hit the dashboard, wanting the truck to go faster.

"Team two, we lost sight of the target. In pursuit." Hunter floored it, the truck careened down into a cattle gap then bounced back up, throwing Ranger into the roof before settling down.

"I said faster, not kill us." Ranger grabbed the oh-shit handle above his head and braced for the sharp curve up and to the right onto the levee.

"Hold on." Hunter spun the wheel, gravel flew and they slid sideways for a second before the truck righted itself.

Aaron's voice came through the comm. "Holy shit boss, you trying to kill us back here?"

"Mind the cattle gap, boys," Hunter answered blithely and then spun up onto the top of the levee. The long winding road built on top of the nearly forty foot tall hill bordering the Mississippi River had been the only obstacle stopping the flood last year from wiping Mercy off the map.

"All due respect, sir, but fuck you."

Ranger couldn't help the grin. Folks not from the south didn't understand its precious beauty or its deadly deterrents.

"Where did they go? Do you see headlights?" Ranger scrutinized their surroundings. The paper mill lit up the sky behind them, its huge column of steam rising steadily into the clouds. Nothing but flat fields lay beyond that to the right. Huge oak and pine trees lined the right side of the levee, and beyond that was the river.

"There, down there." Hunter cut left and dropped into thin air.

"Holy crap, what are you doing?"

"Getting your girl." The truck hit the road halfway down the levee, bounced forward and then back, slinging Ranger's head into the headrest.

They didn't slow down. Hunter increased speed down the gravel road, disappearing into the woods. The road quickly turned into a dirt road littered with potholes and mud puddles. Any other time Ranger would cuss out his brother for driving like this, but not tonight. Not when Amy's life was on the line.

"Straight ahead. He's there." Ranger's heart accelerated with the truck.

"He's stopping at the sandbar turn off." Hunter slowed and then stopped a few hundred yards away.

"Hold back, they stopped at the river." Ranger spoke into the comm.

"Roger."

Ranger pulled out his night vision binoculars. Shane exited the truck up ahead first and rounded to pull the passenger door open. When Amy stumbled out, Ranger's heart stopped. She was alive and okay. For now.

Shane held her with one hand and then reached into the

truck and pulled a bag out with the other.

"What's he got?" Hunter asked.

"I don't know, but let's find out." Ranger opened his door and exited the vehicle, damning himself again for not bringing night vision goggles. The binoculars were great for staking out someone, but not suited for travel. They would have to walk in the dark.

"We're on foot. Follow the road past our truck and flank left at the ramp. Set up a nest and see if you can get a visual."

"Roger," Riser answered through the comm.

Hunter slid his rifle over his back and pulled his pistol from its holster. Ranger did the same. "Ready?"

"Yep." Ranger led, the two brothers moving down the dirt road with sure feet. They'd been down here often enough as teenagers seeking a place to do some necking with a girl. The road curved on to the right, and if you followed, it would lead to an old hunting club. The other option was the boat ramp, which led straight down to the river. Amy and Shane had headed that way, so they would follow.

Ranger stopped at the top of the ramp. He saw two figures standing at the edge of the water. That was it. "What the hell are they doing?"

"Beats me. Maybe going for a late night swim?"

Ranger shot his brother a killer glare and refocused on Amy. She seemed to be bending at the waist and holding her stomach. Had Shane hurt her?

A sound drew his attention. "That's a boat engine."

"Sure is. Team two, you got eyes on that boat?"

"Roger. Merc's locking in now. Hold." Riser answered.

"Who in the holy hell would know he was home? Have you told anyone?" Ranger asked.

"Hell, no. No one has."

"Shit. Mavis came over this morning with Darla and her camera man. Then Cord showed up. They each saw Shane." Ranger recalled the scene. The morning's drama had left him wrung out.

"Never seen Mavis on a boat, and that twit Darla

wouldn't know how to drive one." Hunter pulled his rifle and sighted down the scope. "Can't see a damn thing in this dark."

"Come on." Ranger crept forward, pistol raised and aimed at Shane. He didn't know who was on the boat, but right now the biggest threat was the man standing next to his woman.

They got within twenty feet when Merc spoke. "Son of a bitch. It's Brown."

Ranger and Hunter shared a look of surprise.

Chapter Thirty-nine

"Who is that?" Amy wheezed out the words, the pain in her ribs unbearable now. She kept flickering between some sort of strange haze, walking the edge of conscious and back to her harsh reality.

"That is the man who will help me fulfill my destiny." Amy didn't even cut a glance in her husband's direction. All the way here, he'd talked about his destiny and praise to his savior and what the hell ever else. She'd done her best to tune him out and keep an eye on an escape opportunity.

Too bad none arose. She could have opened the door and jumped from the truck when they'd slowed to turn off the highway, or on the levee, but her ribs wouldn't hold up to that. She could have run when he'd put the truck in park at the top of the ramp, but every step she took was pure agony. Her only other rout of escape lay straight ahead, but she didn't have the strength to fight the currents. "Hope it works out for you."

"It will." Shane stepped forward and raised a hand in greeting. Amy couldn't make out the man on the boat yet, but he waved in return. No help for her there, then.

The boat engine cut off and it continued to float forward, stopping just far enough out so that they'd have to swim if they wanted to reach him. "You got it?"

"Yes. Do you have the package?" Shane asked, his whole body one tight tense wire ready to snap.

"Yep. But I want to see the payment first. Hold it up."

The man bent down and came up with a flashlight.

"You move an inch and I'll kill you." Shane let go of her arm. Amy stumbled to the side without his support and barely caught herself from pitching into the water. He dug into his bag and pulled out the broken picture frame and held it up.

The light zeroed in on the prize. The man let out a low whistle. "Alright, I'll pull closer and throw you a rope. You set that bag down, away from the water."

The boat engine started again and he eased forward, pitching the rope when he was close and killing the engine again. Shane pulled him to the side, onto the grass embankment lining the ramp and river. The man hopped down and extended a hand. "Great doing business. The boat's yours. Head up river a quarter mile, your package is in the barge."

He walked to the bag, scooped the straps over his shoulder and headed up the ramp. Amy watching, wondering what had just occurred and wishing the damn moon would come out so she could get a glimpse of the man's face.

Shane glanced at the boat and then back at the man. He then reached behind his back and pulled out a pistol. Amy gasped as he took aim at the man walking away. He pulled the trigger. A shot blasted loud like a cannon, and she slapped her hands over her ears and screamed. The man fell flat forward and didn't move.

"Oh, my God. What did you do that for?"

"I can't leave any witnesses." Shane strode forward and retrieved the bag. He didn't even check the man. By the time he returned, Amy was a big ball of shaking fear. "Get in the boat."

"No."

He grabbed for her arm but she resisted. He had one hand holding his pistol, the other holding his precious bag. "Get in the boat. I'm not telling you again."

"Never. I'm not going with you."

He slung the bag over his shoulder and made a grab for her, but she stepped back, barely missing his hand.

"The lady said no." Another voice, this one heartbreakingly familiar.

"Ranger."

"You okay, baby?" Ranger kept his pistol trained on Shane.

"Yes. Now that you're here." She wanted to run to him. Hurl herself into his arms and never let go.

"Move another step and she dies."

Amy froze as she felt, more than saw, Shane's gun point in her direction. Ranger stopped, but didn't drop his gun.

"Put your gun down. Slowly," Shane ordered and then he stepped closer to Amy and pulled her in front of him. Shielding his own body.

"Okay. Anything you want. Don't hurt her." Ranger held his hand out and bent at the waist, lowering his gun to the ground.

Amy wanted to weep. Shane would shoot him now and Ranger would be defenseless. "No, Ranger, don't do it."

"How sweet, the whore pleading for her lover." Shane's hot breath touched her neck and Amy wanted to vomit.

"Don't listen to him, baby. Look at me. Focus on me." Ranger spoke as if Shane hadn't said a word. He held her gaze with his own, silently commanding her to look at him.

"That's right, baby, look at him. Watch him die." Shane raised his arm, his pistol aimed straight at Ranger. Amy tensed, ready to knock his hand down.

She heard a whizz past her ear, then a thunk. Shane's arm fell. Amy turned in time to see Shane collapse backwards, a small red hole in the middle of his forehead.

She gagged and the movement nearly ripped her in half. Ranger was there in an instant, holding her in his arms. "It's okay baby. He's gone. He can't hurt you anymore."

"What...who?"

"Damn, Merc, good shot." Hunter appeared from the woods to her left. Merc, followed by Aaron and Riser stepped from the woods at her right.

Merc didn't verbally respond, just nodded and crossed his arms over his massive chest.

"Thank God you're okay. I should have never left you. Ever." Ranger squeezed her to him and Amy cried out. Ranger immediately let go, and she almost hit the ground. He swept down and caught her, holding her loose away from his body.

"What's wrong?" Ranger's sweet tone went deadly serious.

Amy found herself surrounded by four towering men in the next second. "Check her for broken bones."

"Gunshot wounds?"

"I've got a first aid kit in the truck."

She couldn't keep up with who was saying what, all she heard was concern, for her. And for the first time since Shane came home, she felt warm. "I'm okay, really. It's just my side."

"Let me see." Ranger didn't wait for her response but pulled up her shirt to her ribcage.

Aaron produced a flashlight and she cringed away, the bright light hurting her eyes. "Son of a bitch."

She wanted to glare at Aaron, tell him to put the dang light up, but she knew how bad it looked. "I know it looks bad..."

"That's not bad. That's broken," Riser piped in.

Amy stuck out her tongue and he just smiled in return. Ranger turned green. Then red. Then purple. Amy felt sorry for him. "Ranger, look at me. I swear, I'll be okay."

Aaron lifted the light to their faces, Ranger's gaze met hers and then his expression turned black. "I'm going to kill him."

"Too late," Merc said.

Ranger reached a trembling hand to her, skimmed down her face without really touching her. "I'm so sorry. I can never forgive myself for leaving you there, with him."

"I asked you to leave," Amy reminded him and tilted her face into his open palm.

"I shouldn't have listened. I'm sorry." Ranger's tone

was ragged and raspy.

Amy didn't want or need it. "If you apologize one more time, we're through, you hear me?"

"Sounds like she knows what she wants," Aaron broke in.

"It's Lee Brown." Hunter approached the group.

"Are you sure?" Riser said.

Ranger hadn't taken his gaze off her.

"The one and only. What do you think he was doing meeting Shane?" Hunter said from right behind her.

"I love you," Ranger said and she couldn't drag her gaze away.

"I love you, too," she whispered in return. The world seemed to rush around her, the lights fading as the adrenaline left her system.

"Aaron, get that damn kit. Now." Ranger lowered her to the ground, resting her head in his lap. "It's okay. We will get you to the hospital."

Amy licked her lips, her mouth dry. "Look in his bag."

Hunter took off and returned a second later with the bag. He dropped it to the ground and pulled out a black frame, his face a mask of confusion.

"Keep going." Amy said and then coughed.

Hunter dug in and pulled out the right frame this time. He'd shown his flashlight and a cascade of colors reflected back. "The jewels. He had them."

"I'll be damned, that old villager was telling the truth." Riser said.

"Shane was crazy. The man that captured him turned him. He was working for someone named Al Seriq."

The entire group went silent and stared down at her. Amy tried to discern what they were thinking, but hadn't a clue. All she knew was, she wanted them to quit.

"Are you sure he said that name?" Ranger asked.

"Yes. I remember it very distinctly. And he was supposed to give Brown the jewels in exchange for something." Fatigue wrapped its comforting arms around her. Amy let her eyes slide shut, just for a minute.

"For what?"

"I don't know, but Brown said it was on a barge a quarter mile up river." Speaking took all her energy. She didn't know how much longer she could resist the pull of sweet oblivion.

"The weapons." That was definitely Hunter's voice. "Riser, you and Merc go check it out. I'll call in support and Ranger and Aaron can get Amy to the hospital."

Amy heard footsteps, the boat crank and then Hunter talking on the phone.

She heard Aaron unzip his first aid bag.

She heard the crickets and the bullfrogs along the river.

And then she heard a sound much sweeter than anything she'd ever imagined. "I love you, Amy."

EPILOGUE

Amy stood in the grass at the cemetery, holding Chloe. Ranger stood beside her, holding Arturo's hand. All of Ranger's team surrounded them. Hank and Maxine. Hayden. Cheri and Evie. The people Amy considered her family stood behind then as the preacher said the last rites over Pedro's grave.

Arturo sniffled and Ranger, without even asking, scooped him up into his arms. After a minute, Artie settled and laid his head down on Ranger's shoulder. Amy wiped her tears and took Ranger's hand.

They stood together, united, one single unit. A few days after Amy came home from the hospital, Sheriff Lawson had come over with the news. He'd found Pedro's body, a few miles from his house. Apparently, Pedro had made it a lot further than anyone thought possible with the amount of injuries he'd sustained.

Arturo had been hysterical at first. But each day over the past two weeks, he got a little bit better. Amy and Ranger planned to give him all the love he needed to overcome this terrible loss. Together.

After the funeral, everyone paid their condolences and left. Everyone but Hoyt and Jared Crowe, who'd gone on a separate mission a few days ago.

Alone now, Ranger knelt at Arturo's side and placed his hand on the boy's shoulder. His big brown eyes seemed to swallow up his whole face. "Arturo, we can come here as often as you like."

"Why did you put him here, in this place?"

Amy sniffled back the fresh wave of tears, shifted Chloe on her shoulder and knelt beside them. "Because, you are my family now. Pedro was my family too. And this is our plot, this is where he belongs."

"Do you think he can hear me?"

"Of course I do. Your papa is up in heaven and he's looking down on you. Watching out for you. He knows what's in your heart."

"Is he in heaven with Mr. Shane?" Amy's heart clinched and she glanced over to Shane's gravestone, right beside Pedro's. The now familiar mixture of anger and sadness welling up inside, thoughts that had left a permanent scar on her soul.

They had left a scar on Ranger's too.

"Yes. He is," Ranger said. Since Shane's real death, Ranger hadn't left her side. He'd tended to her injuries. Taken care of the kids. The house. Everything.

"I want him back," Arturo cried out and lunged for Ranger, crying.

Amy watched the tender way Ranger cupped Artie's head. The way he rocked side-to-side holding him in his arms. Ranger met her gaze and the look of adoration made her feel strong. She could do this. She could be strong for Arturo. They would be strong together.

Arturo quieted down some after a few minutes. Amy soothed a hand down his arm as Ranger continued to rock him.

Ranger rubbed comforting circles over Arturo's back. "I won't ever try to replace your father. No one can do that. But I'll be here for you, just like your dad would want."

Amy took Ranger's free hand and kissed his palm. "We will be here."

Ranger's eyes watered and he cleared his throat before speaking, "That's right. Nothing will tear us apart. We're a family now."

Before you go...

From the author: I hope you enjoyed Resurrection River. I want to thank you for joining the Men of Mercy on their first adventure. I would like to invite you to post a *review* of the book on Amazon or Goodreads.

–Lindsay Cross

* * *

For updates about new releases, as well as exclusive promotions and giveaways, sign up for Lindsay Cross's insider mailing list here and **be entered monthly to win a $50 amazon gift card.**

www.lindsaycross.com

email: **lindsaycross@lindsaycross.com**
facebook: Lindsay.cross.author
twitter: @lindsaycross101

RECKLESS RIVER
MEN OF MERCY, BOOK 3

They say you can't go home again. Jared Crowe never wanted to.

Home meant facing memories of abuse and neglect. Of dark closets and evil nightmares. Of his own relatives intent on killing him. But now his brother's kidnapping forces him to face those demons. Only this time, Jared isn't a scared little boy. He's a full-grown Special Forces operative bent on revenge.

As a little girl, Sparrow Pickney risked her life to free two abused boys. As a grown woman Sparrow needs to earn a place in her adopted family's business or be forced into a life of degradation. The chance to prove her family loyalty comes when she catches Jared spying on the compound and captures him.

When Jared sees his captor, he realizes she's the girl of his dreams and vows to rescue her from a life of poverty. What Jared doesn't know is Sparrow may not be the savior he remembers...but the one responsible for abducting and torturing his brother.

Jared is determined to find the truth. But that truth may be more than his heart can take.

REDEMPTION RIVER
MEN OF MERCY, BOOK 1
RESURRECTION RIVER
MEN OF MERCY BOOK 2
RECKLESS RIVER
MEN OF MERCY BOOK 3
DAVID: MEN OF MERCY NOVELLA
RAYLAN: MEN OF MERCY NOVELLA
RAVAGED RIVER
MEN OF MERCY, BOOK 6

Lindsay Cross is the award-winning author of the Men of Mercy series. She is the fun loving mom of two beautiful daughters and one precocious Great Dane. Lindsay is happily married to the man of her dreams – a soldier and veteran. During one of her husband's deployments from home, writing became her escape and motivation.

An avid reader since childhood, reading and writing is in her blood. After years of reading, she discovered her true passion – writing. Her alpha military men are damaged, drop-dead gorgeous and determined to win the heart of the woman of their dreams.

FOR YOUR **FREE COPY** OF DAVID, A MEN OF MERCY NOVELLA, SIGN UP FOR MY NEWSLETTER AT WWW.LINDSAYCROSS.COM

www.ingramcontent.com/pod-product-compliance
Lightning Source LLC
Chambersburg PA
CBHW051412170626
46809CB00006B/2123